by

Frost Kay

DEDICATION

To my sissy: thanks for kicking me in the butt when I needed it, being one of my biggest supporters, and demanding chapters when I was scared to hand them over. Love you<3

THE KINGDOMS

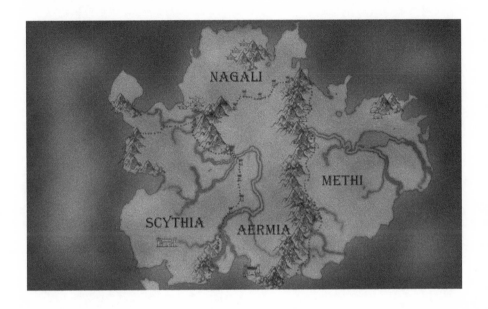

Table of Contents

PROLOGUE...9
CHAPTER ONE..2
CHAPTER TWO...15
CHAPTER THREE...25
CHAPTER FOUR..36
CHAPTER FIVE..44
CHAPTER SIX..59
CHAPTER SEVEN..74
CHAPTER EIGHT...90
CHAPTER NINE...105
CHAPTER TEN...111
CHAPTER ELEVEN..125
CHAPTER TWELVE...139
CHAPTER THIRTEEN..155
CHAPTER FOURTEEN...171
CHAPTER FIFTEEN.. 183
CHAPTER SIXTEEN 197
CHAPTER SEVENTEEN...202
CHAPTER EIGHTEEN...213
CHAPTER NINETEEN...223
CHAPTER TWENTY...233
CHAPTER TWENTY-ONE...245
CHAPTER TWENTY-TWO 257
CHAPTER TWENTY-THREE..266
CHAPTER TWENTY-FOUR...274
CHAPTER TWENTY-FIVE.. 287
CHAPTER TWENTY-SIX..295
CHAPTER TWENTY-SEVEN...309
CHAPTER TWENTY-EIGHT 318
CHAPTER TWENTY-NINE 325
CHAPTER THIRTY...333

PROLOGUE

Life was cruel.

Men were evil.

And hope was lost.

But sometimes, just sometimes, there was a glimmer of something good. Something so sweet that it made all the wrongs, the hurts, the pains, and the nightmares fade just a little.

Sometimes they come in unexpected ways from unexpected people.

Sage's came from a source she'd have never guessed.

Her enemies.

Chapter One

Sage

Sage squeezed her eyes shut and reopened them, though it did nothing to change the scene before her. Her mind was reeling, this couldn't be happening. She couldn't be seeing who she thought she was... She blinked a couple more times.

Swamp apples. Still there.

Two royal figures stood before her, blue eyes staring, one in anger, and one in calculation. Her fingers went numb, and a high-pitched ringing filled her ears.

They were here.

The princes of Aermia were actually here. In *her* family's forge.

Sweat dripped down her spine.

How did they find her? No one had followed Rafe and herself as they made their way home from the festival last night, she had been sure of it. So *how* had they done it then?

She jumped as she felt a touch on her arm. Anxious, her eyes jumped to the one touching her but she relaxed as she met the gaze of her father. It was only her papa.

His eyes narrowed at her. "Sage? Are you all right?"

She nodded slowly and gave him a weak smile, deliberately ignoring the two men boring holes into her head with their eyeballs. "What can I help you with, Papa?"

Her papa grinned. "Actually, I have someone I want you to meet." He wrapped an arm around her and looked toward Sam. "Sage, I would like to introduce you to Samuel."

For a beat, Sage simply stared at the spymaster before her father began again: "This is the Sam your brothers got into so much mischief with over the years."

She started at his words. *Him?* Stars above, it couldn't be true. Life couldn't be that cruel, could it? Apparently, it could.

"It was he who commissioned the dragon sword."

Her gaze dropped to the sword in question. The great dragon broadsword she now held in her hands. Sage then glared at the sword, feeling oddly betrayed, as every foul word she'd ever learned ran through her mind. Of all the bad luck in the world, why did nothing ever go as it was supposed to?

The spymaster cleared his throat, pulling her from her thoughts. As she raised her eyes to his, he arched a brow. "I'm happy to meet you at last. Zeke and Seb have spoken of you so much that I almost feel like I know you."

Sage pulled in a breath and sent him a brittle smile. "I feel exactly the same way."

Sam leaned forward, not breaking her gaze. "The sword's perfect. I've never seen its equal. It's truly a stunning weapon. How long was your apprenticeship?"

Sage hesitated. Sam knew her family, but she didn't know what her brothers had divulged to the spymaster all these years, and she had no desire to give him any *more* information.

Before she had a chance to reply, her father spoke up.

"Actually, she never left my side, even as a little one." Her papa squeezed her. "I used to call her 'my little shadow'. Every time I stepped back, it was onto little toes. Her brothers had no interest in it, so, much to the chagrin of her mother, I trained her instead. Now, here she is: the most talented swordsmith in all of Aermia." Her father's face beamed with pride.

"Indeed," Sam remarked.

"Indeed," Sage mumbled. More like unfortunate.

Sam smiled. "How fortuitous it is to meet you in person." His smiled widened. "Beauty and talent. I believe Colm and your brothers have been hiding you from me?"

"Damn straight," her papa added.

Her eyes flickered to the crown prince's and she registered the barely-masked hostility there. It was time to go.

"Well, it was lovely meeting you." She smiled at Sam. "And thank you for your compliments. I hope the sword serves you well, however, the forge doesn't run itself, so if you will excuse me." As Sage turned away she tried to decide her next move. Should she run to the meadow? Or perhaps go and find Rafe?

"I would like to commission a few pieces."

Sage spun around when the voice cracked through the air like a whip. "I'll be honest, seeing my brother with such a beautiful blade has me a bit envious."

The dark tone sent a shiver down her spine.

Even though she'd warned the princes of the plot to kill the king, they were still her enemies. Their games weren't over: it was just the beginning.

Sage cringed and turned toward Tehl, clenching her hands in her skirt to keep them from trembling. Looking at him again she realized that, unfortunately, he was still one of the most beautiful men she had ever seen. Wavy blue-black hair, sapphire eyes framed with long, dark lashes. The full mouth highlighted by strong cheekbones and a defined jaw. She couldn't believe she had kissed that mouth just last night. She shivered. Though it hadn't been the worst thing to ever happen to her, it wasn't something she wanted to repeat any time soon. Sage blinked. Why was she even thinking about that? Stupid prince.

He shifted and her gaze was drawn up from his lips to his eyes. His eyes held no warmth. Sam smirked while standing next to Tehl and her impassive mask began to crack. Her emotions were all over the place. She needed to rein herself in. But when her father clapped his hands together, she just about jumped out of her skin. She'd almost forgotten he was there.

"Well, I still have a little work to do, so I will let you two work out the details. But it was great seeing you, Sam. Stay for dinner?"

"I would love to, but I'm afraid I've got to get back to work."

"That's too bad, son. Perhaps next time."

She caught her father's sleeve as he turned and gave him a pleading look. "Papa, do you think it wise to leave me here unchaperoned?" She kept her voice low.

He eyed her and then the two royals, patting her hand absently. "I will only be in the forge and can see you the whole time." He turned his gaze toward her. "So have no fear, love." He raised his voice so that Sam could hear him. "I have known Samuel for many years. He would never do anything improper in my forge or make my daughter uncomfortable." The words were friendly but also held a clear warning.

Sam dipped his head, smiling boyishly. "As you say, Master Blackwell. You know, I feel as though Sage is my sister already."

5

Her papa acknowledged Sam with a quirk of his lips before moving back to his workbench. Sage stared after him, feeling like she'd just been left to drown in a river. Her father simply smiled encouragingly before turning away, whistling a lilting tune as he departed.

Sage swallowed hard, locking her knees to stop their shaking. She wouldn't let them detect the fear in her, so she gathered her courage. Grabbing paper and quill, she placed them on the counter before the two princes. The salty smell of sweat caught her nose. Hers or theirs? She had no clue. Steeling herself she asked, "So what would you like?"

Silence followed her question, yet she refused to look up at them. She waited them out a bit but still they said nothing.

"My lords?" she prodded.

When each remained silent she forced her eyes from her paper, eyebrows raised in a mute prompt. Sage found herself under intense scrutiny by both sets of calculating blue eyes. Her stomach clenched.

Suddenly, Tehl smiled fiercely, teeth gleaming. "I think I would like something similar to my brother's. The dragon seems lifelike, which I approve of, but I'd rather you leave off all those pearls and sapphires. Maybe substitute obsidian and black diamonds."

Of course, he wants a black sword, she thought, *it'll match his black heart.*

Sage mulled it over. It would be harder to get the obsidian and black diamonds but it was definitely possible. She grinned evilly as she thought of how much she could charge him. Her father may not have understood whom he'd been dealing with, but she most certainly did.

"It will take time to track down the stones you desire, but we can do it. Of course, you will need to pay upfront; twelve gold marks." Sage smirked when the crown prince's eyes widened just a fraction.

Sam spoke up first. "Come now. I only paid three for mine. His stones can't be *that* costly." Sam gave her a lazy smile as he tried to bargain. "Surely you can give us a deal, I mean we're practically family."

"You are." Sage pointed her pen at Sam before stabbing it toward his brother. "He's not. That's my price so take it or leave it."

Sam sniggered when the crown prince glowered at her before speaking. "I guess I'll need to borrow some gold, brother."

Pulling a bag from his waist, Sam set the coins on the counter.

Sage merely smiled, feigning innocence. "Is there anything else you need?" She kept her tone sweet even as she felt giddy inside. Were she to be locked up today, her family would still be taken care of for a long time.

"As a matter of fact, there is." Sam placed a dagger in front of her. "Something like this."

As she caught sight of it, the blood drained from her face. A rebel blade. More specifically *her* rebel blade. As her gaze snapped to Sam, she caught him taking in her reaction with interest.

So then, what now? Would he punish her family? The spymaster seemed to know she had created the dagger and had no doubt seen others like it on the other rebels. He now had proof she wasn't only a spy, but the rebellion's weapon supplier to a point. She wouldn't be going back to the dungeon, she would hang.

Her eyes darted to her papa, whistling away and working, oblivious to the danger she'd put them in, before returning to the two royals.

Carefully, she pushed the dagger back toward them. "I'm afraid that is an outdated design. Can I interest you in something else instead?"

She hoped they understood the translation: she didn't work for the rebellion anymore.

Sam's brow furrowed at her words before he cleared his

expression. He plucked her dagger from the counter and slipped it back into the sheath at his waist. "Nope, I believe I have everything I need then. How about you, brother?"

She couldn't help darting a glance toward Tehl, but her breath stuttered to a halt when she met his angry eyes. He leaned closer, feigning interest in a dagger on display, but Sage held her ground, refusing to be intimidated. She froze, however, when she felt his breath caress her temple.

"There is only one thing I require here and none of it was forged with metal. So far it has eluded me, but I believe very soon it will be within my grasp." He paused before continuing, "There is nowhere to run, Sage."

Her eyes flew back to Tehl's. Seeing the determination on his face she knew she needed to leave. *Now.* She had planned on never seeing Rafe again but at this point she had no choice. This wasn't just about her own safety anymore.

By then he'd withdrawn from her space, though he continued watching her intently. She smiled grimly and placed each hand on a displayed dagger.

"Only over your dead body," she hissed. He would never find her again and he would never hurt her family. Of that she would be certain.

Both men tensed at her threat and her smile turned deadly. At least they understood that danger was imminent.

"Papa," she called, never taking her eyes from them. Sage heard him as he hoisted himself up to stroll over to her. When he reached her she continued, "I find myself quite fatigued." She then handed him the sheaf of paper with the crown prince's specifications. "Would you mind finishing up?" Sage broke the staring contest she'd been entertaining with the two men so she could meet her papa's worried green eyes.

"Oh, love, I'm sorry. Do you need anything?"

A warm smile split her face as she felt the concern in her papa's voice. "No, no. I'm sure it's just too much dancing last night." Kissing her papa's whiskered cheek she spared the royals a last glance. "It was lovely meeting you, Sam." She hoped to never see him again.

Sam smiled like he knew exactly what she was thinking, which ratcheted her anxiety up a notch. "We'll be seeing you soon then."

Sage turned and forced herself to keep a sedate pace as she departed, until she entered her home. Closing the kitchen door, she then picked up her skirts and ran, revealing the leather pants she always wore beneath them. She vaulted over the table bench and burst into the living room, startling her mum.

"My stars, Sage! You scared me half to death." Her mum took in her facial expression and jumped to her feet. "What is it, love?"

Sage opened her mouth and floundered. What could she say? That she had put them all in grave danger? That she would most likely be hung? That she had let them down? She waved her hands and bolted to her room with her mum on her heels. Sage rushed around the room, ripping her rucksack from a chest at the base of her bed.

"Dear? You are scaring me. You need to calm down and talk to me."

Sage spun to face her mum. "They found me, Mum. I was so careful not to lead them to your door, to put any of you in danger. But of all the wretched luck in the world..." Sage sunk her fingers into her hair.

Her mum pulled her hands away from her tangles and held them. "Take a breath, you need to calm down. I need to understand what is going on if I'm going to help you."

"I don't have time," Sage cried in dismay.

"The quicker you talk, the faster I can help."

Her mum's stern tone penetrated the sea of panic she was swimming in. Her vision blurred as she looked into mum's face, her

9

hazel eyes full of concern. She sat heavily on her bed, pulling her mum with her. "I only wanted to help our people, to make Aermia a better place. I was tired of all the sickness and poverty. Our people were crying out to the Crown but all they received was apathy... I mean, Aermian women on the border are being *taken*. By Scythia!"

"What?" her mum gasped.

"Mum, I was offered a way to help. A way to make Aermia better. I wanted to make it better."

"The rebellion." It was a statement, not a question.

She tipped her head back, gazing at the faded yellow stars painted on her ceiling. "Eventually I was caught. It was the Elite, more particularly it was the crown prince and the commander."

"They are the ones who marked you?" Her mum asked, her voice infused with both anger and sorrow.

"Not by their hand. It happened in the dungeon by their men. When they found me I was on death's door so they brought me to a skilled healer and had me looked after as I healed. I didn't understand why they cared at the time. I figured it was because they wanted information. But I have since learned the man who did this wasn't theirs. He was *from* the rebellion." She barely choked out the last sentence.

A sob broke free from her mum's lips. "Oh, my poor baby."

Sage wanted to mourn too, but she also knew they didn't have time, not now. She swallowed her pain and continued. "It broke me, Mum. Last night was my last night. I told them I was done with it." She paused. "Do you remember the dragon broadsword that I made?"

Her mum's brow wrinkled. "Yes."

Sage barked out a humorless chuckle. "It turns out it wasn't for a regular run of the mill noble. No, it was for a prince, the commander who, it turns out, is intimately connected with our family. Papa wanted us to meet, so he introduced us."

"The Crown's never commissioned any pieces from your father."

Sage smiled sadly. "They have, and my identity is no longer a secret."

Her mother's face tightened in anger. "I can't believe your father did that. How do we know the commander?"

She swallowed, her eyes watering, her mum loved Sam. "It's Sam, Mum. Zeke and Seb's friend, Sam."

"No," her mum breathed. "It can't be."

Sage's heart squeezed. "Of all the rotten luck in the world, right?"

Her mum trembled. "He's been visiting since he was a boy, your brothers love him!" She straightened her spine and lifted her chin. "No one hurts my children. You're right; you need to leave. Immediately." Her mum stood and, in a flurry of swishing skirts, began stuffing things into her pack. "I have a friend who can offer a haven—even your father is not aware of her." She paused. "Is Sam still here?"

"They were when I came inside so I assume so."

"Okay. Give me one moment." Her mum rushed out the door while Sage ripped off her skirts and packed all of her trousers in the sack. She also strapped on as many blades as possible, along with her sword. Hastily, Gwen bustled back in and pushed bread, dried fruit, and jerky into her bag as well.

"This may not last long, but my friend will take care of you before you run out." Her mum also pressed a letter into her hand. "There are directions in here. I will come to you when it is safe, but you need to go now. I could still hear your father talking with them so I will go and say hello. Perhaps I can keep them preoccupied for a while longer."

Sage bit the inside of her cheek, trying to keep from crying, and hugged her mum fiercely. "You'll talk to Papa, right? And tell him I love him?"

Her mum pushed back and cupped her cheeks. "Of course, sweet girl. We will always keep you safe. We all love you so very much, you know that." Sage threw on her cloak and strapped on the sack, eyes watering. She cocked a hip and smiled through her tears. "So...how do I look?"

Gwen grinned back at her. "Improper as ever."

Her heart lightened at her mum's statement. She would be okay. Things would get better. They had to for she would make it so. Sage clambered into the windowsill and swung her legs over the edge. Turning back, she peeked from under her hood, blowing a kiss at her mum.

"Goodbye. I love you."

Her mum scowled for a beat but it soon morphed into a smile. "Never goodbye, love, because I will see you soon. Be safe, tell Lil hello, and that I'll visit soon." She paused. "Remember, Sage, never to judge."

Sage's questioning expression seemed to make her mum's smile widen. Shrugging it off, Sage waved, dropping to the ground on silent feet. There wasn't much to keep her covered, and it was at least twenty-five paces until the homes started. Probably best to sneak into the forest until the homes were a bit closer together.

She kept low to the ground, waiting and watching for movement. Nothing. Her heart pounded as she sprinted through the open before she disappeared into the forest. She heaved a deep breath, only slightly relieved. She was safe for the moment.

Opening the letter, she read the directions. Her mum's friend lived in the fishing district. It was actually close to one of the rebel's bases so she could use one of their tunnels to keep hidden as she made her way there. Shoving the letter into her vest, she began weaving through the forest, feeling calmer almost immediately. There was something about the mixture of vegetation, freshly turned soil, and damp wood that soothed her soul. She breathed deeply, reveling in the cleansing air. If only she could stay here and pretend the outside world did not exist. Mulling it over, she decided she would gladly become a hermit.

A whiff of freshly baked bread floated on the breeze and quickly shattered her daydream of disappearing into the forest. She scanned the modest stone homes that had slowly crept toward the forest's edge. In one, a mother gestured furiously at her son with a loaf of bread. The next, a young woman vigorously washed clothing while humming a familiar tune. Sage continued to move along the tree line, searching for an exit. Unfortunately, it seemed like everyone was home today. Finally, she spotted the perfect place to slip into the city.

The home was clean but in clear need of maintenance. An old man slept in a rocking chair on his back porch, a threadbare blanket covering his slumbering form. Sage paused, observing the place for a few moments, searching for anyone else who might be in the house or the one next to it, yet all remained silent.

She crept from her hiding place to the house in a matter of seconds where she cautiously peeked between the wooden shutters. The home appeared sparse, a stone fireplace dominating the wall across from her, with a worn chair in one corner and a small side table holding a couple of well-loved books. The kitchen was part of the same room, though all that occupied it was a sturdy table and a single chair. She double-checked, but saw neither pantry nor food lying about. Where was the old man's family?

For some reason, it made her heart hurt knowing he could be all alone in the world. Sage dropped her sack and pulled out the food her mum sent with her. It wasn't much, but it was all she had to give. She slipped back to the porch and eyed the sagging stairs. There was no way she could sneak up those—they'd give her away immediately. Ignoring them, she placed a knee on the porch. She leaned closer to the old man's feet and placed the food beside his chair. Soundlessly, she shifted back and slipped quietly between the empty homes, moving in the direction of the fishing district.

CHAPTER TWO

Tehl

Shock pulsed through him even after she'd left. They had actually found her and not only that, but they even knew her true identity *and* her family. She was completely different from when he saw her the night before, less exotic, less refined. Yet she was just as beautiful. When he initially caught sight of her, he'd felt inclined to haul her over his shoulder and lock her up so he and his brother could finally extract some answers from her, and he'd been about to do so when Sam had slid him that look.

He wasn't sure the reasoning behind his brother's decision to let her walk away, but Sam always had a plan. The man had more information, and secrets, than anyone he'd ever met... Except, perhaps, for the rebel girl. She might be the exception.

He pulled himself from his thoughts when he heard the click of a shutting door.

Was she coming back out?

Her excuse of illness was one of the oldest tricks in the book, and it was surprising her father hadn't seen through it.

When he glanced up he noticed an older woman emerging from the curtain. She pushed some silver-streaked hair from the hazel eyes bracketed by fine lines, probably from smiling too often, as it seemed to suit her. She skimmed her eyes over him but lit up with joy as she spotted Sam.

"Samuel!" she exclaimed and rushed toward them. "It has been too long, my boy." She hugged Sam and then planted a kiss on his cheek.

"Gwen, dearest, your beauty has faded not a bit. Colm is one lucky man." Sam grasped her hand, placing a quick kiss on the back of it.

She swatted Sam's shoulder, her lips quirking. "Some things never change, do they? I was hoping you might have finally found a woman to settle you."

"I'm afraid the only woman in my life is my duties, and she's all I've got room for. She's a hard mistress, demanding all my time and energy, so I fear I would have nothing left to give a young woman. For you, however, I think I would make an exception."

Tehl barely kept from rolling his eyes at his brother's antics. Sam couldn't help himself, he just *had* to flirt with anyone that was female.

"Hey, now," Colm scolded, though good-naturedly.

Tehl took the moment to study the older swordmaker while his brother distracted the lady. The older man was a complicated mixture of opposites. He was tall and wide-shouldered, with massive hands, yet his clothes hung loose and his face was gaunt. The size of his clothes bespoke a time of good health and what was most likely considerable strength. Tehl watched as the swordsmith's hands shook slightly while he worked. What had happened to him? Was he sick?

"Forgive me for being so rude but, who is your companion?"

16

Tehl discarded his musings and turned to the woman who was now appraising him. Her smile was friendly, but her eyes were shrewd. As she looked him up and down, the corner of her lips pinched slightly.

Interesting, he thought.

It appeared she didn't like him though he'd yet to speak a word. *Like mother, like*

daughter.

"I am Tehl, my lady." He inclined his head, respectfully addressing the older woman.

"Forget all the formal nonsense. A friend of Sam's is a friend of the family's. Call me Gwen." She brushed her hands against her skirt and looked between Sam and himself. "Would the two of you like to stay for dinner?"

"Colm invited us already, and I do wish we could stay Gwen, but I fear that business waits for no man. Thank you for the offer. However, we really ought to be going."

"That's too bad. Perhaps next time?"

"Next time of course." Though Sam smiled, his expression held a hint of disappointment. "We will be back for the blade in a couple weeks."

"Definitely. Will Zeke and Seb be done with their trading then?"

"Actually, they're home now. They're out running errands for me so I'm sure they'll be sad they missed you."

Sam picked up his sword and passed his other packages to his brother. "Tell them not to be strangers." He then gave Gwen a quick hug, and shook hands with Colm, before turning toward the exit. As soon as he'd turned, the smile slid from his brother's face, grim determination replacing the former levity.

"You're *sure* you don't have time to stay?" Gwen called lightly.

Something in the tone of her question felt off, and Tehl's brows furrowed.

Sam pasted the smile back on his face and tossed over his shoulder, "I am afraid not, dearest, but next time for sure." Sam waved to the couple once more, and they meandered away until they were out of sight from their home. He picked up his pace, urging his brother, "We need to hurry, she's running; I know it. Gwen was trying to stall us." A bitterness had seeped into his words with the last sentence.

"I thought the same thing. I knew something was off when she smiled at me with her lips but it didn't match her eyes." Sam didn't often show his true feelings but Tehl could feel the frustration pouring off his brother. "What's wrong?"

"I have known them for years, Tehl, years. You have no idea how many times I snuck over there to visit their sons, Seb and Zeke. I never met Sage. She was younger and always by their father's side. Neither of the boys had an interest in the forge. I can only guess what Sage told her mother, but my friendship with them just ended. Instead of being honest with me, Gwen shut me out and protected Sage."

"That is, I believe, what mothers are *supposed* to do," Tehl drawled. Odd that it was him making this observation to his brother when it was usually the other way around.

"Believe me, I know. I just..." Sam stopped, searching the surrounding area and running a hand through his hair. "I wish things were different. Everything is so damn tangled." Sam squinted at the forest and changed the subject. "She couldn't move into the city from this direction. If she had, we would have seen her. If I was her, I would have slipped into the trees to sneak along so I could enter the city near the fishing district. The homes butt up against the forest there so it'd be an easier transition for her." Sam met his eyes as he made his way quickly back. "We have to hustle if we want any hope of catching up with her. If we lose her this time I doubt we'll ever discover her again. Our only chance to quell the rebellion peacefully will disappear with her."

Tehl nodded and quickened his pace to match his brothers. They jogged down the lane scanning the area. "We could have avoided hunting her down if you had let me take her at the forge," Tehl pointed out, baiting him. "I understand that you're friends with her family, but this isn't about one family, it's about a nation of people."

Sam scoffed.

Tehl smiled at his brother. Sam loved to tell others why he was right, and Tehl had deliberately created the perfect opening.

"First, we want her to come willingly."

His lips twitched. Hook, line, and sinker.

"As we have seen in the last month, she won't give us a damn thing if we push. We don't want to be seen as the evil ones. If you had taken Sage from her home, we would've become evil, and she would have resisted us with everything she had," Sam continued in a lofty, lecturing tone. "But now, she will run to someone she trusts, someone who can protect her and who is potentially very dangerous."

Tehl let out a snort. So that was it. His brother was brilliant. "The rebellion. She is running to someone in the rebellion."

Sam grinned, huffing out a breath. "Exactly. Two birds, one stone."

They slowed when they reached the end of the forest, and a small cluster of homes gave way to the bustling city's edge, families filling the streets, going about their daily business. Sam paused at an abandoned barrel and dumped his packages into it. Tehl raised a brow. Was he really going to leave his goods in that barrel? Sam saw the question on his face and smiled.

"I can't track a rebel spy if I am weighed down by loot. That girl is fast! Plus, no one is looking to steal from an old barrel, so I doubt anything will happen to it. Stop scowling and blend in, damn it! You keep an eye on the south, and I'll watch the north."

Tehl pulled his hood to more fully shadow his face and scanned the road. Children sat in the dirt, etching games into it with little rocks. Others chased each other or hung onto the edges of their mums' skirts as the women gossiped and shopped. He couldn't help the smile on his face when a baby boy picked up a rock and began gnawing on it, behind his mum's back. His little face sagged in relief with each bite. The little one must be getting teeth. He pulled his gaze from the baby and studied the surrounding people. Tehl inspected each person carefully, even the young men. The first time he had met Sage she was posing as a boy so she could very well be doing so now.

"There," Sam breathed.

Tehl shuffled sideways to where his brother looked. There she was, moving out from between two homes and into the lane. She then flittered from one group of people to the next, looking for all the world like she belonged in each. It was fascinating.

Sam sprawled lazily next to him, groaning about a headache. Sage's head swiveled in their direction. She spotted Sam and appeared to dismiss him before moving down the dirt road. His brother was right. People saw mostly what they expected to see.

Sam straightened and paused next to him. "Shall we investigate a bit?" Excitement gleamed in his brother's blue eyes.

Tehl nodded, gesturing ahead of him. "Lead the way."

Sam's eyes flicked to his boots. "Do try to be quiet, we don't want her to know we are coming."

Tehl glared at Sam. "But of course. Anything that you command, Mighty Lord of The Sneaks."

Sam scratched his chin with a satisfied smirk. "You know, I have always wanted to hear someone say that. Though, admittedly, I'd always hoped it would come from someone of the female persuasion."

Tehl scoffed and kept close behind. They followed Sage at a distance as she made an odd series of twists and turns.

"She's coming to a dead end," Sam whispered, but, when they turned the corner, she was gone.

"Bloody hell," Sam said.

He searched along the street but she was not there. A flicker of movement drew his eyes up. Tehl blinked. She was running across the roof of an alehouse.

"Sam."

"I see her. We need to split up or she'll spot us coming."

He waited for Sam to get a good ten paces ahead before he made a show of sedately meandering down the cobbled street. Her fluid jumps and quick steps made it easy to keep his attention on her. Every movement was precise and athletic, never stumbling or slowing down. He'd have to pick up his pace to keep her in his sight, but, just as he had the thought, his breathing stuttered as she hurled herself across a large gap between buildings. Her dark cloak floated behind her, suspended in the air, until her fingers caught the edge of the roof. Bracing her feet against the building she twisted, and, with her back to the wall, noiselessly dropped to the ground.

He had never seen anything like it.

"I want her. Do you think she'd marry me?" Sam whispered heavily in his ear.

Only years of practice kept him from jumping at the sudden proximity of his brother. Damn his brother and his eternal sneaking. "Was that necessary?" he asked harshly.

Sam shouldered next to him as Sage slipped down the alley. "No, I find it enjoyable, so I wouldn't expect it to stop any time soon. Also, you probably would have heard me if you weren't watching her quite so closely." Sam hitched a thumb over his shoulder. "You passed me a couple buildings back and never even noticed. Not that I can blame you... That woman..." Sam groaned. "Beauty, grace, cunning...and those moves! I bet she's flexible—"

Tehl slapped his brother on the back of the head. "Don't even think about it."

Sam scowled, rubbing the back of his head. "Why ever not? Do you like her?"

Tehl returned Sam's scowl. "No. But it does seem disrespectful to talk about her like that when she is your friend's *daughter*," he defended, stepping down the alley, little shanties popping up in the small areas between buildings. The closer they moved toward the ocean, the poorer the area became. Rusted metal roofs sat atop cheap wooden homes.

"She is skilled though," Sam commented. "If it was anyone other than us, she would have lost any tails long ago."

Tehl agreed. With all the twists and turns, ups and downs, it was hard to keep track of her. He had no clue where they actually were in the fishing district except that the sea was nearby, and he only knew that because he heard the thundering of waves and the smell of seaweed.

They continued on until a break in the endless maze of shoddy homes gave way to the open expanse of sea cliffs. Where was she going to go now?

"She has nowhere left to go." Sam said, obviously perplexed.

The rebel hastily glanced left and right, before sauntering toward a large outcrop of rocks near the cliff's edge.

"She better not shimmy down those rocks. If she does, I'll be very put out," his brother complained.

Sage moved around the rocks and out of sight. Tehl sighed and abandoned their hiding place. Both brothers approached cautiously, keeping an eye on their surroundings, as they slipped around the rocks.

Rocks.

There was not a blooming thing but rocks.

Sam padded to the edge and peeked over. "Nothing. That's odd." Sam turned and scrutinized the rocks. "She can't have disappeared into thin air."

"Maybe it is another of her skills," Tehl said. "Women are tricky like that."

Sam snorted. "*Now* you make a joke?"

Tehl examined the area closely before answering. "It seems to always work for you. I thought I would give it a try."

Sam snarked something back, but Tehl missed it as something caught his eye. There was something unnatural about the moss between two boulders. He approached it and bent down, running his hand along the moss, when his finger snagged on wood. A trapdoor. "I guess I was wrong, Sam. It isn't one of her tricks after all." He felt along it until he encountered a cool metal ring. Tehl pulled it up carefully, so as not to alert anyone who might be below them, but the door moved with ease, gliding along on well-oiled hinges.

Sam squatted next to him. "Well, I've always wanted to go searching for booty by the sea."

Tehl rolled his eyes and swung his legs into the hole, then rolled to his belly grasping the edge with his hands until his boots met a firm ladder. One rung at a time, he lowered himself into the opening, Sam following behind. His brother then closed the hatch, catapulting them into darkness. In the pitch black, they moved steadily, deeper down the chasm. After a few moments, Tehl's eyes sufficiently adjusted so he was able to see a soft light filtering in from the bottom.

Tehl stepped to the side when his boot touched the damp stone floor. He took in the crude porous archway that led to an uneven stone tunnel. The sound of crashing waves echoed around him, making it seem like they were surrounded by water.

Sam brushed his hands off and took in their surroundings as well. "Intriguing," was all he said before continuing down the corridor.

Suddenly, a piercing scream sliced through the air, making his blood freeze. Both brothers slid hidden blades from their stashes and sprinted toward the tortured scream. They burst into a giant cavern with a small opening to the sea. Tehl dismissed the surrounding area, focusing on Sage, who was folded in a man's arms. The man growled and faced them. Just when Tehl thought things couldn't get any worse, they did.

It was the Methi prince.

CHAPTER THREE

Sage

Her heart galloped in her chest. She had been moving so fast that, when Rafe had reached out and grabbed her, an embarrassing shriek had burst from her. Terror filled her for a moment, wrenching her back into her nightmare, and, before she knew what was happening, Rafe had pulled her into his arms and had held her growling. The menacing sound triggered another spike of fear. Sage pushed against his chest, a whimper escaping. She needed to be free, she couldn't breathe.

"I think the lady would like you to release her," a dark, velvety voice commented. Her eyes closed at the familiar voice. Could she never escape him? *How* did he find her? Rafe's arms tightened, trapping her hands between them.

"It seems to me that she was running from you. She reeks of terror. I'm sure that's your doing. She has nothing to fear from me, I would never harm her."

Except that he already had. Sage pushed once more, but he didn't budge.

Rafe continued, "You need to leave me and mine alone."

She lifted her chin and glared up at Rafe. She wasn't anything to him.

"I hate to intrude, Your Highness," the spymaster broke in, "but you have yet to let her speak for herself. From the way you are holding her, I doubt she can even breathe."

And that was how the crown prince found her. Sam. The man of a million faces and lady friends, the spymaster of Aermia. Rafe peered down into her damp eyes and loosened his hold a little.

"Are you all right, little one?" he asked rubbing his thumb along her cheekbone.

Sage jerked her face back. "I will be once you let me go."

Hurt and something else flashed across his face before his arms slipped away. She took a large step back and angled herself, keeping all three men in view. The crown prince studied her, no sign of the anger and shock he wore an hour ago. Her eyes turned to the golden prince. Sam appraised her with a lazy air, while his eyes wandered up her body, making her feel naked. She glared at him when he met her gaze and merely winked.

Damn rogue.

Rafe stiffened, his hands caressed the forearm length daggers strapped on each of his thighs. "Keep your greedy eyes off her. She is not yours to gaze upon."

Sage debated between knocking Rafe on the head or smirking at Sam, but one thing was for sure, the situation was about to explode. Her gaze bounced from one man to the other, pausing on Sam. A devilish twinkle entered his eyes that made her cringe and want to hide. She had been on the receiving end of that twinkle and she'd

26

ended up drugged out of her mind.

"Your behavior is shocking, Your Highness. It was my understanding that women don't belong to anyone but themselves." Sam quipped.

"She's mine."

The dark possessiveness in Rafe's voice made the hair on the back of Sage's neck stand up. She touched her knives and took another step back. "I am no one's, Rafe. Not the rebellion's, not the Crown's."

Rafe turned his glare on her. "No matter what you choose, you will always be mine. *My* family, *mine* to protect."

She looked away from him and locked eyes with the crown prince. He stood silently next to his brother, simply absorbing the situation. Sage wondered if he stayed silent because when he spoke he tended to offend people, or if he truly just had little to say.

Tehl's deep eyes released her and shifted to Rafe. "What is your part in this, Methian? Are you aware of Sage's loyalties?" The crown prince studied Rafe. "She's working with the rebellion. So either Methi's supporting the rebellion or you're a fraud."

"Little one? They have your name?" Rafe hissed, never taking his eyes off the two royals.

Her jaw tensed at the accusation in his tone. It wasn't like she gave it to them.

"We do." Sam rested one shoulder against the rough cavern wall, looking casual. "Sage and I have an interesting history, I grew up with her brothers. Imagine my surprise when I went to collect my sword from Colm this morning, and he introduced me to his elusive daughter." Rafe cursed, causing the spymaster's smile to widen. "I must have been standing under a lucky star, my sword and the lady I have been searching for, all under one roof."

Her breath stuttered. She had heard Zeke and Seb speak about their adventures with Sam over the years. She would never have guessed the outcome of their friendship would be what led to her hanging. How much did Sam know about her family? Even if she ran, her family wouldn't be able to escape. Sage was well and truly trapped. She only had one option left: to bargain. "What do you want, Sam?" she asked, defeated.

"The safety of Aermia," Tehl cut in, his voice echoing like thunder in the small cave. "We want a peaceful resolution between us and the rebellion, no bloodshed. I want to discover why Scythians are stealing our women, and I want to know what the hell you're doing with a Methian prince, if he even is one."

"That was a lot of wants, brother," Sam remarked off-handedly.

"Shut up, Sam. No one asked you."

"I think her question was for me."

"Nobody cares what you think."

Sage gaped at the two royals. She'd seen this side of Sam, but she hadn't seen so much as a glimmer of humor from the crown prince. Shaking off her shock, she scrutinized the men. "You still didn't tell me what you want from me."

"We want you to be the liaison," Sam proposed.

A liaison?

"Between the Crown and the rebellion," he continued. "There is no need to fight. I am sure we can come to an understanding if everyone can be reasonable."

Her eyes widened as his words sunk in. An ambassador? Maybe she could protect her family if she accepted. Sage blinked and her vision was blocked by a large back. How did Rafe move like that?

"You want to *use* her?"

Sage shifted to the side and peeked around him.

"You mean like you? You had the power to help her escape our dungeon." Sam chuckled at Rafe's silence. "Come now, don't pretend like you don't have spies inside the palace. That's just insulting. You left her there with strangers, for a month, so she could give you information."

"You know nothing," he hissed.

"No, I know everything." The humor faded from Sam's eyes. "Including who sanctioned my father's assassination attempt." Rafe stilled. The spymaster held up his hands. "Keep your shirt on, I am not threatening Sage. Despite her best efforts, my father lived."

Rafe's gaze prickled, but Sage ignored it, staring at Sam's exposed collarbone, hoping to hide the deceit written on her soul. She had betrayed the Crown by joining the rebellion, and she had betrayed the rebellion by colluding with the Crown.

She was a traitor to both.

No one should trust her.

"I spent enough time around her," Sam continued, "to know she would have never agreed with that decision. She isn't a murderer, but you tried to make her into one." The spymaster's eyes hardened. "I hold you accountable. You stood by her side last night and let her leave. You are the guilty one. How could you encourage her to do that? To do that to your own family? You and I already carry the burden of death but if she'd taken his life, the Sage you supposedly love would cease to be, we both know it."

Rafe was breathing hard next to her by the time the spymaster finished his tirade. His wide, leather-clad chest heaved like he had just run a race. He inhaled a final, shuddering breath and stilled. Sage shuffled to the side, farther still, studying his profile. His face was blank. Her heart shrank a little. After everything Sam said, never once did he defend himself or capitulate. Rafe thought he was right.

She shook her head, placing her hand across her mouth. To a certain point, she'd understood no one person was greater than their goal, but she never expected Rafe would be the one to demand her sacrifice, forcing her to give up her morality and soul for the rebellion. Except for the crashing waves, silence descended upon the empty cavern, the air thick with regret and pain.

Sage continued to stare at Rafe's profile, her decision made. She couldn't return to the rebellion or forget the responsibility she had toward the people. She stared at the flame of a flickering lantern as she came to terms with her future. Could she do it? Could she deal with the rebellion and the Crown *and* still be fair? Would they hang her if she refused? Her eyes dropped to the crown prince, fatigue riding her. "What would happen if I declined being your ambassador?"

"Then we'd find another way."

That surprised her. Her eyes narrowed. Where were the threats?

The crown prince added, "But Sam, Gavriel, and I believe you would be the best option to avoid bloodshed."

Again, he surprised her.

"You would leave her and her family alone?" Rafe asked, skepticism coloring his tone.

"I have known her family for almost ten years. I have no desire to see any of them hurt." Sam met her gaze. "But if you choose to help, I will send Jacob to your father."

Her world spun. Jacob was the finest healer in Aermia. Her father had been sick for so long, but a healer of Jacob's caliber wasn't within reach for them. It would mean everything for their family if he could be healed.

"You would let her father suffer, knowing he is sick, if she doesn't agree?" Rafe questioned.

"No."

Her eyes jerked to the crown prince.

"We will send Jacob, regardless. Sam was trying to sweeten you up to the idea. Jacob will do whatever he can for your father. But if you say yes, you will help thousands of innocent people, *our* people."

Thousands. How many would suffer if there was a civil war? If she joined the rebellion to help the people of Aermia, if she agreed, she could save lives. Sage turned to Rafe and scanned his face, looking for a trace of his thoughts. He stepped closer, weapons glinting. A little sliver of fear wormed through her. Sage locked her knees to keep from taking a step back. Her nose flared, as anger surged hot on the heels of her fear, why did her body keep failing her?

Some of her tension melted away at the tender look Rafe gave her.

"Little one, I sympathize with how much you desire your father to be healthy. You want to help the people but this..." Rafe paused and watched the royals over her shoulder for a moment. He looked down, citrine eyes warm, and clasped her hands. "I don't trust them, but you will help many by accepting their offer. You are familiar with the Crown and the rebellion, you can make it right for the both of us, and so many others."

Sage studied him then turned back to the royals. Dark blue eyes latched onto her green ones.

"You have suffered more in our home in the last month than I suspect you have suffered in your life. If you decide to be our ambassador, we will protect you." She watched his Adam's apple bob and his jaw tighten. "You don't believe us, but we did not sanction your attack. Despite what I may have threatened you with, I would never treat a woman that way. I take responsibility for my men's actions."

A lump formed in her throat at the sincerity of his apology. She wanted to believe he wouldn't hurt her, but no man was trustworthy except her papa...and Gav. She still didn't like the crown prince, but she wasn't heartless. He didn't deserve to carry the guilt of her attack.

"He wasn't your man; he was the rebellion's." Both royals straightened, rage distorting their faces.

"Serge was a rebellion spy?" the crown prince snarled.

She nodded, bile creeping up her throat at the memory of his smug smile. She swallowed hard when the crown prince's glacial gaze snapped to Rafe.

"You sent your own men to harm her? Was it a test to see if she would give up information? To see if she would hold up under pressure?" he spat, stepping forward, Sam at his side.

Rafe matched the brothers' steps, vibrating from head to toe. "Never," he growled. "That animal did what he did for his own sick pleasure. Mark my word, soon he will painfully disappear from this world."

That was news to her. Rafe scolded her for stabbing him.

"He is not dead?" Sam asked in interest. "I am surprised that you've not already taken care of him. Did he not betray one of your own?"

Rafe glared. "We don't execute someone unless there are evidence and witnesses." Rafe spared her a look before going on. "It was her word against his."

"Were the myriad of scars not proof enough?" the crown prince bit out.

"No, they were not."

Sage's throat tightened.

"She greeted him by stabbing him through the shoulder."

Sam smiled darkly at her. "You stabbed him?"

"I threw my blade when someone yanked my feet out from under me." Sage clenched her hands, feeling angry all over again. "If it hadn't been for that, he wouldn't be around to hurt anyone else."

"A woman after my own heart."

"Indeed." Sage shared a sharp smile with the spymaster.

"It was because of that." Rafe pointed at her face, frustrated. "No one understood why she was attacking him. She outright tried to kill him in front of a roomful of men. To them, it looked like she was acting without provocation, like she..." He hesitated before soldiering on, "Like she was broken, not fit to lead."

Hurt stabbed her as tears burned at the back of her eyes. The rebellion circle thought she was crazy. They didn't believe Serge, or Rhys, or whatever should be held accountable for the trauma he'd inflicted. "Was there a trial this week?" she demanded. Rafe's serious expression told her everything.

"Yes. The decision was passed that since there were no witnesses to validate either of your claims, Rhys would go free."

Her stomach dropped. How could they allow this? They were letting him go. A deranged maniac. Why would they doubt her? Did anyone fight for her? Why wasn't she told?

"Sage," Rafe called to her, pulling her out of her thoughts. "He has been part of the circle for a long time. He had sway, and I had to stand by their decision for the moment." A predatory smile graced his handsome face. "But he will not walk this earth much longer. *No one hurts my family. He will wish for death.*"

Her breath caught at the promise of vengeance in Rafe's eyes. That man would never hurt her or anyone else again, she was sure of it.

"I would like to see your technique or maybe try a few of my own. One for each inflicted on her," Sam offered, his tone flat.

"Don't forget the broken bones and bruises," the crown prince added heatedly. "He ought to pay for those as well."

Rafe regarded them before a vicious smile spread across his face. "I may require your expertise."

The royals mirrored his feral smile, dark promises filling their eyes. All three of them were in agreement: the crown prince, the commander and the spymaster, and the rebellion leader. If she hadn't been in the same room, she would have never believed it. *This brought them together?*

Rafe stalked toward the royals with feline grace, halting in front of them, looking like a warrior pirate. His hands flexed at his sides once before he shoved his hand out. The crown prince glanced at her once before stepping forward and clasping Rafe's forearm. Rafe looked over his shoulder and tipped his head to the side, beckoning her.

Sage steeled herself and glided to Rafe's side. She looked from one prince to the other. This was her last chance to back out, but she was never one to back down from her duty. She thrust her arm out for Sam to take. Sam quirked a smile at her and clasped her arm.

"It will be a pleasure working with you, my lady."

"We will see," she said, making his smile widen.

Sage forced herself to turn to the crown prince. She willed herself not to shake when she reached out to him. With care, he clasped her arm, long fingers overlapping. He stared down at her with solemn eyes. "Thank you for your sacrifice."

"If she is harmed in any way, mentally, emotionally, or physically, our agreement will be void and you will have war," Rafe threatened from her side.

The crown prince's dark sapphire eyes dropped to hers and stalked to the large man at her side. His voice dropped low, deadly. "Agreed. If she is harmed by anyone in the rebellion again, I will burn it down to the ground."

She blinked up at Tehl, shocked at the threat. Apparently, her value as an asset had increased more than she realized. His thumb caressed her arm, and she shifted awkwardly. He hadn't let go. Sage pulled her hand from his grasp, feeling uncomfortable. Time to get down to business.

"It is time for you both to leave. I will arrange a meeting in six days at a location of my choosing." Sage said as she scanned all three men, hoping she didn't sound as inexperienced as she was. "Each of you will meet with whomever you need to. You will only bring six men with you to the meeting in six days' time. Demands will be exchanged, and we can meet three days later for negotiations. Any objections?" Silence met her question. "Good, then it's set. I will see you all in six days' time. Good day." She nodded and turned on her heel.

"I would speak with you before you leave, little one."

She flashed Rafe a sharp smile, knowing what he wanted to talk about. It wasn't going to happen. "And I you, but I have somewhere I need to be. So if you will all excuse me." Sage reached her bag and picked it up, then retreated, forcing her steps to slow so she wasn't seen running toward her escape.

"How will we contact you?" Sam asked.

Sage peeked over her shoulder. "I will find you."

Time to disappear.

CHAPTER FOUR

Sage

Once out of sight, Sage sprinted down the stairs, needing to get away. Her boots pounded against the dirt floor, padding a loud rhythm as she sped from one tunnel to the next. She burst into an intersection of six openings, ducking into the second one on her right without hesitation. She had to get ahead of Rafe; he had a peculiar way of finding her whenever she least wanted to be found.

The floor gently sloped downward, fading from dirt to wet sand. The rough stone walls surrounding her were covered with seaweed, little sea creatures, and moisture. She shivered as the ceiling dripped cool water onto the top of her head and down her neck. Pushing her brown hair from her face, she sloshed through puddles to the mouth of the tunnel. Passing through it, she was momentarily blinded by the sun's brightness. When her vision cleared, her breath caught at the view before her.

Nothing surpassed the turquoise waters of the Thalassian Sea. The ocean glimmered in the light like a million aquamarine pebbles covered its surface. Its waves called to her. She would kill for a swim right now, to explore the treasures under the surface. Sage sighed. She didn't have time for that.

Reluctantly, she peeled herself away from the enticing ocean and scanned the surrounding bay. Ships rolled in the blue-green waves, hulls towering above her. Those moored where the bay met open ocean were actually rebellion supporters. It was brilliant, really, for if anyone left through this doorway it just looked like they had exited in one of the vessels.

Sage eyed the slippery steps carved into the cliffs. They looked awfully slick. With care, she crept up the steps, testing each ledge before placing her weight on it. Finally, she reached the wooden dock; its wood creaked beneath her as she stepped from the stone staircase. People milled about, and she heaved a sigh of relief when the merchants ordering about their workers didn't spare her a glance.

She lifted a hand, shading her eyes from the brightness of the sun, scouring the ships for the Sirenidae. Her eyes landed on an old but well-kept vessel where 'Sirenidae' had been painted in pale green, contrasting the dark wood of its hull.

Gotcha.

Sage meandered among the workers, blending seamlessly and arrived at the massive ship in no time. Oddly enough, there weren't many people around the ship. Where were all its sailors? Unease crept over her, but she steeled herself. She trusted her mum. Gripping the rope rails, Sage marched across the ramp with the churning ocean below, hoping her hosts would not stab her for trespassing on their vessel.

When her feet met the deck, she peered around curiously. The

37

ship was clean and its wooden deck well oiled, practically gleaming in the sun. Large white sails billowed in the breeze, reminding her of her mother doing laundry on sunny days.

Someone takes pride in their work.

A whisper of leather against wood caught her attention, and she focused on the shadowy cove obscuring the new arrival. Sage shifted on her feet and ran a reassuring finger along the blade at her waist. "Sorry to board your ship unannounced, but I mean you no harm," she called out. "I seek refuge, and it was my mum that sent me. She said your captain could provide shelter."

"Blade?" a familiar voice asked gruffly. "What in the blazes are you doing here?" Hayjen stepped forward, his ice-blue eyes regarding her.

"Hayjen?" How did her mum know Hayjen?

"Your mum sent you?"

Sage thought about not answering him for a moment, but she trusted Hayjen as well as her mum. "Yes. Gwen Blackwell." When his face didn't show any sign of recognition, she questioned the directions. Maybe she read them wrong. "I have a letter," she explained, pulling it from inside her vest.

Hayjen's lips pursed before he replied. "I will speak with the captain." Her friend turned back and left, leaving her standing alone on the deck.

Sage frowned. Well. That was odd. Questions swirled through her mind but they would apparently have to wait. She leaned her back against the mast and soaked up the warming rays. If she wasn't careful, she would fall asleep right where she stood.

After a time, her eyes peeled open at the sound of Hayjen's approaching feet. He smiled, his eyes crinkling at the corners. The tension in her shoulders relaxed, this Hayjen was familiar.

"She will see you now."

Now that sparked her interest. A woman captain. You didn't hear about one of those every day. Women could work in any trade but it was still usually frowned upon if she worked in a position or trade dominated by the male gender.

Sage returned Hayjen's smile and followed him down a narrow hallway that smelled of orange oil. They paused at an ornate door painted with swirling colors, and Hayjen knocked twice before opening the door for her. She skirted around him and waited for him to follow, but he simply winked and closed the door. She hadn't expected that.

Sage turned and took in the chamber. A pale blue wooden desk stood in front of three large, clear glass panes that formed a bay window with a plush window seat. Bracketing each side of the window were two massive bookshelves full of colorful books. She found herself gravitating toward them, running a finger along a red leather spine.

"Do you like them?" a husky female voice murmured.

She smiled at the books. Sage had known the other woman was watching her. "They are lovely," she commented. "You have quite an amazing collection. Some of these look to be hundreds of years old." Sage turned to greet the woman but jolted when she met a magenta gaze. She stared blatantly, not able to help herself. She had never seen eyes that color, *ever*. Someone had invented small colored lenses that could be placed in the eyes to change the color, but this was something else, it was obviously natural—and yet it seemed unnatural.

Sage blinked when the captain arched a delicate white brow and pushed her hip off the opposite bookcase. She moved like water, smooth and flowing. She sat on the edge of the pale blue desk and adjusted the emerald silk scarf wrapped around her head and neck, covering damp hair that was seeping through. The scarf dripped down onto unique clothing. Neither buttons nor stitches adorned them. Everything seemed knotted or tied, yet it somehow created a form-fitting dress. A long pale foot dangled from the desk. Sage pulled her gaze from the interesting dress to meet the woman's dancing eyes.

The captain gestured to her eyes. "You will not ask about them?"

Sage quirked her lips at the candidness. "My mum taught me not to ask questions that were rude, and as that would be in that category, I will refrain. But what I am curious about is how you know Hayjen."

The woman smiled at her. "I was a pirate, and he happened to be one of the goods I was stealing, but that's a long story for another time."

Was she joking or serious? Before Sage figured it out, the captain spoke again.

"I've been waiting a long time to meet you, Sage Blackwell. Your mother and I are very old friends."

"Really?" Sage cocked her head to the side, curious, as the woman looked to be only a handful of years older than herself. "This is the first time I am hearing about you," Sage replied carefully.

"No need to beat around the bush, *ma fleur*."

Sage hesitated a moment before continuing. "My mum is a proper woman, and you look anything but proper. No offense."

A smoky chuckle emerged from the woman. "None taken." She smiled with warmth at Sage. "You have spirit which I presume you get from your mum, but your lovely eyes must be from Colm."

Well then. The woman wasn't lying after all.

The captain shifted on the desk and faced her. "And, to answer your question, your mum and I met under extraordinary circumstances. She helped me when I was hurt, and then we grew close, but because of some, shall we say, *unsavory* acquaintances, we had to part ways. We still write letters and every once in a while she steals away to see me, but it's not as often as we would like." The woman's voice turned serious. "Your disappearance just about killed her."

Sage's eyes widened, and the captain's smile sharpened. "There are few things I cannot discover. She came to me but even I could not find you and that is saying something. All Hayjen discovered was that you were on an assignment but we both knew that wasn't the case with Rafe riled up. So that narrowed it down to one man who possessed the skills necessary to make you disappear so entirely."

"Sam," Sage breathed. How was this woman associated with the rebellion? And who was she?

A bitter smile marred the captain's stunning face. "That boy." She shook her head. "Knows more tricks than a whore. He concealed you well."

Sage frowned at the glimmer of respect she saw in the captain's eyes. Whose side was she on then? "If you guessed where I was why didn't you tell my mother? Or even Hayjen? He thought I was dead," Sage questioned.

"Your family would have gotten themselves killed with that information. I was protecting them, even if I couldn't protect you. I knew I could trust Rafe to do that."

Anger and hurt seeped into Sage's blood. "He's a pretty poor protector. I want nothing to do with him or his other aspirations."

"So you're not with the rebellion any longer?"

Sage studied the captain's eyes. Admitting she was part of the rebellion was dangerous. "Rafe is no longer part of my life," she replied cryptically.

"Interesting. What made you want to leave?"

"Not everything is black and white."

"True, but something must have set you off."

"I'm not blind anymore. There are no absolutes when it comes to people. I believe in certain ideals but prefer to go about it in a different manner than certain others."

"How very insightful for someone so young."

Sage snorted. "I am hardly young. Mum has been chomping at the bit to marry me off." She looked down at a scar peeking out from her sleeve. "But I have survived things that have changed my view of the world. Sometimes the enemy isn't someone far off, but a brother wearing a friendly mask."

"All scars heal, *ma petite fleur.*"

Sage's lips twisted. "Some take longer than others." She lifted her eyes and forced a weak smile. "I am in need of sanctuary for a little over a week. I'm willing to work and help here in exchange for you harboring me."

The exotic woman dipped her head. "Done. You will be treated as if you were my own. I have watched over you since you were a child. I look forward to spending time with you." Her magenta eyes flashed. "No one will take you from here. You are safe and protected."

"Hayjen?" she questioned, feeling bad she even asked. Sage didn't want Rafe to know where she was. She had enough to deal with at the moment.

"He will be silent. He is, after all, my husband. We will both protect you."

Sage froze. Hayjen was married? She'd have to come back to that later. "The leader of the rebellion has an uncanny ability to…"

The captain slashed her hand through the air. "That predator will not find you here. Even if he did, he would never set a foot on my ship."

Sage had heard no one call Rafe a predator before, but the description aptly fit. There was something raw and primal about him, a wild danger, like if you got to close you could be bitten. Sage reeled in her thoughts and bowed to the captain. "Thank you for your hospitality, if there is anything I can do to repay you Ms..." She trailed off realizing the captain never gave her name.

The captain leapt from the desk and dipped into an elaborate bow, displaying all sorts of pale skin. "Lilja Femi, at your service."

Sage catalogued the many weapons strapped to the exotic-looking goddess bowing before her. Lilja's scarf slipped from her head exposing wet silvery hair, and her neck! Sage's breath froze at what she spotted: three slits flared slightly with each of Captain Femi's breaths. The captain stood and met her eyes, her gaze inciting a challenge. Sage quickly schooled her features, hiding her fear, and forced her hand from the dagger at her hips.

"Breathe, *ma fleur*, I will not hurt you," Lilja coaxed.

Sage forced a breath in and out. Her mind scrambled. It couldn't be. They weren't real, and, even if they were, they'd supposedly disappeared a thousand years ago. So long ago, in fact, that they'd become a legend, a fable in stories.

"Sirenidae," Sage whispered. The proof was evident. Her mum had sent her to a damn Sirenidae, a living, breathing—sort-of— Sirenidae. This is what she must have meant about not being quick to judge. In all the old stories, Sirenidae were believed to be beguiling, deadly creatures, though so beautiful your eyes would bleed.

Yet, growing up, her mum had never told the stories that way. She'd always painted them as heroes, fierce and kind. Now, Sage understood why. Her mum was hiding a Sirenidae! Sage's fear spiked again. She was standing in a room with one of the most dangerous races ever. The fifth race existed.

The Sirenidae lived.

Sage let out a shaky breath and said the only thing she could think of. "Do you have a tail?"

CHAPTER FIVE

Tehl

He cocked his head and watched the mysterious man track Sage's departure, a wealth of feeling in Rafe's eyes as he watched the girl. How close were they? After she'd gone, the man in question turned to them with outright disdain and disgust evident on his face. Tehl was sure his own expression mirrored the rebellion leader's. He didn't want to work with him; the man was a traitor and a liar.

"Are we going to glare at each other all day or get down to business?" Sam drawled.

Rafe's lip curled as he continued to stare at them with those eerie eyes. There was something off-putting about the man's gaze but he'd be damned if he let the other man realize it. Tehl straightened and stared right back. The rebellion leader's lips twitched slightly, like he was holding back a smile.

"Since the two of you are *still* staring, I will start."

Sam pushed from the wall, breaking their stare-off. His brother was up to something. A million questions lurked in Sam's eyes, despite the carelessness of his expression.

"What is your name?" Sam asked. "We are working together now so that makes us friends."

Tehl snorted but kept silent, waiting for the rebellion leader to answer.

"My name is Rafe."

Sam blinked. "You don't expect me to believe you used your own name last night. You are a better spy than that."

Rafe shrugged, quirking his lips. "Believe what you want to believe, but maybe because I used my name I am the best spy, it keeps you guessing."

Sam mirrored the rebellion leader's smile.

Games. It was always games with these damn spies. Why couldn't anyone just say what they meant? If someone didn't give a straight answer, they'd be here all day. "Are we going to have problems with the Methians?" Tehl inserted.

"No, you will not."

"Are you sure?"

Rafe crossed his arms. "They received your invitation but declined. One of my men intercepted it, and we forged a different one."

"The seal?" Sam asked.

"Borrowed."

"And when the Methians hear that their prince was visiting?" Tehl quipped. They did not need a war with Methi.

"Aermia won't be blamed. The Methi prince will want you to search for the imposter but you won't find him on account of the fact that you're now working with him. Your alliance with Methi is secure."

It was like he took the thoughts right out of Tehl's head. That made him scowl. He didn't like anyone guessing his thoughts. "I don't like you." The words popped out of him. Sam gave him a look of exasperation while a deep chuckle trickled out of Rafe.

"The feeling is mutual, prince. While I would rather rip you from the throne, this way will be a bit less bloody and better for Aermia."

Amber eyes met his, and an understanding passed between them. Both had an interest in Aermia and believed they were helping the people. Grudgingly, Tehl dipped his head in acknowledgment. He would play nice for his people, but it didn't mean he had to like the man.

"You have a few of my people in your dungeon. I want them released."

The corners of Tehl's lips lifted. Negotiations. He could negotiate. "Agreed, if all assassination attempts on my father's life stop now."

"Agreed."

"If one of your people steps out of line and harms my family, I will obliterate the rebellion. It will make what the Scythians did to the Nagalians look like child's play. No one touches my family," Tehl threatened, letting his darker side peek out. A glimmer of respect resonated in Rafe's golden eyes. Bloodthirsty bastard.

"No need for threats, prince. I take my vows seriously. I keep my word." Rafe's eyes darkened, looking almost predatory. The rebellion leader lazily caressed a razor-thin blade strapped to his leather-clad thigh. "But, if one hair is harmed on Sage's head there will be nothing left of your family or its legacy. The kingdoms will forget you ever existed. She is one of the very few reasons I agreed to this."

Tehl studied the posture of the rebellion leader with curiosity. Everything about him bespoke aggression and possessiveness when he spoke of the young woman. Huh. Sage, that petite and devious emerald-eyed nymph was the key to keeping this hothead restrained. He would not forget that little tidbit.

"Her safety is already one of our top priorities," Sam assured the rebellion leader. "We will treat her as one of our own, even provide her with her own room."

Rafe eyed his brother. "Be sure that you do." His threat was clearly implied. "She will not stay at the palace. She will return to where she belongs."

Sam smiled, a sly twinkle in his eye. "And she belongs here, with you?"

That struck a nerve. Rafe's jaw tightened as his eyes glittered with anger. "Yes, here, with her family and me."

"I have spent limited time with the wench, but from my experience I can tell you that no one commands her, not even you. If she stays in the palace it will be at her own behest, not yours nor mine," Tehl spoke, eyeing the man across from him.

"You deny my request?" Rafe bit out, his face turning red.

"I am denying you nothing," Tehl replied. "She is not yours to speak for. She is not your mother, sister, wife, or betrothed. You have no claim on her."

Fascinated, Tehl watched the man's face turn purple. He didn't know that could happen. That had to be unhealthy.

"*She's mine.*"

The words slid along Tehl's skin, full of menace. Tehl opened his mouth with a retort when Sam stepped between them, raising his hands up.

"By all legal and familial accounts, she belongs to no one." Sam paused when the rebellion leader hissed out a breath. "But, if that is a deal breaker for you, you can put it in your list of demands."

The large man deflated like a puffer fish before Tehl's eyes. His brother always knew what to say.

"That is, once you discuss it with the lovely aforementioned female."

And then Sam had to ruin it.

"Fine," Rafe huffed, looking between Sam and Tehl. "Leave the same way you entered, and be quick about it. I'd like you gone so no one stumbles upon you before I've had time to break the news."

Tehl raised an eyebrow at the arrogant tone.

Rafe ignored him and continued, "I will see you in six days." The rebellion leader turned and strode for the door.

"You would turn your back to your enemy?" Sam called.

Rafe craned his neck and smirked at them. "You would be dead before you tried anything. Plus, we aren't enemies, are we?"

Tehl's lips curled at his comment while Sam sputtered. He liked when people were straightforward. They were unwilling allies who would sooner stab each other, but strange circumstances set them together.

Tehl moved back into the tunnel with Sam prowling after him.

"Well that was interesting."

"An understatement for sure, brother."

Tehl ran his hand along the wall, working his way toward the ladder in the tunnel's dim light.

"Aren't you the least bit curious about what other things are hidden down here?" Sam asked.

His brother's curiosity was insatiable. Sam would have spies crawling through these tunnels by nightfall. "Not even a bit. I am sure you will have discovered everything there is to know in a matter of hours though," Tehl replied wryly.

"Damn straight," Sam exhaled.

***

They were both silent, lost in their own thoughts as they returned to the palace. It amazed Tehl how much could change in just a couple of hours. They discovered the rebel woman and her identity. They found out Sam had grown up with her brothers, and Tehl himself had just made a deal with the rebellion. In two weeks' time, the threat of civil war could be over, though he knew things were never that easy.

Various officials and a few of his advisers swarmed him with lists of tasks and questions as soon as he walked through the door. Sam smiled at him and waved, slinking away, the traitor.

After approving the week's menu and a series of visitor requests, he finally made it to his office. Tehl glanced at the sun, realizing it was already time to meet with his war council. What would his council's reaction be to the deal he'd just struck? He straightened a crooked paper on his desk, briefly rethinking his decision but there was no going back. It was done. Nothing he could do now.

He shook his head at himself and abandoned the peace of his office a little early, determined to be the first one in the war council's chamber. He avoided most of the people in the palace halls and slipped into the large, open space. The ceiling curved up, forming a dome with a glass window at its center. His boots echoed on the stone floor with each step of his approach to the round table at the far end.

The dark wooden table stood on a slightly raised dais and was one of the few pieces the palace boasted that was over a thousand years old. Tehl stepped up to his seat and ran his palm along its surface. How many kings and princes had conducted war meetings here?

"Finished watching me, Sam?" he called to his brother, lurking in the shadows.

His brother's baritone chuckle filled the air, echoing around them. "Here, I thought you had lost all of your observational prowess. When did you spot me?"

He glanced at Sam as his brother detached from the side of a bookcase. "I never saw you." He tapped his ear. "The bookcase gave you away. The wood groaned."

"Damn." Sam looked accusingly at the bookshelf. "Traitor," he muttered, under his breath.

Tehl dropped his head, concealing his smile at Sam's antics. He never failed to amuse him. "Is there a reason you were lurking around the war room, brother?" Tehl sank into his chair.

Sam shrugged. "Nothing new, I wanted to listen to any gossip. You know our advisers are as bad as old women. Nothing stays a secret with them."

"Isn't that the truth?"

Samuel strolled to Tehl's side, sprawling into the chair on his right. "How do you want to approach this meeting then? It has the potential to go quite badly."

"There is no need to bring up your past with Sage's family." Tehl stared absently at Sam's glinting earring and continued. "No one in the meeting will know anything about her, save Gav, yourself and I— but I say we tell the truth. That you had some key information which led the rebel to consider working with us instead of against us and that she has negotiated a meeting where we will hopefully do just that."

Sam turned his shrewd gaze from his own boot to Tehl's face. "Do you think it wise to mention that the rebel is a woman?"

Tehl mulled it over for a moment. He knew that some may not trust or respect anything she said just because of her gender and a couple of them had met her last night at the festival. He wouldn't be able to hide her though. "They will meet her eventually, some met her last night and you know as well as I that she has won most of the old men over already."

"True, the use of her injuries was truly masterful. I wouldn't have been able to execute it any better."

"You mean her performance?" he questioned.

"Yes. By her little act she stirred their sympathy, righteous anger, sense of justice, protectiveness, and a hint of lust. Most of them are already wrapped around her finger." Sam sniggered. "I bet most of them would offer for her if they found out she wasn't already spoken for by Rafe. Not that the rebellion leader knows it."

"He is quite covetous of her, isn't he?" Tehl still didn't care for her, but he couldn't deny her beauty or the appeal of her strength.

"He is more than that, brother. That man loves her. If he feels she is threatened at all then we will have some serious problems on our hands."

Tehl sat forward and shot Sam a look before watching the door swing open. "That is why this meeting is important. We need them all to be on our side."

"Precisely."

Both brothers watched as the men filtered in, taking their places. Jaren was the last to arrive. The orange-haired man sauntered into the room as if he owned the place. Tehl couldn't stand the man. When he wasn't looking down on everyone, obviously viewing them as incompetent duds, he was throwing his daughter, Caeja, at Tehl, no doubt hoping for a royal connection.

Jaren lowered himself in his chair and looked around the table. "I hope I am not too late."

Tehl never rolled his eyes at anyone besides his brother, but, at that comment, he almost did. Jaren purposely came in late simply to gain attention. Tehl ignored him and stood. "There have been developments in the last twenty-four hours that will affect how we deal with the rebellion." He gestured to Sam. "Commander Samuel will share with you what he has discovered." Sam stood and bowed to Tehl.

Tehl sat in his chair, nodding for Sam to begin.

"We have been trying to hunt down members in the rebellion."

"Not that it has been fruitful," Garreth interrupted. "I have come up empty-handed every time."

"True," Sam said, placing his hands on the table, "until now."

A series of rumbles and questions erupted.

Sam raised a hand, and the room quieted, faint echoes bouncing around them. "Over a month ago, I received a missive detailing an information exchange that was to happen. I investigated, and, to my surprise, it was accurate. The rebel was caught and brought back to the dungeon."

"Why weren't we made aware of this?" asked the balding Lelbiel. He was a sharp, portly man, but extremely knowledgeable when it came to organizing anything.

"Because there was no information at the time. We interrogated the rebel intensely but they would not break."

"I am sure if you had given me an hour with him, he would have been singing a different tune," Zachael, the combat master, remarked. Tehl didn't doubt it. Zachael knew more about combat and painful uses of pressure points than anyone.

"This situation was...delicate. It required a certain touch." Sam's face hardened. "Some took it upon themselves to interrogate the rebel without our knowledge or permission. When we were informed, the rebel was near death. It was luck they survived."

"How bad was the damage?" questioned the grizzled William.

Tehl eyed the older man with a crazy head of gray hair. The man was an animal when it came to any form of battle on horseflesh. The night of the festival, he had told Sage her scars were a thing of beauty. Tehl was sure that when William figured out who the rebel was, he would be on their side.

"Broken ribs, nose, too many cuts and lacerations to count, bruises, dehydration, and starvation. Also an infection that caused a fever, and fluid in the lungs."

Tehl watched his advisors' eyes widen at the severity of the injuries Sam was listing. "Let it be known that the men who disobeyed me were punished severely. They are no longer with the Guard and are barred from the palace."

Shock radiated through the men. The punishment had been harsh.

"Surely that was a little bit heavy-handed. It was a rebel, after all, a traitor. I am sure those men only wanted to please you as do we all," murmured Jaren, slick as oil.

"Their punishment was hardly sufficient, I assure you."

All the attention focused on Gavriel, who had thus far been observing the table in silence. "They didn't do it for the Crown. They did it for their own sick pleasure and the thrill they received from having power over another person."

Jaren eyed Gav with distaste before dismissing him, looking back at him with a fake smile on his face. "My mistake, my lord."

"So this rebel recovered and agreed to work with us? *Against* the rebellion?" Garreth asked, knowing full well who Sage was. He was the one to carry her to her room when she left the infirmary.

"With time, we were able to reverse some of the indoctrinating that had been taught."

"So we have a spy in the midst of the rebellion?" Jeb inquired, a quiet man with black hair peppered with gray. He had more knowledge about Aermia—how? Geography? Their history? Legally?—and the surrounding three kingdoms than probably all the people of Sanee combined.

"No. We have a liaison," Sam answered.

"You want us to work *with* the rebellion?" Jaren asked incredulously. "That's ridiculous. They are traitors and deserve death."

Tehl ground his teeth to keep from shouting at the idiotic man.

"You would rather we attacked our own people?" William retorted.

Jaren glared at William for a moment before turning his eyes on him. "They are not our people when they are opposing us, they are our enemies."

"They're not our enemies if they will work with us," Sam drawled.

Jaren opened his mouth then wisely shut it when all eyes moved to him, his face turning the color of his hair.

"Have you contacted the leaders of the rebellion then?" Gavriel prodded.

"We have," Sam continued, "and they will negotiate. They are not some group of disgruntled ragtag farmers. They are organized, they are armed, and they have a vast network of supporters. If they attacked right now we could overtake them, but only at significant cost to ourselves and great loss of life." Sam gazed around the table. "If we allow ourselves to be embroiled in a civil war, the Scythians will take Aermia. That is something none of us wants. Our kingdom needs to be united in strength before we can deal with anything that Scythia throws at us."

"What is in it for them?" Lelbiel asked.

"They don't want bloodshed either. We are not yet sure what they want. We are to meet in six days and exchange demands; three days after that, we can begin negotiations."

"You trust this liaison?" Jaren prodded.

Tehl stood and stared the table down. "Yes, I do. Some of you met the rebel last night."

A few confused looks were passed around but a pair of clear gray eyes met him in understanding. William obviously knew whom he was talking about.

"So when do we get to meet this liaison?" Jeb asked.

"You will meet her at the exchange," Sam replied.

All sound ceased in the room. Various expressions of surprise and shock moved over each man's face. Slowly understanding dawned. A series of curses and movements exploded in the room. Each man shouting over the top of one another.

"A woman?" hissed Jaren.

"A woman liaison, how quaint... and exceedingly unusual," remarked Lelbiel.

"It's never been done before," stated Jeb.

Tehl waited for a while, until they got themselves together before nodding for Sam to continue.

"Yes, a woman. An *important* woman," his brother emphasized. "She is high in the chain of the rebellion's command and well loved by them. She will be highly useful to us."

"A woman?" Garreth muttered, as if he wasn't in on the secret. "It's bloody brilliant! No wonder we haven't been able to find their messengers. Women have circles that men never enter. Imagine the network of spies you could form with someone planted among them."

Sam grinned at the Elite captain. "I was thinking the same thing."

"A moment," Zachael growled. All the men looked at the wrathful dark man, vibrating with anger. "Do you mean to tell me that the Guard you removed beat this woman?"

"Yes."

Disgust and rage raced across the combat master's face before he released a breath. He looked Tehl in the eye before bowing his head in shame. "Forgive me, I had no knowledge of their actions."

"You are not accountable for their disobedience. You train the men well, it is their decision to follow your commands as well as mine."

Zachael lifted his head, guilt still weighing down his shoulders.

"Such a trauma can break the mind even if the body heals. I trust your word that she will make a trustworthy ambassador." Jeb hesitated. "But is she prepared for this responsibility?"

"You tell me. Did lady Salbei seem like a weak, unhinged woman last night?" Tehl leaned back in his chair to watch the show.

Half the men gaped at him from the table. It made him want to smirk at their open mouths. They looked like fish.

William smiled at him. "The enchanting siren from last night is to be our ambassador?"

"Indeed, she is," Sam replied.

Jaren's eyes flashed with outrage. *Here we go.*

"You knew she was a rebel last night, and yet you did not think it was pertinent information to tell us?" Jaren haughtily demanded. "How do you know she wasn't the one to try to assassinate the king?"

"Your crown prince does not have to explain anything to you, Jaren," Gavriel spoke up, coldly. "I would rethink the tone you were using with your future king."

Jaren glared at Gavriel for a moment before reining himself in. He gave Gavriel a thin-lipped smile before turning to Tehl. "Excuse my tone, I meant no offense. I was surprised—that was all."

Zachael and William coughed at his lie. Tehl's lips twitched in humor. He despised Jaren, but he was a necessary evil. The man was filthy rich and had a brilliant mind. "These are extraordinary circumstances we are all having to adjust to," he said graciously. Sam gave him a look like he approved, so he must have said it in a politically correct manner.

"The scars?" Lelbiel asked.

Tehl understood what he was getting at. He was sure none of the men in this room would forget her display any time soon: creamy thighs and—

A chair screeching cut his thoughts off.

Zachael pushed his chair back and placed his hand heavily on the old round table. "We did that?" he choked out.

Grim faces surrounded the table, even Jaren looked disgusted.

"No," Garreth interjected. He was next to the combat master. "Sick men did that."

Murmurs of agreement sounded around the table.

"If I remember correctly—" William paused. "She said the captors hadn't been punished."

Tehl eyed the wily old fox with appreciation. Nothing slipped by that man. "The men were punished except for the leader, he escaped. He has been apprehended by the rebellion."

"Are they going to hand him over?" Garreth asked, curiously.

A vicious grin touched Tehl's face. "I asked, but they kindly refused. I doubt we will see Serge again."

"And you are okay with that?" Jaren questioned.

Tehl pinned him with his gaze, his smile widening. "I am more than okay with justice, especially when I sanction it. Anything else, Jaren?"

Jaren swallowed hard. "No, my lord."

Tehl tipped his head. "Very well then. We have six days until we exchange our list of demands. We will meet here in three days and discuss what those will be. Think about it in the next couple days. I don't want to bicker about it for hours. Good day."

His advisors stood at his dismissal and bowed before streaming out of the room, leaving Sam, Gav, and himself as its only occupants. "That went better than I thought it would."

Gav bobbed his head. "It worked in our favor that she was at the festival last night. Her scars had already made an impression."

"You're right. She was a human being already, not some faceless female rebel." Tehl squinted at his cousin. "You're sounding like Sam."

"Hey now," Gav protested.

Sam sniffed. "Eh hem. Everyone wants to be like me."

Tehl exchanged looks with Gav before they both snickered. "You keep believing that if it makes you sleep at night, brother."

"I will tell you what makes me sleep at night. This pretty little blonde..."

"That's enough of that." Tehl cringed. "I don't need those images in my mind." Sam had already scarred him enough.

Sam smirked. "I will *always* want those images in my mind."

Gavriel shook his head. "You understand nothing until you have a wife. Come to me after being married a couple years and then we can swap stories."

Sam looked intently at his cousin, looking intrigued. "Really?"

Smug satisfaction filled Gav's face. "Indeed."

Tehl stretched and stepped off his raised chair. "This has been informative, but I have a date with Damari." Today they were going over the treasury books. He loved pouring over the books. Numbers always made sense. They never changed, and, if something was wrong, it was because there was a mistake somewhere.

"Run off to your accounting then." Sam wrinkled his nose. "I will make inquiries and discover what our various advisors think we should demand."

"No rest for the wicked," Tehl called over his shoulder, heading toward the door.

"I will hold your compliments close to my heart, you know."

"You do that," he retorted, leaving the war room.

CHAPTER SIX

Sage

It had been three days, and Sage still had difficulty grasping the fact that she lodged on a *Sirenidae* vessel. Not only that, but though it'd been mere weeks, it seemed as though her entire world had been flipped on its axis:

The Aermian king wasn't evil.

The rebellion wasn't perfect.

A race thought to have disappeared fifteen hundred years ago somehow still existed.

It was enough to have anyone's head spinning.

Sage mindlessly peered at the glistening waves as they lapped against the hull, fascinated that, despite the movement, its waters were clear as glass. She marveled as little schools of fish darted around below, shimmering purple and silver in the sun. She cringed, though, when it served as a reminder of the abrupt question she'd carelessly blurted to her host, and she had to fight the impulse to bang her head against the quarterdeck. Thankfully, Lilja had only laughed instead of seeing fit to drown her. The unusual captain had then slapped her on the arm and showed her to her quarters.

Sage leaned her elbows on the railing, deciding tonight she would finally ask about the Sirenidae. For the last couple of days, she had found herself staring at Captain Femi's scarf, curious about the gills she knew it hid. She had been sorely tempted to ask at the time but quickly decided it was better to wait for the right moment. Since then, Sage had been filling her time by helping Lilja, doing whatever was needed.

There'd been a few instances where she'd thought of sneaking from the ship to her family's smithy, just to see if they needed her, but reason always prevailed. It was too much of a risk, for she knew both Sam and Rafe would have her home watched, hoping to catch her doing just that. Also, she was certain she had seen Rafe skulking about the docks shortly after her arrival. That man was an expert tracker, so it was best not to tempt fate.

As she sat, silent in her contemplation, the sun slowly sunk below the horizon, streaking the sky in shades of gold, orange, red and pink. Abandoning her perch, she skipped down the stairs and onto the deck. Sure-footed, Sage moved to the opposite side and down into the galley, and her stomach growled as the savory smells of herbs and warm bread greeted her.

Lilja smiled and waved her forward. Sage stepped up to the table, watching as Lilja added spices to what seemed to be a stew. "What can I do to help, captain?"

The captain flashed her a smile, pointing to the bread and vegetables. "Could you cut those for me?"

Sage plucked a heavy blade from a wooden block and began doing so. "It smells delicious," she remarked, glancing at the stew, and paused. It was almost the same color as Lilja's eyes. "It's an...unusual color though."

"A question but not a question. I find you refreshing, Sage."

Sage's brows wrinkled.

The captain tossed her a wry look before continuing to stir her soup. "It's apparent you are filled with curiosity, and yet you have not asked me a single question."

It was true. She was brimming with a million questions, but she also didn't know what sort of burdens came with the answers. Sometimes it was best to remain ignorant. "On some occasions, it's safer to keep your questions to yourself."

Lilja considered her for a moment before setting her spoon down. "True, but without questions how would one learn? Knowledge is power."

"It also means danger," Sage answered, not looking up from chopping her sea onion.

"Another wise answer for one so young."

"You age quickly when your innocence is stripped from you," Sage replied, keeping her cuts in perfect, even slices. She may be young but she felt like she'd aged years in the last month.

"You have suffered many things, *ma fleur.*"

A pale hand settled on hers, ceasing her cutting. Sage lifted her gaze to Lilja's and saw in her unusually-colored eyes that the captain understood what she was suffering. Sage dropped her eyes back to the onion, waiting for her to speak.

"It will pass with time, love. You have strength beyond anything you can imagine." The captain removed her hand and paused. "So to answer your question-not-question. I muddle a special seaweed into the soup, and that's why it turns that color."

Sage appreciated the change in subject. Her time in the dungeon wasn't something she wanted to think of; she dreamed of it often enough each night. Hayjen and Lilja had burst into her room the first night thinking she was being murdered, but she'd only been screaming in her sleep, and poor Hayjen had received a blow to the face when he woke her. She still prickled with guilt whenever she thought of it. She'd been so out of sorts she hadn't known what was real or what was the dream.

"Where do you find the seaweed?"

"It grows about three hundred arm-lengths below the ocean's surface."

Sage's eyes rounded. That was incredible. She had never heard of anyone being able to dive that deep. Maybe asking a few questions wouldn't be too offensive. "That must be an interesting trip," she ventured, tipping her vegetables into the soup.

"It is unlike anything you can imagine."

"As a little girl I always wanted to be a Sirenidae," Sage remarked off-handedly, scrubbing the sharp blade in a wash bin. "I've always loved swimming, and I feel like the ocean is my second home."

"There are so many treasures down there. It is truly a completely different world."

Sage wiped the blade dry and placed it back on the wooden block, turning to Lilja. As she again eyed the woman's scarf she fought her nerves, jerking her chin toward the royal blue material concealing the mysterious white hair and gills. "How do those work?"

White teeth flashed at her in a deep smile. Lilja brushed away the scarf and drew a long pale finger down the side of her bare neck. "They filter the oxygen from the water, and my body keeps the oxygen and injects it into my blood while forcing out the water."

Her brows furrowed. "Oxygen?"

"Air."

What a perplexing thought. But fish had to breathe some way so she supposed it sort of made sense. "I didn't know there was air in the water."

Captain Femi gestured for her to sit at the table. "It is all part of science."

Sage pierced her with a serious look and sat slowly, thinking. No one practiced science after the Scythians did what they did. Everyone lived and used what they could from nature. Science had caused the Nagalians' genocide and no one wanted that again.

"Don't give me that look, *ma fleur*. I will not turn into a murdering barbarian before you." Captain Femi's eyes glinted. "Remember: knowledge is power."

"Indeed." Sage cocked her head, studying the woman across from her. "How are you still alive? Sirenidae are now just myths."

"Through secrecy, deception, and cunning."

Sage didn't doubt that. "Do others exist?"

Lilja lifted her scarf and patted it into place without looking away. "That is a secret I can not give you, but our race will never die off."

Sage respected her answer and moved on. "Are the stories true? Do you drag men into the ocean and drown them?"

Lilja stared off, like she was seeing something else. "That is one fable that sprung up after we disappeared. During the Nagalian purge, we did wage war from the sea and drowned our enemies. But we never did it as sport, as the fables say, it was against the law."

"Whose law?"

Lilja's gaze sharpened. "The king's."

"Are you speaking of Poseidon?"

"The one and only."

Her mum had told her stories about the unearthly ruler of the Sirenidae. "Did he have magenta eyes and white hair as well? Is that a racial trait?" she asked curiously.

Lilja smiled. "The silvery-white hair is a Sirenidae trait. We are born deep in the ocean where the sunlight doesn't reach, so we have no color in our hair." Captain Femi gestured to her eyes. "As for the unusual color, they change once we eat the rose seaweed. It has properties that enhance our vision, enabling us to see in the ocean's depths."

"So you weren't born with pink eyes?"

"No, my eyes were a lilac color. They fade back if I'm unable to regularly eat rose seaweed."

"Does the sun affect your hair?"

Lilja shook her head. "No, I've spent too much time in the sea. Between the lack of sunlight and the salt, it is permanently colorless."

"What would happen if a Sirenidae was born on land?"

"They would look like anyone else."

So they could blend in. "What about the gills?"

Captain Femi laughed. "If I stay out of the sea, they seal shut until I swim and need them again."

Sage opened her mouth to ask another question but paused when Hayjen stormed in, wearing a blustery expression. Her burly friend halted at the edge of the table, scrutinizing her. Sage glanced to Lilja, the captain's face sobering as she eyed her husband warily.

Sage's heart flew to her throat. Something bad had happened. "Is my family okay?" she asked, her tone sharp.

Hayjen's blue eyes softened a touch. "Your family's fine, Sage. I checked on them myself today." He blew out an irritated breath. "Rafe called a meeting of the rebellion. It is to be in less than half an hour."

Sage pondered that for a moment. "Why is this the first time I am hearing about it?"

Hayjen's nostrils flared. "It's my belief he intended to exclude Sage."

A small noise of outrage escaped Lilja.

Frustration bubbled under Sage's skin. What game was he

playing? She had every right to be there. She'd certainly earned it. Was she now the enemy because she was a liaison? She was merely seeking the best outcome for *all* citizens of Aermia. "I will have to sample some of your fabulous soup later, I'm afraid. It seems I have business to take care of."

Capitan Femi cocked her head, eyes twinkling. "Give them hell, *ma fleur*. Show them what you are made of."

The look in Hayjen's ice blue eyes stopped her. "Rhys will be there."

Every muscle in her body tensed at his name. Nightmarish images flashed through her mind and she bowed forward, clutching the end of the table, her fingers turning white as the wood bit into her flesh. She let go the breath she'd been holding and tried to regulate her breathing.

Could she handle seeing him again?

She barely registered the scraping of a chair when an elegant pale hand entered her view. Sage focused on the hand settling on her own. The slight pressure caused her to glance up into magenta eyes filled with understanding but no pity.

"There is no shame in weakness. There's strength in knowing your limitations, but this is not one of your limitations, Sage. You are better than that animal. You know he will never hurt you again. The strength of your inner person shines brighter than the dawn's first rays. He has no power over you. You are not in that dungeon, you are here with Hayjen and me. He will be by your side in place of your family. You have allies. You are *not* alone." Warm hands cupped her cheeks. "You will never be alone. Dig deep, and use all that anger and desire for vengeance to do something good. Use it to protect your people."

Sage's eyes blurred, and she dropped her eyes to Lilja's chin. She needed those words. "I want him dead," she whispered, speaking the ugly truth out loud. "I know I shouldn't feel that way; it's wrong. But he haunts me every time I sleep. I am so tired, Lilja, worn out. Why is that monster free?" She lifted her watery eyes back to Lilja's.

"Everyone is punished for their actions one way or another. I don't care what the rebellion decided. He will be held accountable for his actions, mark my words, *ma fleur.*" Her eyes darted to Sage's emerald ones. "Can you do this?"

She pulled in a stuttering breath and nodded yes. She would not let her fear rule her. Lilja's hands dropped from her face while Sage blinked back her tears. She sucked her lip in and bit it. She would let no one keep her from this meeting.

She twisted her head back to Hayjen. "Are you ready?"

He walked around the table and wrapped both Lilja and Sage in his burly arms. "I am. Everything will be all right. I will never leave your side." He dropped a kiss on top of the Captain's head, releasing them. "We will be home in a couple hours, my love."

Sage trailed him before glancing over her shoulder at Lilja. "Do you want to come with us?"

Captain Femi snorted and waved her off. "Those men would run for the hills if they met me. I would be a distraction more than anything. Watch that man of yours, he has quite the reflexes. I doubt you will escape him easily tonight. Keep your wits about you."

Now it was Sage's turn to snort. "Never lost my wits to a man yet."

She jogged up the two stairs and across the shadowy deck. Reaching the rail, she swung her leg over and shimmied down the rope ladder. At the bottom, Hayjen reached for her and pulled her to the dock.

"Are you ready to face the beasts?"

Determination filled her, and she used it to force back some of her fears. "Indeed."

Hayjen grunted and began a clipped pace along the dock that had quieted. Most of the laborers had gone to their homes or ships by now, yet it was still early enough that they hadn't drunk enough to be noisily inebriated. Hayjen led her to the same tunnel she'd escaped from and Sage dropped down, noting the water was three inches higher than the last time she'd done this.

Her friend noted. "The tide is coming in. We will have to take a different route home."

Home.

That word resonated with her.

Where was home?

It wasn't safe for her family or her to stay with them anymore. Much to her chagrin, the palace had started to feel like home. There was also Lilja and Hayjen. She felt safe with them. They expected nothing from her, but offered her everything. Where did she belong? Where was home?

Hayjen took the lead, and Sage followed in his wake, each tunnel blending into the next in her mind. He hesitated outside a thick wooden door, looking to her before opening it. She shored her defenses and nodded, so her friend soundlessly pushed it open and entered. She hung back for a moment, taking a deep breath. A chorus of masculine salutations greeted Hayjen. Sage then stepped forward into the room and met seven narrowed gazes.

Silence.

Sage had to fight her panic at being the subject of so many male stares, but it was time to play at being collected and unaffected.

She smiled warmly at the room, avoiding a pair of muddy brown eyes glaring daggers at her. She kicked the door, and it thudded shut behind her. She then glided to Hayjen as he pulled out a chair. Pulling in a shallow breath through her nose, she sat, placing her hands on the worn table.

"Good evening, gentlemen." She peeked up at them from

underneath her lashes and gave them a soft smile. The stern faces melted into more welcoming expressions. Bitterness welled inside her at how easily they were manipulated. Rafe had taught her well.

"Why is she here?"

Sage covered her flinch and kept her serene mask in place at his voice.

He couldn't hurt her here.

Hayjen's hand settled on her knee in silent support. She maintained her smile as she faced down her own personal demon. Rhys looked the same to her, completely unremarkable except for his height. Nothing to indicate the sadistic monster living inside him. And here she was, sitting at the same table like everything was okay. His eyes roved over her, causing bile to burn her throat. Everything in her body revolted against the lecherous glint in his eyes.

A low growl emanated across from her, snapping her out of trance.

Sage pasted a bland smile on her face and clenched her hands to stop them from trembling. "I am part of the rebellion circle, am I not?" She couldn't stand looking at him anymore so she looked into each face around the table, skipping over Rafe.

"Of course you are, dear," spoke up Mason from her right.

She gave him a kind smile. He was an older man with a fierce love for his family. "How is your daughter doing? I heard you have a new grandbaby to love."

His moss green eyes lit up with joy. "The wee babe is doing well."

"I am happy to hear it."

"I am glad as well that your family is doing well, Mason. But maybe we should focus on the task at hand." Rafe's low, baritone washed over her, irritation coloring his tone.

Sage slid her eyes to the mountain of a man staring her down. Rafe's amber eyes bored holes into her. She felt like prey just before it was pounced upon. He was obviously not happy with her. He broke their stare down and swept the table with his gaze, her breath rushing out once she was no longer the subject of his scrutiny.

Finally, he started to speak. "There has been a development that is beneficial to the rebellion."

Sage held her breath as the circle of men leaned forward.

"Thanks to Sage's negotiating skills, we have a meeting with the Crown."

Sage noted the various expressions of shock and revulsion that crossed their faces. Sputters of indignation and curses exploded around the table.

"What do you mean by that?" demanded Noah, a merchant with a heart of gold and a shrewd mind for numbers.

"He means—" Rhys's insidious voice cut through the din, "—that the princes' whore used her wiles on Rafe and the princes of Aermia."

Goosebumps rose on Sage's arms as his eyes brushed over her skin.

"What did you do to get them to agree to such a farce?" Rhys continued.

Sage clenched her teeth so hard her jaw ached. She refused to look at him, focusing instead on Hayjen's face. She would not dignify that with an answer. *Breathe in and out. He cannot hurt you,* she chanted to herself.

"That is enough young man," Mason chastised from the end of the table.

Her eyes darted to the stern older man. His eyes flicked to hers briefly, softening a touch. Sage was grateful to him for sticking up for her when no one else did.

"She must be something special to keep the attention of that many men." Rhys released a loud groan that made her stomach heavy, and saliva fill her mouth. "I overheard she could do this one thing with her…"

"Enough!" Rafe snarled, a low growl rumbling out of him.

Sage flinched in her seat, eyes snapping to the seething man across from her. The hair on her arms stood up at the sound he'd made. Lilja was right: he was a predator. Everything about him screamed danger from head to toe; black leather and numerous weapons were strapped all over his muscular frame. His eyes glinted with rage, burning an intense gold. She'd begun trembling again but stilled as Hayjen put pressure on her knee, letting her know he was there for her.

"Don't you ever speak about Sage that way or you will find yourself with more than a shoulder wound!" Danger was woven into each of Rafe's words.

"Is that a threat?" Rhys questioned, a small tremor in his voice.

The corner of Sage's mouth twitched. It seemed even monsters were afraid of Rafe.

"It is a *promise*." The rebellion leader's lips twisted into a sinister smile. Sage would hate to be on the receiving end of such a look. Rafe eyed each man before pausing on her for a moment. "We do not speak about our comrades in this way. Even if the lies Rhys is spouting were true, we all understand there's a heavy price to be paid to accomplish our goals. We do what we need to in order to survive."

"I thought you were done after your assignment, Sage?" Madden, who had been quiet up until this point, asked.

Sage ripped her gaze from Rafe and held Madden's hazel eyes with hers, flashing him a rueful smile. "As did I, but life has a funny way of playing tricks on you."

"So what of this meeting?" Hayjen rumbled from her side, taking the attention off her. "How does a meeting with the Crown benefit us?"

"We have had information that the Scythians are mobilizing their warriors. One can only guess what they are up to but..."

"War." Madden supplied, not looking surprised.

Rafe nodded. "We believe so, yes."

"But why now?" Badiah asked, confusion clear on his slender face. "They've been silent since the construction of the Mort Wall and that was a good two hundred years ago. It's always been their pattern to *send away* their unwanted kin. Now they're *taking* people? *Our* people?" He shook his head. "It makes no sense. They hate outsiders and anything that doesn't meet their ridiculous notion of perfection. This does not bode well for any of us."

"Which means we can't afford a civil war," Sage supplied.

Badiah eyed her as if he was reading the thoughts in her head. "You mean for us to seek a treaty with the Crown."

"What?" Madden asked, incredulously. "We can't trust them as far as we can throw them! Is *that* the source of your Scythian information?"

"No, it is not." Rafe didn't elaborate.

"We have the advantage," cried Rhys, shooting to his feet, his chair falling to the dirt floor with a dull thwap. Sage tensed but maintained her calm façade. "We are so close to starting a new regime. Have you all forgotten about why we are here in the first place? Our families are starving, our crops are dying, and our people are now being stolen! Where has the Crown been all this time? What have they been doing? Hiding in the stone palace, doing nothing. Meanwhile we suffer."

Mason eyed Rhys skeptically before glancing to Rafe. "We sanctioned the assassination of the king not even two weeks ago. It seems naïve to think the princes would forgive such an act and now seek peace between us."

"You have never steered us wrong, Rafe," Badiah cut in. "But none of us are infallible. Are you certain this isn't a trap of some kind?"

"It isn't," Sage murmured. Suddenly, she was the center of attention. Sage forced false bravado into her voice, raising her chin. "During my time at the palace they tried to recruit me, and so I listened, and I learned from the things they were willing to share as they attempted to win me over. The king was a wealth of information." Her face hardened. "The Scythians *will* strike. If we do not unite as a kingdom, they will destroy us and swarm Aermia like locusts. There will be nothing of us left to rule." She let them mull that over before continuing. "Our goal is to save the innocent lives, to give them a better life, to give them a voice. This is our chance to do just that but without the bloodshed. No one need die. We still have control. Arrangements have been made to exchange demands three days from now. You have until then to decide what you want."

"The decision has been made?" Madden growled.

"Yes, it has." Rafe deliberately rose from his seat, muscles bunching with the controlled movement, and crossed bulging arms over his wide chest. "This will greatly aid our cause. Now, it is up to you to decide what we need from this."

"How does Sage fit into this?" Hayjen asked, shifting in his chair.

"She will be our liaison. She knows the rebellion and the Crown. Sage is perfect for the job."

She doubted that.

"If she is supposed to be the liaison then what is she doing here?" Madden asked. "This doesn't seem very neutral of her."

Sage tried to not to be offended, but she was. She had done everything they had ever asked of her.

"I agree."

She gasped, looking up into Rafe's serious face. He stared back without emotion. Betrayal burned through her. He planned on kicking her out. Sage looked around the table hoping to see someone disagree with him, but from their blank faces she knew they agreed with him. Her gaze trailed back to Rafe. For a moment, she had thought that maybe she could trust him, but, once again, he'd betrayed her. She didn't even know him anymore. Her thoughts must have shown on her face because his eyebrows creased and his face fell, ever so slightly.

"Little one..." he murmured softly.

Sage shoved down her own personal feelings and maneuvered her face back into her mask. She pulled her hands from the table and reached down to squeeze Hayjen's hand, and then scooted out her wooden chair, her heart hollow. She'd spent years of her life with these men. She'd trained, schemed, fought, and laughed with them. Yet as she stood, it was like they were strangers to her. They had sanctioned regicide, sent a monster to hurt her and then protected him, and now, they had cast her out. She was done.

"Well then, gentlemen. Be wise in your choices, you have the chance to heal Aermia. Don't be foolish or hotheaded in this." Her features hardened. "If any one of you tries something stupid at the exchange, it will mean the obliteration of the rebellion and all the resulting bloodshed will be on your head. Don't overestimate yourselves, and don't underestimate the Crown." She bared her teeth at Rafe and took perverse joy in how his fists tightened in response. Someone wasn't happy. "I wish you all the best." She touched Hayjen's shoulder, signaling him to stay, before striding out of the room as if it had been her choice.

As soon as the door thudded behind her, she fled. She suspected Rafe wouldn't be far behind.

CHAPTER SEVEN

Sage

She hastened through the labyrinth of tunnels, twisting left and right until she finally spotted the dock. Her breath heaved in and out of her chest as she paused and admired the sparkling stars in the colorless night sky. They winked at her like gems haphazardly strewn across a bed of midnight silk. The sounds of bawdy sailor songs filled the air, merchants and corsairs alike already deep in their cups.

She startled as a large man crashed into a crate before slumping onto the wooden deck and laughing, obviously inebriated. Sage crept around him, picking up her pace as she headed to the Sirenidae vessel. A wooden ladder dangled against the ship's hull, and Sage eyed it with skepticism. There had to be at least four feet between the ship and the dock so it'd be a stretch to reach it. She pursed her lips.

Would it be better to call for Lilja's help?

Nope. She could make it, but she couldn't hesitate.

Sage backtracked a few paces, focusing on the ladder as it swayed in the light breeze. She loosened her arms and released a deep breath before pushing off the balls of her feet and sprinting to the dock's edge. Her muscles coiled and sprung as she pushed from the wooden surface and she caught hold of the rope, her momentum crashing her into the wooden hull and nearly knocking her senseless. Her feet dangled below her, and she scrambled to get her feet onto a rung. Her right boot finally caught the ladder, and she made quick work of climbing it, vaulting over the rail as soon as she'd reached it. She allowed herself a satisfied smile at the fact that she'd made the leap despite being so short.

"For a moment, I thought you would not make it, *ma fleur*. Quite agile, aren't you?"

Sage didn't take her eyes from the dock below even though she hadn't heard Lilja's approach. "You watched me the whole time but didn't offer help?"

A husky laugh reached her ears. "You didn't need my assistance. Besides, it was amusing."

Sage rolled her eyes and peered into the inky corner Lilja was lurking in. "And if I hadn't been able to make it?"

Captain Femi waved her hand and uncoiled from the barrel she was sitting on. "You would've gotten a little wet. It might even have done you some good. After all, the ocean contains healing properties that aren't found anywhere else in the world." The captain sauntered to her side and ran a hand down her brown locks as if she'd been doing it all of Sage's life, scrutinizing Sage's face. "What has you so riled up, child? And where is Hayjen? He was not to leave your side."

"I was relieved of my position among the circle." The words felt like ash on her tongue. She swallowed hard, feeling bitterness well in her. "I am the best asset they have and a wealth of information, yet they threw me away like I meant nothing." She dropped Lilja's knowing gaze turning back to the rail. Little lights bobbed along the ships, illuminating a series of card games, storytelling, and cleaning. "I fit nowhere," she found herself saying. "I have no home. The Crown doesn't trust me because I am part of the rebellion, and the rebellion doesn't trust me because I was imprisoned for so long with the Crown. Neither wants *me*, but both want something *from me*. I only have value in what I can give them, not as a person." She blew out an angry breath, glancing at Lilja. "What rubs me is that I thought Rafe, of all people, would stick with me, that he was my friend. But he is nothing but a pretender. He cast me out today."

Captain Femi hissed. "Aye, you need to beware of that one. You couldn't find a more pigheaded man if you tried."

That perked her interest. "You know him?"

Lilja's eyes shuttered but her smile was sharp and knowing. "I know of him. That man is about as flexible as a hundred-year-old oak tree. He may be wise but he's stuck in his ways. By the time he figures you out, it will be too late."

Sage's brows furrowed. What was she talking about? "Too late?"

"To correct his mistakes, *ma fleur*." Lilja brushed a hand along her cheek and yawned. "It is time for me to find my bed. Don't worry about the ladder, Hayjen will pull it up when he comes home. Goodnight, love."

Sage smiled at the quirky female and whispered a soft goodnight as Captain Femi glided across the deck, her skirts swishing seductively behind her. She shook her head and claimed Lilja's abandoned spot. Weariness filled her, making her ache for her own bed, but she didn't want to miss Hayjen so she'd just have to keep her vigil.

***

A whisper of sound had her eyes springing open as she observed Hayjen heaving himself over the rail in the dim moonlight. As he pulled up the ladder, Lilja slipped into view, wearing a translucent robe that was most indecent. Sage blushed and averted her eyes, instead stretching the crick in her neck. Hayjen glanced over the ship's side and jerked his head to his wife. She froze for a beat before stomping over to the rail and glaring down at the dock.

"You are not welcome here," Lilja glowered. The captain's white waves slipped from the emerald silk scarf wrapped around her hair, displaying her face. Danger carved her face into sharp planes that could cut glass.

Something about the captain's look and her tone made the hair on Sage's arms stand up. One thing was apparent, she never wanted to be on Lilja's bad side.

Sage leaned forward to listen, shivering when a menacing growl rose from the dock.

"You will not hide from me what is mine!" That made her spine stiffen, she knew that voice.

"There is nothing on this ship that belongs to you, I can assure you of that."

"Come now, Lilja, you and I both know you harbor what is not yours."

Captain Femi tossed her head and glanced to Sage's shadowy corner before glaring back down. "Leave. There is nothing here for you."

"I will have what I came for. Do not make me come and retrieve her."

Lilja's face hardened into angry lines. She leaned over the rail, her silvery hair making her seem almost ethereal in the moonlight. "You set one foot on my ship, and I will drag you to the bottom of the ocean and watch with glee as you drown."

The malice in Lilja's voice shocked Sage. There was a danger lurking in her new friend that she had heretofore never witnessed. Perhaps some of the myths were true after all.

When Hayjen placed a large hand on her shoulder, the currently ferocious woman turned to him. Whatever she read on his face seemed to calm her. She smiled up at her husband and placed a quick kiss on his hand before turning to Rafe. "My threat stands."

Sage finally stood and strode to her friends, staring down at the handsome man seething below her. His eyes flashed to hers, roving her face.

"Sage."

In that single syllable, he had infused a wealth of meaning. She reached over and pried one of the captain's hands from the railing. "It's okay. Why don't you go back to bed and I will handle our unwelcome guest?"

Lilja searched her eyes before nodding. She spared one last glare at Rafe before turning on her heel and striding to her chamber. One side of Hayjen's lips turned up, before he whispered, "Don't let him step foot on this ship. Heaven knows I can't control her if he does."

Sage returned his smile before turning back to their audience. Rafe stayed quiet as Hayjen's footsteps faded away, gazing intently into her eyes as if trying to peer into her soul.

"Little one... "

Sage stiffened at the endearment, her lips pinching. "What do you want, Rafe?" she barked.

He scanned her face before he spoke. "I want many things, but, first, you need to return to those who love you."

"Home?" she scoffed. "I can't *go* home, Rafe. I need to keep my family as far from this as possible. You know that. A treaty hasn't been signed. I won't put them in any more danger than they are in already."

"I didn't mean to your parents' home." A pause. "I meant mine."

Sage gaped. *His* home?

"I will have you protected the entire time."

"From the rebellion?"

"Yes," he drew out.

"The same rebellion that cast me out for having the unlucky happenstance of being caught and tortured by the Crown?" she hissed. "The same rebellion that sent a monster to check on me but did the opposite, damaging me in a way that will never heal? The same men I thought to be my brothers in arms but who kept that monster in their midst, even letting him decide what's best for our people?" Sage seethed with righteous indignation. "The same rebellion that commissioned me to murder our king? *That* rebellion?"

"You weren't cast out..."

She slashed a hand through the air. "That is exactly what happened! You sanctioned it! You sought me out in the woods. You offered me a chance to help protect people, yet the men you are working with have done the hurting."

"No one is perfect, Blade."

Oh, he'd used her nickname—something he only did when *really* pissed. Well good. Maybe he would now feel a fraction of the turmoil she was feeling. "You're right, but I refuse to be blinded by honey-coated words meant only to incite loyalty." She stabbed a finger down at him. "I have had a few weeks to think on our first conversation in the cave. I was too distressed after my escape and dealing with that low life to notice, but I remember your face. You weren't shocked when I told you of the king's illness. And I very well know that you never agree to something you don't know inside and out. You *already knew*," she accused. He didn't drop her gaze or look ashamed. Disgust filled her. "You were willing to sacrifice an innocent old man for what you wanted."

"No one is innocent."

"You're right." She stared pointedly at him.

Rafe cursed and threw his hands in the air. "He wants to die, Sage. The old man misses his wife, he can't function. It would be a kindness to put him down."

Revulsion filled her. "Like a lame animal? Are you even listening to yourself? Who made you the judge?"

"You are still young, little one, and naïve. We're at war."

"What war?" she cried, flinging her arms out wide. "There is no war, save the one you're trying to create!" His condescension made her blood boil. "Don't you dare patronize me! My youth was ripped from me in that cell. Don't you dare call me naïve after what I have seen and experienced."

His face dropped, and he raised his hands, attempting to placate her. "It's not my intention to argue with you."

"No," she said hollowly. "You came to cage me."

His hands curled into fists, his face turning red. "Why are you being so difficult? I can see Lilja's influence already. I should have stolen you away earlier."

"Excuse me?!" she growled, rage pulsing through her. Sage leaned over the rail, glaring furiously. "Lilja has been nothing but kind and honest, unlike you. I am where I want to be, I am not leaving!"

"Oh, yes, you are," he retorted. Rafe sprung from the deck and slammed a blade into the side of ship.

"What the bloody hell? Lilja is going to skin you," Sage yelled.

"If she can catch me," he grunted, climbing the side of the ship. Her eyes widened and she took a step back as Rafe cleared the railing in no time. He crouched there, eyes brimming with a tumult of emotions.

Stars above, he was angry.

"I will not leave you here."

He reached for her arm, but she pulled just out of his grasp.

Rafe's eyes hardened. "Do not make this difficult. I will protect my family. You're part of it."

Her chin jutted out. She was *not* leaving with him. "Family doesn't betray each other. I am nothing to you."

His jaw clenched before he shifted onto the balls of his feet. "No, you are everything."

A moment of clarity hit her.

He wasn't going to take no for an answer. She would have to out maneuver him. Rafe would never hurt her intentionally, but he wouldn't give up. Time to put her skills into action. She would have to fool the master.

Sage softened her face a little and stared at him with resignation and exhaustion. She didn't have to fake being tired, she really was. "I am tired, Rafe. I haven't slept a full night in ages."

He reached a hand out and cupped her cheek, his palm rough but gentle. "I know, little one, I will you keep you safe so you can sleep."

She swayed into his body, placing a hand on his chest. "Will you protect me from my monsters?"

A small smile flashed in the dark, breaking what was left of her heart. "Always, little one, always."

Sage smiled back, steeling herself, and then shoved with all her might, ducking down to avoid his grasping hands. Startled amber eyes met hers just before he disappeared, a loud splash sounding below. She peered over the rail at Rafe as he flailed in the water. He sputtered and kicked to the wooden dock, heaving himself up as water pooled beneath him.

"Sage," he bellowed.

She grinned impishly at him and waved, ignoring her churning stomach. "I will send a message on the day of the exchange with a location. If you come up here uninvited again, I will have Lilja take you for a swim." Incense filled her nose just before Captain Femi appeared at her side.

"And it would be a pleasure," the Sirenidae purred.

Rafe looked between them, his fury mounting the longer they stared at each other. He stabbed a finger at her. "We will talk about this Sage Blackwell." He straightened his soggy leather vest then turned, prowling down the dock.

Sage released a breath she hadn't been aware she was holding. She felt so many emotions that she couldn't differentiate them anymore. She swallowed and pushed Rafe from her mind. There were too many things to deal with, and his obvious control issues were at the bottom of the list. She glanced at Lilja from the corner of her eye. The captain was still squinting in the direction Rafe had gone when she spoke. "Did you enjoy the show?"

"There's been more excitement around here in the last three days than the last three years combined." The sound of Hayjen's deep voice rumbled from a nearby alcove.

Sage rolled her eyes and hid a smile. Privacy? More like the illusion of. "Eavesdropping?" she hummed.

Lilja quirked a white brow, a smile on her lips and her eyes bright. "Of course we were spying, as if we would truly leave you alone with that bully. For a moment, I thought he would snatch you from my ship and abscond with you into the night. You're lucky you're so quick." The Sirenidae sniggered. "The look on his face when you pushed him will provide me with amusement for years to come."

Sage turned to rest a hip on the rail, trying to figure out the woman next to her. Lilja spoke of Rafe as if they knew each other intimately. "How do you know him? Is he a former lover?"

Lilja choked and shook her head so furiously her white waves flipped around her. "Stars above, no. Let's just say he and I have run in the same circles over the years, and I don't approve of his highhanded ways."

Sage snorted. "Highhanded is a mild term. Do you truly dislike him?" Despite his obvious failings, Sage still felt he had a good heart.

Captain Femi's magenta eyes caught hers. "No, he wants good things. I just disagree on how he gets them."

Hayjen popped out of his darkened corner to join their conversation. He wrapped his arms around his tall wife and grinned broadly over her head. "He has a will as strong as Lil's, and she doesn't like when someone challenges her."

Lilja scowled and swatted at his arm. "Not true."

Hayjen peered down at his wife, a silly grin on his face. "You and I both know it's the truth." Before she could argue, he swept her into his arms. "Now, my contrary wife, it is exceedingly late, and well past my bedtime." He lifted his eyes from his wife to Sage. "Time for you to seek your bed as well, I believe."

Sage scoffed at him. "When did you become my keeper?"

Hayjen grumbled under his breath like he was prone to. He shifted Lilja in his arms and stared up at the stars. "Lord save me from feisty women."

Lilja touched his face. "Ah, but you love it."

His lips tugged up at the corners before he addressed Sage. "Well... I am a glutton for punishment. I only meant that you might be tired as well. I know you didn't sleep last night."

She smiled sheepishly and bid the couple goodnight. Sage paused by her door, watching Hayjen cart away the giggling Lilja. A stab of envy struck her at their companionship. She hoped someday she would have that. Sighing, she slipped into her room, most likely for another night of nightmares.

***

Over the course of the next few days, Sage continued helping Lilja and furthering her own training. Captain Femi was a wonderful sparring partner. The woman's movements were smooth and fluid, yet quick as a viper. Training aboard the ship added another element of difficulty. The dipping and swaying of the vessel caused her to stumble a time or two, but over time it improved her balance.

The day of the exchange arrived speedily. She sent messages to both the Crown and the rebellion with the meeting location, praying that Lilja's contacts proved trustworthy.

Sage had encountered and persuaded a merchant to lease the entire space of his home for a few hours. Calling him a merchant was perhaps bit of a stretch as he was more pirate than anything, but she didn't care. She was most likely living with pirates. If Lilja was a legitimate trader she'd eat her own hat.

The home she'd secured suited her purposes well. It was neutral territory with plenty of escape routes. The peaked roof was perfect for surveying the surrounding area. It also boasted a hidden trapdoor between the chimney and tallest peak, making it easy to lurk in the rafters of the house.

Sage perched in the rafter with the hatch slightly raised, peeking out of the trapdoor. She scanned the street below with interest. She had been sure to arrive early specifically so she could observe the interactions between the Crown and the rebellion before she made her entrance. She was still piqued by the fact the rebellion's demands had not been revealed to her. Over the last three days she had tried to needle it out of Hayjen, but it seemed that the man was skilled in avoidance and, occasionally, in disappearing into thin air.

A laugh drew her attention. A blond deckhand was chatting up a washer girl. Her eyes narrowed on the familiar frame.

Sam.

If he hadn't laughed she wouldn't have known it was him. That man was certainly good at what he did. She snorted. But he was always chasing women. If Sam was nearby it meant his group had already arrived as well.

Sage clicked the trapdoor shut and waited in the darkened beams for her guests to enter. A door creaked open. She watched with interest as a cloaked figure slipped into the room and searched it. After a moment, he threw back his hood and whistled softly. His disheveled dirty blond hair almost covered his eyes. Sage scrutinized him. He was familiar, but she just couldn't place him. He moved to one side of the room and waited.

The door creaked open again and a heavy tread moved across the wooden floor as Hayjen entered her line of vision. He stopped across the room from the cloaked man. "So, they sent us in first?" The blond remarked while chuckling. "Either they trust us implicitly, or we're expendable."

She could see Hayjen's lips crack a smile. "No doubt the latter," he joked.

Both men turned to the door when it opened, both cataloguing the newcomers. A man with black and silver peppered hair glided into the room. Sage would bet her best blade he was an assassin by trade or, at least, exceptionally skilled in combat. The man trailing behind him was someone familiar. It was the older gentleman that had said her scars were beautiful the night of the banquet. They both moved to the blond's side, assessing Hayjen.

Light footsteps slipped into the home, adding Badiah to the mix. The slender man perched on a chair next to Hayjen making him appear like a child when contrasted with the other man's hulking frame. Sage smiled. None of them would suspect the small man's skill with daggers and hand-to-hand combat was perhaps unparalleled. Badiah was deliberately using his short stature to his advantage; no doubt the other men would underestimate him. She held in a snigger.

Badiah wasn't anywhere near as mild and delicate as he was portraying.

"God damned pirates," exploded a voice behind the door as it was flung open. Noah. He never changed, he still couldn't whisper.

"For all that is holy, lower your voice, Noah," Madden grumped behind him. "You could wake my dead mother with your bellow."

Both men quieted as they got a good look at the room. "Well, isn't this a regular old tea party? Crumpets anyone? I heard that's what the Crown's lackeys eat these days," Noah taunted.

Sage pursed her lips, searching the Crown's representatives for trouble. She slowly exhaled when she found none. Noah couldn't be more contrary if he tried.

Sage cocked her head when she heard the back door open beneath her. Mason strode into the room followed by a large figure hovering in the doorway, but, before she could examine him, her eyes snapped to the opposite door as it opened as well. Three more cloaked figures entered and paused, watching the man below her. One of the three threw back his hood, exposing blond curls, stepping into the room. "Well isn't this a happy occasion," Sam cried gaily.

"Really?" Gavriel's smooth voice chastised.

Her heart clenched. Gavriel. She hadn't seen him since she left him behind at the festival. The look on his face still haunted her. Sage shook her head and focused back on the events playing out below.

Sam's eyes swept the room and up into the rafters. She stilled, knowing her cloak hid everything but her eyes. His eyes narrowed into a squint, then a small smile tugged at his lips. That was the moment he spotted her.

Damn the spymaster.

She placed a finger to her lips, and he dismissed her immediately. None of the other men had noticed her yet.

Idiots.

What she did notice was that the two figures in the opposing doorways still stared at each other.

"Your Highness," Rafe intoned below her.

The crown prince nodded to the rebellion leader. "Rafe."

The room crackled with anticipation and tension. Both men went to stand with their representatives. Twelve men in one room. Both sides distrustful, looking like they'd rather be anywhere else. Madden whispered something, and the black-haired man she had labeled as dangerous narrowed his eyes.

"Where is our liaison?" the gray-haired man asked.

"She is not yours," Noah corrected blandly. "That's the purpose of a liaison, is it not?"

Madden rolled his eyes even as Sam smirked.

Sage didn't feel ready to leave the safety of her hiding spot, but she focused on the fact that she had numerous escape routes. None of these men could cage her again. It was time to get things started before there was any bloodshed.

Sage shifted on the balls of her feet and dropped from her perch to the floor, landing in a crouch. She lifted her head, considering the room. Weapons glinted in almost everyone's hands.

She smiled and straightened lazily, projecting confidence. "You called, and I answered." Sage sauntered toward the middle of the room, keeping her back to the front door. Men stared at her from both sides, a range of expressions on their faces. The blond man's mouth was still hanging open. She slipped to his side and placed her finger under his chin, closing his mouth, and fought the temptation to wipe her hand off after touching him. Instead, Sage winked at him, her heart thudding. "If you leave that open long enough it could stay that way."

She moved forward to stand next to the dark one. She cocked her head to the side to give him the impression she was sizing him up even though she already had. "You," she murmured, watching him tense, "are someone everyone should be afraid of."

He stared down at her with banked intrigue. "And are you afraid of me?" he asked just as softly.

"No," she answered, realizing it was true. The two of them were similar. It was the ones who hid what they were you had to watch out for. "There are worse things in the world than you."

"A realist?" the dark man mused. "A pleasure to meet you, my lady. I am Zachael." He bowed from the waist.

"Charmed." She dipped her head in acknowledgement, gliding down the middle of the men.

"My offer is still open," the grizzled older man remarked from her left. Rafe hissed from his side on her right. "Still spoken for I see," he added, lightly.

"I wasn't spoken for then, neither am I now."

The older man arched an eyebrow as the room went completely silent.

Sage shrugged and shot Gavriel a real smile before spinning around to face the room again, her cloak sweeping the floor. "Let's not dawdle. Please hand over your demands."

Mason and the older gentleman stepped forward and each handed her a scroll. She glanced at the scrolls, butterflies fluttering in her stomach. This determined their futures. Sage lifted her head and handed each gentleman the opposite side's proper scroll. There. It was done.

She copied the smile her mum used when she was proud of her children. "Now, that wasn't so hard was it? We will meet in three days at a location of my choosing. Once negotiations begin, they will not end until an agreement is made. Think wisely, gentlemen. As for today, if I find out that anyone was followed," she looked pointedly at Sam, who flashed her an innocent smile. "There will be consequences." She jerked her chin toward Zachael. "If you think he is dangerous, you don't want to see me angry."

She turned to her former comrades. "That goes for you as well. No threats, no tricks, no violence. If I catch wind of any shenanigans, I have a friend who is fond of tying a barrel to one's boots and dropping that individual off the dock to see how long he can hold his breath. Understood?" she barked.

The group of men straightened under her unflinching regard.

"I have things to attend to. Good day."

Sage spun, taking a few steps, sprinted to an older chair, using it to vault herself up and into the beams. She pulled herself up and looked down at the curious faces below her. She allowed a grin to touch her face. "Be safe, gentlemen," Sage imparted as she escaped through the hatch up onto the roof. She ran sure-footedly across the roof and leapt to the next roof, rolling out of her landing. She popped up and sprinted across. They wouldn't be able to follow her this way. Only six more days until the future of Aermia would be decided. Hopefully, they wouldn't all kill each other.

Not likely.

CHAPTER EIGHT

Tehl

He gaped at the trapdoor like a fool. She had catapulted herself off a chair and into the rafters, then disappeared. Sage somehow still surprised him.

"What a woman," Sam muttered. "Did you see how she twisted her body and pulled herself up? Imagine what she could do..."

"If you value your life, you will not finish that thought," warned the giant across from them. His glacial eyes stared daggers at Tehl's brother but that was not the person his brother needed to worry about. It was the golden eyes that had locked onto Sam with such malice it had him elbowing his brother in the side.

Sam glanced first to him and then to Rafe. His brother's smile dropped to a scowl. "Your minds are filled with filth. Before you so rudely cut me off, I was going to say imagine what she could do for the Elite."

Tehl schooled his face. He was sure that wasn't what Sam would have said. What made him wary was that Rafe's amber eyes still hadn't moved from his brother. Stars above, they didn't need any fights. He shuffled to the side, blocking his brother. Tehl crossed his arms as aggressive eyes snapped to his face. "Do we have a problem?" he asked, feigning boredom. Rafe could try to intimidate him all he wanted, but it wouldn't accomplish anything.

Rafe blinked and then relaxed. "No, we do not."

"We will see you in six days then."

Tehl nodded, signaling that it was time to leave. Zachael, Garreth, William, and Gavriel circled Sam and himself. They quickly parted ways with the rebels and quietly chatted about inconsequential things on the way back home. He itched to know what was held in the scroll, but it would have to wait until they arrived.

**

"What do you mean they want representation on the council?" Jaren barked.

The bickering and arguing had started as soon as the demands were read:

1. Money sent to the families who'd lost their loved ones or homes to the Scythians.

2. Any service provided by a rebellion member would receive compensation.

3. Lower taxes.

4. Restoration on the Mort wall.

5. No seizure of rebellion weapons and assets.

6. A rebellion member has the choice to accept an assignment or decline without punishment.

7. All previous unlawful acts pardoned.

8. Equal representation of the rebellion on the council.

"It means exactly what the letter says, Jaren." William retorted.

Jaren threw his hand in the air. "This is ridiculous! Why are we negotiating with them?" He leaned forward in his chair with a gleam in his eye that Tehl didn't care for. "We have access to something they care about." He paused. "The rebel woman."

The whole table of men stared at him.

"We do," Gavriel said, carefully, his violet eyes shuttered.

"She is a bargaining piece. If we captured her, we would force their hand. Not to mention we'd have knowledge of their main base."

"It's not a bad idea, in theory, but the consequences would be heavy," Jeb, the strategist, inserted.

Tehl kept the bored expression on his face, waving away Jaren's idea. "It's an option, but the whole point of this treaty is to avoid bloodshed. No doubt if we pursued this course many lives would be lost. The matter is closed. The rebel woman won't be harmed or touched." His voice rang through the room. Some looked ready to argue. Time to change the subject. "Which of these are reasonable to you?"

"Home reconstruction and monies for the families is doable," Lelbiel answered. "I can check with Demari, but I'm certain we can afford it."

"Good." Tehl thought so too. "Next."

"Compensation for the rebel members," Garreth added. "We're paid a wage for our service to the Crown. It's logical for them to receive it as well." The blond man hesitated a moment. "I think they also should have a say in assignments. They aren't part of the Guard or Elite. The rebels aren't soldiers. They are not bound like we are."

Zachael eyed Garreth, then bowed his head in agreement. "I agree, we do not want unwilling men. That only leads to danger, confusion, and, possibly, dissention."

"Two down. What else?" Tehl asked.

"I don't think they all should be pardoned just because their leaders made a treaty with us," William stated. "I believe in actions speaking louder than words. Hard work deserves rewards, so they must work with us, help us; only then will they receive pardon. "

"I couldn't agree more." Tehl liked that idea. No charity. You work for your privileges.

"The restoration of the Mort Wall is not possible." Jeb looked around the table. "The time, labor, and assets it would take to fix it are unreasonable. A project on that scale isn't possible. It would take years. The Mort Wall is more memorial than protection anyway. Not to mention it would put our laborers near the Scythians. We would knowingly put them in danger and possibly even lose them to their raids."

Tehl thought about the Mort Wall. It had been built after the last war with Scythia, hundreds of years ago, after the Nagalians' genocide. Shortly thereafter, a deadly plague spread throughout the Scythian people with rumors that it had something to do with their questionable use of science but little more was known. What they did know was that the wall went up to keep the Scythians out, and all the danger they presented. But now it was mostly rubble.

"It's a waste of time and resources," Sam put in. "I say we veto that one."

"Agreed." Tehl looked at Jaren, who was examining the wood grain of the table. "What of the taxes, Jaren?"

"We can't lower them." Jaren winced. "I wish we could, but there isn't a way. The taxes are levied based on what a household *can* pay, not everyone pays the same thing. We are not out of line. It been a rough couple of years for everyone." Jaren slumped into his chair looking like he'd aged ten years.

"Thank you, Jaren, moving on."

"The weapons," Zachael spoke up. "We need them. It would save money if we were spared the necessity of forging more by using the rebellion's weapons. We'd be that much closer to being prepared for a Scythian attack."

"That could kill two birds with one stone," Lelbiel commented.

"All right." Tehl swept the table looking for someone brave enough to bring up the final point, representation on their council.

Gavriel stood and placed his hands behind his back. "I think that having their men on our council would round us out and give us a fresh perspective. Many of us don't live among the people or make a living in the city. The only information we receive is secondhand. It could prove to be both informative and helpful to us to know what the people are thinking."

"Once a traitor, always a traitor," Jaren muttered.

Lelbiel nodded in agreement.

All eyes turned to him in question. Tehl didn't like the idea of Rafe having a seat of power because his motives were still questionable. The men in the room all had their flaws, but they were trustworthy. Out of all the rebellion's demands, this one seemed like it would be their most important, it would no doubt be non-negotiable. His personal feelings aside, it would actually be a smart move. No one from the rebellion could cry foul because they would have representation and therefore be a part of the decisions. Tehl didn't like it, but he would do it for the people of Aermia. And they could no doubt work around it, should the need arise.

Tehl cracked his neck and straightened in his chair. "We will grant them this request in exchange for their weapons. I also would prefer not to have them on our council but it matters not what I want, but what is best for Aermia." He met each man's eyes. "We are bound by duty." Solemn nods followed his statement.

"And if they choose women?" William proposed, a sly glint in his eyes.

"Perhaps you don't recall in your old age, William, but my mother was part of this council. We wouldn't dream of treating the fairer sex any differently than one of you." Sam's teeth gleamed white against his tan face.

William sat back, satisfied, while the rest of his council seemed to ponder the last statement. Tehl knew what old William was thinking. No doubt Sage would be among those chosen. He would never be rid of her unless she resigned. That thought perked him up as she would no doubt detest being so near him. She was bound to disappear after a short while. That was what she was best at.

Lelbiel pulled the smaller letter Sage had slipped to Garreth and examined it. Lelbiel's eyes narrowed, pinching at the corner before he smiled. "It seems that the lady liaison didn't restrict the number of men this time to six. You can bring your full council, and an addition of four Elite. It's interesting that she wouldn't allow you to bring protection the first time but now she will allow it. I wonder what that means?"

Zachael snickered. "It means she expects violence. She is warning us to prepare for the negotiation."

"Indeed," Sam mused at his side.

Tehl stood, staring at the room. "Unless something comes up in the next six days, we have no reason to meet. If you need me, request an audience." With his dismissal, chairs screeched across the floor as his advisors stood and bowed. One by one they left the room.

That had been easier than he thought. Out of the corner of his eye he caught Sam frowning, and a faint wrinkle appeared in between his golden blond eyebrows. "Something on your mind?"

Sam peered at him, blue eyes full of calculation. "Sage allowed us four Elite and your full council. She expects mischief." His brother blew out a frustrated breath. "I hate not knowing the location. I can't scout or place any sneaks."

Tehl's mouth twitched from the effort to keep a smile from his face. "I believe that is the reason she did it this way," he deadpanned.

Sam's eyes narrowed. "Stop making fun of me, this is serious. Your life is going to be in danger."

That sobered him. "We need to be prepared then."

***

The next six days sped by in a flurry of day-to-day activities and training with the Elite every chance he got. Sam was right, he'd gotten soft spending so much time in the palace. Every night he fell into bed, aching and exhausted, but content.

The missive arrived early that morning announcing the time and place of the meeting. When night fell, all of his men were armed to the teeth. They were to meet at a pub between the fishing district and merchant district. Tehl and his twelve men set out in pairs to Sanee, it was less conspicuous that way. Sam paired with Garreth and disappeared in the blink of an eye.

Zachael walked beside him, assessing every person as well as their surroundings for any potential threats to his person. They wound through the city in companionable silence. Zachael didn't talk for the sake of talking, and Tehl appreciated that about his combat master.

After a while, Tehl at last spotted the pub. It was ordinary, but, after a second look, he noted that the quality of the craftsmanship stood out. It had a thick wooden door framed by two small windows with iron welded in patterns across it.

"Smart," Zachael commented. "The windows look like art, but they're built for protection."

The pair moved up three stone steps and onto the deck. Zachael reached for the door only to have it jerked back from his grip. The light haloed the alluring curves of a woman with shocking silvery white hair.

"Please come in."

Her smoky voice draped over him. The woman was dressed most unusually with fabric draped here and there to cover her body. Was it one piece? He wanted to roll his eyes, thinking how Sam would love to investigate such a type of dress. The purple scarf wrapped around her head emphasized her shocking magenta eyes. A knowing smirk played along her lips while she watched him gawk at her.

Tehl flashed her an apologetic smile before muttering a speedy, "Thank you."

A black curse tore his attention from the unusual female he'd been examining. Tehl quickly snagged Zachael's arm just before he lunged forward.

"Let me go. I've a traitor to deal with." The weapons master snarled quietly.

Tehl scanned the room and stiffened as he spotted the source of Zachael's anger.

Serge.

The smug bastard was leaning against the bar sipping a brew, watching Zachael with obvious amusement. Tehl wanted to rip the man's heart out, but he also knew now was not the time. He reeled in his friend, whispering harshly in Zachael's ear. "Now is not the time, old friend. He *will* get what he deserves in time."

Zachael nodded that he heard Tehl but didn't drop his eyes from the traitor lounging ten feet away. Tehl turned away from Serge when the man waved at them lazily. Two long narrow tables sat in the room with an open space in the middle. Men lounged around the room but there was a definite division between the two groups. Tehl nodded to Rafe when he caught the rebellion leader's eyes.

Tehl stood behind an empty chair at the odd table, waiting for the meeting to begin. A hush fell over the room as light steps echoed from a hallway intersecting the bar. Sage glided into the room in a pair of skin-tight black leather breeches, a white linen shirt, and a snug green vest, making the most of her every curve. She smiled at the group, stopping in the center of the room, demanding every man's attention.

She cocked a hip and ran her hand over a dagger sheathed to her arm. Sage looked up from underneath her lashes and spun in a slow circle inspecting the men. Tehl straightened when her gaze ran over him before moving on. The wench was bold, he would give her that.

"As you can see, I am armed." She gestured to the dagger on her arm and smiled. "But that's my prerogative being the liaison." She lifted her chin. "Captain Femi and Hayjen will collect your weapons."

Protests broke out. She raised her hand, and the room quieted. "This is a peace meeting, you will not need them." Her face hardened. "If you keep a weapon and use it, there will be consequences." Her harsh gaze swept over the room. "Captain Femi knows of some unique ways to punish. I believe one of her favorites is to drop you in leviathan-infested waters and see if you can swim back to shore."

Utter silence filled the room. Leviathans were nasty creatures. The vicious creatures were similar to dolphins, but that's where all similarities ended. They had row after row of sharp teeth, and a love of flesh that made any man shudder.

She quirked a grin at Zachael. "That is if she gets to you before me. There is a reason they call me Blade."

Dark chuckles rumbled through the rebellion's men causing Sage to smile.

She clapped her hands together. "This is how we will proceed. I will flip a coin, whomever wins gets to start the negotiations. Please pass Captain Femi and Hayjen your weapons and we can proceed."

The weapons collection was a slow-going process. Every man boasted a sword and daggers. Sam grumbled the entire time while stripping his off beside him. Sage winked at his brother before barking at Madden about a dagger in his boot.

Tehl removed his weapons, this time ignoring the exotic woman. He couldn't keep his gaze from the green-eyed vixen running the meeting. Despite her bold act, he noted how uncomfortable she was with all the men. Every so often her hands would shake. He pulled his eyes from her as the last person was relieved of their weapons.

Rafe.

Apparently the man carried an entire armory with him.

The giant man, Hayjen, gestured to the wicked looking daggers strapped to both legs. Rafe shook his head, staring straight at Sage. Her face was cool as she strode across the room, stopping in front of the rebellion leader.

"Is there a problem, gentlemen?"

"He won't hand over his blades," Hayjen explained.

Tehl leaned forward in his seat along with the rest of the room. How would she deal with the defiant rebellion leader?

Sage peered up at Rafe, tension in her whole body. "You need to hand over your weapons, there are no exceptions."

Rafe's eyes trailed over her face as he unbuckled the belt that held them in place. "These blades are special. The only hands to touch them are myself and my family." Rafe gathered the daggers and held them out to Sage.

Sam chuckled under his breath. "The smooth bastard. He is claiming her in front of all these men so they know she is close to him. Conniving, but effective."

Only her back was visible, but she didn't move to take them.

"Only you can keep them." Rafe rumbled.

Irritation nipped at him for Sage. Of all the times to try something, the rebellion leader had to do it now. He must be desperate. The thought made his lips curl. She must have been avoiding Rafe. That put a full-blown smile on his face as the captain relieved him and his men of their weapons.

With reluctant fingers, Sage plucked the daggers from his grasp, avoiding touching him, Tehl noted, before she dumped them onto a chest behind the bar. His brother sniggered. Rafe may have been trying to make a point, but hers sounded loud and clear.

"Will the leaders please join me?" Sage asked.

Tehl strode to her side, Rafe on the other.

"Coral for rebellion, dragon for Crown." She flipped the coin, the dragon landed face up. They both nodded to each other and moved to their seats.

"The Crown begins. Please take your seat. Remember not to shout, all your concerns will be heard. No one leaves until an agreement has been struck. This gets decided tonight." She bowed. "For Aermia."

A chorus of *Aermias* thundered through the room. Captain Femi placed two cushioned chairs at the head of the room. Both women sat and looked at Tehl. He placed his elbows on the table and eyed the men across from him. "We have read your demands, and this is what we can offer: payment and support to the families that have been affected by the Scythian attacks. You are not part of our army so you can choose to accept or decline any assignment. You will also receive wages for any assignment you carry out." Murmurs of triumph reached his ears.

Don't get too excited, he thought. "Punishment for unlawful actions will be removed with an exception." He met Serge's brown eyes. "You must work off your debts by accepting work with the Crown. If you don't contribute to the peace and betterment of Aermia, you live your life in the dungeon. Last, we can offer four places on my council." Tehl sat back and waited.

"What of the other demands?" Rafe asked.

"Not possible," Sam replied. "Taxes are based on what each family makes, the food shortage was not caused by taxes, it was caused by Scythians."

Roars of outrage erupted around the rebellion leader. He raised his hand, never taking his eyes off them. "And the others?"

"The Mort Wall," Jeb supplied. "The wall is a symbol, not protection. It would be a costly, colossal waste of time and resources. Scythia has been raiding our borders for a year now, for no reason we have discovered. If we embarked on such a thing, it would put more people in danger."

"War with Scythia is imminent, we need your weapons. That is one of our demands," Zachael added, bluntly.

Sage stood. "The Crown has made their offer, what say you, rebels?"

"We will supply men for the war with Scythia. We will share our expertise on training. As for the weapons, we will part with some, but not all. Once we sign the agreement, there will be peace, anyone who acts is on their own and subject to your laws."

Reasonably, they agreed to meet four out of six of the Crown's demands.

"And the others?" William asked, echoing Rafe.

The rebellion leader zeroed in on William, dripping aggression. "We will not impart all the names of our members and put their families in danger." His amber eyes pierced Sam next. "I will not contribute to your sneaks. I will not put them in your hands, just for you to send them into Scythia never to return."

"What do you suggest? Let all the traitors go free?" Jaren cut in. "Can you assure us that your people are completely loyal to you?" Jaren waved his hand. "And this new venture?"

"We're not thrilled to be getting into bed with the Crown," the mouthy man from last time supplied. "But we are loyal to Rafe. He has never led us wrong."

Sage stood again. "Are these terms agreeable to you, prince?"

"They are," he supplied. "Jaren's concerns are valid. To the Crown, you are traitors. If they are willing to betray their kingdom, what is stopping them from betraying you?" He stared evenly at Rafe. "If we don't have their names we can't keep an eye on them to make sure they are behaving as law abiding citizens."

"I can see your point," Rafe conceded. "I will check on them and will take along another person."

Jaren opened his mouth to say something when Rafe cut him a look. His advisor snapped his mouth shut.

"This person will be someone whom we both trust." Rafe's gaze slid to Sage. "Our lady liaison."

"I am sorry, but I will not be available. My place is with my family," she replied, firmly locking gazes with the rebellion leader.

"This is important to both the Crown and the rebellion. Could you not care for this *and* your family for the sake of peace?" An older man with moss-colored eyes asked Sage.

Her eyes softened at the old man's expression. She let loose a sigh, defeated. "I accept then. Are the terms laid out by the Crown acceptable to the rebellion?"

"All but the number of weapons. We will not part with all of them."

"That is up to neither of you," Sage interrupted. "I know I am the neutral party but this concerns me."

"How does this concern you?" Garreth asked.

She smiled wickedly. "Because they are mine. I made them."

Surprise flashed across several faces. Not everyone knew who she was.

"I will give three quarters of the weapons to the Crown, and the rest I will keep. Did you get all of that Captain Femi?"

The exotic woman lifted her white head from her record. "Indeed. Continue on."

"So this leads us to the final agenda. Who will join the Crown's council?"

"Hayjen, Madden, Sage, and myself," Rafe supplied.

"I see an issue here." Serge's voice carried through the room. He stood up, a stupid smile on his face making Tehl want to punch him. "Having members on the council is fine and all, but we will still have less representatives than the Crown."

Every word out of his mouth made Tehl's hackles rise.

Serge moved to the bar and leaned against it. "What is the council? They are advisors. They may advise, but they have no real power." Serge stabbed a finger at him. "He still makes the final decision. The council is a farce in its actual power of execution. The only way the people would have real say is if we had equal representation."

Rafe glowered at Serge. "What is the meaning of this, Rhys?"

Rhys, so that was his name. Tehl filed that away. Rhys was going somewhere dark, deep, and miserable.

"The Crown is trying to trick us."

What was that leach getting at?

"How dare you!" thundered Jaren as he stood up. "We are extending mercy to you traitorous lot." Zachael grabbed Jaren by the shirt and yanked him back down into his chair, hissing something into his ear.

"You see?" Rhys said, smugness in his tone. "They feel like we are below them, untrustworthy. They will never respect us, despite having a place among them."

Men nodded their heads in agreement.

Tehl saw what was happening. Rhys was trying to sabotage the peace treaty, but why? It didn't make sense. Did he loathe the Crown so much? He had served in the Guard for over four years. Was it because they stripped him of his title? Revenge?

"We need someone to check his power," Rhys continued. "Someone who will stand against him and hold their own. Someone who shares his power."

More men were nodding and shouting encouragements while Rafe looked like he was ready to blow.

"And how would you do that?" the rebellion leader questioned tightly.

Tehl wanted to know that too.

"By uniting the rebellion and Crown permanently." Rhys gave Tehl an arrogant look. "We know of someone who isn't afraid of you. Someone of strong moral character, who stands up for the weak and has a strong sense of duty. Someone who challenges you."

Rhys breached the distance between Sage and himself. Rafe, Gavriel, Sam, and Tehl surged to their feet as she paled and leaned away from him. She stilled when he ran a finger down her white cheek. Captain Femi hissed and slapped his hand away. Rhys smiled down at Sage then rolled his shoulders and faced the room.

"The rebellion wants equal representation."

"What exactly do you propose?" Gavriel asked, rage in his voice.

Rhys smiled directly at him. That monster should be locked up, not conducting a negotiation.

"I propose a union between the Crown and the rebellion: matrimony."

Tehl's breath stilled.

No.

"Between the crown prince and the rebellion's blade, Sage."

CHAPTER NINE

Tehl

Pandemonium broke out in the room. The rebels were cheering, and his advisors were cursing and shouting at each other. He blocked everyone else out and focused on Rafe, Rhys, and Sage. Rhys looked extremely pleased with himself. One glance at the rebellion leader, and Tehl knew he was one second away from murder. Last there was Sage. Her face was blank. Not one glimmer of emotion even in her eyes. Why wasn't she reacting? Something wasn't right.

"Are you okay?" he mouthed. Nothing. Captain Femi was stroking her brown hair and whispering to her. "Is she okay?" he asked louder, his voice carrying over the din. Captain Femi's pursed lips thinned in answer. He didn't care for Sage, she was a thorn in his side, but he didn't want to see her hurt.

Gavriel pushed through the men and knelt in front of her knees. His cousin took her hand in his and spoke to her. Still nothing. Tehl couldn't hear Gav's words but he could see him pleading with her, trying to coax her out of her mind.

"This is how you lead your rebellion?" Zachael bellowed. "You wouldn't know your head from your ass. Get your dogs in line, or I will do it for you."

Rafe stilled. He swiveled his neck to stare at Zachael. "What did you say?" Rafe rumbled.

Zachael leaned over the thin table. "I said: get your dogs in line, or I will do it for you. Control them. That's your responsibility."

The room quieted at the challenge.

"I control nothing. I direct them, but they have a choice. That's the difference between the Crown and the rebellion. The Crown forces and takes. We each choose and give. We work as a group, no one has the ultimate power. Which is why Sage will not marry the Crown, she will not be forced into anything."

"Rafe is right," an older man inserted. "We make the decision together." The older man shot Rhys a thoughtful look. "But Rhys is right. We need someone to check the Crown's power. I propose the rebellion vote. Those in favor of Rhys's demand?"

A myriad of hands rose, except for the old man, Hayjen, and Rafe. Bloody hell. They would demand he marry the rebel woman.

"It's settled," the old man said reluctantly. "You marry her or there will be civil war."

Tehl's brain scrambled to catch up to what was going on. This couldn't be happening.

Sam cursed. "Be reasonable. Surely, you wouldn't subject Sage to a lifetime of misery?"

The old man stared at Sage with sad eyes. "She is a good girl. Sage does what is necessary and needed. She has a good heart. She will do this for Aermia, for the rebellion, and for her family."

Tehl's men looked at him, waiting for him to give the signal to leave, but he couldn't move.

"This is extortion," Jeb muttered.

And it was.

He had to choose between his happiness and the welfare of Aermia. Tehl had spoken about finding a wife weeks ago, but this wasn't how he wanted to obtain one. He had planned on picking out a mousy woman to bless him with children then stay out of the way. Tehl never wanted what his parents had. Love was dangerous, but this was something else. He would be tied to a woman who hated him. His life would be hell. Tehl doubted she would let him touch her, but that was a necessity for heirs. Was he selfish enough to say no? He thought about all the men who would die in a civil war and the possibility of Scythia invading Aermia. Blood would run through the streets. Bitterness filled him. He didn't have a choice. Duty above all.

"You're not considering this, right?" Sam asked pulling him from his thoughts.

Tehl tipped his head back, a bitter laugh spilling out of him. "There's nothing to consider, I am surprised you even asked."

Sam regarded him for a moment. "I wasn't asking you as your tactician, or as your duty as the crown's shield, but as your brother."

"There's no choice, and you know it."

His men circled around him wearing grim faces. "There hasn't been an arranged marriage ever in our history, my lord," Jeb remarked. "That's what makes the monarchy so strong, a strong marriage based on love."

"They would have to keep it a secret," Garreth said. "If the people found out it was arranged, they would lose confidence in the Crown. We need their support now more than ever. If you decide on this, you both must act like you love each other anytime you aren't alone. Can you live like that?"

"He will have to," Jarren despaired. "That's a hard life, sire."

They all knew that if he refused, many lives would be lost. He couldn't live with that on his conscience. His mother told him that with privilege and power also came responsibility, duty. He had a responsibility to his people. He rose from the chair on wooden legs, his men fanning around him. Tehl met Rafe's angry eyes.

"Is this really what you want?" Tehl was sure that Rafe understood what he was asking. Would he let Sage go for the sake of his lofty principles? The rebellion leader's hands clenched so tightly his fist turned a splotchy white.

"It has been decided."

Tehl felt oddly detached when he spoke. "Very well, I will take her as my wife. But I have a few demands of my own." He glared at all the men across from him. "Firstly, since you hold personal choice so dear to you, you will extend the same freedom to Sage."

"Done," piped up the old man.

No one disagreed.

"Secondly, none of you will ever have contact with her again except for the old man, Hayjen, and Rafe. You have used her over and over as a sacrificial lamb." The hothead, next to the old man, sputtered. Tehl ignored him, letting menace seep into his voice. "You sanctioned the death of my father and sent her back to the place where she was tortured and almost died. Again, you offer her, damning her to a fate that will kill her every day." Most of the men shied away from his piercing gaze like cowards. "She is to be nothing to you. She will not be your blade anymore, but my future queen, my consort. I will make this simple. If you even breathe in her direction, you will disappear." And he meant it. "She has three days to come to me, willingly." He peered at Captain Femi, hovering protectively by the girl's side. "Will you ensure this will be done?"

Captain Femi scrutinized him for a moment before bowing her head. "It will be done."

"Make sure she knows what she is getting herself into. Our people need harmony. She must play a role when we're not alone. It won't be an easy life." He hesitated a moment before voicing what needed to be said. "I am the crown prince, so heirs are a necessity. I will have children, several of them. Make sure she knows this is a requirement." Tehl spared one last glare for the group. "We're done here."

Captain Femi stood, leaving Sage with Gavriel. She flowed toward him, carrying the treaty she had been working on all evening. She smoothed it out on the table and held a quill out to him. Tehl looked over it, making sure nothing they'd discussed was missing or additional points added, before stroking his name across the parchment. The woman relieved him of the quill and blew on the ink. With care, she picked it up and placed it before the rebellion leader. He carefully read over it, allowing a few of his men to do the same. Once he received their nods, he scratched his name down.

It was done. Peace was secure even as his own life and peace was signed away.

Gavriel stood from his crouch. "My lord, I request to stay as protection for your betrothed."

Tehl hid his flinch.

His betrothed.

He would be married, but to someone who'd rather eat glass than share a room with him, much less a bed. Tehl nodded his permission and strode toward the door, ready to escape.

"Betrothed?" a feminine voice accused.

Tehl halted in his tracks and spun to meet horror-filled green eyes. She darted glances around the room, panic evident in her movements. Her eyes stopped on Rafe. "What have you done?" she whispered.

"Forgive me, little one."

There was so much pain in those four little words.

Betrayal and rage filled her face, warring with one another. She jerked to her feet. "I will never be yours, I will die first!" she spat.

Taking everyone by surprise, she leapt over her chair and sprinted the opposite way down the hall she entered from. Gavriel scrambled after her, shooting him an upset look.

He now knew for sure what she thought of him. Tehl may have secured peace for Aermia, but make no mistake, he had just started a war all the same.

CHAPTER TEN

Sage

Escape.

Escape.

Escape.

The hallway seemed to stretch forever ahead of her; no matter how fast she ran, the walls still pressed inward. Sage couldn't breathe. It was like a giant hand had reached inside her chest to squeeze her lungs until there was nothing but panic and pain. Her boot caught a rug, and she stumbled, slamming her hip into a table she hadn't spotted. The pain was acute, but it actually helped her regain focus. Heavy footsteps pounded in her direction. Terror filled her. No doubt the monster was coming for her again.

Sage knocked over the small table behind her and sprinted through the exit. Hopefully that would slow him down. She burst outside and the dark of night engulfed her. Normally, she welcomed it, but tonight the tendrils of darkness were clawing at her, trying to pull her apart and feed her to the nightmare. Her surroundings blurred as she tried to escape the nightmare behind her.

She registered only snatches of the startled faces she passed as she ran for her life. She slowed ever so slightly when she gained a moment of clarity. Did she even know where she was running to? Home? No, she would lead the monster there, and that wasn't an option. The hair on her arms rose. He was hunting her, she felt it in her bones. Shuddering, she picked up her pace and soon she could see the glimmering waves of the bay.

Lilja's ship.

Safety. She needed to reach the ship, there she would be safe.

As Sage cut through the fisherman shacks, the sound of her boots on the wooden dock soothed her frantic heart; she would make it. A manic smile had just split her face when an arm caught her waist, jerking her back. Terror filled her once again.

He had found her.

Sage screamed, but a large hand hastily clamped over her mouth, her screams muffled. She flailed and struggled, but it did nothing to loosen his grip. Nor could she hinder his progress as he dragged her away.

She sucked in huge breaths through her nose, tears blurred her vision as panic overwhelmed her. As the world around her began to fade away, Sage absently concluded that perhaps death wouldn't be so bad. One thing was sure, she was taking her monster down with her. His harsh breaths touched her neck, making her shiver, not in revulsion, but in anticipation of her next move. He would hurt no one ever again.

"Sage! It's me."

She frantically searched for the source of that familiar voice. Maybe she would have help after all. Sage increased her struggles.

"Sis, it's okay. Calm down. I've got you. You need to stop screaming." The hand released her mouth.

Gav? Where was Gav? Who was screaming? A high-pitched ringing filled her ears, along with the wailing of a dying animal.

"Sis, it's Gavriel. You're safe. No one is going to hurt you." The hands holding her, shook her roughly. "Sage! You need to calm down. I will never let anyone touch you."

Confusion filled her. Was that dying sound coming from her? Sage sucked in a hiccupping breath, her throat burning. Did Gavriel slay her monster?

"Sage, love, there is no monster. Just me."

Without her permission, her whole body sagged against his. She tried to command it to move, but it simply wouldn't cooperate. He shifted her around so she was facing him, her head against his chest. Her eyes latched onto his. He had saved her once again, even after her deception. More tears poured down her face as gut-wrenching sobs tore out of her. Gav crushed her even tighter to his chest, cooing soft words of comfort. In her distress, she barely registered that, at some point, they had returned to the Sirenidae vessel, and she vaguely registered being placed in a soft bed. Desperately, she clung to the man who'd slain her monster and held back the nightmares. "Please," she begged, "please don't leave me alone."

"I won't. I won't." Calloused hands pulled the covers up to her chin and then a heavy weight settled next to her, gathering her into his arms. In the security of his hold, she finally calmed and darkness claimed her.

***

The next day's weather matched her mood.

She stood, watching, as a storm rolled in from the south. Gray clouds adorned the sky, the water shifting from its usual brilliant turquoise to a murky blue-gray. The ship bobbed with a bit more ferocity as the waves rocked her to and fro. Drifting, just like her. Last night had not gone at all as she'd imagined. She wished she could erase it from her memory.

When Rhys had touched her, it was like he'd stolen her will. She had frozen, as if she was locked in her own body, watching everything play out. No matter how much she railed from the inside, beating against the walls of her mind, she couldn't break through. She couldn't even lift her hand to swat away his disgusting fingers as he caressed her cheek. Even when a concerned and familiar gaze met her own, his violet eyes pleading with her to respond, she could not do so. She could see mouths moving, as if speaking, but no sound reached her ears. What were they saying? What did they want? Why weren't they disposing of that disgusting wretch?

Sage shivered and scrubbed at her cheek with her palms, as if the action could erase the memory of his touch. She tipped her head back, looking from the swirling sea to birds moving about the sky. They seemed playful, dipping and gliding on the wind, utterly free. She wanted that. But it seemed that she would never be free.

The previous day was still a blur, save the memory of intense terror and her own need to flee. How she had arrived at the dock was a mystery to her. By her sore body, she guessed she had sprinted the whole way. When Gavriel had grabbed her she'd been prepared to die. She was so tired of fighting the nightmares, night after night, never getting more than a handful of minutes of sleep. Sage was fairly certain Rhys would kill her, and the thought had been strangely relieving. She had been ready for death, to finally be at peace. In the light of day, now that she was capable of rational thought, she couldn't believe how selfish that thought had been. How could she even think it? It would gut her entire family. They had suffered so much already.

She dropped her elbows to the rail and placed her chin in her hands as she turned her thoughts to Gavriel and the role he'd played in events. She grimaced at her vague recollection of clinging to him as she sobbed her heart out and begged him not to leave her. When she'd woken this morning, her hands had been wound into his shirt, crushing the fabric with her fingers. He had kept his word and stayed. Dark smudges had bruised the area underneath his eyes.

I did that, she'd thought.

She'd released him and crept out, leaving him snoring in her bed, grimacing at what a needy fool she must have seemed to him.

A crash and heavy footsteps made her glance over her shoulder, and a very disheveled Gavriel stumbled out of the hallway and onto the deck. He urgently scanned the area, his eyes panicked, but he calmed as soon as he spotted her. He paused to brush his shirt out and strode to her side, mimicking her pose. Gav didn't speak; rather, he simply watched the ocean, waiting. She examined him from the corner of her eye. His black, wavy hair, so much like the crown prince's, stirred in the ocean breeze, slipping around his square jaw. She had left him without even a goodbye. He must be so angry with her, but even so, he'd protected her. She owed him an apology.

Sage traced the grain of the wood beneath her arms for a moment, preparing herself for the biggest apology of her life. "I'm sorry," was all she got out. She wanted to bang her head on the rail. He deserved better, but she could find no words to make what she'd done okay. Her mouth parted, ready to grovel, when he spoke.

"What are you sorry for, Sage?" He turned to the side, propping a hip against the rail, and stared down at her.

She didn't feel ready to handle the disappointment and accusation no doubt written on his face, but she steeled herself; she was no coward. She slowly turned and, with great difficulty, raised her eyes from his bare feet to the open collar of his shirt, pausing there, still struggling to meet his eyes.

His hand cupped her chin. "Sis? You need to look at me."

Tears pricked her eyes as she met his warm gaze. He had called her 'sis'—he still used the endearment. When she had called him her brother, she had not been acting. She had meant it, and she knew he had too. She bit her quivering bottom lip. Sage had never felt like she was much of a crier, but in the last two months she had cried more than she ever had in her entire life.

"Gavriel, I am so sorry I didn't say goodbye. I needed to go. I couldn't stay locked up like that indefinitely...and I didn't want to be used."

His face pinched. "You thought I was using you?"

She blanched. "No. I just meant that I understood why you were saying certain things. You wanted to turn me into a Crown sympathizer, but I couldn't give you what you wanted. Our friendship was real, I know that, but in the back of my mind I couldn't be sure if part of you was still befriending me because you wanted something from me." She looked away as he dropped her chin. "I was an intelligence officer for the rebellion. In order to get what we need, it sometimes means lying or even becoming someone else. I wasn't sure if you were doing the same. I hoped not, but...we do things for our family that we might never do for others."

"It wasn't fake."

Sage met his eyes. "I know. It became painfully clear to me when I saw the look of betrayal on your face that night of the Midsummer Festival." She exhaled a disgusted breath. "That was supposed to be my last night."

"You helped the Crown."

She smiled ruefully. "No, I helped Marq. Murder is never the solution. He may be sick, but he's a wonderful old man with a good heart, he didn't deserve what they had planned for him. I had no choice but to accept the assignment. It was the only way I could protect him.

"And you did, despite the danger to yourself."

Sage shrugged. "It was supposed to be my last night with the rebellion anyway. I'd already decided that, although I believed in the cause, I couldn't work with them if the end was accomplished through such methods." She snorted. "Not that it mattered. I ended up in the middle of it anyway, despite my best efforts to escape."

"Why did you agree to be the liaison?"

Sage raised an incredulous eyebrow. "Do you really think I had a choice? I had led the crown prince and his spymaster to the rebellion, even if unintentionally. Many people I knew and had worked with could have died because of my mistake. I did what I had to do to ensure their safety." She placed a hand over her heart. "I believe in what the rebellion wants for Aermia, I too love her people. I joined for the chance to help restore our lands, to create a better life for so many innocents, and to help protect them. And, now, serving as the liaison, I can continue to do so, only this way we may spare the lives of so many on both sides."

"And now the rebellion is asking something more from you." Her eyes widened at the bitterness in his words, and she simply stared while his eyes searched her face. "Do you remember much of last night?"

She looked away, gripping the railing so tightly her fingers ached. "Most, until Rhys touched me." She forced out between clenched teeth. "I only have pieces of the rest." A pause. "Thank you for your support and help last night." She flicked her eyes to the side, smiling at him briefly. "The meeting did not go as I..." She halted when a sudden flash of the previous evening formed in a picture in her mind. The crown prince speaking to Lilja, discussing the need for children.

Their children.

His and hers.

Sage gasped and stumbled back from Gavriel.

Marriage, that was the bargain. The rebellion had sold her to the Crown for power. Rafe had sold her. She was chattel, no better than a whore. A warm womb to grow more princes.

"No." Her friend's eyes widened at the vehemence in her voice. "I *won't* do it. I don't care if he's not the devil I thought he was at first! He still is an arrogant, thoughtless pig. I will never wed him. He will *never* touch me."

Gavriel's face cooled during her tirade. "He is still your crown prince, and, as such, you should accord him with due respect when speaking of him."

She let loose a harsh laugh. "He will receive my respect when he damn well earns it. From the moment I met him, he has threatened to harm me. In his home, I was starved, left without adequate clothing, drugged twice, tortured, and... " Her throat clogged, but she pressed on. "...and my innocence was almost stolen. He has bullied and yelled. I was his prisoner for weeks! So excuse me if I'm not singing his praises, my lord." She spat the words.

"You leave out all the positive things you experienced. Perhaps you should meditate on those as well." He shook his head, frustrated. After a moment, his face cleared. "Whether you accept it or not, your rebellion used you as a pawn, *not us*. They were the ones demanding you marry Tehl; it was not our idea. It was *our* crown prince who made certain to set up stipulations for your benefit, not his, because your people did not seem to see fit to do so. The rebellion promised war if he did not do what they asked, and so he thought, not of himself, but of others. Do you think he wants you for a wife any more than you want him for a husband?"

That pierced her. She was broken, used up. No man would want her.

"Instead of grabbing you and taking you back to the palace where you would have no choice, he gave you three days to decide. It is in your hands, not his. Tehl gave you that. Your crown prince gave you the option of freedom, not Rafe, or the rebellion. Just Tehl." Gavriel's chest heaved, and he ruffled his midnight hair in agitation before picking back up. "Those men you call friends sold you while you were defenseless. Tehl stood up for you. If you return to the palace, none of those men will see you again."

Sage gasped at that. How dare the crown prince dictate whom she saw? "He will never tell me how to run my life."

Gav's face reddened. "He wasn't trying to control you, but protect you from your betrayers," he hissed.

Sage wanted to scream. She stepped closer to Gav, not quite knowing what she would do, when a musical voice called across the deck to them.

"You have had your say, my lord. Maybe it is time for you to leave her to my care. Your prince left it to me to be certain she was apprised of the previous night's events."

Gavriel's eyes left her to stare at the woman behind her. He sucked in a breath before looking back down at her. "I have been stationed here for your protection for the next three days. If you need me simply call for me."

He dipped his chin and stalked toward the ramp. Even with all the anger and confusion swirling around her, she didn't want them to part ways angry at each other. "Gav," she called. He peered over his shoulder at her. "Thank you for everything. You have gone well beyond what is necessary."

"I am always here for you," he said, just before he disappeared.

Lilja sidled over, ogling Gav as he placed himself on a barrel overlooking the sea and the Sirenidae. "Such a handsome man, that one. Such unique eyes."

"You're one to talk," Sage remarked.

The aforementioned magenta eyes turned back to her, somber. "We have serious matters to discuss, *ma fleur*. Let's go to the kitchen, and I will make us some tea and biscuits."

Lilja took Sage's cold hand and drew her into the warm kitchen, sitting her down on one of many luxurious pillows in the corner. She closed her eyes, listening as her friend bustled around the area. Before she knew it, a cup of something hot that smelled like lavender and chocolate was pressed into her hands. Sage sniffed as something sweet tantalized her nose. She cracked her eyes, squinting suspiciously at Lilja.

"It's just a little lavender oil, nothing which could affect you adversely." Lilja *tsked*. "So untrusting."

"Well, events these past two months have given me good reason to be," Sage retorted. She leaned into the pillow and relaxed, listening to Lilja hum and cook. The swish of her skirt alerted her to Captain Femi at her side. Her exotic friend folded herself gracefully onto the pillow across from her, examining her.

"He shouldn't have touched you." Lilja's eyes darkened. "You were fine until that cur dared to touch your cheek. If Gavriel hadn't pushed him out of the way, I was planning on grabbing one of Rafe's Griffin blades and stabbing that man." Her lips pursed. "Yet you froze, gone from the world. What happened?"

Sage looked down into her tea. "Terror. And memories. I was trapped."

Lilja touched her foot in comfort. "Are you ready to discuss what happened last night?"

Sage's face hardened. "I don't think I need to hear anything from you."

Lilja gave her a stubborn look. "You will listen to what I have to say." They glared at each other in stony silence before the captain

120

continued. "The treaty was signed by both sides last night, but it hinges on your decision. Hayjen informed me that your marriage to the prince had not been contained in the original list of demands from the rebellion. They believe that the advisors don't hold real power, and, to an extent, this is true, but I don't feel a forced marriage is a good solution. Unfortunately, it's not my decision. It's important to note that every representative from their side voted for it, save Rafe and Mason." Lilja frowned. "Rafe wants you for himself, you know. Hence the little display with the Griffin blades."

Sage dropped her eyes, glaring at the floor. "I know."

Lilja's laugh rippled through the room. "Indeed you do. That was abundantly clear when you plopped his blades onto the bar without a care. It was an excellent move, but I am afraid we're digressing." Lilja sighed. "I observed the crown prince wrestle with his decision before he agreed to their demand regarding you. Despite his ire at having been put in the situation, he made efforts to protect you. He required that you might be given time to choose—three days—and if you acquiesce, none of the rebellion circle are to have contact with you again. This was not high-handed, you know. It prevents them from using or hurting you again." Lilja sent her a severe look. "The crown prince also didn't want you to go into it blind. If you marry him, it will not be an easy life. You will be on display, your life will not be your own."

A harsh chuckle burst out of Sage. "Has it ever?"

Lilja's mouth turned down, but she continued. "The kings and queens of the past have always been bound by love which foments mutual respect and loyalty for one another. Your marriage won't be based on that, you will have to try to succeed without it. For a large part of this, you may need to live a ruse. Any moment you are not alone you will have to play the part, you must pretend to love the crown prince. You know the nation requires heirs as well. It would

121

be your duty to give them to him."

Sage blanched, horror choking her. Heirs? Never. Mutiny must have shown on her face because Lilja gave her a stern look. "He entrusted me with this information. The prince did not want you agreeing to this treaty blind. There is a huge responsibility set on you both."

"I won't do it."

"Then many will die."

Sage blinked at her friend, hurt. "I thought you cared about me. You agree with them? You support this"

Lilja shook her head fiercely. "You misunderstand me. I would spirit you away tonight if you wanted, but you need to consider the cost. Can you live with the civil war that will spring up when you say no? Some could, but I doubt you are one of them. You have a strong sense of duty and love for people. Every person that died in the rebellion, you would feel personally."

"So you would condemn me to life in a gilded cage? I've been a sword maker's daughter, a peasant, an officer of the rebellion even. I am not a princess. I am not a queen."

"All of those things will make you a brilliant queen. Just think about it."

"I don't need to, I don't want it." Having to spend the rest of her life with the crown prince made her want to throw up.

"In three days, if you want out, I will protect you, but think carefully until then." Captain Femi rolled onto her knees and kissed her forehead. The Sirenidae sauntered to the oven, pulling out the buttery biscuits.

Sage's decision would affect everyone in their kingdom. Lilja was right when she'd said Sage would feel each death keenly if she refused. *Could* she live with that? An unreasonable part of her said she could, but she knew herself better. Loneliness and uncertainty filled her. What was she doing? She needed someone to support her, someone to talk to. "I need my mum."

Lilja flashed a smile over her shoulder. "Done. I've already sent for her."

***

Her mum's arms felt wonderful around her. She wasn't a little girl anymore, but there was something comforting about being hugged by her mum. What would happen to her family if she married? Sage shoved the thought away and enjoyed the day with Lilja and her mum. They regaled her with stories of their youth. Sage was still curious how they met, but they skirted around that story with skill that would make the spymaster proud. Sage laughed until her belly cramped. But when the sun set, so did her happy mood. Her mum would go back to the family, and she would stay here.

"Love, I know you have a lot on your mind, but I wanted to let you know that your papa and I love you so much, and we are so proud of you. We raised you to be strong, independent, hardworking, kind, and loving. You are all those things and more." Her mum softly brushed her cheek. "You have taken care of us for so long. You have a weighty decision to make, but we don't want you to base it on us. You have done enough." Her mum's eyes grew damp. "I wanted to thank you for the doctor. Jacob has been a miracle. Papa is already doing better."

So they'd kept their promise. "They already sent Jacob to you?"

Her mum smiled. "He has been visiting every other day for two weeks."

Sage hadn't expected that. The Crown had kept their word. "After everything I went through, Mum, I knew I wouldn't find a fabulous match, but I hoped to find someone who would love me like you and Papa love each other. If I choose this life, I will never have that. My life will belong to someone else." She shuddered. "I am required to give him heirs, and I don't think I can do that."

"We will support you in whatever decision you make, baby girl. Never sell yourself short." Her mum wiggled her eyebrows. "From my understanding, you have yet to give him *your* demands."

Sage smiled. Her mum was brilliant. She crushed her mother against her, trying to memorize how it was to hug her. "I love you, Mum."

"And I you, daughter."

Her mum said her goodbyes, and Hayjen escorted her home. Sage waved to Lilja and slipped into her room. She ended up staring at the ceiling most of the night arguing with herself, trying to rationalize saying no. By the time morning came, exhaustion plagued her, but knew she had no choice.

She had to marry Tehl.

CHAPTER ELEVEN

Sage

Sage stomped across the deck to the captain's cabin. She felt ready to tear apart the world. Was there no justice in the land?

Roughly, she banged on the door. Hayjen yanked open the door, blinking furiously, his enormous torso on display along with bare feet and loosely-laced breeches. She winced, feeling badly for waking him, but grateful she hadn't been subjected to the sight of Lilja's naked body. Sage studiously stared at his collarbone, embarrassed. "I am sorry to wake you, but I will need you to arrange a meeting with the circle for this evening."

Hayjen smiled, his ice blue eyes sparkling. "Raising a little hell, are we?"

Sage's smile was wicked. "Indeed." She nodded and spun on her heel, concluding that she would spend the day however she pleased. Soon, her life would belong to someone else; she had to make the most of the time that was hers.

She spent most of the day lying in the sun and gossiping with Lilja. The highlight of their time together was when the two of them went for a swim. It was pure joy to spend time with sea creatures and experience the ocean the way Lilja experienced it, beneath its surface. Living as a part of it. Then, as soon as Sage would lose her breath, the captain would shoot them to the surface. Again and again, they dove. It was another world, entirely foreign yet wondrous. The only time she'd been alarmed was when a pair of leviathans became curious about them, even following them around for a time. Lilja had assured her they wouldn't attack, but Sage's heart still pumped frantically when one bumped her with his smooth snout. Later, when her lungs could take no more, they made their way back to the Sirenidae and dried in the sun, napping wherever they fancied.

Sage flopped her head to the side, smiling drowsily at Captain Femi. When was the last time she'd had such a peaceful day? "Thank you for today. I suspect I'll not have many more days like this in the future."

Lilja's smile dimmed. "Always find time for days like today. You will always be welcome here you know."

Sage snatched her hand and squeezed. "I will visit." Sage scanned Lilja's face, noting again the absence of the fine lines found in her mum's face. "Why do you look so much younger than my mum? You're the same age." She'd been wanting to ask it for so long.

Sadness tinged Captain Femi's features. "I am actually older than your mum. It is a Sirenidae trait. The sea rejuvenates us and so does a certain algae that grows deep in the ocean. We live longer lives."

"Hayjen?" she asked.

Lilja smiled. "He looks younger than he is."

Now that surprised her. "Is he Sirenidae too?"

"No, but the algae heals and restores the human body."

Sage mulled that over. It must be a well-kept secret. The Sirenidae would no doubt be hunted if word spread. "That is dangerous information."

"It is. And, as queen, you will handle such information."

She froze, and then forced her body to relax. "I will be queen in name only."

"Only if you allow it."

She smiled weakly before standing up, noting the hour. "We will see. For now, it's time to wreak havoc."

***

Rafe's voice carried through the thick door, and her ire increased, fueling the sense of betrayal she already felt. Sage smiled to herself. She would go down fighting. She kicked the door open with the heel of her boot and sauntered in. Startled eyes snapped to her as she gave them a sharp smile, stopping at the end of their table. She had their attention. "Good evening, *brothers*," she said, a hard edge to her voice. "Sacrificing virgins, are we?"

Everyone flinched save Hayjen, who was grinning like a loon, and Rafe, who looked like he wanted to leap over the table and throttle her. She noted that the monster wasn't at the table... She hoped maybe someone had stabbed him. Brushing aside her morbid thoughts, she focused on the table of traitors before her.

"Sage—" Mason started but cut off when her angry eyes landed on him.

"I joined the rebellion to help our people. I believed you were my brothers in arms, but there have been several times now that you have betrayed me." Sage jabbed a finger at the empty spot. "That man is despicable, yet you turned a blind eye to his crimes and blamed me for protecting myself. You are corrupt."

"How dare you..." Madden began.

"Yes, I dare," Sage shouted over him. "You lot sanctioned the king's murder! Not only that, but you sent *me* to do it! And you knew what going back there would be like for me!"

"If it was so wrong, why agree to be a part of the assassination then?" Noah questioned.

She smiled, baring her teeth. "Of course I agreed, I could never let you hurt someone I love. Had I refused you would've only sent someone else. How could I protect him if I wasn't there?"

The room stilled, the air thick with tension.

"What?" Rafe grated out.

Sage met his furious eyes, her own gaze unwavering. It hurt when someone deceived you, she knew that. "It's not pleasant, is it? To wonder what other secrets have been kept from you? What things were real and what was fake?" His jaw tensed. She smiled at the table. "No matter what the rebellion meant to me, I will never compromise my own honor or morals. Not for you. Not for anyone."

"So you didn't make an attempt on the king's life?" Badiah asked, incredulous.

Her lips twitched. "I attempted, just not very well."

"You lied to us?" Mason inquired in a hurt tone.

"Traitors don't belong in the circle," Madden snarked.

She laughed humorlessly. "I agree." She met his stare squarely, and, after a moment, he dropped his eyes. "I relinquish my place in your circle. Never will I work with or for you again. I hope never to see your faces again, which will most likely be the case as you've already sold me off."

Mason and Noah's faces blanched.

Her smile turned grim. "I was vulnerable the night of the treaty, it was obvious—but, rather than having a care for me, you made your grab for power. You used me to get your own way, without even bothering to get my consent, as if I were merely a bag of goods to exchange. You disgust me." She sucked in a breath, trying to control her rolling emotions. She met each of their gazes, one by one. "You got what you wanted. I will marry the prince." A stunned silence followed her statement. "This is goodbye, gentlemen. The crown prince made himself clear. If any of you seek me out, you will be harshly dealt with. You're wretched, but I don't wish for you to be harmed, so listen. You *will* honor the treaty, or I will personally hunt you down." Sage lifted a brow. "And I know all of your tricks. Don't forget why you've called me the rebel's blade." After issuing her threat, she confidently sauntered from the room, though her heart beat furiously in her chest. A giant roar came from behind her and Sage's eyes widened, the back of her neck prickling. One of Rafe's famous tempers was about to ensue.

"SAGE!"

Sage picked up her feet, full out running down the tunnels.

"Don't you dare run from me!" he shouted.

Her breath caught at how close he sounded. Damn, he was fast! She rounded a corner and sprinted toward an intersection of many tunnels, but she skidded to a stop when Rafe stepped into the middle, not even ten paces away.

How did he do that? Sage blinked, quickly scanning the tunnels. He must have shortcuts. "What do you want?" she bit out.

His chest heaved violently while he watched her. "What are you thinking?"

"That I only have one more evening of freedom before I am chained to my enemy because of you. Excuse me." She straightened, as if to walk around him. "I don't intend to spend it with *you*."

He took one step forward, and she countered it, watching him warily. He cocked his head in an almost canine way, studying each move as she made it. It was creepy. Something in her eyes must have given away her thoughts because he raised his arms carefully, like he

129

was trying to calm a skittish horse.

"It was taken out of my hands. They outvoted me. But all of that is unimportant." He squared his shoulders, holding his hand out for her to take. "You don't have to marry that toad. I can take you away from here. To freedom. Come with me to Methi."

She paused, her brows wrinkling in confusion. What was he talking about? "Methi?"

He took a step closer "Yes, my homeland. I can protect you. We can take care of your family. Just say yes, and I will take care of everything."

Homeland? How could that be? He wasn't Aermian? "What are you talking about? You're from Methi?" Sage accused, her mind scrambling to catch up.

"I am."

Sage gaped. Who *was* this man? "But why lie?"

Rafe exhaled a frustrated breath. "There are many things I need to tell you, but for now just know that I was sent here to help. I came to make Aermia stronger."

"Make Aermia stronger? You're a damn Methi spy leading *our* rebellion!"

"You're making it sound worse than it is. If Aermia is weak, they would open a path for the Scythians. We could not allow the fate of Negali to become ours."

Her mind reeled, but at the same time, many things clicked into place. That's why he'd been so sure Methi wouldn't retaliate when he'd impersonated their prince. It had, no doubt, already been sanctioned. They had sent spies to Aermia to cause mischief. His style of combat was so unique, unlike anyone she'd ever seen, and, in her innocence, she chalked it up to not being well traveled. But they had all been merely pawns. Had Rafe ever cared for Aermia or its people? She placed a hand against the stone wall to keep herself upright. This secret impacted everything. "And what of Aermia?" She eyed his outstretched hand mere paces from her.

He shrugged, as if this wasn't any of his concern. "They can fend for themselves. The crown prince isn't a complete moron. The treaty was signed, so the rebellion has to uphold it." He took a step closer. "Aermia has been solidified now. There is no chance for civil war."

"You're the one who stirred up the rebellion in the first place! We wouldn't have to deal with the threat of civil war if it wasn't for your meddling."

He waved away her statement. "The people were working themselves up to it already. I only shaped the outcome so that it could lead to something successful. It worked out for everyone."

Rage choked her. Worked out well for *everyone*? Her face heated. It most certainly did not work out well for *her*. This man was not the man she had come to know, love, and trust. Every time he opened his mouth, he unlocked another great secret. Did he know how to speak truth? What was she to believe? Sage stood upright, lifting her chin in challenge. "You're a liar."

"I am a spy."

No remorse. Like everything he had done was justified. It wasn't. Not everything was black and white, but right and wrong still mattered. Sage stormed forward and shoved past him. A large hand gripped her wrist, a deep growl emanating from him. Sage halted, her hair lifting on the back of her neck at the menacing sound. Sucking in a deep breath, she faced the beast of a man, ready to defend herself. She caught a brief glimpse of pain etched into his face, just before Rafe dropped to his knees and wrapped his muscled arms around her. Sage tensed as he curled his back, resting his forehead below her breasts.

"Please, please, forgive me. I have been trying to protect my people, help Aermia, and protect you as well. It's too much. I can't control everything, no matter how much I try. Sage, I am so sorry."

It was surreal to have the man she'd always viewed as her mentor kneeling at her feet, begging for forgiveness, his voice full of remorse. His actions would affect the rest of her life and others' lives too. Rafe had lied to her from the beginning, while she had gulped it all down, never doubting for a moment. Sure, she understood he kept things from her—that was a necessity of the life they had chosen. But she never dreamed everything she had grown to love about him would be a complete lie. Could she forgive him for what had taken place? Maybe a year ago, she may have. However, she was, in many ways, a different person now. She hesitantly lifted a hand, running it through his dark wine-colored hair. Her hand looked so small and pale in contrast. Sage's eyes widened as a gentle purr vibrated against her stomach. "What is that?" she whispered.

"It means I love you," he mumbled into her vest.

Sage froze, her hand clutching his hair. How dare he say that after everything! No, he didn't mean it, he couldn't.

Rafe lifted his head and gazed up at her, golden eyes gleaming. Carefully, he untangled her hand and stood, slipping his hands along her waist. She braced her hands against his strong chest, squeezing her eyes shut. A sob tried to escape, but she pinched her lips. Why was he doing this now? Everything was so messed up. He dropped his forehead to hers, soft breath puffing into her face.

"I have adored you ever since I saw you in the forest practicing swordplay, each of your movements graceful and smooth. I almost believed you to be Methian until I caught sight of those stunning green of your eyes." He moved, his nose grazing her temple, ruffling the hair there. "You were mine from the beginning."

Her breath whooshed out of her when he tipped her chin up. Sage opened her eyes to meet the serious gaze searching hers with an intensity she'd never before experienced from him nor anyone else.

Rafe must have found what he was looking for because he closed the distance, and pressed his lips against hers.

This wasn't happening.

She kept her lips still as he gently explored, holding her breath. When she couldn't hold it anymore, her lips parted as she exhaled. Rafe's arms tightened around her, pressing her along his hard body. She jerked back when he nipped her bottom lip. Rafe rumbled his displeasure and opened his liquid golden eyes.

"Finally, you're mine," he sighed, a gorgeous smile lighting his face, and puckering his scar. "Mine. My companion, my mate, after all these years," he murmured, a look of wonder on his face.

Sage struggled to form a complete thought with the whirlwind of emotions battling inside her, she felt like a ship in a storm. She wanted to cry, scream, punch, and hug him all at once but she was still hung up on the word 'mate'. What an old-fashioned word for spouse. She wasn't ready to be anyone's *mate*, and yet she already had a betrothed. Despite all the deceit and anger swirling inside, she couldn't dismiss him. Sage wanted to say ugly things and hurt him as he had hurt her, but she wouldn't. This would be the last time they would see each other. She had to send him away with peace between them.

Sage hesitated a moment before cupping his cheeks. He tilted his face into her touch then turned his face, kissing her palm tenderly. She swallowed her emotions and focused on the man gazing at her in adoration. "Rafe." She paused, licking her lips, him following the movement with heat in his eyes. Fear spiked through her at the look, but she tamped it down and focused on what she had to say. How was she going to let him down without hurting him? "I... I forgive you, but that doesn't change the fact that if I do not marry the crown prince, there will be civil war." Sage dropped her hands and pulled his from around her waist. She clutched them to her chest and kissed each hand. "I am not your mate." She gave him a pleading look. "Even if I had the choice, I wouldn't marry. Marriage needs honesty, and you have proven yourself not capable of it. You're a stranger to me." She gentled her words by squeezing his hands.

Sage braced herself when Rafe stilled, all warmth evaporating, his face looking like it was carved from stone. "You are. You belong to only me. I know it." His tone brooked no argument.

Her lips thinned while she attempted to control her frustration. "I am not, nor will I ever be, yours. You cannot own someone. They have to give themselves to you, and you give yourself in return. I am sorry." The sadness in her heart made it hard to speak. She dropped his hands and stretched to her tiptoes, kissing his stubbled cheek, which still hadn't so much as twitched. "Forgive me," she whispered, sparing him a final glance before stepping around him, eyes burning with unshed tears.

His hand wrapped around her bicep, halting her. "Please, I didn't mean it," he whispered in a broken voice.

Sage looked down at his overlapping fingers, then her eyes trailed up to his anguished face. "I understand that you are, but I can't right now. Please let go." When he didn't move she added, "Don't make me fight you, Rafe. Let us part with peace between us."

She watched as his eyes seemed to ice over and he looked fierce once again. "I will never let go of my mate. What is it really?" he said coldly. "Are you anxious to run back to the royals' beds? The three princes seem to hold more affection for you than seems ordinary."

His accusation pierced her, and any remorse she felt for hurting him evaporated. Sage wrenched out of his hold and slapped him with everything she had. Her hand pulsed as she pulled back, pain radiating up her arm. Rafe touched his face, abandoning his stone impression, regret softening his face. Sage tucked her hurt hand against her belly and stabbed her other hand at him.

"You *know* those rumors to be false. How dare you! You may have sold me to the Crown, but I am not a whore. How dare you speak in such a way!" She glared at him, a tear slipping down her face. "You can only belong to someone if you give yourself to them, I never did, Rafe."

"But you've always been mine."

"What does 'mine' even mean? Yours to play with? Manipulate? Train? Lie to? Sell? What Rafe? What?"

A vicious growl rumbled out of him. "Just *mine*. Mine to protect, possess, love, and care for."

"Why would I trust you with any of those things after what you have done?" Sage swallowed hard. "You've hurt me deeper than anyone has. You claim to love me, to want to protect and care for me? But Rafe, you broke me," she whispered. "*You* broke me, no one else."

Understanding dawned, and shame blanketed his face. He heaved, clutching his stomach like she'd kicked him, and stumbled to the wall, leaning heavily against it. Rafe gurgled twice trying to speak, but it was like words were stuck in the back of his throat. "Breezes of old, what have I done?" he choked out. "Forgive me, little one. I—I failed you."

Once again, he dropped to his knees. But this time it didn't look like he would get up. He looked as broken on the outside as Sage felt on the inside.

She swallowed and shook her head. How could she forgive him? How many times must she turn the other cheek just for him to stab her again? But the broken man on the floor tugged at her heart. Anger stirred in her gut as guilt still managed to prick her conscience over his feelings. "In time, perhaps," she muttered woodenly. "But I can't deal with you right now. Goodbye, Rafe." She spun, half running to get away.

"I love you, little one. I'm so sorry. " His strangled voice echoed behind her.

Sage pushed herself harder, hoping to outrun the pain, guilt, hate, and love swirling inside her.

Once she hit ground level, Sage wove through the streets of Sanee toward the castle. The closer she got, the sicker she became. She couldn't trust Rafe not to disappear with her in the night, and she didn't trust that one of the rebellion wouldn't try to have her killed or detained until the three days were up. To go back home, or even to the Sirenidae, would place those she loved in much danger. She slowed her pace and let herself finally process all the feelings she'd held back until now, the tears pouring down her face. Tucking her mussed hair beneath her cloak, she pulled the hood up, wanting to mourn the loss of her freedom with a measure of privacy. She mourned the loss of a life she always thought she could have, the trust and friendship she'd lost with Rafe, and, throughout this whole ordeal, the loss of her very self somewhere along the way. The betrayal, the rejection, every tumultuous feeling in her heart broke free. She wandered around, letting herself settle and trying to get herself together. When finally she'd found a measure of peace, her last tear dry, she'd neared the castle's outer wall. As she approached, it felt very much like she was walking to her execution. It was then that Lilja materialized at her side. No doubt the Sirenidae had been following her for some time.

"Heading in early?"

"No other choice."

"Come back with Hayjen and I for the night, or, if you need, we could set sail, perhaps spirit you away from here for now."

Her heart squeezed at the sincerity and concern she detected in Lilja's voice. She didn't know what she did to deserve such a wonderful friend, but was certainly grateful for Lilja's support. "Thank you, but no." She smiled softly. "I have made my choices, and they all lead me here. I cannot let others suffer when it's within my power to prevent it, nor can I continue to sacrifice the safety of my family for my own freedom, no matter how I long for it."

"Difficult as this may be, I hope you know: you *are* making a wise decision, *ma fleur*."

Sage nodded, swallowed, and stepped through the gate. Her heart raced as they passed through the second gate and into the courtyard. She spotted the Elite training on her right, and she watched briefly, before a familiar head of salt and pepper hair caught her attention. She meandered toward the training yard, pressing past several Elite who sent questioning glances her way. Pretending not to notice, she leaned against the fence to watch the sparring. Zachael slammed his sword into his opponent, twisting and striking with a speed that made her smile. Finally, the older man placed the tip of a dagger underneath the younger man's chin. The young soldier nodded, and the combat master removed the dagger from the man's throat. He glanced her way, and she registered surprise on his tanned face. Apparently he wasn't expecting her. Sage forced a grin. "Is that all you've got, old man?" A sea of eyes turned to her, the attention prickling uncomfortably under her skin. She suppressed the desire to run away, panicked, and lifted her chin.

His eyes sparkled as he placed the tip of his sword in the dirt. "Old man? Who, exactly, are you talking to, Sage? I don't see anyone of that description here."

"That last trick an infant could have executed." Male sniggers surrounded them. Lilja muttered something about picking a fight and being upset, but she ignored it for now. "Plus, that's not how you handle a sword."

"Why don't you show me how it's done, little miss?"

The sniggers stopped at the combat masters taunt. She smiled inwardly at the looks of interest from the elite. She may have to put on a false front in every other area of her life right up until she died but this was one place she would never have to. Clambering up the fence, she swung a leg over and dropped into the practice ring.

"Daggers or swords?" she questioned.

"Both?"

This time, her grin was genuine. Daggers were unquestionably her favorite blades. Zachael returned her grin with a wicked smile, though it was not unfriendly, and she decided then that she would like this man. Maybe she would spend her time here, training with the Elite. It would certainly be both beneficial and enjoyable. She pulled her own sword from its scabbard, excitement bubbling inside her for the first time in a long while. She clenched her teeth together to keep them from chattering. It was an odd thing that always happened, that and her blood sang just before she sparred. Sage loved a good bout. She stepped toward the combat master and allowed herself another smirk.

"I hope you're prepared to lose."

The older man grinned. "En garde."

CHAPTER TWELVE

Tehl

He finally finished up the stacks of necessary paperwork to restore the homes destroyed by the Scythian raids. Tehl sighed and sat back, trying to work out the kinks in his spine as he admired the pink evening sky. Sunsets were his favorite.

A knock sounded at the door, interrupting his moment of peace.

"Enter."

Sam sauntered in, a smile plastered on his face in a way that put him on edge. That particular smile never boded well.

"I have some interesting news."

"Oh?" he asked, warily.

His brother's smile widened. "It seems your betrothed is putting Zachael through his paces."

Tehl blinked. Betrothed? So she had arrived then? She actually came? Mixed feelings of anxiety and relief warred within him. There wouldn't be a civil war, but it meant fighting his own mini-war at home, one he must battle alone while seeming at peace in public. Sam's words finally registered in his mind, distracting him from the depressing direction of his thoughts. Paces? "She's doing what?"

"She's annihilating him. Come and see for yourself."

Tehl stood, rushing toward the door, but just as suddenly, jerked to a stop before actually going through it. Once he was on the other side of that door, everything would change.

Sam bumped his shoulder, studying him with serious eyes.

"Are you prepared for this? From this moment on, things can never go back to how they are now." He paused. "You know I will be by your side. I will support you every step of the way in this...and I'll do the same for Sage."

Surprised, Tehl stared at his brother with raised brows.

Sam rolled his eyes. "Don't give me that look. You don't have to leave your home, friends, family, and everything familiar behind. You were born into this life. As a matter of fact, it's all you know, yet despite this, it's still difficult at times. She's being thrown into this mess without any preparation and very little understanding."

Tehl nodded, acknowledging his brother's point. He couldn't begrudge her the support she would obviously need. Ruling was no cakewalk; it was a grueling set of ever-present responsibilities and burdens. He straightened his spine and stepped forward. Time to move ahead.

He shoved the door open, moving down the stairs and through the castle with Sam trailing behind him, silently. Tehl strode into the training yard but quickly halted to marvel at the match taking place in the ring. Sage and Zachael were engaged in a deadly dance: twisting, spinning, lunging, and blocking so fluidly that a surge of pride welled up within him. He may not have asked for this bride, but Sage had potential to be a remarkable queen. She was ferociously beautiful with sweat beading her brow and a slight smile touching her lips, her sword flashing. For the first time since Tehl had met her, she looked truly exquisite; she looked free.

"My god," Sam breathed. "You're marrying a damn warrior goddess. I think I've got betrothal envy."

Tehl snorted, never taking his eyes off the green-eyed woman currently out maneuvering his combat master. "You love too many women."

"I would be a one-woman man for her."

He winced as Zachael landed a heavy blow, knocking her to her knees, but in response, she swept his legs out from underneath him. The combat master crashed to the ground in a cloud of dust. Before he could rise, she touched both her dagger and sword to the man's neck.

"Yield."

Tehl tried not to gape when his combat master broke into the largest grin he had ever witnessed on the older man's face.

"Well done, missy, it has been a long time since someone could best me."

Sage threw her head back and laughed, the joyful sound putting smiles on the faces of all in the area. Tehl hung back, still observing, as the Elite moved in on her. One helped her up from the ground, another flirted, and yet another one inquired about her blades. Shortly, though, she shied away from them, the genuineness of her smile bleeding away as it turned forced.

"You better go claim your betrothed before another attempts to steal her away." Sam clasped him on the shoulder. "Ready yourself, brother. You need to play a ridiculously besotted version of yourself. Everyone knows you're awkward."

Tehl flashed Sam a filthy look and marched toward his men as they circled Sage. One caught his gaze and bowed before moving. In the blink of an eye, the others followed suit, and he found himself standing before her. Sage blinked repeatedly, her hands tightened on her dagger. Warily, he closed the distance between them. Before he could second guess himself, or give her the opportunity to stab him, he wrapped his arms around her hips, lifting her so they were the same height. Gazing into her startled eyes, he pressed a chaste kiss to her mouth. It wasn't even a kiss, rather it was simply a pressing together of mouths. She dipped her head so her loose hair curtained around their faces. Sage slipped her arms around his neck, never looking away, and her eyes narrowed. Her expression promised retribution. He scowled back. He hadn't even really kissed her.

Whistles and crass jokes interrupted their stare off. Tehl pulled back and slowly lowered her to the ground, like he was reluctant to let her go. In reality, he was only hoping her arms could stay where they were so he'd know she wasn't grabbing her weapons.

She dropped her gaze, now staring at his wrinkled shirt. He ran his hands down her arms to cup her elbows, wishing he could see her face. If he could see her face, he could anticipate her next move. Her body tensed under his hands, and she tilted her head just enough so that the flat line of her mouth was visible. So concerned about selling his performance, he didn't think about how she would react. If she didn't wipe the rage off her face, everything would be ruined before it even started. He leaned down to her ear. "Smile, darling."

Sage darted a quick glance to the Elite but wiped all expression from her face when she seemed to spot something. Tehl followed her line of sight to the exotic woman from the treatise meeting, Captain Femi. The white-haired captain gazed back evenly at the girl. They stared at each other as if in silent conversation.

Sage's eyes shuttered as she turned back to him. He could tell she reeled in her anger, and then she slipped into character.

"I came early. I hope that's all right." She peered up at him through her lashes, placing a hand on his chest. "I just couldn't stay parted from you," she murmured with a sly smile.

Tehl blinked at her, coughing once. She was good when she wanted to be. "This is where you belong." She blinked at him and raised an eyebrow.

Heat scorched the back of his neck. *That was the best he could come up with?* He wanted to bang his head on the fence. Tehl slid one hand to the back of her neck and licked his lips. Maybe he should just kiss her again and stop making an ass of himself.

Something flashed through her eyes when he leaned toward her. Then the world tilted, and his breath was knocked out of him. Tehl blinked, disoriented. How had that happened? A smug feminine face entered his vision as she squatted beside him, her hand still on his wheezing chest.

"My prince," she cooed. "I think you need to keep your hands to yourself. We are yet to be married. What would your people think of such displays of affection?"

Tehl growled at her, his lungs screaming. His focus shifted to the Elite leaning closer to catch every word. Gossip whores. Sometimes, his men were worse than the old biddies of his court.

Zachael stepped next to him, teeth flashing in an amused grin. "You need practice, my prince. She swept your feet clean out from under you well before you knew what was happening."

"She tends to do that," Tehl remarked in a dry tone.

Sage brushed her chestnut hair from her face as she stood. Tehl waited to see if she would extend her hand. When you knocked someone down during a bout, it was good sportsmanship to help them up. A moment passed and another. Well, he had his answer. He started to sit when she shoved her hand into his face. Tehl eyed it like it was a snake. Would she help him up or try to drop him again?

Her hand wiggled in front of his face impatiently. An idea took root in his mind that made him want to grin. It was time to channel his brother. He grasped her hand and jerked it, pulling her off her feet. She stumbled and fell onto his chest in a heap. A bitty growl bubbled from her throat. Check mate. "My lady, I am not concerned about what anyone thinks." She struggled to stand, but he kept her still, banding his arms around her waist. Raising his voice, he asked, "I assure you that most of the surrounding men are green with envy, am I right?"

A chorus of male agreement thundered around them

"Let go, my lord, you are causing a scene," she hissed between clenched teeth.

"This is entertaining, but you have yet to introduce her to the men," Zachael commented.

Sage flashed the combat master a thankful smile even as Tehl scowled, making the men around him chuckle. Tehl kept an arm around her small waist and stood, facing his men. She tried to escape, but he linked their fingers and squeezed her hand. Sage halted her wriggling and stood placidly before him. Her hand felt oddly small in his. When was the last time he'd held hands with a woman? Even though her fingers were delicate, there were calluses on them. At least she was a hard worker. Tehl cleared his throat and raised their linked hands. "Men! Meet my betrothed."

Ear-rupturing shouts and congratulations were flung their way. Sage stilled, her fingers tightening when his men circled them. Tehl felt her shudder when Garreth kissed her free hand, murmuring his congratulations. He met his brother's eyes, darting a glance to the overwhelmed female beside him.

Sam eyed her and shoved everyone aside. "You came home at last! I always wanted a sister to bother. Think of the trouble we can cause." Sam grinned wickedly.

Some of her unease slipped away as Sam approached. Tehl noted her lips twitching, like she was fighting a smile.

"Come give me a hug, sister." Sam held his arms out.

Sage tugged her hand from his and tapped the arm circling her waist. Tehl released her, grinning at the way she stared his brother down.

"I would rather eat coral."

Stubborn wench. At least it was directed at someone other than him this time.

Much laughter and teasing erupted around them. Sam pouted for a moment, pretending to be heartbroken. Sage raised a winged brow at his attempt to sway her. Finally, dropping all pretenses, he lunged for Sage, taking her by surprise. A startled yelp burst out of her when he swung her into his arms like a bride. "You and I both know how dull my brother can be. Why don't we settle you in and see what mischief we can cause?"

"I know exactly what kind of mischief you cause, and I want no part of it."

Sam winked at him and marched toward the castle. "How would you know?"

Tehl sniggered as his unlikely betrothed struggled with Sam, starting in on a huffy rant. "I heard all kinds of stories from Zeke and Seb about..." Her voice faded out as they disappeared through the castle doors. He glanced at the captain as she untangled herself from one of his men, heading in the direction Sam had taken Sage.

That was his cue to leave. "I better rescue my bride before my brother tries to steal her from me."

He said it only half joking. Tehl saluted Zachael and trotted after them. When he found Sam, his brother was whispering something in Sage's ear. She went rigid in his brother's arms and glanced over Sam's shoulder at him.

"We have much to discuss." Sage said.

Tehl nodded. "In private."

He jogged up the stairs, preparing himself for the battle ahead. They arrived at his study more quickly than he would have liked. He held the door open until all three filed in after him. Tehl shut the door and locked it before turning around.

Sage wiggled out of Sam's arms, almost landing on her face in the process.

"Don't be an idiot," Sam scolded. "I wouldn't hurt you."

"I didn't want you touching me and look! Now you are not," she retorted. "Mission accomplished." She turned to him. "As for you, my lord, don't you ever put your slobbering lips on me again without my consent."

Slobbering lips? Hardly. "If I was slobbering on you, you would feel it. I am sure nuns have experienced more passionate kisses than what I gave you. You can't even call that a kiss."

He ran his hands through his hair and shot Captain Femi a look. Did the woman wear nothing but bright colors? Just gazing at her hurt his eyes. "You explained everything to her?"

"Yes."

Tehl turned back to Sage.

The rebel.

Also his betrothed. That was odd.

"I did what I had to. It was only to keep our secret. I was *not* making any advances. You know as well as I do that I needed to make them believe we're in love. Not sure if we did, but at least *I* did my best." He took in her crossed arms, cocked hip, and agitated expression. She wasn't happy to be here. "Have you come of your own free will?" The question lingered in the air.

Her jaw tightened, and she nodded once. "Yes." She lifted her eyes from the floor and met his gaze head on. "No one forced me. The thought went through my mind to run."

He appreciated her frankness. "I understand."

"No, you do not." A shrug. "But I could never condemn our people that way. If this prevents bloodshed then I am duty bound." A sardonic smile twisted her pink lips. "In my line of work I have become well acquainted with acting. We both have our respective roles, but I would appreciate it if you warn me before you touch me, though it would be better if you didn't have to touch me at all," she added.

His head whipped to the captain. Sage didn't sound like she had been apprised of all his stipulations. "All?"

"All," Captain Femi replied tersely.

He blew out a breath. They needed to speak about heirs. It wasn't a conversation he wanted to have, but he was never one to beat around the bush. "And what of heirs?" Tehl's stomach clenched at the horror that passed over Sage's face leaving her ashen.

She gulped and threw her shoulders back. "As the crown prince, I understand the need for heirs to secure the throne. I thought of a solution that will suit both of us."

"Okay," he drew out, not knowing where she was going.

"I don't care for you and you don't care for me. You shall not be receiving heirs from me. I would rather stab you than share your bed."

That pricked his masculine pride, but Tehl pushed it aside.

"That would make for interesting bed sport," Sam joked.

"Imbecile," Captain Femi muttered. Sam merely smirked, taunting her.

Tehl ignored them both, still trying to figure out what she was talking about. She wouldn't have his children? He fought an odd sense of rejection and disappointment as he stepped toward her. Why was she even here if she wasn't planning on cooperating? "That was one of my stipulations to the ridiculous demands of *your* rebellion. I will *not* be denied children," he warned. He'd always wanted a big family, and he loved having a brother. Tehl would compromise on many things but not this. He braced himself for a fight when her chin jutted out.

"You shall not be denied children, my lord. You may have as many children as you desire, but they won't be coming from my womb. I suggest you keep a mistress."

Sam whistled.

Captain Femi cursed up a storm.

And Tehl stared at her in confusion. "I beg your pardon?" He must have heard her wrong. "You can't be serious." But from the expression on her face perhaps she was. She wasn't his first choice to share a bed with either, but it was just something they both would have to deal with. He actually felt a little insulted. "I have never kept a mistress, and I will never keep one," he stated firmly. "It would shame you, not to mention my entire family line, if I did such a thing. Plus, it would easily undermine our ruse of love." He stared at her. "And even were I to do as you wish, they wouldn't be legitimate. Your plan will not work."

"Have me declared barren."

Tehl froze. That was one of the most humiliating things you could do to a woman. He would never do that. She'd rather be humiliated before the entire kingdom to escape his affections? He did not really desire a love match, having seen the devastation it caused his father when they lost their mother, but he had hoped to at least like, or have a friendship with, the woman he would spend the rest of his life with. They were to raise a family together after all.

"That way it would not bring any reproach on you or the Crown," Sage continued, excitement in her voice. "I imagine your advisers would urge you to take a mistress."

Captain Femi gasped. "Sage, no. This is a very serious decision.

Just because you don't want to have children now, doesn't mean you won't."

"I want children, just not his."

That was a punch to the gut.

Silence engulfed the room, and his pulse pounded in his ears. Tehl had never been so insulted in his life. She wanted children but not his? His hackles rose. Whose children did she mean to have? Did she expect him to let her have lovers? Because that would *not* happen. He may not have chosen her, but stars above, they were stuck together. No one would touch his wife. If she wanted children, he would damn well give them to her. He was done. She wasn't thinking clearly, even her friend saw it. "This is not something you can negotiate. It has been written into the treaty. Are you willing to break it and cause civil war?"

"The rebellion had their demands, the Crown had theirs, you had yours, but I did not," Sage seethed, her hands shaking. "While I was being touched by the monster whom Sam promised to take care of, you and Rafe were haggling over my sale. You had no right!"

"It was not like that." His voice rose. "That rat changed the demands and your leader backed them."

She visibly flinched, hurt pinching her face. He needed to calm down. She was as much a victim here as he was. Tehl swallowed the angry words on the tip of his tongue. "I made the best of the situation. I did not snatch you up and lock you in a tower like an evil villain. I gave you a choice unlike your comrades."

"Some choice," she scoffed, tugging on her loose braid. "Marry you and lend you my womb, or live my life and let innocents die. I joined the rebellion to *prevent* loss of life. It wasn't much of a choice in reality," Sage mumbled, staring at the wall above his head.

"And that's why you'll make a good queen."

Her eyes shot to his, her face showcasing her shock. The words had accidentally tumbled out of his mouth, but they were true. She would be a troublesome and cantankerous wife but she cared for his people. Ever since he met her she'd proven to be loyal and hardworking for those she loved—both were fine qualities for a queen.

"I don't want it. I am a sword maker, not royalty."

"That makes you a perfect candidate for the job, Sage," Captain Femi spoke up. "Your humility, sense of duty, and compassion will be what it takes to make you a capable ruler."

"Indeed," Sam agreed.

His betrothed looked around the room and finally settled her eyes on him.

"We were thrown into this mess, both of us. We're bound; there is no escape for either one of us." He stated the facts bluntly. It was better to be honest than play games. "You and I are alike in this. We share that strong sense of duty." Tehl opened his mouth to continue but closed it. What he needed to say had to be said in private. He looked to the captain and his brother. "Leave us."

Captain Femi ignored him and looked to Sage who nodded her consent. Sam unlocked the door and opened it for the tall woman. "My lady."

Tehl watched them leave and gazed at the door after it shut. "I noticed how you trembled when the Elite surrounded us earlier," he began, turning his attention from the door to Sage's apprehensive eyes. "Gavriel told me of your nightmares. I watched you at both meetings. You can put on a fairly flawless mask, but I still saw your terror, though you tried to bury it deep, at being around all the men, even ones with whom you seemed to be familiar."

"What of it?"

He had to tread carefully here. "You fear me."

Her cheeks reddened at his comment. Apparently, that was the

150

wrong thing to say. Sage's eyes narrowed into a glare.

He rushed on to avoid another argument. "Not in the instance you fear me, but my touch. You reacted that way with any man who touched you, even Rafe. But know this, I will not force myself on you for children." His eyes scanned her face. "Honestly, you may be lovely but a woman who loathes me has no appeal."

A tremulous smile touched her mouth. "Agreed, my lord."

Stars above, something they agreed on. "I don't plan on having children soon. I don't want to bring a child into a world with the threat of war looming. It'll be years before I want them." Now it was time to see if she would compromise. "It's wrong to have a mistress and you know it. The sanctity of marriage is precious. And I won't tell the world you are barren to save face. I understand you need time to heal from what happened. Would you be willing to give me children if we waited?" Tehl held his breath.

She bowed her head, then her gaze returned to his face. "Would you let me choose when?"

He wanted to say no because he didn't trust her. If he gave her that power, she could push off children for forever. But they needed to work together if they would survive this marriage. He needed to give her a little trust, maybe then she would return the favor. "My offer is five years." Tehl watched her throat bob.

"That is acceptable to me... Maybe then my skin won't crawl at the thought." She tacked on.

Tehl's mind flashed back to their kiss in the hallway, at the Midsummer Festival. Heat stirred in his veins, surprising him. A cinnamon smell teased his nose. How did she still smell like cinnamon when she was sweaty? He shook himself and got back to the matter at hand. "Was it so terrible at the festival?"

"I was playing a role, that was different," she huffed.

"Truly?"

"Truly," she echoed.

"Let's try something. Slip into your role."

"What?" she stammered as Tehl strolled toward her, giving her time to step away or tell him to stop. She didn't, but he noted she shifted onto the balls of her feet, slightly at an angle, a defensive pose. Her distrustful look brought a genuine smile to his face. He slowed in front of her and held his hands out for her to take. She was in control, she had the choice to accept or decline. Sage reminded him of a skittish foal, untrusting and wary, not that he would ever tell her that. She would probably punch him in the face. His smile widened. What would his court think about his warrior woman? Sage would cause quite a stir, he was sure of it.

She only hesitated a moment before slipping her hands into his. Tehl bit back his smile of triumph. It was a small step, but at least they weren't fighting. Tehl ran his thumbs along the top of her hands. "See, not so bad." She watched his thumbs for a moment before pulling away. He let her go and stepped to his desk, leaning against it. "What do you want, Sage?" If they were open and honest, they could understand exactly what to expect from each other. If they treated this marriage like a business, it meant they could be partners. Not friends, but not enemies either.

"The impossible." Her smile was sad.

"You will be queen eventually, nothing will be out of your reach."

Her smile turned bitter. "Except for freedom." She rolled her neck, closing her eyes. "I want nothing from you, but I find myself asking anyway. My family." She peered at him. "I have been the one running the smithy because of my father's health. He can't do it anymore. By marrying you, I will leave them helpless."

"Your family will be well taken care of. We can move them here."

"What of the forge? That has been in my family for generations. My parents would never leave. They wouldn't be happy here."

"What if we sent someone to work for your father?"

"They wouldn't be able to afford to pay them," Sage whispered. He could see her pride stung admitting it.

"You're entitled to wealth once we marry. Did you not realize this?" Tehl eyed her. Most women he met were very interested in the Crown's wealth, in the jewels. Yet she acted like the thought never crossed her mind.

She glowered at him. "I don't want your gold. My needs are little. If I have food to eat, clothing on my body, and a roof over my head, I am content. I'm not asking for charity. I am asking you for a solution."

Tehl wracked his brain for a moment, pushing his black hair out of his face. "What if I sent an apprentice from the palace to your forge? There are many, and they are not getting as much training as they would at your father's side. They would still be under the Crown's employ, so your father wouldn't need to pay them. We could rotate an apprentice out every half year or so." Something warm seeped through him at the small smile that put on her face.

"That would work." Her lips pursed. "Though I would still like to work in a smith and continue my training."

Tehl could think of many reasons why she shouldn't do either of those things, but by her stance he knew she would not budge on these either. He nodded. "We can make arrangements for you to continue both. Anything else?" "No."

"I will send for Mira and have her settle you." He clasped his hands. "Just so it doesn't take you by surprise, the betrothal will be announced tonight."

She paled. "So soon?"

"Yes." He grimaced. "The Elite are the worst gossips; I guarantee word has spread already. I need to hunt down my father and somehow convince him to show up and give us his blessing." Tehl grumbled to himself. Finding him would not be an easy task.

"I can do that."

He glanced at her in surprise.

Sage lifted one shoulder. "He visited every day I was here. I think he will find me even before I go looking."

One less thing off his plate. "Thank you." Silence filled the room. Tehl stared at her, not knowing what to say. He was never good with small talk. "Is there anything else you need?"

Sage shook her head. "Nothing that needs fixing now, my prince."

Tehl stood and stretched, aware of Sage's eyes observing him. He ignored her and strode to the door, opening it, revealing a smug looking captain and an irritated Sam. What kind of trouble had his brother gotten into this time? He turned back to his betrothed. "You know the way?"

"Same room?"

He nodded.

"Then, yes, my prince." She brushed past him, ignoring Sam, and continued down the hall.

If she kept referring to him so formally no one would continue to believe them besotted.

"Sage," he called. She stiffened and stopped, regarding him over her shoulder. "Use my name."

"Of course, Tehl."

He liked the way his name sounded when she spoke it. He scowled at the thought. Sage dismissed him and resumed her clipped pace, disappearing from sight with the captain trailing behind.

"She's trouble," his brother remarked.

"Yes." Sage would make his life very interesting.

CHAPTER THIRTEEN

Sage

"You know where you are going, *ma fleur?*" Lilja's ironic words sounded from behind her.

Sage ignored the comment, focusing instead on the stone walls and the lanterns casting flickering shadows across the smooth surfaces. It was odd how soundless her footsteps were in the vast arching hallway. It was almost as if she wasn't really here. The disjointed feeling made her uncomfortable in her own skin. She needed to get out of here.

Sage spotted the staircase to the royal wing and sprinted up, eager to leave the hallway behind. The fist on her lungs eased as she reached the top but the eerie silence of the hall brought the feelings rushing to the forefront as she caught sight of her old door. Goosebumps lifted the hair on her arms.

The door itself may have been unremarkable but that which it represented, at least to her, was highly impactful. It had been her prison of sorts before, but once she entered this time it would start a lifelong sentence. The very thought of being trapped again had sweat pooling between her shoulder blades. Was she really doing this? Could she subject herself to a lifetime of loneliness? The people of court weren't like her. Sage could pretend all she wanted, but she was different, real, common.

What she did for the rebellion and her family shaped her into who she was. Who would she be after abandoning everything she knew? Would Sage still be herself? If she didn't know herself how could she govern others?

Sage panted heavily as her biggest fear rose in her mind. Children. Children needed strong mothers, ones who'd protect them from the world. That wasn't her. Sage knew the truth. She was weak and broken inside. Weak women made for terrible mothers. How could she raise the next rulers of Aermia? Panic clawed at her chest. She wasn't ready. It was too much to ask. Sage had no unearthly clue how to be a princess, queen, or mother. She had no business being here.

"Take a deep breath," Lilja murmured in her lyrical way. "It will be okay. You are not alone."

Sage squeeze her eyes closed. Now was not the time to panic. Opening her eyes, she stared at the ordinary handle for a beat before reaching for it, but her hand stopped, hovering just above it.

Stop being a coward.

Sage clasped the cool metal with determination, pushing it open. The room looked the same. The giant four-poster bed, carved from an aqua colored jardantian tree, still dominated the room. She willed her feet to move and she slowly made it farther in. Each step of her boots sank into the luxurious blue carpets as Sage absently ran her hand along the abalone adorning the mantelpiece. After a moment, she abandoned the fireplace in favor of large windows set into double doors. She pressed her face against the cool glass, trying to get a glimpse of ocean but it was too dark to see much at this hour. The sound of the water crashing on the rocks below still reached her though, and she felt a small measure of comfort. She turned, bracing her back against the door, watching as Lilja took her turn, inspecting the room.

The curious Sirenidae tested out each chair, even remarking on the comfort of each, before standing and moving to investigate the bathing room. Sage watched her friend disappear and waited for the explosion of excitement she knew was coming.

"*Plumbing?!*" Lilja shrieked.

Sage bit back her smile when Captain Femi poked her head out of the bathing room. "I could live in here. I would pay a fortune for the bathing tub alone."

Sage nodded and returned her attention to the large bed, its fluffy white coverlet seeming to beckon. Exhaustion and longing overwhelmed her. All she needed was a nap, then she could start to process everything else. She pushed from the doors and flopped onto the bed, the blanket encasing her face, creating a fluffy cocoon. She lay there, enjoying it, but soon her lungs burned, so she was forced to roll over just so she could breathe. The last time she had been *kept* in this room, it had been her cell. Luxurious to be sure, but a cell nonetheless, and yet here she was again, still a prisoner of sorts but this time she'd chosen the fate.

Lilja's *oohing* and *ahhing* over the bathing space and its luxuries pulled her from her bout of self-pity. There were certainly worse places to be.

A moment later, the door burst open, causing Sage to jump and Lilja to rush over. The room's newest occupant carried with her the scent of herbs and tonics.

Mira.

Sage took a fortifying breath, preparing to grovel. She lifted her arm only to meet a pair of angry blue eyes.

"I'm sorry," Sage blurted the first and only thing she could think to say.

Mira grabbed her arms and yanked her into a hug. "I am nowhere near forgiving you." Mira's arms tightened around her. "But I am so glad you're safe." Mira released her and stepped back to glare at her some more. "I knew you wanted to leave, but I thought you would at least say goodbye before slinking off into the night like a damn thief. You could have trusted me."

Sage swallowed. She should have, she knew that now. "I know, and...I should have. But, at the time, I just didn't want any blame shifting to you for my actions. I said as much of a goodbye as I could without alerting Gav to my plan."

"Was anything you told me true, Ruby?"

"... My name is actually Sage."

"Of course it is." Mira huffed out an angry breath, looking away. "You weren't honest with me. That's not to say I don't understand that you have reasons. I know you had people you were protecting," Mira's face turned red, and Sage could hear the hurt in Mira's voice as she continued. "But color me shocked when my presence was requested to attend you. Why didn't you come to see me as soon as you arrived?"

Sage tugged on her braid, embarrassed and a bit ashamed. "I haven't had a moment. I arrived, was whisked into a meeting, and then immediately sent here to get ready for dinner." Her excuses sounded pathetic, even to her own ears. She should have gone straight down to the infirmary. She shot Lilja a glance, who had made herself comfortable in a chair, both legs thrown over its arm. The captain winked and pretended not to listen. The little eavesdropper was enjoying this.

Sage turned back to the irate healer. "Do you know why I am here?"

Mira's face morphed into amusement. "The current ridiculous rumor is you've been betrothed to the crown prince." Mira sniggered. "I laughed when I first heard it. You detest the crown prince. Of all the men in the world he's the *last*—"

"It's true," Sage choked out.

Mira's jaw unhinged, gaping, but only for a moment before her face blanked. She took a few steps back and sank into her customary chair by the fire. Her blond friend looked to have no words. She opened and closed her mouth several times before she could get anything out.

Sage's stomach churned.

"How?"

Sage paced before the fireplace and began her story, explaining everything from the very beginning. Mira listened carefully, never once interrupting or even questioning. Some parts were ash on her tongue, and she had to muscle through them, the sting of betrayal still somewhat fresh. It was odd recounting everything that had come to pass, but it was also surprisingly freeing. When she finally stopped talking, Sage felt a little lighter.

Mira's eyes dipped to the floor for a moment before returning to Sage's face. "Thank you."

That wasn't the response she'd expected. "For what?"

"Your sacrifice. I know better than most how you feel about the Crown."

Sage turned from Mira's knowing gaze, instead watching Lilja pretend to sleep. "How I feel isn't really important at the moment. There is too much at stake. I have no idea if we'll succeed, and I don't know what I'm doing, but I'm also all the Crown has. If this is our only chance at peace, what choice did I really have?" Sage took a shaky breath, whispering her next words. "Honestly, after everything that I've been through, it's not as though I have any semblance of appeal." She paused, chewing her lip before continuing. "No respectable man would have wanted me anyway. I should be happy, after all coming here has given me an opportunity. At least now I might have a family of my own."

"How many grandbabies should I expect then?"

Sage yanked out her daggers and pivoted toward the voice. She saw in the corner of her eye that Lilja had done the same, crouching with a long, wicked-looking dagger in one hand. Where had that come from? Sage brushed the thought aside and focused on the person speaking. A section of wall slowly pushed open, revealing the king. He took in their weapons and smiled gaily.

"That's no way to greet family."

Sage gaped as he moved into her room like he owned it. She supposed, technically, he did. "Can I help you, your majesty?"

"Did my ears deceive me, or are you to wed my son?"

Sage floundered for a moment, unable to respond. When she recovered she sent him a scowl. "Were you *listening at my door?*"

"You shouldn't leave the door open, anyone can listen in." Sage mentally rolled her eyes at that. The king continued, "Now, answer the question. Sage, are you betrothed to my son?"

Sage straightened but couldn't meet his eye. She chose to examine the rug instead of Marq. "I am."

Heavy footsteps moved toward her, and brown boots entered her line of vision. A large hand cupped her chin, lifting her face. She met his familiar blue eyes and something about the warmth there had her fighting tears. He searched her face, giving her a sad smile.

"From the Elite, it sounded to be a joyful reunion, but from your face it seems that, for you, at least, this is not a happy occasion." He could not hide his disappointment with this revelation.

Sage forced a smile upon her lips. "We want people to believe it to be."

He studied her, his face sharpened. "You are marrying to protect Aermia, yes?"

She gulped. "Yes."

"That's a weight."

"It is. May I be honest with you, sire?"

"Please."

"I have no desire to be either queen or your son's wife. But I give you my promise that I'll do whatever I can to help the kingdom mend and weather the storms ahead of us."

"And what of my son? Will you do your best to help him as well?"

She met his eyes, the eyes of a concerned father. "I will help him run the kingdom. I will give him children. Don't worry, the royal line will continue."

"That's not what I was talking about. Will you be a good companion, helpmate, and consort?"

"I will advise him to the best of my ability."

"He doesn't need an advisor, he needs a wife."

"The crown prince should have thought about that before he bought me." Sage winced. She knew she sounded unreasonable but she couldn't help what she felt, or change what happened.

Marq's lips thinned. "You feel he bought you?"

"Essentially." She shrugged, looking to Marq hopefully. "I know I am not what you imagined for your son. I am sure he feels the same way, but I'm all that you and our country get." Sage clasped his hands. "As I'm sure you overheard, the lives of many depend upon this. I cannot have the consequences of failure on my conscience; it's why I'm here in the first place. But, in order for this union to succeed, we *need* your permission and blessing. We need your support. The prince told me we have to make the announcement tonight. Would you... Do you think you could come to dinner and be the one to do so? Please?" Sage pleaded.

Marq watched her, an unreadable expression on his face, before pulling her into a gentle embrace. "I can do that, dear. Thank you," the king whispered into her hair.

Sage squeezed him once and stepped back.

"I will leave you so you can make yourself ready then." The older man strode from the room, disappearing as quickly as he'd appeared.

"Stars above." Lilja fanned herself. "He sure is a handsome man for his age."

Mira snorted. "You should see his sons."

Captain Femi flashed the blond healer a smirk. "It's true. They are pretty easy on the eyes."

Sage scoffed. "Beautiful on the outside they may be, but the insides definitely leave something to be desired."

"You better keep that opinion to yourself, lest someone hear you. Don't ruin everything because you can't keep your mouth shut," Lilja chided.

Mira stood, eyeing her leathers with disdain. "You need a bath and change of clothes before you join them."

Sage smiled at the promise of a bath but it fell when she remembered that she'd have to wade into the leviathan-infested waters of court immediately after. Her scowl deepened. Hopefully it wouldn't taint the joy of her bath.

***

Sage sunk into the deep tub letting the warm water lap at her shoulders, as spicy oil teased her nose. Cinnamon. Her favorite. She tilted her head back, eyes closing, her neck cradled along the tub's edge. She'd needed this.

She could hear Lilja and Mira discussing dresses. Sage liked pretty things, but it still irked her to think that the worth of many extravagant pieces could feed a family for months. She didn't need something that was such a colossal waste of coin.

"Something modest," Sage hollered, and the voices paused as two sets of footsteps moved into the washroom.

"You are now the betrothed of the crown prince thus your dress needs to be impeccable," Mira argued. "Any flaw will give the harpies of his court reason to rip you to shreds. You represent the Crown now."

Sage sniggered. "I don't care what they think. I am not here to impress them, so I will dress as I please. I'm to be the prince's consort, am I not?"

"*You* may not care but in so doing you will make a mockery of the Crown. Is that what you want?"

Mira's harsh words made Sage pry her eyes open. "No," she said, serious now. "But I will not dress in a way that mocks the suffering of our people either. Queen Ivy never wore shoes. I will not shame myself, nor the crown prince, no matter how much I might dislike him. I believe that something both tasteful and simple is not too much to ask."

Lilja shot Mira a look, a small smile on her face. "She sounds like a queen already."

Mira lifted Sage's heavy fall of hair and poured some delicious smelling soap into it, working through the tangles. Sage let out a happy sigh.

"Sage, I wasn't criticizing you but you must remember that how you dress matters from now on. I want to protect you from the judgment you will no doubt face tonight. Many of these women are not kind. Behind pretty little smiles may be a coiled viper."

Sage placed a wet hand on Mira's arm, meeting concerned blue eyes. "I'm aware of what they may be like. But do not fret, I can handle myself. I am not without skills myself when it comes to pretense, and no one here can say anything worse than what many said when I returned home before. Their words only hurt if I let them. I truly don't care what they say, I am here for one purpose and one purpose only and it has nothing to do with them." Sage patted her friend's arm before resuming scrubbing herself. She met Lilja's magenta eyes. "The only dress I have fine enough for tonight is my costume from the Midsummer Festival, and that is inappropriate. What would you suggest I wear?"

Captain Femi entered the room and ran a fingertip along her bathwater. "I sent someone to the Sirenidae for a dress of mine."

Sage eyed her skeptically. They were shaped nothing alike. Lilja was tall and willowy whereas she was short and curvy. How exactly would *that* work?

Captain Femi snorted. "I am a merchant."

"Pirate," Sage teased. In truth, Sage had discovered a few things while staying on the Sirenidae. Lilja was a legitimate business woman, but she also had some *interesting* enterprises on the side. She also had things Sage had never seen before, stuff not of Methian or Aermian origin, and very old.

Captain Femi sniffed but ignored her comment. "I am having dresses brought here for you. They may need to be altered, but I am sure we can find one that fits enough for tonight."

Sage eyed Lilja's colorful outfit, hoping whatever it was wasn't quite so brightly colored.

Lilja caught her expression and swatted the air. "Don't give me that look. Many wish they could wear the colors I do."

Mira squeezed the water from her hair. "They are exotic, but I'm afraid only someone with your coloring can pull off that yellow. It's quite...vivid."

Lilja smirked. "I am sure that, with your golden hair, you could wear it reasonably well."

Mira stood and picked up a towel, beckoning for Sage to get out. She paused for a moment, self-conscious, but steeled herself knowing Mira had already seen her at her worst. She stood, water sluicing down her body, and stepped from the tub as Mira wrapped her in the warm towel. She was led to the vanity to sit as Mira begun working on her hair.

Lilja followed them into the bedroom and met Sage's eyes in the mirror. Sage shivered when she saw the anger plain on her face. "He will pay, *ma fleur.*"

She didn't need to ask whom, but, seeing her friend so fierce, she realized the woman could be quite frightening. She imagined this is what the stories referred to when they referred to the Sirenidae as bloodthirsty fighters. She glanced away from Captain Femi into flashing blue eyes and winced when Mira jerked the brush through her hair. Noticing her discomfort, Mira gentled her brushing with an apologetic smile.

"Sorry. I am not a lady's maid, though I am sure you will be assigned someone soon."

Sage gaped at her in horror. "I hope not. I don't have a need for one. I appreciate your help with my hair, but I am capable of washing and dressing myself. It would be a complete waste of a maid's time." She thought for a moment before continuing. "Why would anyone aspire to do such a thing anyway?"

"Mostly it is the distinction that comes with the title. In this case they could boast being entrusted to work with nobility, perhaps even the ruler of our nation, which would no doubt help them in their own pursuits of husbands or networking. Sometimes it is one who has performed their duties well, and they are assigned the task as a reward. A lady's maid isn't nearly so hard as many other positions. There are many reasons, some fine, others less so." Mira started worked more oil into her hair.

Sage didn't want someone she didn't know hanging around all the time. "What about you?"

The blond healer laughed. "I have no desire to ever be a lady's maid. I am a healer through and through. Give me blood and tonics over dresses and hair pins."

Mira finished Sage's hair and stared at it like it was a puzzle. Lilja scooted to the side, bumping Mira out of the way with her hip. "Move, healer, I will take care of this. Hmm..." she mused. "Me. A hairdresser. Who would have thought?"

Sage closed her eyes and let Lilja turn her from the mirror, as she plaited her hair, and Mira applied a few cosmetics to her lips, cheeks, and eyes.

"Not too heavy, please." She hardly wore the stuff, it always melted off in the heat of the forge, so what was the point? Plus, her mum had always said she didn't need it.

A soft knock at the door made her eyes pop open as Mira moved to get it, her skirts rustling. Mira let out a startled squeak and Lilja paused and called, "Hayjen?"

A grunt answered her.

"Please come in."

Hayjen scanned the room and, noting the bed, carefully laid the dresses there, grumbling all the while. "I had to practically fight my way here." He turned, his grumpy face lighting in a tender smile when he spotted his wife. His eyes moved to Sage. "Don't let her fool you, she loves dressing women up." A pause. "You left early." A statement, not a question. "That was wise of you. Rafe was not happy when he returned. Wouldn't happen to know anything about that, would you?"

Sage gave him a hard look, choosing not to dwell on the memory. "I'm afraid I couldn't give him want he wanted."

Hayjen's lips thinned as he leaned against a bed poster. "He is determined."

Her stomach rolled. Sage understood Rafe better than anyone else. "There is nothing to be done."

"Now is not the time to be speaking of such things," Captain Femi chided. "She has enough to deal with tonight."

Hayjen, her longtime friend, strode to her side with a smile. He leaned down and pressed his lips to her forehead. "You will make a wonderful princess and, someday, a wonderful queen. Let no one convince you otherwise."

Warmth infused her at the demonstration of affection and his kind words.

He pecked Lilja on the cheek and made his way to the door. "I will stand outside until you ladies are ready."

Lilja finished up Sage's hair and began digging through the beautiful fabrics on the bed, humming as she sorted. The Sirenidae finally settled on an emerald silk dress and shook it out. It was sleeveless with a shallow scoop that cut across the collarbone. It was form-fitting and long enough that it looked like it would probably puddle on the floor. An angled golden sash draped around the hips and fell to the floor. It was simple, but it was also very elegant.

Sage smiled at Lilja. "It's perfect."

She stood and lifted her hands above her head. The smooth fabric glided over her skin like the kiss of a butterfly's wing. Both women tugged gently until it was settled onto her, hugging her body perfectly. Sage marveled at the panels that had been sewn inside so she wouldn't need a bustier. She brushed her hands down the dress, smoothing its fabric, trying not to think about how it clung to her hips and thighs. Sage glanced over her shoulder and released a squeak. The material plunged down, showcasing her back with a sheer material sewn over it with a row of dainty round buttons running down it. The emerald silk pooled at her feet, flowing into a modest train.

It was certainly beautiful, but Sage was slightly aghast. "Who cut out the back of it?"

Mira sniggered.

Sage began to step forward when her dress split along the thigh. She stared at the sash that wasn't a sash. Rather it was part of the dress, sewn to lay over a thigh-high slit. She frowned down at it. "I thought this was supposed to be modest."

"It is. Nothing inappropriate is showing."

Sage gave Lilja a droll look. "Half of it seems to be missing."

Lilja rolled her eyes and tossed her a pair of matching slippers. Sage grinned, stopping to slip them onto her feet.

Gingerly, she lifted the dress and approached the mirror. Her wavy hair was swept back from her face, three braids crossed over the waves, starting from behind one ear and fastened behind the other with gold feather pins. Her waves tumbled down her back in wild array. The stunning green dress made the green of her eyes pop, like gems. Sage stared at her reflection, scrutinizing the woman in front of her. She still looked like herself but more refined. Lilja had certainly outdone herself. She lifted a hand to touch her cheek and stared as it trembled. Lilja shifted to her side, clasping Sage's hand with her own.

"You made a tough choice, *ma fleur*, but it was the right one. You will be okay."

Sage took a breath, trying to release some of her nerves, and smiled at both women. "Thank you, both, so much."

Mira blushed which Sage found entertaining. The healer could sew up all sorts of body parts but as soon as you praised her she couldn't take it and blushed crimson.

Sage lifted her dress and sidled to the door, staring at the handle once again. It was now or never. Gritting her teeth, she yanked it open before she could stop herself and stepped through. Hayjen cocked his head and raised a questioning eyebrow at her determined expression. No doubt she looked exactly as she felt, like a martyr.

"You don't want to know," she grumped.

"Sage, we need to return to the Sirenidae, but I will visit as much as I can. If you need me all you need to do is send for me." Lilja clasped her hands and searched her eyes. "Be brave, *ma fleur*. There is nothing you can't do or accomplish. You are never alone."

Sincerity shown in the captain's exotic eyes. In the short time she had known this strange woman, they'd grown to be good friends. Sage wrapped her arms around her. "Thank you for everything you have done." She leaned back and stepped around to hug Hayjen as well.

"You're not weak, so don't let anyone walk over you. You're their equal, perhaps even their better, in all things," his gruff voice whispered into her hair. His arms tightened for a moment before releasing her. Lilja kissed both her cheeks and then returned to Hayjen's side, clasping his hand.

"We will see you soon," the Sirenidae called, just before strolling down the corridor, her husband in tow.

"They make an interesting pair," Mira remarked.

"That they do."

Mira pushed passed her to the staircase and shot Sage a questioning look. "Are you coming?"

She hadn't moved. Sage shook herself out of her stupor, struggling with the urge to run far, far, away. Mira started down the staircase as soon as Sage reached her. Following behind, Sage took each stair deep in thought. She felt as though every step toward the dining room was one step further away from herself, from her life. Contemplating this, by the time she'd completely descended the two enormous flights, she had come to a realization. The life she felt bleeding away from her, the girl she had been, both had died in that cell somewhere beneath her feet. Ever since then, she had been trying to become that same girl, but she finally understood that it would never happen. She may have the same body, but the passion, the joy, and the hope had been scraped from inside her. Perhaps taking on this role for the Crown wouldn't be so difficult after all, since she was really just a shell anyway.

Chapter Fourteen

Tehl

Tehl longed to pace. He had come into dinner earlier than normal so he could be settled before Sage's arrival. He leaned back and studied the goings on around him. Members of his court flitted about, some laughing, some plotting, some merely enjoying their meals. Tehl took a healthy gulp of his wine and hid his smile behind his cup. He couldn't wait to see the stir his betrothal announcement created.

Soon, Sage would have to deal with all this tedium. There were so many things she could take over; the staffing, the meal plans for the week, planning for visiting nobles and dignitaries, and the blasted letters he both received and sent. And that was only a few of the things he couldn't wait to be rid of. His grin widened at the thought.

"Why are you smiling like a lunatic?" Sam asked while winking at a woman across the room.

"I was thinking about how my betrothal arrangement will benefit me. No more ridiculous tasks that I have very little patience for and even less skill in. Soon all of that, and this, will be her domain." Tehl spoke the words with unadulterated glee.

Sam tilted his head, lips twitching. "I am sure she will *love* that. I imagine she'll work to escape from those duties even more vigorously than you do. But, at least you have time to ease her into everything, the wedding won't be until spring, I imagine. It's a pity though, for, if not, you could get started on that heir-making all the sooner."

Tehl narrowed his eyes at his brother. "It's a little early to be talking of children."

His brother's gaze moved past him and widened. Sam blew out a deep breath, straightening. "It is never too early when you have a woman like that."

Tehl swung around as Sage enter entered the room in a gem-green gown that seemed to flow down and over her curves. It accentuated the shape of her bust, small waist, and flared hips. Her hair was swept away from her face so he could admire her heart-shaped face and green eyes. A small slit gave a preview of a toned, feminine leg every time she stepped.

"You're gaping," Sam muttered.

Tehl snapped his mouth shut as Sage met his eyes, her expression unreadable. Very quickly though, her face morphed, and a happy smile replaced the odd expression, her eyes crinkling like she was truly happy to see him. If he hadn't known any better, he would have truly believed he'd imagined the change. She was good, he'd give her that.

Tehl stood and began descending the steps, ignoring the myriad of curious eyes on him. His betrothed added extra swing to her hips as she approached and, having reached him, sunk into a deep curtsy before standing proudly before him.

172

"My lord," she murmured, throatily.

Tehl reached for her hand and placed a kiss on it. "My lady." Her hand twitched in his grasp, the only evidence of her desire to no doubt pull away. He released her hand and placed a hand on her back. Her *scarcely covered* back. He snuck a glance at her attire. Where was the rest of her dress? Tehl offered her his hand to escort her up the dais and eyed her back, displayed for the world to see. There was a piece of fabric but it was so fine and sheer she might as well have worn nothing. There was little he could do about it now, so he tried to dismiss it from his mind. He sat her between his brother and himself while allowing him a moment to survey the reactions of his court.

Astonishment was most prevalent. His advisors gazed at her with curiosity but not anger. Many men looked at Sage with lust in their eyes, but that didn't particularly bother him. She was a beautiful woman; they could look so long as they didn't touch. He cleared his throat, gaining everyone's attention and motioned for the meal to begin. Servants brought out dishes and placed them on the table, serving himself and those around him first, then continuing on down the table. He waited patiently, curious to see who would be the first to start the inquisition.

"Madam, you look ravishing this evening," William complemented, his gray eyes twinkling.

Sage put down her spoon and grinned at the old advisor. "Why, thank you. I do prefer boots and trousers, but a woman likes to dress up every now and again. Makes her feel good."

A few women gasped.

"Boots and trousers?" Jaren's daughter scoffed.

Stars above, he disliked that woman.

"How very vulgar. Truly, you jest?"

Sage snuck a glance at the various people pretending not to listen before answering. "Vulgar? I think not. There is nothing vulgar about hard work is there?" His betrothed gestured to her dress. "How can I clean, or wash, or do anything useful in a dress so fine as this? It would be ruined. And don't you think it would be a shame to damage such a lovely creation?"

Many of the men and even a few women around them chorused their agreement.

"We wouldn't want to ruin something that looked so enticing on your body, would we?" Sam drawled, leaning toward her.

"From what I hear, you rarely leave anything on any woman's body. So, excuse me if I doubt your expertise, my prince," Sage retorted.

A glint entered his brother's eye that Tehl didn't like. "Perhaps you're right. Are you requesting I demonstrate my expertise then?"

Tehl tucked away his smile as everyone leaned forward to hear what Sage would say. She tipped her head back; a peel of laughter escaped her as her hair tumbled down her back. Once she seemed to gain control of herself, she gave his brother an appraising look. "As intriguing as that sounds, I have heard of your exploits, it seems you always come up short. But what would I know of such things?" she asked too innocently.

Sniggers surrounded them at her slight. Sage ignored Sam's gaping reaction and sipped her soup as dainty as any lady, not like she had just insulted Sam's manhood.

Sam recovered quickly, a genuine smile flashing. "Point to you, my lady."

Each question that Sage was asked, she answered in a way that delighted and amused but at the same time gained respect. Several times, Tehl said what seemed to him to be a perfectly logical phrase or response, but, when he received odd looks, Sage would make a comment or joke that would smooth out any conversational hiccups.

She was better than some of his dignitaries, a born diplomat. By the close of the meal, she had most of his court enchanted, if not half in love.

"Have I missed dessert?" his father's voice called from behind his chair.

All eyes snapped to the man behind him in surprise. Tehl slid his gaze to Sage, catching her eye. His father had not attended dinner in over a year, no matter how many times Tehl had asked. But one conversation with Sage, and here he was. His gratitude must have shown on his face for she gave him a small nod in response.

His father stepped beside him and clasped his shoulder. "Tonight is a special occasion." His father plucked a goblet from the table and held it aloft. The court followed his example glancing around in confusion. "I am happy to announce tonight the betrothal of my son, Tehl Ramses, to the lovely Sage Blackwell."

The lots were cast. Tehl stood, never taking his eyes from Sage and stretched out his hand to her. She stared at it for a beat before a radiant smile bloomed on her lovely face. Sage slid her hand into his confidently, like a woman in love. Only the tiny quiver of her fingers betrayed her.

Tehl slowly brought her to his side and reached for his own wine. Carefully, he held it to her lips, the ritual a demonstration of their future life; she would share what was his. She sipped it and pulled away, licking her lips. She then reached for her own and smoothly held hers up to him, her fear seeming to have dissipated. He took a healthy gulp and pulled the cup from her hand placing it on the table. He wiggled his lips slightly, trying to prepare her for what was next. They would seal the betrothal with their kiss. He wrapped his hand around her neck, and she shifted on her toes to meet him halfway. Soft, plush lips met his, and he gave her a quick, innocent kiss. The sounds of cheering and applause met his ears. It was done.

She shifted back, smiling at him like she hadn't told him hours ago that she didn't want to have his children largely because she couldn't stand him personally. Tehl needn't have worried about her ability to pull this off, she seemed to be as good as his brother. His father's voice pulled him from his thoughts.

"The happy couple will be married in two weeks' time."

Sage's nails dug into him.

Two weeks. Bloody hell.

Tehl wiped any expression from his face and pasted on his smile. Two weeks. He would have a wife in two weeks. Though her expression remained unchanged he could see that panic filled her eyes, which, thankfully, never left his face. Tehl pulled himself from her and held their entwined hands in the air. More shouts of congratulations and a general feeling of excitement filled the room. He knew it was time to escape because he didn't have the patience to answer everyone's questions, not after what his father had just done.

He put his mouth by Sage's ear. "May I carry you?"

She turned her face, lips resting against his jaw, for all appearances a lover's gesture. "As long as you take me away from here."

Cinnamon wafted from her hair, making him sniff. Where did that damn scent come from? Cinnamon was one of his favorites. Before she changed her mind, he swung her into his arms and carried her away from the chaotic excitement in the dining room. Hoots and hollers followed them, echoing in the spacious hallway. She exhaled a sigh of relief against his collar, causing the hair on the back of his neck to stand up. He rolled his shoulders to rid himself of the feeling. After a few twists and turns, he placed her back on her feet and offered his arm. "May I escort you to your room, my lady?"

She stepped to his side and took his arm, her breast brushing his sleeve, and his body warmed at the contact. Tehl scowled for a moment before smoothing his face into an appropriate expression for strolling with your beloved. It irked him that something so simple affected him. The logical part of his brain told him it was a good thing and that it meant there'd be no issue when they did decide to have children. She was a beautiful woman. He still didn't like it though.

Tehl slowed his gait to match hers as they ascended the staircase. Her legs were so much shorter than his. Again, much to his displeasure, he noticed that with every other step she took, her bare right leg peeked out. "Where did that gown come from?" he asked gruffly, censure in his tone.

Sage kept her eyes on the marble stairs answering. "It was a gift. I came here in a rush so I did not have time to collect my things, and, even if I had, I wouldn't have had something suitable for dinner. The only thing I own that would be fine enough is my costume from the Midsummer Festival. And, somehow, I didn't think you would want me wearing that tonight."

The revealing costume she'd worn popped into his mind. It had been seductive, way too much skin on display. "It would have been inappropriate."

She sniggered. "I thought so too, hence, this gown."

His mind caught on that thought. She wasn't a traditional bride who brought a hope chest with all the things deemed necessary for marriage contained therein. She'd come to the palace with only the clothes on her back. He hadn't spared a thought for what she would wear tonight until she showed up looking like every man's fantasy.

When they turned the corner, entering the royal wing, low and behold, Sam lay in wait for them. Leaning casually against the wall, one boot braced behind him, he was the epitome of casualness.

"How did he arrive so quickly? We left before he did."

Tehl shook his head. "I stopped asking that years ago. I've grown up with him, yet even I don't know all his secrets."

Sam straightened and opened Sage's door for the two of them. She pulled free from Tehl and was across the room before he'd even clicked the door shut behind him. She made it apparent that she didn't want him to touch her, at all. The door opened again, this time admitting his cousin.

"By all means, invite yourself in," Sage replied sarcastically.

Gavriel and Sam both stepped to Tehl's side to watch the strange female pacing across the room. She eyed them unhappily, her dress flaring around her legs with each turn. She was like a caged griffin, regal in her bearing, but dangerous if you moved too close.

Sam was the first to move. He strutted to her bed and plunked down, groaning. "This bed is so comfortable." His brother stretched out his hands behind his head, ankles crossed. The feisty brunette squinted at Samuel and crossed to the opposite side of the bed, scowling at his brother.

Sam gave her an approving smile. "You did well tonight. I don't believe there was a single person in the room who was not at least partially in love with you by the time you left. The only ones who probably shall hate you are those who were hoping to take your place in my brother's bed."

"They can have him," she grumbled. Tehl watched as a calculating gleam entered her eyes as Sam lazed on her bed. "That still doesn't explain why you are now in my bed. Get off."

"It would be my pleasure," Sam purred, the devil in his eyes.

Sage's narrowed dangerously. "I will tie you up and drop you off my balcony if I have to."

Tehl fought a grin. His brother would no doubt have something to say to that.

"Tie me up? I must admit that sounds rather appealing, there are so many options." Sam reached up and caressed the head of the bed. "This would be the perfect bed for..."

A dull thud sounded and suddenly a blade quivered in between Sam's fingers, embedded in the headboard. Sam's face was a mask of shock. Tehl's eyes snapped to the smirking female. He hadn't even seen her throw it. She stepped back from the bed and glided to a nearby chair. With fluid grace she placed her foot on the chair, so reminiscent of the Midsummer Festival's night, when she'd displayed her scars. His betrothed then hitched up her dress exposing a thigh sheath. She plucked two more blades, placing them at a precise angle on the bedside table. She switched legs and pulled three more from another sheath there. Sage dropped her foot, lifting her hands to the flowers in her hair, gently tugging. He then noticed they weren't just hair ornaments but weapons, very long, dangerous-looking needles. She shook out her hair and released a happy sigh. Last but not least, she pulled the fine chain that dropped into her dress and revealed a very pretty looking dagger that dangled on the end. She was a walking armory.

She clasped her hands in front of her. "Now, as I was saying, get off my bed."

Sam obeyed this time, though he took his own sweet time, taking a moment to pry the blade from the bed. His brother *tsked* when he saw the gouge in the beautiful wood. "Look at what you did, Sage. This is jardintin wood."

"You should have gotten out of her bed then," Gavriel replied dryly. His cousin turned his attention to Sage, disapproval on his face. "Did you not even think to warm me when you snuck off the ship today? At first, I panicked because I couldn't find you, but when I discovered Hayjen and Lilja had also disappeared I hoped you were only with them, so I waited, just in case. But none of you returned. I'd just decided to make a search for you when Rafe appeared, very much unhappy." Sage cringed. "That man was beyond angry. He demanded I tell him where his mate went."

Tehl's brows rose at that. Mate?

"I could only guess he somehow meant you so I let him know I hadn't seen you for hours. He stalked off, cursing up a storm. Fortunately, I then spotted Hayjen, and he was able to inform me of your whereabouts. If I hadn't been detained by the rebellion leader, I would still be out there, looking frantically and praying that I wasn't going to happen upon your carcass instead."

"You left Gavriel behind?" Tehl growled.

Sage shot him a mulish look. "He is not my guardian. I can do as I please."

"That may be so," Tehl replied coolly. "But he is also your friend. How could you do that to him?"

His betrothed looked chagrined and held her hands out to Gav. "I am sorry, Gav. I didn't mean to worry you. There were a few things I needed to wrap up tonight. I truly meant to come back though. It's just..." She hesitated. "There were complications."

"Ah. The rebellion leader," Sam deduced. "How long have you been together?"

"Never."

Tehl shifted, arching a brow at her. "You appeared very cozy at the Midsummer Festival. I got the impression you had been together a long time."

"I merely played a role much like I did tonight. We only faked love and affection for each other."

"*He* wasn't acting, sis," Gav spoke up softly. "Every man at the table that night felt his claim on you. Be honest with us. Are you attached to him?"

Sage sunk her fingers in her hair, frustration in the movement. "I have always admired him. Rafe is brave, loyal, intelligent, and kind. I have worked with him closely for over a year. Of course, I was attached to him. He was my mentor... He was my friend."

"Was?" Tehl questioned.

Anger stiffened her body and she glowered. "Yes, *was*. It was he who sent that monster to me, and he was a part of the Circle who also decided to protect him, the very same which almost condemned me for attempted murder." Her body shook, angry tears spilling onto her cheeks. "Then he sold me to a man he knew I loathed, sentencing me to live in the same place where the worst horrors of my life took place."

"What of our conversation in the cavern? I thought Rafe had plans in order for Rhys."

Sage laughed, slapping her leg like what he said was comical. There wasn't anything funny about what he'd said as far as he knew. He slid a glance to Sam but neither was his brother laughing. Good, he hadn't missed anything, though her behavior remained a mystery.

"You did see him at the negotiation, right?" She raised her hand above her head. "About this tall, utterly ordinary until you see the rot of his demented soul? The man who pawed at me and orchestrated this whole farce?" Another hysterical giggle escaped her. "Mark my words, he will go free. He is rather like the wind. You know, he's there only because you see the effects of his actions, but as soon as you think he's in your grasp, you open your hand to find nothing." Her bleak eyes turned to Sam. "You told me he would be punished and would never hurt anyone else, yet he is, this very day, running around free in Sanee. I stabbed him, trying to free the world from his particulate brand of evil, yet the Circle protected him and blamed me." She then turned to Tehl, accusation in her eyes. "Once again, after your conversation with Rafe, I was relieved that he might disappear from my life, but no. Instead, he is the one who somehow has the power to orchestrate my enslavement to the Crown once again." She chuckled without mirth. "And now his destruction is impossible. If he were to go missing now the rebellion would blame you and all the hotheads itching for a change in government would just use it as an excuse to start their fight back up again."

"We will..." Gavriel started.

"No. She's right," Tehl cut him off, never taking his eyes off Sage. "Our hands are tied at the moment." She deserved to know they would protect her. Their situation was not ideal, but she would become his family in a matter of weeks. They may not be best friends, but they did want the same thing.

Tehl marched over and knelt in front of her. She had given up much, so he could do this much for her. "In two weeks you will become part of our family. You could have done as you pleased, you owed no loyalty to me, but you did it out of love for my people, and I will not forget that, ever. We are unlikely allies, and now we are to be partners. I promise you this: you will be safe here. I will protect you to the best of my ability, and when the time comes in which I may act without fear of the repercussions you spoke of, then there will be nowhere he can hide. This I vow."

Her green eyes glimmered. It was obvious many emotions roiled around inside her. "I will hold you to that, my lord. The same goes for you, and yours. I'll protect your family to the best of my ability."

She stepped back and shoved her arm toward him, watching him carefully. Tehl clasped her forearm, his fingers overlapping.

"Allies then."

"Yes. Allies," he echoed.

CHAPTER FIFTEEN

Sage

Her conversation with Tehl the week prior fueled her anger. Allies, what a joke.

Sage lunged, meeting her opponent's sword with her own. Her muscles strained against the weight of the larger man's brute strength. She bared her teeth at him and spun away, blocking one of his strikes. They circled each other, wary, searching for weaknesses. Sage loved sparring, being as she was so small, she often had to figure out how to take down opponents much larger than she. And when she was able to best them there was nothing so invigorating as that glorious win.

She continued to eye her opponent, trying to anticipate his next move. He was good, she would give him that much, but she knew she was faster. She smiled inwardly. He'd just given himself away with a slight movement of his torso. By the time he'd attacked, she was already in motion, slipping under his guard and knocking him to his knees. She leaned over his shoulder and placed her blade at his throat.

"I yield," he huffed out, black hair shining in the light. His purple eyes peered up at her, crinkling at the corners. "I also had you though."

She sniffed and stepped away, ignoring all the male eyes watching her with interest. Her unladylike pursuits made quite the impression on courtiers and soldiers alike, setting tongues-a-wagging.

"Sage."

Spinning, she caught the rag he'd thrown and wiped her face and neck. It was warm out, already causing sweat to trickle down her spine as well as in between her breasts. That was the worst part about training, the breast sweat. She wrinkled her nose and tugged her leather vest back into place. Most of the time she wore a linen shirt underneath but when sparring on days like today it was much too hot. That left her in trousers, boots, a leather vest, and arm guards. Sage placed the towel on the fence and leaned against it to inspect Gav as he ran a towel over his own face and hair.

"You weren't giving it your all." Irritation colored her voice. "I will not break. I am not made of glass. Again," she demanded, as she pushed off the fence and strode to the center of the ring.

Gav scowled at her but didn't move from his spot. "I understand you will not break but it still feels wrong to spar full force with a woman."

"So you let me win?" Sage clenched her teeth.

Gav looked at her hesitantly. "No, not necessarily...but I could also never hurt you."

"If you will not spar with me, then I will find someone else." She scanned the area locking onto combat master. "Zachael! Would you spar with me?" The combat master grinned at her and moved their way.

"You have been at this for two hours already today. Don't you think you should take a break or finish making plans?" Gav asked.

That had her seeing red. She shoved her sword into her scabbard and stalked to Gavriel. "That's exactly why I am out here, to *escape* wedding plans."

Garreth glanced up from sharpening his sword. "I thought most women loved that sort of thing."

Sage rolled her eyes, placing her hands on her hips. "Do I seem like most women?" The men around her snickered, and she smiled in spite of herself. In the twelve days since she'd arrived, she had trained every morning and afternoon with the Elite. It had taken her a while to get used to being surrounded by men again and several times she'd felt herself start to panic, but Gavriel never left her side and the men never touched her. They were always courteous and respectful. After a week, being around them felt familiar, similar to being around her brothers. If someone pinned or surprised her, she usually had to fight some anxiety, but she managed.

In the beginning, Sage was relieved that the only time she had to interact with the crown prince was for dinner. But as the days wore on, she realized that he had, in fact, abandoned her so that she alone had to manage *all* wedding preparations, and in just two short weeks too. That first day she'd taken Marq to task for announcing their betrothal in such a way. She'd begged him to somehow give them more time, but, despite her pleading, he wouldn't change his mind. She'd seethed at the comments she'd had to bear from the women she was forced to spend time with. Everyone thought she was already carrying the heir as it was the only reason they could think of for such haste. The thought made her nauseous. Thank goodness that wouldn't be for some time.

"You are definitely one of a kind." Zachael's words pulled her from her thoughts.

Murmurs of agreement followed his comment, and she blushed. Sage waved away their words when Gav leveled her with a look and asked, "What is so bad about planning a wedding? My wife loved it."

She turned from his searching eyes to stare at the sky. How could she explain herself without giving away her true feelings, or rather the lack thereof, for the crown prince?

"I wasn't born to this life," Sage whispered. "I always imagined myself marrying behind my family's home in the forest, or maybe in my meadow." She shrugged, trying to cover the emotion rolling in her gut. "I figured I would know each and every face in the crowd and it would be a simple affair. I'd be surrounded by friends and family with the man I loved. I only wanted simple. I still want simple." It was the truth and her dream. She dropped her head and gestured to the palace behind her. "This is anything but." Sage pulled a face. "What is the difference between ivory or eggshell? Anyone?" She spun in a circle and received shrugs. "That's my point. Who cares what color of cream the napkins are? And my betrothed has dumped it all on me."

"He hates it as much as you do. Perhaps he thought you would enjoy it," Garreth tossed in. "But it's all worth it, right? The responsibilities come with the man." Garreth raised a brow, as if daring her to say something to the contrary.

Sage swallowed a bitter retort and spoke sentiments more suited to a woman in love. "He is worth any trial, even suffering through wedding plans." The words were ash on her tongue.

In two days, she would say her vows, promising her life to a man she cared nothing for. Just the thought had her feeling stifled. She needed to get away for a while. "You are probably right." She pasted on a smile and turned on her heel. "I think I'm about done, I need to get out of the sun. Gav, I will meet you here two hours before sunset."

186

Sage fled the training ground in favor of the palace, slipping into one of its shadowed coves. Gavriel appeared several moments later, striding briskly down the corridor. Once he'd disappeared around the corner, she slipped back outside and snagged an abandoned cloak from the pile with a mental note to return it later.

She needed to see her papa. Her mum visited every day, even her brothers, Zeke and Seb dropped by a time or two, but she had yet to see her father, and she craved his company desperately.

Slipping past the walls was all too easy as no one had noticed her departure. Sage took her time walking to the forge, finding comfort in the familiarity of the town as she meandered from one street to the next. Being so cooped up inside the palace had started to feel unbearable, so, with each step away from it, she could feel her tension falling away.

The hustle and bustle of the community brought a certain amount of solace as well. Grubby children laughingly chased one another, whipping around the scolding merchants and gossiping laundresses, their little bare feet slapping against the ground. Their bright eyes and joyful smiles brought forth one of her own.

Every home and business was familiar, and she felt as though each one she passed was welcoming her home. Sage rounded the final corner, her heart leaping in her throat. Everything looked the same, from the open stall displaying their wares to the scrolling vine shutters decorating the window. Each piece that adorned her family's arched door widened her smile. Every year, she made a flower and presented it as a gift to her mum, and her mum displayed each one with love and pride. Sage flew to her home, kicking up dust behind her. She skidded to a stop when she slipped into the forge, the sweltering heat welcoming her home. Jacob was leaning over her father, checking his chest and both men jerked when they heard her abrupt arrival.

"Papa."

Both adoration and relief were evident on his face as he stood, opening his arms wide and she ran straight to him. He wrapped her in his warm arms, and, immediately, she felt both comforted and safe. Sage grinned against his tunic when she realized that, as she wrapped her own arms round him, his waist seemed to be a bit thicker.

"Sage," his warm voice curled around her. "I am so happy to have you home, love."

Sage couldn't believe the difference in her father. She lifted her head, taking in his altered appearance carefully. His face now had a healthy glow to it, and his cheeks were no longer sharp and gaunt but rounded. Even his breathing seemed less labored.

"Are you well, Papa?"

He cupped her cheek and kissed her on the forehead. "Still a worrier, I see. But yes, love, I am well."

Sage squeezed him once more before throwing her arms round the Healer. "Thank you," she whispered in his ear, a wealth of emotion in those two little words.

He tweaked her nose, his bronze eyes twinkling. "All in a day's work. Think nothing of it." Jacob released her and turned to her father, clasping his hand. "Keep taking the tonic I gave you, and I will visit again in a week."

Jacob retrieved his bag and winked at her before exiting the room. Sage watched the curtain ripple in the wake of Jacob's departure. There was no way to express the depth of her gratitude to the Healer. She hadn't seen her Papa in a month, and it was like looking at a different man. A tiny voice in her head whispered that she was lucky to have been asked to be the liaison for this peace treaty and that here was the silver lining to her storm. Her papa was healing and that made every sacrifice well worth it.

"You're staring at that curtain awfully hard. I assure you it is the same as it has always been."

His poor joke pulled a reluctant smile out of her. She shrugged off her cloak and wiped her forehead, luxuriating in the forge's familiar warmth.

"You are looking well, Papa, and I'm glad of it."

His chest puffed up, preening, his reaction so typically male that she had to bite back another smile.

"The tonics from Jacob have done their job."

"Tonics?" she asked, curious.

Colm's face soured. "Disgusting liquid. But your mum threatened right away to pour them down my gullet if I didn't take them so here I am." He widened his eyes. "She's intimidating when she wants to be."

"Imagine having her as your mum."

"Imagine having her as your wife," he shot back.

They both sniggered and plopped down in a seat. Sage plucked a blade from the stack and began cleaning it out of habit. She had so many things on the tip of her tongue, but each time she opened her mouth they seemed stuck there. Her papa's gaze rested on her but he stayed silent, cleaning blades at her side, waiting for her to speak. They didn't speak for some time, each content to simply spend time together doing the same thing. What was she going to say to him, anyway? That she was sorry for making such a big mistake that tore her from their family? That she couldn't fathom how she would survive the years to come? That the thought of overseeing the palace's day-to-day affairs made her want to jump off a cliff? Where did she even begin?

Her papa's large hand closed over hers, pausing her vigorous scrubbing on a hilt. He uncurled her clenched fingers and took the rag from her. Sage lifted her head and met her papa's gaze, hoping her every emotion wasn't written all over her face.

"What is on your mind, my little shadow?"

She could feel her eyes stinging so she turned away, hoping to stay the flood of tears threatening to spill over. Her mind was a muddle of guilt and anxiety, so many thoughts of 'what if' when it came to both her future and her past. It was enough to drown her, but there was no use crying over something she couldn't change. The course of her life had been set and she needed to just accept it.

"Love, you need to speak to me. I can't read your mind. What's going on?"

"Why haven't you visited me?" she twisted toward him, surprised by her own question. "Mum has visited every day, even Seb and Zeke, but not you. Why? Are you—" She swallowed. "Are you ashamed of me?"

"No," he gasped and scooted next to her, forcing her to meet his eyes. "It wasn't that I didn't want to come and visit, but I know you don't need me there to help you pick out things for the wedding. I also knew you would need to escape all of that at some point and the forge has always been the place for you to do so. Thus, I have waited for you to come here. Now tell me what's on your mind, love. I am listening, and it's obvious you need to get it out."

Sage stared at his dear face, the warmth in his eyes encouraging her to bare her soul, so she did. "I don't know if I can do it, Papa. I could feel confident keeping a small house but not a kingdom. I never wanted to be a lady, and yet that's the role I'll be forced to play *for the rest of my life*. When I think of spending my whole life in that palace it's like I can't breathe. I want to just run away and never look back."

He placed a hand over hers. "Your mum, brothers, and I will pack up right now and flee with you if that's what you need. Just say the word and it will be done. We want to see you happy."

Sage clutched his hand tighter "I know, Papa, but how could I do such a thing when so many would suffer?"

Colm caressed her face. "You have grown into a wonderful woman, Sage, and your heart is filled with more compassion and love than most people's. You have a selfless heart, and I'm proud of you for it."

Sage pressed her face into his hand as if she could soak up his love through her pores. But his words weren't enough to erase the guilt. Sage wasn't selfless, for her accepting the assignment had been with ulterior motives. Primarily, it had been to secure a healer for her father. If she was truly selfless, she would have done anything to help the people, healer or not, and done so without the anger and resentment currently festering inside her.

"He came to see me."

"Rafe?" It was painful to even speak his name.

"No, your betrothed."

She stared at him blankly. The crown prince had done what? "I don't think I heard you right, Papa."

"You heard me right."

A dull ringing filled her ears. Betrothed. Her soon-to-be husband had visited her home. *How dare he come here, what audacity!* She tried to control the rage rising up in her, suppressing it as best she could. "Oh?" she asked mildly, her voice wavering just a bit.

Her papa eyed her expression and began cleaning another blade. "He offered us a place in the palace and to buy our home."

Sage was sure her face was an alarming shade of red. She and Tehl had already spoken on this subject and she *thought* they had already agreed on a solution. "I assume you declined?"

"I did. The forge has been in our family for generations."

"How did he react to that?"

"He offered me a compromise."

"Which was?" Sage asked through clenched teeth.

"He is looking to expand the knowledge of his palace apprentices. The crown prince wants me to train some of them. I agreed." Colm paused his cleaning. "He also left a generous amount of gold for your acquiesce toll."

Acquiesce toll, what a joke. She hadn't acquiesced to anything. The crown prince had well and truly bought her like horseflesh. "Did I fetch a good price at least?" she asked sarcastically.

Her papa snorted. "Your brothers and I had to stash gold in the walls and bury some behind the forge. We have more than we could ever spend in a lifetime." He met her angry eyes. "But you're worth far more than any treasure. No matter how much he left, it would never equal you. Sage, you are precious."

His loving statement soothed and pierced her heart. Even if the only people who valued her for just herself were her family, she could live with that. Many didn't have a loving family. Sage counted herself lucky to have the overwhelming love and support that she did.

"He is nothing like Sam."

She smirked. That was the damn truth.

"He is very serious. He assured me you would be well looked after and want for nothing."

Sage's smile slipped. Materially, she would want nothing, but the one thing she longed for would be out of her grasp forever: her freedom to do as she chose. She forced her lips into a weak smile, just for her papa. She didn't want him worrying. "He will keep his word."

"He will, or he will have your brothers and myself to deal with." Colm chuckled darkly. "I don't care who he is. No one hurts my daughter and gets away with it."

Sage didn't doubt it for a moment. Her papa would go to the ends of the earth to care for his family. Soon she would be part of a new family, though. She stiffened as a thought occurred to her. She would no longer be a Blackwell, but a Ramses, and, for some reason, that angered her. Not only was she going to be assimilated into a new life and family, but she would lose her name too. Sage snatched up a scythe and polished it like she could scrub away all the hurt, anger, and confusion fighting inside her.

She and her father worked in silence until there were no more pieces to polish. Sage stared at the blade in her hand, her reflection distorted in its uneven surface. It felt poetic as it was also a fitting description of her inner self: indistinguishable, distorted, ruined. Sage thrust the blade onto a bed of velvet and quickly stood, stalking to the window. The lush green forest beckoned to her, immense trees standing like soldiers at its border, and she was filled with a longing to visit her meadow. The wind whistled a melancholy melody that spoke to her battered soul. Sage felt her father's eyes on her but she didn't turn. She just soaked up the picturesque scene before her. Her eyes sketched every limb as she tried to imprint each in her mind for she had no idea when she could next visit.

She frowned at the trees when yet another thought occurred to her. For anyone desiring to do so, it would be extremely easy to sneak through the forest to the back of her family's home. The Mort Wall may be miles away but that didn't mean it wasn't within the Scythians' power to make it this far. "Please lock your doors and windows every night, Papa, and never leave Mum alone washing clothes in the back." She tore her eyes from her forest to her father.

Alarm was evident on his face. "It is so dangerous?"

She turned to lean against the window frame. "It may not be now, but it is only a matter of time. Be vigilant."

"Is there nothing you can tell me?"

Sage debated a moment before answering. "People have disappeared, and it has been confirmed that the Scythians are sneaking over the Mort Wall and that, for some reason, they're taking them captive."

"My God," her father whispered. "Do you know what's become of them?"

"We have no idea, but I can only imagine the worst." Looking back outside she grimaced, finally realizing the hour. Gavriel would skin her alive for being late to their training, and he would no doubt lock her up if he knew she'd slipped out for the day.

Her father eyed the fading daylight and stood from his stool. "It's best you be getting back, love. I am sure you are being missed by now."

Sage scoffed, for, in her mind, no one truly missed her. They were just worried about what it would mean if she didn't marry the crown prince. She rushed into her papa's arms, once again surprised at how much stronger he was since the last time she had seen him. "I love you Papa, so much."

"I love you, too." His arms tightened, crushing her against his chest. "I am always here if you need me."

She would miss seeing his twinkling green eyes every day. He always made time for her, treating her with patience and kindness. In her mind, there was no better man.

She inhaled the familiar smoky scent of her father one last time and squeezed her eyes shut to keep more tears from falling. All she had to do was make it out of the forge. He kissed the crown of her head and released her. She stifled a sob when she saw his eyes were damp too.

He cupped her cheeks and smiled. "You are my only daughter, and I don't want to give you up. When you came into this world, you were the most breathtaking baby I ever beheld. I spoke to you, and you turned those big green eyes and looked right at me. At that moment, I was lost to you, I knew you would make my life challenging, but in the best way. I've loved raising you and watching you grow up into a fine woman." He stared into her eyes solemnly. "I know this was not your choice, I want a different future for you from the one you've ended up with." He sucked in a deep breath like he was fortifying himself. "But you will make a fine ruler." A smile. "A warrior queen. You are exactly what Aermia needs right now so never doubt yourself. You have much to offer, don't forget that."

She merely nodded, lips trembling. When she spoke, she could not prevent her voice from cracking with emotion. "Okay, Papa." Sage lifted herself onto her tiptoes and kissed his whiskered cheek. "Love you." She stepped back and strode toward the door.

"I will see you in two days, love."

Her stomach dropped at the reminder.

She peeked over her shoulder with a wobbly smile. "I will be the one in green."

Sage slipped through the curtain and out of the forge, and a cool breeze chilled her warm body. She shivered and set a brisk pace toward the palace as the sun sank below the horizon.

After a time, she halted in her tracks and just let people flow around her. She was already late, someone would have missed her by now, so it mattered little if she was even later. She might as well enjoy her evening. Enticing music drifted from an alehouse across the lane, so Sage stepped from the throng of people into the dim parlor. She scoped the area and moved to an empty table in the corner. When she gestured to the barkeep, a serving wench came quickly over and slapped a mug of warm ale in front of her. Sage flipped her a coin and lifted the tasty brew to her lips. She leaned against the wall, watching the room.

The three-person band in the corner attracted all attention. The music caressed her, soft and seductive, begging her to move with it. Sage gestured to the serving wench for another ale when she'd emptied hers. The place continued to fill with people, each seeking some sort of solace or escape, just like she was. Torches were lit, casting soft light across the room.

Sage brushed off any attempts of conversation by interested men, ignoring the lingering looks she received. She snorted. It was funny that she was a betrothed woman now, not that you would know. She had no cuffs or rings to signify she was already taken. Chuckling, she took a swig of her drink when a large man suddenly plopped down across from her, his hood up.

"Seat's taken," she said gruffly. He didn't move though. She scowled at him and fingered the blade at her thigh. "I am not interested."

"Oh, but I am so interested in you and what exactly it is you're doing." As he said this, he tipped back his hood, revealing golden curls and sapphire eyes.

The damn spymaster had found her.

CHAPTER SIXTEEN

Sam

He raised a brow, waiting for her answer.

Sage rolled her eyes and sipped her drink, watching him over the edge of her mug. "I would think it was obvious."

He placed his elbows on the sticky table, squinting at her green eyes. Her pupils were a little larger than normal. He cast a disgusted look around, noting each of the exits just in case. How long had she been in the alehouse? "Are you drunk?"

She glowered at him. "No, that would be dangerous and stupid."

He scoffed. She sat in an alehouse, surrounded by men, many of whom were no doubt criminals, and most of them were eyeing her like they each wanted a bite of her. Not that he could blame them. She certainly was beautiful and she shone brightly in contrast with the tarnished wenches whose breasts were tastelessly falling out of their dresses.

"So is drinking alone when you are the target of so many enemies." His lips thinned in disapproval. "Also, leaving the palace without telling anyone."

Sage grinned at him and lifted her leg onto the bench, placing her half-full mug on her elevated knee. She tossed her brown hair, looking haughty. "Am I supposed to ask for permission? Am I still the Crown's prisoner?"

Sam would never forget how she looked battered and broken in that cell. He'd make sure that never happened to her or anyone ever again who was under their care.

Her grin grew brittle at his silence. "That didn't work out so well for me before. Mark my words, I will never again be held against my will."

She took another sip, her eyes darting over his shoulder. Sage scowled at someone, presumably the oaf who had been ogling her since he walked in. Sam cleared his throat, and her gaze returned to his face.

"You are no one's prisoner."

She sniggered behind her hand. "Mmmhmmm..."

Sage was acting childish. In the time he'd known her, Sam had never experienced this blasé attitude from her, and it irked him. He'd been searching for quite some time, praying no one had stolen her. In the two weeks she'd been at the palace there had already been three attempts on her life which, thankfully, the elite foiled. Sage was being careless with her life and the future of Aermia.

"Did you ever stop to think of the worry you would cause by leaving?"

She let out a charming laugh, causing more than one pair of male eyes to turn her way and linger—not that she appeared to notice. Sam gritted his teeth, wishing she could be more inconspicuous. Sage drained the rest of her drink and slammed the empty mug on the table. "Worry for the Crown, I am sure."

His anger lifted a notch. He snapped his hand out and grabbed her wrist, pulling gently, but firmly, so she leaned over the table. Sam touched her chin, forcing her to meet his eyes. Her careless smile melted and a knowing light entered her eyes that made him uncomfortable.

"I was wondering when you would show yourself."

What was she talking about? "What do you mean?" Sam asked, never taking his eyes from hers.

Sage leaned closer, like she had a secret. "I saw a glimpse of the real spymaster." Her lips turned up into a smug smile. "You can fool everyone else, but you cannot hide from me."

"What am I hiding?" Sam ran his eyes over her features with deliberate slowness, trying to gauge her meaning.

She shrugged, her gaze just as intent. "Anger, pain, guilt; a number of things really. I bet the only people who truly understand you are your cousin and brother, but I doubt either of them knows the true extent of your façade. I think you've worn it so long you don't know yourself what is real and what isn't."

Sam kept his face impassive, despite the fact that her words hit disturbingly close to home. He'd played so many parts over the years, he sometimes felt like he'd lost himself. She was very keen to have noticed, and he idly thought it was a shame she wasn't one of his sneaks. He quickly pulled himself from his thoughts. He wasn't here to have a heart to heart with Sage; he was here to retrieve her.

"Over the last few hours, Tehl, the Elite, and I have searched high and low for you. We were worried that you had been taken or worse. Now you can imagine how I feel finding you, instead, sitting here, drinking in a pub."

Sage's eyes narrowed, and she tugged her arm from his grasp. "Don't you dare judge me. I have done nothing but comply over, and over, giving everything of myself to help everyone around me. So what if I wanted a drink before I shackled myself to a man, a title, and cage I want nothing to do with? It's a very little thing to let me have this small moment to myself."

Sam tensed when silver flashed into her hand. Where in God's name had that blade come from? The longer he spent around Sage, the more intrigued he became. His new sister was a mixture of soft and hard. If only she could get over her aversion to his brother, she had potential to be a fine asset to their kingdom. He snorted. That and if his brother finally learned some tact. It was going to be a long road to success.

She stabbed the blade at him. "I have seen you with new, let us call them *diversions*, every day of the week. You do not get to judge me, or counsel me on my actions and morals. I wanted a chance to think in peace, so I took this chance as it is the only one I shall probably be afforded for some time."

"Yes, but at the expense of others," he retorted.

"That's rich coming from a representative of the Crown. When have you had to make a sacrifice that cost you everything?" Her eyes dropped for a moment before returning to him, filled with ire. "So forgive me if I don't feel bad for taking a couple hours to myself so I could say goodbye to my life and family. After all, I'm *only* continuing yours at the expense of mine."

Sam shot to his feet when she stood from the bench suddenly. The last thing he needed tonight was to hunt her down. Again. Sam scrutinized her as she shifted to the balls of her feet. He was sure he could keep up, but it would be a bloody waste of time. He had several meetings he needed to make tonight so he needed her to come *now*.

"Are you ready then, my lady?"

Sage stared at the back exit for a long moment before tossing a glare his way and stalking to the door, her cloak swirling around her.

Sam smiled behind her back. She may be tough on the outside, but she was warm and passionate once you got past her walls. He'd enjoyed making her scowl. They would be great friends; she just didn't know it yet.

CHAPTER SEVENTEEN

Tehl

Where the hell had she gone? When her ladies complained that she hadn't shown up for her dress fitting he figured she was out practicing, as was her custom every morning and evening, much to the shock of his court. When Gavriel barged into his study, worried that she didn't show up for her customary bout, he felt behooved to send a few Elite to discreetly search for her. It wasn't until all four Elite showed up empty-handed that he finally got frustrated and, while grumbling under his breath, stomped from the room, determined to find her himself.

His first thought was to visit his father, for he knew they shared an affinity for hiding out whenever there were royal duties to attend to. When he got there, however, he was surprised to learn she hadn't been there all day. Next, he checked the infirmary, but Mira, likewise, had no idea of her whereabouts, and, by then, Tehl had started to actually worry. By a stroke of luck, Jacob overheard Tehl's inquiries and casually mentioned Sage visiting her father. He'd stalked out of the room irritated that she hadn't notified someone of her departure. Was it too much to ask that she use good sense and take measures to protect herself?

He took Sam, Gavriel, and a few Elite to the forge, but yet again she'd evaded him. Even her father, Colm, didn't know where she was, having thought she'd headed home already. Now more concerned, they broke up into three groups, his team searching the fishermans' district. They checked everywhere they could think of, even visiting Captain Femi, but to no avail. By the time they returned to the training yard, Gav's group was already there, still empty-handed.

"Anything?" he growled, already knowing the answer.

"Nothing," Gavriel said tensely. "We need to form a larger search group and soon. Something could have happened."

Tehl nodded and pushed back the thread of panic twisting inside him. Sage was smart. If someone had stolen her, she'd escape. They just needed to find out where to. The Elite surrounded him and someone procured a map and a lantern. His men squatted down next to him as he spread the map across the dirt. He squinted at it. Was she stolen, or did she run? It would narrow their search if they knew if she ran or was taken. He tugged on his hair, frustrated that he didn't know her mind well enough to make a guess. Worried purple eyes caught his attention. Gav was the closest to her. He would know.

Tehl caught Gav's eye and jerked his chin, standing. Once the two of them had walked out of hearing range he turned and looked his cousin straight in the eye. "Is she running?"

Gav blew out a frustrated breath. "No. Sage was upset this morning but she wouldn't leave like this."

"Why was she upset?" He had barely seen her so it couldn't have been his fault at least.

"You dumped the wedding on her."

Tehl blinked at him. "Women love planning weddings. Emma loved it."

Gavriel tossed him a droll look. "Is Sage anything like Emma or even most of the women of your acquaintance?"

"No," Tehl drawled, thinking of her colorful word choices and warrior skills. In all his life, he had never met a woman like her. Her boldness, fortitude, and compassion set her apart from the women he'd been raised with.

"Then why would you think she would enjoy planning a wedding?" Gav lowered his voice. "She's been forced into it with a man she hardly knows nor cares for? I mean, think about it. Do you remember how you felt planning the Midsummer Festival?"

Tehl grimaced. What a bloody nightmare.

"Exactly." Gav pinched the bridge of his nose as he continued, "You had months to plan it. You threw her into this without any prior experience and worse still, your father has given her a scant two weeks to do so. It's an event most of the kingdom will attend so you can see why she'd be, not only upset, but more than a little overwhelmed."

He was an idiot. He'd been so relieved that it was no longer his responsibility that he hadn't stopped to think about how she might feel. Tehl simply assumed she had plenty of help and that it wouldn't be a problem. He sighed. What was done, was done. Now they could only move forward.

Tehl returned to his men, crouching next to Zachael who had joined the group after he'd stepped away with Gav. Zachael sent him a look that promised questions later as Tehl filled him in on their progress so far.

"We searched here and here." Tehl pointed to the fisherman and merchant district. "Gavriel will lead a group south and..." A commotion at the gate drowned out his voice. He stood and caught Sage shoving his brother away from her.

"Who knows where those hands have been so keep them to yourself."

She was safe.

Something loosened in his chest just knowing that, but with the relief came anger. He quickly ran his eyes over her, seeking any sign of abuse, but not a hair was out of place. He found that to be, somehow, both reassuring and frustrating, especially when she unclipped the oversized cloak and sauntered up to Garreth, batting her eyelashes as she spoke.

"I borrowed your cloak this morning, I hope you don't mind." Tehl's jaw clenched when she next lifted her hair up, baring her neck, her back slightly arched. Garreth's eyes very briefly skimmed her curves before snapping to him, a question in his eyes.

Before he could do anything, Sage touched the Elite's arm, effectively returning his attention to her.

What was going on?

"You're not upset, are you?"

"I don't mind, darlin'."

Garreth placed a hand over hers, his thumb running along her skin while the entire group just stared at the spectacle before them. She was flirting with one of his men, *right in front of him.*

What. The. Hell?

A sturdy hand gripped his shoulder. "Calm down, she isn't propositioning him," Sam whispered.

"Like hell she isn't," Tehl ground out. "Where did you find her?"

"In an alehouse."

He saw red.

Tehl considered himself a calm and logical person, but there was something about Sage that made him lose it. Here he had been, worrying over her, searching high and low, just hoping nothing terrible had happened, while she'd actually been out drinking.

"Do you understand what you put me through?" he thundered, without thought.

Sage dropped her hand and turned to him, cocking a hip. "My lord, I went to visit my family."

Tehl jerked forward, out of Sam's grasp. "We searched for you for hours. You left without notifying anyone, leaving your protection behind. Neither your father nor Lilja knew where you had gone."

She smirked.

She bloody smirked at him. Like his words were funny.

"My men wasted their personal time searching for you. Did you want to punish me?"

Her mocking laughter floated over the silent group of men. "Not everything is about you, my lord. I needed to get away and say goodbye to my family. Would you deny me that? Keep me here forever?"

Reason filtered through, causing him to bite his tongue to keep his damning words from spilling out. "No. But your actions put you in danger."

"I wasn't in any danger." She jerked her chin toward the men surrounding their display. "Your men can attest to that."

"You are not infallible; I have had you before."

The expression on her face made him pause.

"You will pay for that comment," Zachael muttered under his breath.

Tehl's brows furrowed in confusion as a round of sniggers erupted around him.

"Not the best choice of words, brother," Sam imparted.

He stiffened, realizing his mistake too late. Sage's face turned an alarming shade of scarlet at the blatant reminder of her capture. Her hands clenched at her sides.

"You've never had me," she emphasized, glowering at the surrounding men who were now trying to disguise their laughs as coughs. "You surprised me one time."

"One time is all it takes. My enemies are your enemies. You can't wander around doing whatever you want, you have responsibilities."

"Responsibilities?" Sage hissed.

Tehl froze. He knew that tone, it was the same one Gav used before he ripped someone's head off. Seething rage.

"You want to speak of *responsibilities*? With *me*?" Her pitch rose, almost screeching.

He wanted to rub his ears, but he didn't think it would go over well. Her arms gestured wildly, a crazed look on her face.

"Where have you been the last week? Not once did you help or give me guidance. I never even *wanted* a big wedding. I'd be fine with a quiet ceremony in a meadow but *YOU*—" She jabbed a finger at him, eyes blazing. "*YOU* are the royal. We're doing this because of *you* so this should all be on your shoulders, not mine. I will not be your rug or dumping grounds whenever you have undesirable tasks. We will be equals or nothing at all."

"Nothing at all? You are *already* mine, I paid the acquiesce toll not even five days ago. In two days, you will wear my cuffs, my ring. It is already as good as done." The red in her face deepened with every word he spoke. Why was she getting so angry this time? He had merely stated the truth.

"Now you've done it, you bloody idiot," Gavriel whispered.

Tehl spared his cousin an annoyed glance before focusing on the woman spitting fire in front of him. She stormed up to him, stopping two strides away.

"Do you enjoy humiliating me?" Sage spat, her eyes burning.

"What are you talking about?"

"Don't play stupid, Your Highness. Did it ease your conscience to pay my acquiesce toll?" She gestured to her curvy body. "You may have bought me like a whore, but I will never wear your cuffs."

That was downright offensive. He had never treated her like a whore, not once. When he visited her father, he'd been respectful and was trying to do the right thing. This union might not be what either of them had envisioned for their future, but he still wanted to follow the proper protocol of a groom as best he could. The curious looks from his men were problematic. Sage was *very* close to giving them away.

"Leave us," he bellowed. The Elite bowed and removed themselves, leaving only Garreth, Zachael, Gavriel, and Samuel. Tehl scowled at Sage, every inch of her body radiating defiance. "Are you out of your mind? Do you not recall the need for secrecy?"

"I didn't forget, I just don't care."

That heated his blood. The troublesome wench. "Well you better start caring," he said, through clenched teeth, "we have an agreement."

"We do, but don't you dare tell me how I can react to something. I can say what I want and how I feel. You will not silence me. I have my own mind."

"Even if it reveals us?"

"You mean reveals *you*?" she challenged, tossing her silky brown hair.

Tehl stepped toward her. If Sage made threats, she needed to know he wouldn't back down. He had no problem discussing things or working through problems, but he'd be damned before he was cowed on something this important.

"If you fail to keep your end of the deal, then I will forgo mine. You're the one who asked for time." Tehl wrapped an arm around her waist and pulled her against him, smoothing his hand down her back.

She paled but held her ground, still as stone in his arms, not an ounce of give. "I would kill you first." She twitched, and he felt something sharp pressed against his stomach.

A blade.

Always with a damn blade.

Tehl scowled at her, wondering where she pulled the dagger from without him noticing.

"Listen, and listen well, my lord. I will marry you, but I will never wear your cuffs. I belong to only myself, even if you paid my father more gold than a dragon could horde. You can't buy my loyalty, compliance, or affection." Her dark green eyes glittered dangerously. "I am to be your wife in name only, we are enemies that happen to have a common enemy, nothing more."

Cuffs. There was that word again. It was the second time she'd mentioned it. When a couple married, tradition mandated that both husband and wife wear cuffs, his on the biceps and hers on the wrists. It was a fitting symbol of them being bound to each other forever. It also served as a sign to others, as well as a reminder to themselves, of their union. Whether she liked it or not, they would be bound to each other in two days.

Tehl studied her, attempting to discern the turbulent thoughts swirling around in her head. His gaze dropped to her wrists, and he stared for a moment before gently sliding his fingers along the twisted flesh. Sage jerked her arm away like his fingers burned her. Was that a reaction to his touch? Or was it born from the things she'd suffered?

He raised his eyes back to her face, and he actually felt pity for her. Her whole body was defensive but behind that he could see there was embarrassment and pain. Tehl kept his face impassive. If she saw his pity, she would only shut down. Instead, Tehl set her away from him and stepped back. As soon as he did so, she flipped her dagger and stowed it in an invisible pocket on her thigh. Momentarily distracted, Tehl leaned closer, intrigued.

Where did it go? Did she have special pockets in her trousers? Tehl shook himself. Thoughts for another time.

"It's perfectly clear you'd rather not wear my cuffs but it doesn't really matter; you must." Tehl held up a hand when her mouth opened. Probably to curse him to the leviathans or something. He brushed his sleeve not meeting her eyes. "Have you not thought about the fact that I will wear yours as well?"

Her mouth opened and closed a couple of times before she huffed out a breath. "I... I hadn't considered it."

Sage's honesty cooled some of the frustration, and he was able to respond more calmly. "Look, we need to learn from each other." Tehl ran a self-conscious hand through his hair, giving her a small smile. "As you have already observed, I am not gifted with words or a great understanding of people. You must tell me what you mean or want, preferably in private, or I won't understand. After what you suffered, I can understand your aversion to something that represents being bound, but keep in mind you're not the only one who is bound in this. You're not alone."

"I don't believe you."

Tehl reined in the spark of anger her stubbornness set off and merely raised a midnight brow. "Have I ever lied to you?"

Sage pursed her lips, squinting at him. After a moment, she turned her head to the side. "No," she mumbled.

"What was that?" Tehl baited.

She finally turned to him, glaring, and crossed her arms. "No," she said, more loudly this time.

"Exactly. Stop treating me like I will stab you in the back every time you turn around. Since you came here, I have put your health and wellbeing above everyone else's whereas *you* have lied repeatedly. Don't punish me for crimes I did not commit." Tehl lifted an arm toward Sam, Gav, Zachael, and Garreth. "And these men have protected you from more than you realize. I would appreciate it if you could keep your disdain for everything about your life to a minimum when in their company. They deserve more."

She studied the group of men. "I understand. I will make an effort not to let my bitterness bite them." She turned back to him, both brows lifted. "My health and wellbeing? If my wellbeing was really your priority you wouldn't have dumped the entire stress of this wedding on my head."

"It was my understanding that women loved that sort of thing." Tehl winced as her scowl deepened. "I have since been informed that you, however, do not share that sentiment."

"Of course not. I mean, would *you* find something like that enjoyable?"

"No, planning the one festival was more than enough for a lifetime." His nose wrinkled in distaste. "It was a nightmare, and I hated every moment."

"Precisely. At least we are in agreement on one thing." Sage twisted her lips. "I will not do the tasks you discard because you can't stand them. We have to do them together, share the burden."

Tehl wanted nothing to do with the celebrations, but what she proposed made sense, it was only fair. Thus, much to his surprise, he reached out and, for the second time in two weeks, shook the hand of his betrothed. And when she didn't jerk out of his grasp immediately, Tehl counted that as a small victory. "Agreed."

She gave a brisk nod and strode away, returning to the four men still waiting for them. Tehl trailed behind, allowing her to speak with his brother before she strolled toward the palace. Tehl arrived at Zachael's side, noting that all the men stared after his betrothed. Sam was obviously both intrigued and a bit lustful, Gavriel was undoubtedly concerned, and Zachael seemed to feel admiration. Tehl, too, watched her disappear and, for the first time, counted himself lucky. She drove him crazy but he could have done a lot worse.

"That one right there is a gem. She may be rough around the edges but she will surprise us all, mark my words," Zachael commented.

"Sage is full of surprises," Sam grouched.

Tehl smiled at his brother's tone. Sam always hated mysteries he couldn't solve and it was obvious that Sage was one of them. She didn't quite fit into any category: rebel, nobility, common, or royal. Sage just was.

Chapter Eighteen

Sage

The following day passed in a flurry of fittings and last minute wedding preparations, such as wine tasting, not that Sage complained. The wine certainly helped when it came to practicing the wedding dance. Normally, she loved dancing but the shrew teaching was a real stickler when it came to form. When Sage finally spied her door late that evening, relief eased some of the tightness in her shoulders; her bed was close.

Sage pushed her door open and shut it, leaning her back against it, tipping her head up. Silence. Sage smiled as she was at last able to enjoy a moment of peace. No judging looks from her ladies in waiting, no instructor correcting her, no one demanding her attention. Just blessed silence. She dropped her head to admire the faint light filtering through the glass doors of her terrace. The sky was clear so the stars on display were breathtaking.

It was at that moment that a most unwelcome thought popped into her head: The next time she gazed at the stars she would be a married woman. She rubbed her arms as a chill ran up her spine at the thought. Her eyes darted to the cold hearth of the fireplace; sitting by the warmth of a fire would feel marvelous.

Sage bolted the door and wove around the furniture, avoiding the areas where darkness clung. She stooped in front of the fireplace and pulled pitched-soaked pine kindling from the basket. She was thankful one of the servants left the kindling, knowing she appreciated her privacy. She strategically placed the kindling in the cold hearth and struck her sulfur match. The spark caught the pine few after a few tries. Carefully she breathed on the precious flames, coaxing them to life. Soon, she had a roaring fire and it chased away the darkness, or most of it anyway. There was still a pool of darkness perched in her chair, which, up until now, she had studiously ignored.

Without turning around she addressed it, "I was wondering when you would show up. What do you want, Methi?"

A deep masculine laugh raised goosebumps on her arms. Sage scowled and rubbed at her arms, irritated that he'd been able to get a rise out of her before even saying a word.

"I was wondering if you had lost some of your edge when you didn't seem to notice me."

"Not at all," she muttered, offended. "I deemed a fire more important than giving you the attention you're seeking." Sage pushed herself up and spun around to face Rafe who was sprawled comfortably in her chair like he owned the place. She'd known he would eventually seek her out, but she still didn't feel ready for it. The lies he'd told her and the sting of his betrayal was not something she was yet able to let go of, nor her confusion over their last meeting. His hatefully spoken words still echoed in her mind, but now was not the time to dwell on those things. She pushed those thoughts aside and stood erect. Looking him in the eye, she said, "You have my attention. What do you want?"

He ran his eyes along her body, and though it was not overly sexual, she could still see heat in his gaze. "You look well."

Sage snorted. She looked horrible. The lack of sleep combined with the exhausting schedule and the palace training had already etched black bags beneath her eyes. "Now, now. We both know you can lie better than that."

His face pinched at her comment, but she wouldn't take it back. These were consequences of his actions and losing her trust was one of them.

Rafe straightened and pushed himself from her chair, making her suddenly very aware of how far she was from the door. She felt a wave of sadness at the fact that she felt the need to be wary around him, but she also knew that, despite her having spent over a year in his company, he was very much a stranger to her.

"I wanted to offer my apologies."

She blinked. That was unexpected.

Rafe inhaled deeply and released his breath through flared nostrils, his eyes solemn. "I was out of line and had no right to say those things to you. I am fully aware that you are not that type of woman. I was angry and upset, but that still doesn't make it right."

Sage nodded. She understood saying something you don't mean in anger. "I understand. Our last conversation was difficult for both of us." That was the truth. Sage understood his duty to protect his own kingdom, and therefore his identity, but it didn't make his dishonesty any less hurtful. The fact was it had been *his* decisions that ultimately led to her torture, as well as being ousted from the rebellion and sold to the Crown. Sage might even have been able to work through these things and forgive him, except she had no idea if the man she thought she knew even existed. She had given everything to Rafe and his rebellion but gained nothing but pain and heartache. The entire situation had left a brand on her heart; she would not make that mistake again anytime soon.

"What are you thinking, little one? I can see the gears of your mind have been set in motion."

Sage returned her focus to Rafe. "I'm wondering if I ever knew you, or if it was all a façade." Her body tensed when he stepped toward her.

Rafe froze at her reaction. A frustrated breath huffed out of him before he began approaching her again, this time holding his hands out to his sides in supplication. "I've been myself with you from the beginning. I *never* changed who I was, and, although there were certain aspects of myself pertaining to my purpose and identity that I didn't tell you, I was *always* real with you."

Sage stared at him, trying to decide if she believed him or not. She supposed it was true, that in all her time with him, their relationship and his treatment of her never changed, so either he was the best actor the kingdom had ever seen, or he was telling the truth. After a beat, she decided. "I believe you."

His shoulders slumped, as if a great weight had finally been lifted off.

"You don't know how glad I am to hear it, little one. I have agonized over this every moment these last weeks. It was all I could do not to come straight here and get you." Rafe ran a hand through his silky hair and shot her a scowl. "Don't think I didn't know you ran straight here."

Sage crossed her arms and glared right back. How dare he! "If I wasn't worried for my safety and that of my family, I wouldn't have *had* to leave early. I just couldn't trust you not to try and spirit me away in the night. I had no choice, thanks to you."

He gave her a rueful smile. "I'll admit that was my plan that first night. Color me surprised when I didn't find you on the Sirenidae."

Sage smirked. "And how did Lilja react to that?"

He mirrored her smirk. "She never knew I came aboard."

Her smile slipped. Lilja's race had some unique qualities, one of which was the ability to hear things that most people couldn't. There wasn't any way he could have slipped aboard unknown without sprouting wings. Her eyes narrowed. "How?"

Rafe smirk grew wider. "You will never know."

Did he do something to her? Sage's brows knit. "You better have not touched them."

Rafe's smile disappeared altogether. "How could you accuse me of such a thing?"

"I don't know you." Sage shrugged. "Just because I believe you didn't lie about *absolutely* everything doesn't mean I can trust you." Pain flickered across his face, and she felt a twinge of guilt, but she immediately stamped it down. She wouldn't allow him to make her feel bad for a situation that he himself had caused. "You didn't answer my question." Sage took a small step back, toward her bed.

"No, I did not hurt them."

She relaxed slightly. Fatigue settled over her like a warm blanket. Sage snuck a glance at the pitch-black sky that seemed to swallow the light of the stars. It was very late. She should be in bed already.

The pop of the fire brought her attention back to her surprising guest and it occurred to her to wonder, *Why was he still here?* He had said his piece. Why hadn't he taken his leave? She heaved out a weary sigh as she moved to pull back the covers of her bed. Propping a hip against the tall bed, she raised her eyebrows expectantly. "Is there something else you need?" She covered her yawn with her hand as best she could, then touched the soft coverlet. "Tomorrow is a big day for me. I need my rest."

Rafe's face darkened and his body tensed, putting her back on alert. She glanced at the bed, trying to gage how quickly she could get to the other side. She had a couple of blades on her, but her stash was at the other side of the room and she would need it if anything happened.

Rafe cocked his head and took a cautious step toward her. "I may have a solution to your problems."

"Problems?" Sage repeated, confused.

"Your marriage to the prince. I've found a way out."

Her eyes widened as wariness turned to a tremulous hope. What was he talking about? There was no way out, the rebellion had made sure of that, hadn't they? "What are you talking about? Are you saying I need not marry tomorrow?" Even as she held her breath for his answer she viciously tried to stomp out that little seed of hope. There was no escape for her, and it would do no good to imagine otherwise.

"No, you will need to marry him."

Sage glared at the rebellion leader. "Why would you get my hopes up?" she barked, her heart picking up speed. For a brief moment, she thought she might have a chance at freedom again. All the worse to realize it was not so.

"I meant what I said. You have to marry the crown prince but when we go to war, and we will, we can fake your death."

Sage blinked, her hand clutching the blanket. Fake her death?

"Before you tell me I am addled, mull it over." Rafe stared at floor and began pacing. "You're known as the rebel's blade and now also as the warrior princess to the court. When Scythia attacks you won't be waiting here, you will be among those fighting. War is chaos. We can make it seem like you fell in battle, which will be glorious and honorable and you would be free of the prince without giving the rebellion cause for retaliation." Rafe paused his pacing to look at her.

"You can have the life you always wanted. You can be free of this marble prison."

Her mind scrambled to keep up with the things he was suggesting. War. Chaos. Escape. Freedom. Living her life as she sought, not as someone bid her. But what of her family? "It sounds like you have put a great deal of thought into this, but what of my family? Where would we live? My face will be recognizable."

"You and your family will come home with me, to Methi."

Her jaw slackened. Methi. He wanted to take her to Methi. "As what?" she choked out.

Rafe looked at her with confusion. "What do you mean?"

If her life experience thus far had shown her one thing it was this: everyone wanted something. "What do you expect of me if I accept your help in escaping my nightmare?"

"Nothing," he drawled softly. "I will take care of you like you are my own."

"As your sister? Or like a daughter?" Sage pushed, knowing that was not what he had in mind.

"As my mate."

Mate. There was that odd word for a wife again. Sage shook her head. She would not jump from one man to another. "Would you make me a harlot?"

He looked at her, aghast. "I would never dishonor you that way. We would have a ceremony that combined both our traditions."

"That is not what I meant." She made sure to look him in the eye as she spoke her next words. "Even if I agreed to what you are asking I could never be with you."

The predatory glint in his eyes had her feet moving before she'd consciously decided to do so. The next thing she knew was that she was on the opposite side of the bed with both blades in hand.

Rafe glided to the opposite side and placed his hands on the mattress, leaning forward, his temper only just reined in. "Why," he bit out, "do you keep scorning me? I have offered you exactly what you want. There is no one but yourself keeping you from the life you want." His back heaved as he sucked in a breath before pinning her to the spot with his amber eyes. "I want you above all others."

The sincerity of his words reverberated in her mind and pierced her heart. She looked at him, a sadness shadowing her face. "I could not marry you even if I wanted to, Rafe. Even if we faked my death I would still be married to the crown prince."

"Annulment."

"And if the war doesn't come for years?"

Rafe ran his fingers around one of the post of her bed, then followed her, almost like he was hunting.

"Time doesn't matter. As long as you remain untouched you can go free." He paused, his smile gentle. "You can be free with me."

Her heart squeezed with his words. Everything in her life was out of her control. If she said yes, she would not only be choosing her own path, but that of her family as well. She couldn't leave them, but would they go with her? Would they even want to? Sage wanted to be reckless, throwing caution to the wind just to get out the depressing life she felt was ahead of her, but her head knew better than her heart. Rafe was, in a lot of ways, still very much a stranger, and he had hurt her even more than the Crown at this point in time.

Overcome with exhaustion, she lifted her fists and rubbed at her eyes, being careful not to gouge herself with her daggers. A whisper of sound reached her ears just as big hands wrapped around her wrists. Sage gasped, and his earthy scent filling her lungs.

"This is not a decision to be made lightly little one." He tugged on her hands. "I will wait for your decision."

Sage pulled her hands from his grip and stepped away. She needed to be alone. Everything he was saying and doing was just too much for her to handle, especially tonight. She sheathed her daggers, unlocked the door, and opened it, peering into the hallway outside. Two Elite had posted themselves there. Sage grimaced and briskly nodded at them before stepping into the hallway. Rafe wouldn't go unseen so his presence would no doubt get back to Tehl. Sage levelly met his gaze and gestured down the hall. "Please leave."

His lips thinned and the corners of his eyes pinched, but that was the only indication that he was less than happy with her dismissal. He stalked through the doorway, ignoring the looks of interest and suspicion the Elite were throwing his way. He didn't stop until he was toe to toe with Sage. He cupped her chin and lifted her face, staring into her eyes. "Hold your head high tomorrow, little one. Through your strength, bravery, and honor you have become the savior of kingdoms. People will not understand your sacrifice. Royalty doesn't come from just your bloodline but from your character. You are just as much royalty as the crown prince."

Sage swallowed thickly, tears pricking her eyes, touched by his sudden sincerity. "Thank you," she whispered.

His eyes dipped and Sage turned her face just in time, his lips brushing the corner of her mouth in a kiss. He lingered there.

"What is family for, little one?" He breathed against her skin before pulling back and caressing her jaw. "Until tomorrow."

Sage watched him stride away, disappearing into the shadows of the castle. His black cloak seemed to soak up light. A throat cleared, catching her attention. Sage turned to the Elite guards who wore disapproving looks on their faces. She ignored their looks and stared down the hall. She trained with them, but it didn't mean she owed them any explanation.

A flutter of color flickered down the hall. A familiar head of hair whipped back, disappearing around the corner. Caeja, Jaren's daughter, the harpy mooing over the crown prince. Sage shook her head before trudging back into her room. She closed her door and leaned back against it. It amused her that the vicious noblewoman was spying on her, but it also created a problem.

Sage didn't doubt that by morning everyone would think she was entertaining other men. She could run to Tehl and explain what happened but she was sure he'd approach her about it later. That was the thing about rumors, you could never catch them or control them. She sighed, exhausted. These were all problems for another day.

Closing the door behind her, she stumbled toward her bed, discarding her clothes as she went. She lay down on her side and stared at the crackling fire. By this time tomorrow morning, she would be a princess. A royal. She shivered at the thought and pulled the covers tighter. Her mind and heart were heavy, so she feared she wouldn't be able to rest this night. As it turned out, however, the call of sleep was stronger than the worries of the day. She slipped her hand around a dagger beneath her pillow even as her eyes were drooping. Maybe tonight she wouldn't have nightmares.

CHAPTER NINETEEN

Sage

Sage jerked awake, dagger in hand, startling the serving women who had bustled into her room. She winced as a couple let out startled shrieks. Sheepishly, she waved her dagger at them, mumbling words of apology. She flopped back onto her bed and just listened, the soothing sounds of the women stoking the fire and preparing a bath relaxing the tenseness of her shoulders. Nightmares had awoken her all through the night. It felt like she hadn't slept a wink.

Today she would marry.

Marry a man she cared nothing for.

She would be royalty.

Trapped.

Morning had come too soon.

That thought had her lungs constricting, and she suddenly felt unable to breathe. She focused on the ceiling above, calming herself by counting in her mind. After what seemed like forever, her breathing slowed and eventually evened out. Everything would be okay.

"What are you still doing abed?" Lilja teased.

Sage turned her head to meet the magenta eyes of her friend and gestured with her dagger. "What does it look like I am doing?"

Her mum, Mira, and Lilja were all gathered by her bed, smiling down at her. Lilja examined her face and cocked a hip. "It rather looks like you got into a fight with a leviathan. That hair."

Sage scowled as she patted her crazy nest of hair. Sometimes it defied nature. Nothing she could do about it.

Her mum slapped Lilja's arm and strode to the bed to sit beside her daughter. She looked down, a soft smile upon her face. "Aren't you ready, love?"

No, she wasn't.

When Sage forced a smile and nodded once, the smile on her mum's face slipped. Apparently, she wasn't as convincing as she thought she was.

Addressing the mass of women gathered to assist her with her preparations, Lilja commanded, "Leave us. We will attend the prince's betrothed. I will send for you when you are needed."

Swiftly they filed out, the soft click of the door signaling their departure. Sage's tension from being watched all the time eased as soon as the room quieted.

Mira plopped down next to her mum and grasped Sage's hand, squeezing once. "Are you hungry?"

That brought a real smile to her face. Mira knew her well. She was always hungry.

Lilja gathered together a few trays and placed them on the enormous bed before stretching out on the other side and raising a brow. "Eat. Now."

"Bossy wench." Sage sat up, searching for something that might go down okay. She finally settled on a flaky pastry dotted with berries and plucked it from the tray.

"That's Captain Femi to you," Lilja sassed.

Sage blew her a kiss before taking a distinctly unladylike bite of her pastry.

"You would think we raised her with no manners," her mum grouched before cracking a smile.

Their jesting finally lightened the atmosphere enough that they were able to pass the rest of the morning in luxury. They ate, drank, and laughed. Sage was lighthearted and relaxed by the time Lilja called back the ladies to assist her in preparing for the ceremony. She was scrubbed and buffed to perfection. By the time they were finished, her skin had a healthy glow and it was softer than it had probably ever been. Her hair even shone with auburn and honey highlights she'd never before noticed.

Lilja rubbed her hands together. "Now we get to the fun part."

Once again, the serving women were ushered out. Sage tipped her head back, allowing her hair to cascade down the back of her chair and onto the floor, and she sighed as her mum and Lilia began carding their fingers through it. Nothing felt better than having someone play with her hair.

Mira shuffled in front of her. "Close your eyes. I'm starting on your cosmetics."

Sage narrowed her eyes. "Nothing extravagant?"

Mira gave her an eye roll and pointed to her own flawless face. "Does mine look extravagant to you? No. All I'm doing is highlighting your features and enhancing your natural beauty. Now, close your eyes."

She obediently closed her eyes but couldn't help mumbling, "Hmph. Everyone is so bossy today," earning some chuckles from her companions. Somewhere between Mira working on her face and the other two working with her hair she drifted off. It wasn't until someone pressed her arm several times that she awoke. She opened her eyes to her mum, who was leaning down to cup her cheek, eyes suspiciously damp.

"You're done, my love. It's time to put your dress on."

Her stomach dropped and her pulse quickened. It was almost time.

Her dress lay across the bed, its fabric spread across the duvet. It was the softest green, almost white, for Aermian brides always wore green on their marriage day. It represented a fresh start, the beginning to a new life.

As Mira lifted the dress, Sage took an unconscious step back. Once she donned it there was no going back.

Mira, Lilja, and her mum all paused, their faces carefully blank.

"Are you all right, *ma fleur*?"

Sage swallowed, nodded, and lifted her arms. The three women helped lift the dress up and over her head. The sleeves slipped down her arms as the dress fell to the floor, caressing her body. Its neck was cut wide to expose her collarbone. Each end edged her shoulders and ran to her elbow where the silky material met lace sleeves. The silhouette followed her curves, flaring slightly at her thighs, like a calla lily. She felt Lilja's cool hands touching the skin of her back, tugging softly to adjust the bustle. All three women stepped back, awed.

Sage shifted, uncomfortable. "How do I look?"

"Like a queen," Mira breathed.

Tears filled her mum's eyes and then spilled over, tracking down her face. "You're beautiful darling. And as regal a bride as ever there was, I'm sure."

Lilja took her hand and led her to the mirror.

Sage gasped. The dress was stunning. The work they'd done on hair and cosmetics was beautiful, but she still couldn't get used to seeing herself like this. It looked like someone had painted a picture of her but enhanced it so that her features seemed more striking and more polished. She grabbed a handful of the dress and turned, eyeing the back. It was open with dainty bows tied in the center to keep the dress in place. Lilja had left her hair loose with a lone braid that started at the crown of her head and wove down behind her ear and under her heavy fall of hair.

She hated it.

Not so much the dress in itself, rather what it meant. She bit the inside of her cheek to hold back the bitter words ready to spill out. Sage flashed her family a grateful smile. Despite her personal feelings she refused to make it harder on them. She met Lilja's eyes and knew by the knowing look that she wasn't fooling her. Lilja touched her hair, offering silent comfort and support.

"Not only stunning on the outside but on the inside as well," her mum murmured from behind her.

Sage turned into her mum's arms and hugged with all her might. "I love you, Mum."

"I love you too, more than you understand." She pulled back and gave her daughter a watery smile. "I should go and find your father. Do you need anything else before I do so?"

"No."

"Okay then. I will see you in a bit my love."

Lilja kissed her cheek and squeezed her hand. "Courage, *ma fleur.*"

The two quit the room, leaving only her and Mira, the latter staring at her through the mirror. Her friend looked conflicted as she laced her fingers with Sage's. "I have been with you from the beginning. I know how you feel about Tehl. If you want to leave, I will help you."

227

Sage froze at the seriousness in both Mira's voice and eyes. Her friend meant it. Mira would risk everything for her. She would lose her life and the only family she ever had to help Sage. Her throat felt thick. She didn't deserve such wonderful friends. She lifted their entwined hands and kissed the back of Mira's. "Thank you for such love, but I am needed here." Despite the brave face she was putting on, she still felt the beginnings of panic setting in. She needed to be alone. "Would you mind giving me a moment to myself?"

Mira nodded. "I will send someone to retrieve you when the ceremony is starting." She then hugged her and disappeared through the door.

Sage turned back to face the mirror. Her mum had spoken true: she did look beautiful. Everything about her shone, except for her eyes. They were dull. Sad.

An ugly sob escaped, her face contorting. Blindly, she clutched the dresser in front of her, leaning heavily against it. She blearily glanced at the cosmetics and jeweled pins scattered atop it as each sob continued to wrack her chest. Why did this happen to her? She wasn't perfect, but she didn't feel like she deserved to be punished for the rest of her life. It was just so unfair. She shoved the items off the dresser, the jeweled pins plinking onto the stone floor. With shuddering breaths, she stumbled to the side table, and, hiking it up carelessly, with shaking hands, she clumsily attempted to attach her thigh sheath. She had to get out of here. Now.

"Do you need a hand?" a deep voice asked.

Sage blinked and looked to the door. Gav and Sam both stood in her room. She tried to rein in the frayed threads of her emotions but it was impossible. She couldn't control anything. Another sob rose, and, in her attempt to stifle it, only accomplished an embarrassing strangled cry. Their figures completely blurred, leaving only fuzzy blob shaped masses. She looked down to her trembling hands. She needed help. There she admitted it. "Please," she cried holding the sheath out.

The blob with golden hair moved to her side and gingerly took it from her, kneeling next her. She tipped her head back, trying to ignore Sam's large hands touching her thigh. Her tears rolled down her cheeks and dropped into the hollows of her ears. Gav moved behind her and wrapped his large arms around her, causing more desperate sobs to slip out.

"Next."

She dropped her leg and lifted the other one to the bed. Sam worked quickly and was standing before her. His deep blue eyes watched her with concern and a deep sorrow that somehow made her only cry harder. Sam stepped forward and wrapped his arms around her too. The tears kept coming. "I don't know if I can do this," she cried over and over again. Both men whispered to her and held her until she'd calmed enough to take gulping breaths.

Lifting her head, she stared at the wet mess she had made of Sam's vest, hiccups jerking her body. His large hands cupped her cheeks and lifted her face. "I am so sorry."

Sage closed her eyes, blocking the pity she saw in his eyes. She'd made a fool out of herself. Why was she so weak? They knew as well as she did that there was no escape for her. She shook her head, fighting off the embarrassment overwhelming her. "No, I am sorry you had to see that."

Sam's rough fingers tenderly brushed away the tears dampening her face. Sage sucked in a stuttering deep breath and forced her eyes open. Sam smiled sadly before looking over the top of her head to Gavriel.

"This is wrong," Gavriel whispered, his breath ruffling her hair.

The spymaster's eyes dropped to hers and she simply stared back at him. In his eyes was a wealth of information. He was truly saddened by the situation but there was nothing to be done. Just as there was nothing to stop the sun from rising each morning, there was nothing that could keep her from marrying the crown prince. Sage nodded once and took a deep breath. She could do this. She had survived so many other things, she would not allow this to break her.

Sage turned to step away from the princes, though Gav's hold tightened a moment before he let her go. She returned to the mirror and examined the damage she had done. Her face was flushed with a map of trails where her tears had fallen. Her eyes were puffy and a shiny clear green. Sage dropped her eyes to smooth out the dress, erasing the wrinkles Sam and Gav had caused. She felt more than saw both men move to stand on either side of her.

Carefully, Sage lifted her face and watched them in the mirror. What did they think of her now?

Gavriel smiled. "You are lovely, Sage."

She gave him a weak smile. "I should with what it cost. I bet I could feed a family for a while if I sold this," she joked.

To her surprise, Sam reached down and clasped her hand, his eyes never leaving her face. "It's not the dress but the woman who wears it. The dress is beautiful but you are what gives it worth."

"It's because of my mother's good looks."

"No," Sam shook his head. "That's not what I meant, and you know it. You're beautiful but it is your inner self that draws people. Your courage, compassion, and love shine, touching everyone around you." He paused. "You know, our mum would have loved you."

Her throat tightened. Where was this coming from? Sage had never seen this side of the spymaster. "I am only doing what anyone else would."

Sam pinned her with a look. "Anyone else would have condemned us to death and ran away. You have gone above and beyond what anyone else would do." Sam turned her from the mirror and knelt in front of her and Gavriel. "From this moment forward, I want you to know you can always come to me for anything. I will support you and love you like my sister, this I promise. And I would like permission to call you such."

Sage gasped and stilled, staring down at the blond prince. She never expected to receive such an oath from *him*. She assumed she would be alone in her gilded cage. Was this a cruel ploy? But as Sage searched his eyes, she found nothing but sincerity and the barest hint of vulnerability. Sam actually meant what he said.

"I would be honored," she whispered.

His radiant smile just about blinded her. "Excellent! I always wanted a sister."

A small chuckle slipped from her. "Just remember that when I am annoying you. Remember, too, that I grew up with two brothers."

Sam sprang up and crushed her against his enormous body. "The same goes for you, sis."

Gavriel cleared his throat breaking up their moment. Sage turned to him, staring into his dear face. He reached out and smoothed her hair from her face. "Do you remember our conversation before you left?"

Sage nodded, guilt pooling in her stomach.

"That was never a ploy to get you to trust me. I meant it then, and I mean it now. Despite the circumstances that brought you here, you are a part of this family, and we take care of our own." Gav held open his arms and she rushed into them. "I am always here for you."

Sage gave him a final squeeze before stepping back to look at both men. Never in a thousand years would she have expected to have two of the princes of Aermia call her family. Sam still threw her off balance, but that was just his personality. "I don't deserve this but I will cherish you both as my brothers, my family."

Twin smiles split their faces, calling one to her own face.

Reluctantly, Sage turned back to the mirror and stared again at her reflection. Gav picked up a cloth she had flung to the floor and handed it to her, and, with it, she cleaned up her face. She then fixed the damage to her hair as best she could and squared her shoulders. Now was not the time to be a coward. She gave her word and now she needed to fulfill it. Sage smoothed her dress one last time, turning to her new brothers to inquire of them, "How do I look?"

"Like a queen."

Sam's eyes glinted. "My brother won't be able to stand it when he sees you."

Sage grimaced. "I highly doubt that, but thank you for the compliment."

Gavriel held out his arm. "Are you ready?"

No, she would never be ready but she kept that thought to herself. "Yes."

CHAPTER TWENTY

Tehl

Tehl paced.

Guilt had his stomach turning. Sage's broken sobs still echoed in his ears. He'd merely gone to see how she fared before the ceremony, to double check that she hadn't run off, and show her his surprise. When he'd reached her chamber though he'd stopped when he saw Sam and Gav standing in the hallway. Neither moved. They just stood there, staring at the closed door, faces bleak. He joined them, leaning close to the door to listen, but when he'd heard the desolate cries emanating from the other side, his own throat had thickened and he couldn't help feeling a little sick. He had leaned forward, resting his forehead against the door, unsure of what he was supposed to do. He couldn't just let her suffer like that but how could he possibly help?

She put on such a tough exterior, despite the fact that she was torn up inside, but he knew she'd never accept comfort from him or want him to see her in such a vulnerable state. Part of him wanted to rush in and wrap his arms around her with an assurance that everything would be okay. But the logical part of him knew he'd more than likely make it worse. A large part of the reason she was so upset was no doubt due to him.

Turning to his cousin and brother, he'd whispered, "Take care of her," before he returned to his own chamber, the burden placed upon them both by their kingdom weighing heavily upon his mind.

Life was simply not fair.

His pacing was abruptly interrupted by the sound of a voice.

"Getting cold feet, my lord?"

He blinked, trying to shake himself from the memory. "No." Tehl tugged at his hair. "Am I doing the right thing?" he blurted.

Zachael studied him for a moment. "Only you can answer that."

Tehl sent him a pleading look. "Please, old friend. Speak your mind. I could use an outsider's input."

The older man exhaled, dropping his eyes to the marble floor. "She has been through much, but she hasn't stopped trying to tough it out. Sometimes, women hold it in for so long they just break down. She will be fine later. I think she just needed to get it out of her system since she probably hasn't done so until now." Zachael met his gaze. "You both need time to adjust. All will be well, Tehl. Be patient."

No. All would not be well for either of them.

The combat master glanced at the window. "It's near time. Ready?"

He pulled in a deep breath and tried to steel himself.

It was time.

Tehl nodded to Zachael and strode through the door, to the courtyard full of people. At his approach, all stood and bowed as hundreds of eyes turned his way, following him as he took his place on the dais beside his waiting father. Carefully, he ordered his features into an appropriately blissful expression for his court and waved to the crowd.

His father shifted closer and asked underneath his breath. "Are you nervous, son?"

Tehl glanced from his father to the Elite mingling among the throng of people. He hadn't been before, but, somehow, his father's words had him starting to be. What if she didn't show up? What if she did? His gut clenched. He shook his head to clear the thought.

Never show any fear, never let them see you sweat.

"Not at all," he answered, infusing it with as much confidence as he could. A deep chuckle had him turning and scowling at the king. "She will be here," he muttered, more to himself than his father.

Tehl turned back to the crowd and fought the intense discomfort he still felt when under the scrutiny of so many people. He never was a people person. He rolled his neck and took to examining the shine of his boots, staring at his warped reflection. Tehl relaxed his clenched jaw and drew in another deep breath. Once this was over things would be better. He would make it so.

Suddenly, the crowds quieted.

She was here.

Abandoning the examination of his boots, he mentally prepared himself and lifted his eyes toward the doors. He could make out Sam and Gav first and then the two brothers of his betrothed, but Sage was thus far unseen. A thread of panic seized him. Where was she?

Music started, and the wall of men parted, and, suddenly, she appeared. Tehl's breath stuttered and he gaped.

From the crown of her head to the tip of her toes she was breathtaking. Her whiskey mane glistened in the late sunlight, its locks waving in the slight breeze.

"Breathe, son."

Tehl let out the breath he'd been holding and snapped his mouth shut. She'd always been attractive but today she seemed ethereal. Her pale green dress made the green of her eyes seem even brighter than ever. He couldn't take his eyes off her.

"Your mother would have loved Sage. Well done, son. Your bride will do Aermia proud."

His bride.

Such a beguiling creature would be his. Tehl stood a little taller as a feeling of satisfaction settled inside him. He watched as she smiled at his people and took in, with wonder, the decorations strewn about the outside garden, creating a version of her meadow, yet she did not meet his eyes. She hadn't even glanced his direction.

Look at me, he thought.

He continued to focus on her, willing her to turn to him. At that moment, her head lifted, like she'd somehow heard him, and their gazes clashed. A jolt went through him at the mix of emotions displayed there.

She dropped her eyes and stopped at the dais, turning to bestow a kiss upon Sam, Gav, and then her brothers. Next, her mum stood and hugged and kissed her. Her father did the same before taking her hand and turning her toward Tehl as he descended the steps, focusing hard on each one so as to not tumble down them like a drunken fool. Colm's serious eyes met Tehl's, an obvious warning in them.

"Are you prepared to bind yourself to my daughter?" he said, somberly.

"I am," Tehl vowed.

Colm studied him for a beat and then placed Sage's small hand in his own. Tehl's fingers wrapped around her dainty hand and he gently led her up the stairs. Sam, Gav, Mira, and Lilja, each a member of the wedding party, followed in their wake. Tehl turned to Sage and reached for her other hand, scowling when he noticed he trembled.

He glared at the offending appendage, willing it to stop its infernal shaking. He tried clenching his fist, but it was to no avail. Sage too stared for a beat before stretching her hand out instead, a slight tremor evident in hers as well. His eyes snapped to hers and she gave him a wobbly smile, which he returned. It seemed they both were nervous.

"Are you ready?" he whispered.

Her slight smile dropped as she swallowed thickly, and biting her lip, jerked her head up and down. Neither of them were ready, but they were doing the best they could.

"Are you ready, my dear?" his father's deep voice interrupted his thoughts.

Sage turned to his father. "I am."

When she turned back to Tehl, his heart clenched. His people saw a serene bride about to blissfully wed their prince, but they couldn't see her eyes. He, however, did and they were anything but blissful. Depression. Exhaustion. Resignation.

There was no turning back now, their lots were cast.

His father's voice rose, and a hush fell over the crowd. Tehl tuned out his father's words, never taking his eyes from the woman standing before him. Tehl hoped his gaze conveyed to her his commitment to this arrangement of theirs and that somehow it would comfort her, at least slightly. A hand touched his shoulder, breaking his attention from his betrothed. Tehl blinked at his father. "What?"

A laugh burst out of his father followed by many from the crowd. The king smiled and nodded toward Sage. "It's time for the binding."

Tehl tightened his grasp on Sage's hands as she began to pull away. He gave her a stern look before dropping her hands; now was not the time to be having second thoughts.

Sam stepped forward and handed him a silk bag containing a pair of silver cuffs. The silk slid through his fingers while he unwrapped them. Carefully, he extracted the metal bands and stepped up to the rebel, the tips of his boots touching her sandaled feet.

"Do you accept these cuffs of mine and therefore agree to be bound together until we both depart this world?"

Her breaths came in and out in quick succession while she stared at the cuffs in his outstretched hands. Tehl shifted as murmurs rippled through the Crown at her. Silence. Stars above, would she to refuse him? "Sage?"

Her fingers twitched, and she blew out a breath. Sage shoved her arms out baring her wrists but still not meeting his eyes. "I accept."

Relief rushed through him as he hastily placed a silver band on each of her scarred wrists. The cuffs were simple in design: plain metal with small waves etched along the brushed silver edge. It was the simplest cuff ever worn in the Crown's history, but, from what he knew of Sage, he felt they were the most suitable; she wasn't an extravagant woman. Tehl watched her face carefully but she gave nothing away, carefully maintaining a practiced smile. Disappointment pricked him. She didn't want to wear his cuffs, but he hoped she would at least enjoy the design he'd created just for her.

Sage turned to Lilja, who'd stepped up behind her to hand over a roughly woven sack. Sage pulled out a single, larger cuff and turned toward him. His heart stuttered as she stepped closer, her dress rustling. Sage tipped her head back and met his gaze squarely.

"Do you accept this cuff of mine and therefore agree to be bound together until we both depart this world?" Her voice rang out loud and clear among the assembly, giving no evidence of her true emotions.

Tehl searched her face before answering, noting the tightness around her eyes. "I accept."

She reached for his hand and slid her cuff up his arm, her soft fingers teasing his skin. His eyes rested on the cuff adorning his bicep. It was nothing like what he was used to seeing. Most men wore cuffs made of bronze, silver, or gold. But Sage had created something new. The cuff was a series of leather and silver strips woven into a complex braid that was sturdy yet flexible.

"It is done," his father announced. "Please kneel."

Both knelt as his father moved toward them in all his kingly finery, a delicate crown in his grasp. He stood in front of Sage, a tender smile upon his face. "Do you, Sage Blackwell, promise to uphold Aermian law in all your ways, to protect the kingdom with your very life when necessary and to rule with justice?"

Sage lifted her chin and straightened her spine. "Yes."

"I know you will, my dear," he said quietly, for their ears only.

The king then placed upon her head an intricate silver crown embedded with pearls. When his father caressed Sage's cheek before stepping back, Tehl stared in wonderment. His father truly loved his bride.

"Please stand."

Tehl helped Sage to her feet, his own crown feeling heavy upon his head. The king clasped their joined hands, raising them in the air. "Proudly, I present to you the bound Crown Prince Tehl Ramses and his consort, Princess Sage Ramses."

Deafening applause erupted from the Crown. A faint ringing filled Tehl's ears as he beheld the woman beside him who was surveying the cheering crowd with fake enthusiasm.

It was done, he was bound.

A strong sense of satisfaction filled him at the thought. He had a companion and not just any, but one who had just as much at stake. Both of their lives were equally vested in his kingdom's interests. After a moment, she gave him a look from the corner of her eye, a question on her face. He shrugged and smiled, enjoying the shock on her face.

"Now, my son, make your bride yours."

Sage's nails sunk into his hand at his father's words. He barely kept from wincing. Tehl slipped a hand around her waist, pulling her toward him but it was like holding a statue. She didn't give at all. Her wide frightened eyes met his before she slipped a sultry mask into place, stealing the breath from his lungs. Stars above, she was good.

Sage turned to the king and winked. "What if I make him mine?"

His father let loose a booming laugh, gesturing toward Tehl. "By all means."

Sage popped up onto her toes and pressed her lips against his.

Flames.

Bloody hell.

Tehl didn't expect the fire in his veins at her unexpected touch. Heat followed her hands as they skimmed their way up his arms and around his neck, fingers sinking into his hair urging him closer. His thoughts turned to mush when her mouth opened against his. Without her permission, he found his arms snaked around her waist, his hands clutching her dress as he hauled her against him until every inch of them touched. Time seemed to stop as he devoured the promises on her lips. When she finally pulled back, he chased her lips once again only to be thwarted by a finger pressed against his mouth. He blinked a few times, feeling like he'd been awoken from a dream, jolting when he met a pair of very serious green eyes.

Damn.

Any lingering heat in his blood chilled at the carefully composed look on her face as realization dawned.

It was an act.

It was for the crowd.

Tehl cursed his own infernal weakness and fumed. How could his damn body betray him like that? He lowered her to the floor, attempting to compose himself. He was better than this.

Control, Tehl. Control.

The roar of the crowd filled his ears, and Tehl shook his head once before pasting on a smile of his own.

"Are you all right?" Sage muttered.

He grunted. He refused to talk about what just happened.

"Let the celebrations begin!"

Tehl wove Sage's arm through his and muttered. "Let's get this over with."

***

Wading through the crowd of well-wishers was a nightmare. It took forever just to make it to the raised dais where the ceremonial dinner was to be served. Then, dinner passed in a flurry of conversation and courses. Sage ate next to him, conversing with anyone and everyone like a true princess. She listened and empathized with those she spoke to, building a personal connection with each interaction. She made people feel comfortable and important, her conversation a good blend of sense and witty remarks. The chords of a soft and slow tune began, reminding him of their last ceremonial responsibility. Tehl scooted back his chair and stood, holding his hand out to the rebel looking up at him through her lashes. "My lady, will you dance with me?"

"Of course." She placed her napkin on the table and placed her hand in his, rising. Turning to the table she gave them a nod and a smile. "Excuse us".

Tehl lead her down the dais and to the stone dance floor, the stars serving as their backdrop. People emptied the floor and gathered in a circle around them so they were the only dancing couple on the floor. Tehl twirled her once before bringing her into his arms. With practiced ease, he began the twirling steps that had been drilled into him as a child. The crowd smiled and whispered as they pranced and whirled. Tehl looked down, scanning Sage's profile. He was pretty sure he hadn't said more than two words to her since the ceremony. She raised a silent brow in question. Apparently he'd been caught staring. In response he simply said, "It's done."

"Indeed, it is." Her lips twitched.

"What's so funny?"

"You."

"Why?"

"I know it's done. If you'll recall, I was there too."

Tehl snorted and looked over her head, amused at himself as well. "True."

"One word answers, my lord?"

He shrugged. "Are additional words necessary?"

Sage glanced up at him briefly before looking away. "I suppose not, sometimes simplicity is the best." A pause. "The decorations are beautiful."

Tehl blinked at the change in subject. "I am glad you like them."

"It looks like my meadow."

"I wanted you to have at least one thing you'd always wanted tonight."

She gave him a genuine smile, one that reached her eyes. "It means more than you know. I won't forget your kindness."

He cleared his throat, slightly embarrassed. "It was nothing."

"If you say so, my lord."

They finished their dance in comfortable silence, neither feeling the need to fill it. By the time the song drew to a close, Sam was already at his side, ready to sweep away his bride for the next number. After a few hours of dancing, he was done with the night. Tehl thanked his last dance partner and strode toward Sage and her

242

current partner, Zachael. He stopped and sketched a shallow bow.

"If you don't mind, old friend, I am here to retrieve my bride."

Zachael kissed her on the cheek and handed her over to him. Her smile dimmed some at the change in companions but did not disappear completely. Cheering went up as they exited the dance floor together. Tehl guided her to her family and bowed over her hand. "I will see you soon, my lady." Tehl nodded respectfully to her brothers and father before making a quick exit. Swiftly, he made his way to his rooms, thinking about the awkward evening ahead of him.

He jerked to a stop when he opened his door. Every surface was covered with lit candles and a fire blazed in the hearth. Someone had placed sweet treats and a few bottles of spirits on the table between two wingback chairs that sat a comfortable distance from the flames.

Grimacing, Tehl skirted the bed and pulled off his boots. He reached the spirits and poured himself a drink then wandered passed his closet. Frowning, he took a couple steps back and eyed the mass of feminine clothing items now in it. The staff had certainly been busy. He rolled his eyes and downed the alcohol, relishing its burn at the back of his throat. He then plopped into one of the chairs and stared into the flames, mulling over the fact that his wife would arrive soon.

He froze.

His *wife*.

Tehl jumped out of the chair and poured another drink. He had a wife. He was married. There was no reversing what had happened today. For better or worse they were bound forever. The door slammed open and he startled. He spun as Sam, Gav, Rafe, and Sage pushed into the room, all of them shouting. Sam shut the door and latched it while Sage shook off Gavriel and brushed by Rafe to pour herself a drink.

"What in the name of hell?" he barked and stabbed a finger at the rebellion leader. "Why is Rafe in our room?"

Sage glared at him before downing her drink. "Well, Your Highness, the issue is that someone just tried to kill me."

CHAPTER TWENTY-ONE

Tehl

Tehl brows furrowed. Did he hear her right? He tore his gaze from her face and glanced to the room's other occupants. By the murderous looks he saw on their faces, he must have indeed heard correctly.

"What happened?" he asked firmly but calmly. They'd been expecting something like this, so there was no need to completely lose it.

"I'll tell you what happened," Sam exploded. "An assassin strolled right through the crowd to congratulate our new princess on her marriage and, in front of everyone, attempted to cut her heart out!" Sam's hands shook as he ran them through his hair.

Tehl blinked. Sam never lost his cool. If his brother was upset it had to have been a very close call.

Tehl glanced to the seething brunette beside him, and an image popped into his mind of her lying there on the stone floor, her body in a pool of blood. His stomach soured at the thought.

"If Sage hadn't been carrying one of her daggers she would be dead," Sam added.

The words hung in the air, leaving a sense of darkness on the room. Tehl breathed through his nose, frustrated. He bit out his next question, "Where is he?" He expected an attempt on her life, it was part of being a royal, but it still rankled. How dare someone attack Sage, his wife, a woman under his protection.

"Dead," Sage answered, flatly.

"By whom?"

"His own hand, the coward," Rafe growled.

That grated on Tehl as well. Apparently the man had no honor at all and now they had no way of getting any more information. "Did any of you recognize him?" He pointedly looked to Sage.

"I didn't know him. He wasn't part of the rebellion if that is what you are asking." Sage massaged her temple and stomped over to his chair, plopping herself into it. She scowled in the rebellion leader's direction. "Did you know him?"

"No."

"You're *sure* neither of you knew him?" Gav asked again.

"I never forget faces, and I would have remembered his for a certainty. It was exotic, beautiful even. The planes of his face seemed perfectly cut." Sage interjected. She turned to Sam, "You noted it as well."

His brother nodded. "He was pretty for a man, hardly inconspicuous."

A pair of burning golden eyes met his. "And what of your enemies?"

Tehl studied Rafe. "What enemies? You mean the ones you've incited against me?"

"You can't tell me you don't have enemies of your own?" Sage asked incredulously, pulling his attention from Rafe's glare. "Nobody's perfect, and you're about as companionable as a porcupine. Who have you offended recently?"

"The names would be too long to list," Gav grouched.

"Mmmhmmmm..." the rebel hummed in agreement.

Tehl gave Gavriel a black look. He didn't have great people skills, but he wasn't that bad. A thought occurred to him. He smiled wickedly at Sage. "Now I'm married to you I don't have to worry about that, you can put out all my fires."

Her mouth snapped shut. That silenced her.

"We won't figure anything out tonight. Tomorrow morning we can look into it," Gav reasoned.

"I will reach out to my contacts," Rafe added, inserting himself into the investigation.

Swamp apples, he would never be rid of this man.

Sage yawned and tipped her head back against the chair. "How long do I need to stay here before I sneak back to my rooms?" she mumbled.

All three princes darted glances to each other.

Oh hell.

"Did no one tell her?" Tehl asked, ignoring Rafe's narrowed eyes. How could no one have mentioned anything? And how in the world did it fall on *him* to do so now?

"Tell me what?"

Tehl pinched the bridge of his nose and gestured to the closet, preparing for the huge fight ahead. "Take a look for yourself."

He placed a hand over his mouth, waiting for the explosion soon to come as he watched her heave herself from the chair and onto her feet. She then proceeded to do as he'd told her. She opened the door.

One, two, three...

"What in the bloody hell?" Sage stormed from the closet and to him, scowling. "What is the meaning of those dresses?" she demanded, stabbing a finger to the closet.

Tehl lifted his drink and took a fortifying sip. This wasn't a conversation he really wanted to be having as a group. He faced Sage, but he made sure to track Rafe's reaction in his peripheral. The rebellion leader was unruly at best when it came to Sage. "Exactly what you think it does."

Her eyes narrowed. "I am not staying here."

"It has always been this way. There is not a ruling couple in our history that did not share the same room." Tehl tried to sound as reasonable as possible. Maybe if he showed her the advantages, they could avoid an argument as this was not something he could compromise on, it simply had to be done. "Everything about this ruse will be easier to keep up if you stay here."

Her eyes narrowed so much they were thin slits. "I'll not do it."

Rafe stepped to her side, placing his hand on her back. Tehl arched an eyebrow at him.

"I would listen to the lady." Tehl could detect a touch of malice in Rafe's voice. The rebellion leader was playing with fire, he shouldn't even be in the room and here he was commanding Tehl and touching his wife. This was not heading the direction he'd hoped.

Tehl blew out a breath. *All right*, he thought, *unreasonable it is.*

"In this we have no other choice. Do you think I want to sleep in the same bed as you?"

"She will *not* share your bed," Rafe hissed.

Sage's face turned an alarming shade of red. "Sharing a room doesn't mean sharing a bed."

"No, it does not," Sam said, sounding reasonable. Then he grinned and wiggled his eyebrows. "As a matter of fact I frequently share be—" Sage grabbed a pillow from the bed and launched it at his brother's head.

Sam held up his hands. "Now, now. No need to be feisty. I was just pointing out the differences."

"Enough," she growled, turning her glare from his brother to him. "I promised to marry you, but I never agreed to this. This was not included in our negotiations. I can never sleep knowing you're in the same room."

Tehl scoffed, a little offended. "What do think I will do? Knife you in the middle of the night?"

"Among other things."

Tehl rolled his eyes. "I have no designs on you tonight or any other night. Contrary to your absurd opinions about me, I am absolutely not interested in unwilling women." Tehl threw his hands in the air and stomped to his bed, yanking back the covers. "Listen. There are guards posted outside our door, they will see you if you sneak out so it's ridiculous to keep arguing about this. Tonight, and every other night, I am sleeping in my bed. You are welcome to sleep wherever you wish, be it in the chair, on the floor or somewhere else. But it will be in *this room*. You agreed to this marriage, and this is just a part of what it entails."

He could see her start to fume. "This was thrust upon me, I had no choice in the matter so I didn't actually agree to anything," Sage spat.

"Sage, it's true about our kings and queens sharing the room," Gav added gently.

She held his cousin's gaze for what seemed an eternity and finally spoke. "It seems I once again have no choice in the matter, just as in every other aspect of this mess." She then swung her infuriated gaze back to him. "If you so much as twitch in my direction..."

Her hand flashed and a dull thwack sounded very close to his head. Tehl twisted to find a dagger embedded in the bed poster a scant three inches from his ear. "Did you just throw a knife at me?"

he asked, incredulously.

The smug smile the rebellion leader now wore had Tehl fighting the desire not to walk over and punch him in his interfering, smug face.

"That was a warning. You stay in your bed and I will stay in mine." She whirled around and snatched something from the closet before slipping into the bathing room. The clicking of the door was followed by the sound of running water.

"Well," Gav sighed, "that sure went well... "

"I guess the traditional wedding night is out," Sam deadpanned. That pulled a low growl from Rafe.

"Enough," Gavriel chastised, elbowing his brother. "It's well past time we be leaving. If she has nightmares," Gav paused and winced, "*when* she has nightmares watch for her blades and call for me. I'll use the secret passage ways so as not to stir up gossip."

Gossip about their new marriage was the last thing they needed, Tehl thought.

He nodded to them both so Sam bellowed, "We're leaving!" in the direction of the bathing room. Sage burst into the room, and, when Sam opened his arms, to Tehl's surprise, she walked right into them.

"Thank you," she whispered.

His brother caught his eye and, over the top of her head, flashed a real Sam smile. "Anything for you, darling."

Sage smiled softly. She stepped from of his arms to Gav's, giving him the same treatment. When she reached Rafe, she hesitated a moment before sliding her arms around his middle. At that moment, a spark of jealousy ran through him as he observed the rebellion leader run his hands through her hair. He gritted his teeth when Rafe looked him in the eyes and, maintaining eye contact, kissed her forehead. The man was dangerous. Tehl would have to keep an eye on him just to make sure the lecher didn't steal his wife right out from under him.

Sage pulled away and retreated once again to the bathing room, sparing Tehl only a brief, annoyed glance. When he looked at the other men in the room, they all stared at the door with varying degrees of affection in their eyes. The damn woman had wiggled her way into all of their hearts.

"You better not mess this up," Sam mumbled. "She is worth her weight in gold. I hope you know how to handle something that precious."

"I run a kingdom."

"Women are more difficult."

"You'll not find me brooking argument there."

"You'll be dealing with more than her family if you hurt her," his brother said, eyeing him.

"I will not harm her."

"I'd kill you if you did," Rafe tossed in.

Tehl didn't doubt it.

"You better not," Gav grumbled. "Okay. It is now well past my bedtime and there is still much for me to do before I can even think of sleeping, so I'm going to bid you all goodnight."

Sam rolled his eyes. "Come along, *old man*," he said, exasperated.

The two princes left his room, bickering, while Tehl had a nice little stare off with Rafe. The door closed, the room filled only with the sounds of running water and a crackling fire.

After a few moments, Tehl finally grouched, "Out with it, I haven't got all night." He really was tired. Today had taken a heavy toll on him and he needed to rest.

"She may be your wife, but she is not yours."

Tehl's hackles raised. Their marriage may be a business deal, but that certainly did not mean Rafe could speak of Sage with any sort of possession. "And who pray tell, does she belong to? You?" Tehl asked, holding his eerie gaze. "From what I hear, she has rebuffed you at every turn."

The rebellion leader's eyes turned murderous. "You—"

Tehl held up a hand, cutting him off. "She doesn't belong to either of us," he said frankly. "But legally she is mine, and I will care for and protect her."

"I don't make idle threats. I meant what I said. Do not hurt her."

"I would expect nothing less."

"We have an understanding then?"

"Indeed."

Rafe dipped his chin and stalked from the room.

Tehl grimaced, the rebellion leader was nothing but trouble. For the next while he went about blowing out the ridiculously large amount of candles that had been placed in their chambers. He slipped into a soft pair of sleep pants and sat on the bed, elbows resting on his knees and hands clasped, just thinking.

Not that much had been altered in it but his own chamber felt so different having Sage here. He had moved to these rooms when he became of marrying age, and, until this moment, Tehl never thought about what it would feel like to bring a woman here. When he imagined getting married, he thought that it would be a sedate occasion to some mousy bride eager to do his bidding. Obviously, he could have never imagined that he'd get a coerced bride who wouldn't spit on him if he was burning.

The bathing room door opened, interrupting his thoughts. Steam billowed out, announcing Sage's arrival. Her skin was pink and shiny, her dark hair dripping water onto the white linen shirt she was wearing, making it most-becomingly transparent.

"Keep your eyes to yourself," his new wife barked. She then strode purposefully to the other side of the bed, ripping pillows off it.

Tehl raised brow. "Keep my eyes to myself? Really? That's the best you could come up with?"

She growled at him and yanked the coverlet out from under him, apparently refusing to dignify his comment with a response. She then ripped off her cuffs, slapping them onto the side table, and stormed toward the fire where she began constructing a nest on the floor.

"You really intend to sleep there?"

"I do," Sage sniffed. "It is better than being in the same bed as you." A dagger appeared in her hand, and she pointed it at him. "You stay on your side of the room, and I will stay on mine."

Exhaustion tugged at him. He didn't have the energy to spar with her. Wearily, he ran a hand down his face and returned his gaze to the hostile woman watching him. "I won't argue with you there. Do whatever you like as long as you don't disturb my sleep." Tehl stood and yanked back the remaining sheets and crawled into bed. He stared at the ceiling and listened as Sage shuffled around, mumbling to herself or cursing under her breath every so often. He couldn't help but smile at a few of the black oaths that came out. A docile wife she most certainly was not. At least his life was about to get a bit more interesting.

"Goodnight, Sage."

Her rustling paused. "Goodnight, my lord."

"Tehl," he insisted.

"Tehl," she repeated

***

Tehl's eyes snapped open, instantly awake. Darkness weighed down on him blanketing the room. His hand crept toward the dagger hidden under his pillow. What woke him? Tehl's brows knitted when he heard a small whimper. What the devil was that?

He sat up and scanned the room, pausing at the slumbering figure before the fire. The tension drained from his body when he realized it was only the rebel. He grumbled and stashed his dagger, irritated at having been awoken needlessly. A dry chuckle fell from his lips as he settled back into bed. Sage was tiresome even in her sleep.

A sharp cry had him bolting upright. "Sage?"

No response.

Tehl yanked back the covers and hissed when his feet touched the cold stone floor. He strode around the foot of the bed, avoiding pieces of furniture, intent on Sage. He barely made out her features in the dark, illuminated by the dying embers in the hearth. She struggled against the covers knotted around her.

"No!" she shouted and struggled harder. "Don't touch..." She broke off with a cry, tears slipping out the corners of her closed eyes.

Tehl's heart seized. This is what Gav was talking about. Sage was having a nightmare. "Sage, wake up." She thrashed harder and let out a wail he was sure would have the Elite crashing through their door. He sank to his knees, trying to decide the best course of action. Sage was so wrapped up in whatever horror she was experiencing he couldn't get through to her. Gavriel warned him about her weapons. It wouldn't do to get stabbed while attempting to wake her. If, however, he could clamp her arms to her sides, he might be okay. He would not become her pincushion.

Tehl blew out a breath. Here went nothing.

He snatched Sage and pulled her back against his chest. "Wake up, you're dreaming."

A feral cry burst out of her, and she exploded into motion, bucking frantically and throwing her head back, clipping him in the chin. Losing his balance, Tehl landed hard on his butt, his legs hugging her hips. He threw both legs on top of hers, tightened his arms, and pushed his head into the side of her neck to pin her to the ground. Meanwhile he spoke in a soothing voice. "It's a dream, it's just a dream, love," he found himself saying over and over.

Her fighting gave way to teeth rattling shudders and sobbing. He released her legs and rolled up to his feet, standing with Sage hanging in his arms. Tehl shifted her in his arms and carried his broken rebel wife to their bed.

"Shhhh...it's okay. I have you."

He set her in it and stared down at her frightened eyes while she fought her way back from whatever hell held her hostage. Tehl ran his eyes over her shadowed features once more before walking around the bed to sit down himself. Emotions washed over him in waves. Guilt. Sadness. Disgust. Anger. He may not have been her attacker, but, to a certain degree, he still felt responsible, as it was his actions that had set the stage for her to be so taken advantage of and hurt. Sage's defiant face when he'd flung back her hood flashed through his mind followed by the memory of her broken cries before the wedding. Tehl sucked in a ragged breath and scrubbed a hand over his face. The vibrant woman he'd first encountered was a dim remnant of her former self, and he hated that he'd had any part in that. He wasn't sorry that they'd thus far subdued the rebellion, but he did regret the way some of it came about.

"We're never to speak of this," Sage's sleep roughened voice pulled him from his reverie. Tehl looked over his shoulder. In the darkness, he could barely make her out as she lay on her back, staring up at the ceiling. "I am not weak," she insisted.

"I never said you were."

"You were thinking it, I could hear it in your silence. You were pitying me."

Tehl pulled one of his legs beneath him and turned to get a better look at her. "No."

"No? I don't believe you, husband."

Tehl stiffened at the title. It wasn't said in an inflection he remembered his mother using to his father, but as a joke. For a reason he could not quite define, that bothered him. After taking a moment to ponder it, however, he realized it made sense since their marriage was a joke anyway.

"Believe it or not, I was raging at the injustice of what befell you, especially since the burden of guilt is partly on my shoulders," he said heavily, his confession hanging in the air.

Her profile turned his way, studying him. "You may have contributed to the circumstance, but you are not responsible for everyone's actions. I have to take responsibility in my part as well. If I hadn't taken part in treasonous acts, I would never have found myself in that situation in the first place. We must all face what we have done."

He was momentarily shocked by her humility, he couldn't believe she was willing to see, much less speak of, her own burden of guilt in this. It was a surprisingly mature response and he respected her for it. "What you speak is true, but, still, I am sorry for what you have suffered. I dare say I will carry a part of the burden all my life."

"Good."

Tehl winced and dropped his head. He supposed he deserved her cruelty.

"I don't mean it like that. I don't want you to suffer, but I believe if you carry the memory with you always then it will inculcate a lesson into your heart. It will influence the way you rule and how you deal with others. That can be a good thing." Tehl lifted his head, watching her watch him. "I won't ever forget what happened to me, but, one day, I will be able to forgive both you and I, it's just not today."

Tehl nodded. He knew the feeling. Forgiveness could be an elusive thing.

CHAPTER TWENTY-TWO

Sage

Sage's eyes sprung open. She blinked at the unfamiliar ceiling. Where was she? Something warm shifted against her side. Sage turned her head to the side and stilled. There was a man in the bed. A half-naked man. She blinked a couple times and then let loose an earth-shattering scream.

As soon as she did so, his eyes flew open and he bolted upright. Sage scrambled backward on her hands, kicking at him as she tried to escape. One of her kicks clipped him on the chin, clacking his teeth together and sending him off the bed. Her whole body trembled as she scrambled to find a weapon of any sort and figure out what was going on. Burning pain seared her hand as she clumsily grabbed the blade of the dagger hidden under the pillow. Ignoring the pain and blood, Sage rolled off the bed and fell into a defensive crouch. How did she end up here? She darted a glance around the room searching for an easy exit. Blast. The only door was on the other side of the bed.

"Stars above, what are you doing, woman?" a familiar voice demanded.

A large hand gripped the edge of the bed and irritated dark blue eyes peeked at her over its edge.

"What was that for?"

After a second, recognition dawned. Tehl. The crown prince. Her husband. Sage pushed her unruly hair out of her face and tried to calm her heart as it tried its best to beat right out of her chest. She scowled at the bed then looked at her abandoned nest on the floor. "Why did you move me?"

A snort pulled her attention back to her husband as he hauled himself from the floor, attempting to untangle himself from the bedding. "Do you not remember?"

Sage stared blankly at his naked chest for a beat before shifting her focus back to the rumpled bed, her brows furrowed. She remembered taking a bath, slipping into bed, and then—suddenly it came crashing back. Muddy-brown eyes, traipsing hands, and pain. Nightmares. She'd had a nightmare. Sage's jaw tightened when she remembered how she had lain in Tehl's arms, crying like a pathetic victim. How scornfully weak he must think her.

Sage's eyes snapped up to find Tehl regarding her evenly. She scrutinized his face, searching for any hint of condescension or pity, but, miraculously, she found none. His eyes wandered down her arm and paused, a flicker of concern on his face. Sage followed his gaze to her crimson stained hand. She blinked. She'd forgotten she'd even done that.

Tehl grabbed the sheet and ripped a strip off, moving around the bed toward her. He halted in front of her and held his hand out. Sage eyed it before unclenching her hand and carefully placed the bloody dagger onto the side table, and, immediately, she felt the pain begin to pulse from the wound. Reluctantly, she laid her hand in his. It had already bled quite a bit, making it look worse than it was, but fortunately it wasn't deep enough to require stitching, however, it would prove to be annoying in the coming weeks.

As he examined her hand, palm up, his calloused hands were surprisingly gentle. Sage winced when he used his fingers to probe the cut, ascertaining its depth, and focused on a soot mark marring the fireplace. An uncomfortable silence filled the room as he wrapped the cloth and bound it. After what seemed like an eternity of awkwardness, he finally said, "All done."

Sage pulled her hand from his grasp and shifted backward, clearing her throat. "Um, sorry about kicking you off the bed."

He took a step back as well and leaned a bare shoulder on a bed poster, crossing his muscular arms against his very bare chest. It irked her that he cut such a nice figure. Sage was no stranger to the male physique; she did, after all, grow up with two brothers and had spent plenty of time training with men. For some reason, however, she was discomfited by it when it came to the crown prince.

"Would you put a shirt on?" she snapped.

"No, I won't. I have slept without a shirt for as long as I can remember and that's not going to change just because I have a wife. If it makes you uncomfortable, don't look." The crown prince turned on his heel and left, entering the bathing room. Just before slamming the door, he called out, "You're lucky I wore pants."

Sage glared at the door a moment but soon left that to examine the room. The bed looked like a wild beast had been let loose on it. Blankets and pillows were strewn about the room, the sheets ripped and blood stained. Feathers decorated the bed, its side-table, and the floor. When did that happen? And how?

A sharp knock at the door had Sage scrambling. She rushed to pick up her nest of blankets and threw them on the bed. No one could know they weren't actually together. She plucked a pillow up and lobbed it at the bed.

No doubt hearing her scrambling around, Tehl yanked open the door, frowning. "What?"

"There's someone at the door!" Sage hissed.

Tehl's eyes widened. "Put a robe on over your clothes."

She dashed into the closet and tugged on the first robe she found. "One moment," she heard the crown prince call out. It was so large the sleeves covered her hands and it dragged on the floor, but it would do.

Sage stepped out of the closet just as Tehl placed the bloody dagger into a drawer. He turned to her and nodded. "Good. My robe is a nice touch."

That's why it was so big. She was an idiot sometimes. He moved to her side and reached for her braid. "What are you doing?" Sage barked, batting his hand away.

"Making it appear like you have been tumbled all night," he growled.

"I can do it!" Speedily, she unwound her braid and ran her fingers through her locks. Sage bent forward and flipped her hair back, tousling it. "How's that?"

The crown prince stepped into her space and speared his fingers through her hair, ruffling it. "There. Now you look tumbled."

She jerked away from him with narrowed eyes and opened her mouth to retort.

"Enter," Tehl called, plopping into a nearby chair, yanking her with him. She fell with a grunt into his lap. Annoyed, she stiffened and tried to get right back up.

"Sit back and relax," his deep voice whispered into her ear. "They are bringing breakfast to a newly married couple. What do they expect to see?"

Sage had no choice but to curl into him as the door opened, admitting one of her ladies-in-waiting and a few servants. A large hand settled on her thigh, and she couldn't help the blush that crept up her cheeks.

"How are you today, my lady?" Lera, a plump serving woman, asked while spreading a feast before them.

"I am well, Lera. Thank you."

Tittering drew her attention to her ladies-in-waiting that she avoided since they had a tendency to gossip and she had no interest in such things. They were glancing from the bed to one another, whispering furtively. Sage's brows furrowed as she tried to figure out what they could possibly find *that* interesting. One of their gazes flickered again to the bed, curiosity evident on their face. Sage glanced to the bed, but she noted nothing worth commenting on. Dismissing it she was about to turn away when her eyes snapped back to the bed in horror.

The blood.

That's why they were staring.

Her cheeks burned at what they must be thinking. Lera noted her preoccupation and looked to the bed, stilling for only a moment. The sweet servant smiled softly, kindness on her face. "Would you like me to draw you a bath? I have lavender. It is wonderful for soothing all sorts of aches and pains."

"Please do," Tehl responded, "for the lady and I."

Humiliation burned her at the knowing glint in Lera's eyes. "Of course, my lord."

Sage blocked out everything and everyone in the room and instead focused on simply appearing comfortable and relaxed. What was she doing here? She rubbed her wrist and blanched. What did she do with her cuffs? She scanned the room frantically, attempting to be subtle in her search. Her heart banged against her ribs when she caught sight of them under the bed. A rough shake pulled her out of her stupor. She blinked and turned to stare at narrowed dark blue eyes. "What?"

"You can get off of me."

Her own eyes narrowed at his tone. "Excuse me?"

"They're gone, you can drop the act."

Sage leapt from his lap and tugged off his robe, tossing it onto the bed with disgust. Her new husband remained seated, relaxed in the chair slouching with his legs splayed in front of him, still without a damn shirt. His blue eyes were thoughtful as he rubbed at his chin, musing.

"I think that went well."

She snorted. "*Hmph.* What part?"

"All of it," the prince gestured to the bed. "I couldn't have planned it any better. In an hour the whole palace will know what ardent lovers we are."

Sage sniggered. "*Ardent* lovers?" she asked, her nose scrunched.

Tehl's lips turned up. "Yes. Ardent lovers."

Sage rolled her eyes and swiped her cuffs from under the bed, plopping down on it. "What do we do now?"

"Our court already knows we aren't leaving for a bonding period like some do, so they'll be expecting us to be holed up here instead for a while."

She stared at him in horror. How long would she have to stay in the same room as him? She didn't think they could survive; one of them would surely murder the other. "How long?"

"Two weeks."

"No."

"Yes."

"I will not be trapped in this room for two weeks. Who will run Aermia?"

"Sam, I imagine."

"You can *not* be serious."

"What would you have me do?"

"One week. I will stay here one week and one week only, not a moment more," she said severely.

"We could get away with one week, I suppose. That would be ideal since I don't relish being stuck in here either."

Sage blew out a breath. "One week."

"One week," Tehl echoed.

***

The week wasn't as horrid as Sage had imagined. She discovered, to her delight, her new husband felt the need to avoid her as much as she did him. The worst part was being cooped up in a single suite. She read books, practiced, and lounged in the sun on the terrace to pass the time. At one point, she'd become so bored that she convinced Mira to bring her a sewing basket. After hours of trying, and nothing but knotted thread, a wounded finger, and jabs from Tehl to show for it, she finally just threw the blasted thing over the balcony.

Sam popped in a few times with updates on her assassin, or rather, the lack thereof. They could find nothing so far. They had a body but no names or connections. So many times she wished she could go and investigate herself but was always politely reminded that Rafe was looking into it as well and that it was more important that she stayed where she was.

She also missed her family. It was lonely being stuck with just the prince. Gavriel stopped by for a few games of chess but never for very long nor frequently enough to fill her need for company. Sage grew so desperate she even attempted to converse with her husband but he was dense. He couldn't hold a conversation to save his life.

Husband.

She'd never be comfortable with him wearing that title.

Her biggest issue, however, was every night. The crown prince dropped into a deep sleep as soon as his head touched the pillow, whereas Sage would curl up by the fire, staring at the ceiling for hours until she finally succumbed to sleep. She envied his soundless sleep night after night for, inevitably, she would have a nightmare. Thus, every morning, she woke up, not only exhausted, but irritable because the stubborn man wouldn't leave her in the nest on the floor. She hated that every morning she awoke plastered to his warm side.

When Sage woke on the eighth day, she couldn't hold back her excitement. She was free. She shoved her feet into boots and snatched her daggers from their various hiding places. Tehl rolled from the bed and watched her.

"You're chipper this morning." His voice sounded like two rocks being rubbed together.

"We are free of each other." Sage grinned at him in the mirror while she quickly braided her hair.

The crown prince pushed up from the bed and plucked something from her side-table. Sage turned to him when he stopped behind her. Her lips pinched when she saw what he was holding. Her cuffs. Sage held her wrists out to him, keeping her face neutral. She hated them. She shivered when the cold metal kissed her skin. Tehl ran his thumb over one cuff and released her. Sage plastered a bland smile on her face and slipped out the door with a quick goodbye.

The surge of excitement she felt at her newfound freedom added a skip to her step. She ignored the Elite following her and lengthened her stride. Finally, she burst through the doors leading to the practice ring and tilted her face to the sun, basking in its warm embrace.

"You appear mighty satisfied." Sam teased.

Sage's lips twitched. "I am indeed."

"Oh?"

She opened her eyes and peeked at Sam who was lounging against the castle wall. "Married life suits me well."

Sam smiled widely at her with twinkling eyes. "I am inclined to believe you. You're ravishing this morning."

"Always the flatterer," Sage replied, a hand on her hip. "How many women have you said that to?"

Sam clasped his hands over his heart. "You wound me."

"I doubt that. There'd have to be a heart in that chest before I could wound it." Sage left him sputtering.

"I have a heart full of love."

"You love too much," she called over her shoulder.

"There's no such thing!" he insisted.

His feet marched behind hers, chasing her toward the practice courtyard. "It's not so much about quantity as it is quality."

"So you're saying one woman is better than many?"

Sam tugged on her braid and threw his arm over her shoulder.

Sage elbowed him in the stomach and shrugged off his arm. "Better be careful or you might have a horde of women thinking you love them."

Sam's face blanched and she giggled. After patting his arm, she attempted a sympathetic expression. "Don't fret, I'm sure you'll figure out some way to thwart them. After all, I've heard you're an excellent liar."

"Says the pot to the kettle," he mumbled.

"You and I are going to be great friends."

He smiled down at her. "Yes, we are."

CHAPTER TWENTY-THREE

Sage

The crown prince was in so much trouble.

She'd kill him.

Without so much as a word she blew past the two guards holding the dungeon doors open. Her footsteps echoed on the stone walls as she descended the steps leading to the dungeon, her jaw clenched.

She had to be wrong. When she had stumbled across a pair of Elite speaking about a woman in the dungeon, Sage had frozen, hardly able to believe her ears. There was another woman being held captive? There was no way Sam and Gav would keep this from her, she had to have heard wrong. Jeffry's head jerked up as she slammed into his office, halting just before his desk.

The old man blinked and steepled his fingers beneath his chin. "Yes?" He leveled an assessing gaze at her. To many, his silver eyes would be off-putting and intimidating, but she'd already known him for quite some time. She was not deterred.

"Where is she?" Sage growled.

"Who?"

So he was going to play dumb. How original. "The woman!" she spat.

Pity filled Jeffry's face. "She's been well taken care of."

A stone settled in her stomach. It was true. Stars above. "That's not what I asked."

He glanced to a soldier stationed in the corner of the room. "Jacque, show the princess to cell nine-twelve."

Dismissing the Keeper, she followed Jacque's wiry form into the labyrinth of hallways which made up the dungeon. How could they keep this from her? She rubbed her arms as chills ran up and down them. The walls seemed to inch closer, the deeper they descended. How she hated this place!

A dirty prisoner caught her eye when he held a limp hand out to her. Old insecurities rose. What did these people do to deserve their sentence? Were they all guilty?

Lost in thought, Sage failed to pay attention to her footing and stumbled, stiffening as a hand wrapped around her bicep. She glanced up into Jacque's angular face with a frown.

"Be careful, my lady. That one is in here for crimes you couldn't imagine. Preys on women and children alike."

All her pity disappeared. Children were to be protected, not preyed upon. Sage bared her teeth at the man and continued to follow Jacque. They turned a final corner and the soldier stopped at a cell at the very end of the hallway.

Her heart fell to the floor when she made out the sleeping prisoner on the other side of the bars.

A woman.

How could they do this?

Sage pushed closer and grasped the bars. She scoured the woman for injuries, but, apart from being loosely shackled to the cell, she looked thus far unharmed. Beneath the dirt, the woman was stunning. Her mocha skin was perfectly smooth, faint swirling patterns somehow etched or painted on it. She had hair so dark it seemed to soak up any surrounding light.

"How long has she been here?" Sage croaked. She wet her lips waiting for the guard's answer.

"I would say almost three months. They brought her in about the time you were taken to the healer."

Bile crept up her throat.

Three months.

They had kept her in here for three bloody months. Sage pulled in a deep breath through her nose, trying to keep from heaving. All she could see was herself hanging above the grate, bleeding. The pain. The terror. The iron bit into her palms, but she didn't feel it. The sensation was lost in the memory.

"My lady?"

Sage blinked and shook away the memories. She turned to Jacque. "What?"

He hesitated for a moment. "Are you all right?" he asked gruffly, jerking his chin toward her face.

Sage lifted her hand to her forehead and followed the bar's impressions down her cheek, discovering it was wet. She hadn't even realized she'd been crying. Sage scrubbed her face with her arm and dismissed the guard's concern, choosing to focus on the cell and its occupant.

The prisoner had woken, and she stared at them with midnight eyes so dark it looked like she had no pupil. The perfect symmetry of her face struck Sage as odd and then the breath in her lungs froze. What had the princes done?

A Scythian.

She had seen few Scythians growing up. The ones who sought refuge in Aermia tended to live in relative solitude, but when she did come across them, she had always admired their beauty, but this woman looked like none she'd ever encountered. She was unearthly, as if her features had been carved rather than born of flesh. Sage suppressed a shiver. In a way, the woman probably was. She didn't doubt for a second that this woman was one of the 'Flawless' Scythia manipulated into existence.

Sage watched the woman watch her. "What's your name?"

The woman cocked her head. "I have been asked many questions since I have arrived here, but none of them have been in regard to my name." She spoke with a faint, lilting accent. "Why would you ask me such a thing?"

Sage shrugged. "It's fairly standard practice when meeting a new person to ask their name. You're a person, aren't you?"

The Scythian woman let out a short, harsh laugh. "I am indeed." She lifted her wrists and rattled her chains. "But in here I am little more than wasted space."

"I doubt that."

"Why are you here, princess?"

Sage regarded the woman with interest. She knew more than a prisoner should know. Interesting. "You know who I am?"

The prisoner waved her hand. "I'll not answer your questions. Did the commander send you? Did he think a woman would goad me into speaking? Have the last three months taught him nothing?" She lifted her chin and looked at Sage with haughty eyes. "I am unbreakable."

"No one is unbreakable." Everyone had a weakness.

"Lies." She scanned Sage from head to toe. "You are a close companion to the lie. Your new nuptials are not as perfect as everyone believes."

Sage kept her expression blank as her mind spun. The only ones who knew about their agreement were the Circle and the Crown's advisors. How did this woman have that information? Was she guessing? Or had someone passed it along to her? Either way boded ill. The question was, did they have a traitor or a spy?

This was nothing like what she had expected to find. She thought she'd encounter a broken woman in need of care, but what she found was a woman strong enough not only to converse but to play at words and toss out threats. She'd bet her best hat the woman was a spy. She smiled and crossed her arms, she knew how to deal with spies. Lie. Believe the lie.

"I love my husband."

The woman snorted. "Indeed. You love him like you love a snake in your bed." A sly smile appeared on the woman's face. "You're good. Your façade at the moment is flawless but that is also your tell." Her eyes slid to the guard, hovering just behind Sage's back. "It won't be long now."

Sage refused to inquire further for she wouldn't rise to the bait, as that was what it was. Time to throw her off guard.

"Are they feeding you?"

Confusion wrinkled the woman's brow at the change in subject. "Yes."

"You're not sick? Or wounded?"

"No." She jiggled her wrists. "I have sores but nothing life threatening." Her eyes narrowed. "What is your angle? Are you going to befriend me? Attempt to have me betray my people? What do you want?"

Sage squatted in front of the bars to better look her in the eye. "Nothing."

The woman froze and suspicion filled her gaze. "Nothing? Likely story. No one wants nothing."

Sage smiled sadly. "What a bleak world view." Sage shook her head. "In truth, all I want is for you to be healthy."

"I don't trust you."

Sage sniggered. "And I you, but that doesn't mean I want you to suffer."

Silence.

The woman scrutinized her for long minutes. "You mean that." The woman squinted at her, obviously baffled. "I am your enemy."

"You have done nothing to me. Have you hurt any of my loved ones?"

"No."

"Then I harbor no ill against you."

The woman lunged toward the bars, chains jerking her back a touch. Sage was careful not to flinch; instead, she simply watched the woman who was now a mere hair's breadth away.

"You're dangerous," the woman whispered.

"Indeed."

A sharp smile flitted across the prisoner's face. "I like you, so I will tell you a secret."

"I don't want a secret. I would like your name."

The woman brushed aside her comment without breaking their stare. "Darkness approaches your land. You think you understand its magnitude..." Her eyes unfocused. "But you do not. It is like nothing you have ever seen." She focused back on Sage. "Prepare yourself. It will not be stopped, and there will be war, the likes of which will put the Nagalian Purge to shame. Prepare yourself now or you will all die."

Sage pushed aside the spike of fear she felt at this revelation. It was not so much the words but the way the woman seemed to feel about them as she said them. She hid it well, but there, at the end, fear had seeped through for she had not been able to stop her voice from quivering when she spoke of all their deaths. Sage was an expert at hiding fear. She had to do it every day when someone touched her unexpectedly or surprised her. Whatever was coming terrified this warrior woman.

"Why tell me this? Why lose the element of surprise?" Tactically, it made no sense to share such information.

"No one likes an easy fight and..." The Scythian hesitated. "The strong deserve to live. You are built from strength. You wear it like armor."

Sage tilted her head. "I believe you and I are alike in that way."

"Indeed, princess."

"Sage."

"Your visit has been interesting, Sage."

"Likewise." Sage stood and began walking away.

"And Sage?"

Sage peered over her shoulder.

"My name is Blaise."

Sage smiled and nodded before continuing. A name. She counted that a success.

Jacque took the lead, making their way out of the maze of cells. When Jeffry came into view, she slapped a hand against his desk.

"Is she being given food?"

Jeffry eyed her hand and brushed it off his documents. "She's given rations and cared for by no one but myself. She has not been harmed."

Not like her.

Sage jerked her arm back and closed her hand into fist. "Are they interrogating her?"

"One of the princes has been here every week since she was first imprisoned."

That was at least twelve times. "Excuse me, Jeffry. It seems I have some business I need to take care of."

Sage sprinted up the stairs and burst into the courtyard, startling a few doves pecking the ground. She stalked into the palace, ready to tear someone's head off. Demari's eyes widened when she stalked over to him. "Where's the crown prince?"

"In the war room," the royal steward answered.

Sage nodded and stormed through the castle toward the war room, irritated even further. She should have been invited. Were they keeping her from other meetings as well? What else was she being kept in the dark about? Did they think her merely ornamental? If so, they had another thing coming; she was not a pretty thing the prince could take out when he wanted and then shelf when he felt she wasn't useful. The closer she got to the war room, the more she fumed. The whole reason for their marriage was for her to check his power. Was this the first war meeting since their marriage? She doubted it. How many had she missed so far?

Sage smirked when she finally caught sight of the doors. They weren't prepared for the storm they had coming.

CHAPTER TWENTY-FOUR

Tehl

"Where is she? She's your consort, your check to power. Why isn't she here to represent us?"

Tehl pinched the bridge of his nose. This was their third meeting since adding the rebellion leader and it wasn't going well. They rarely agreed and it usually ended in them arguing with one another until he shouted over them all.

He lifted his head and glared. "I agreed to make her my wife and consort, but I never agreed to her sitting in on the war council." That shut the little rebellion weasel up.

"The attacks along the border have stopped," Zachael put in, but he said it like it wasn't a good thing.

"That's a good thing, right?" William asked.

"No," Rafe's deep voice rumbled. "It means they've focused on something else. Something we know nothing about. So now we're blind."

The group quieted.

"Have you no spies in Scythia?"

Sam stiffened and sat forward at the question. "No, not at the moment. I have sent many but, as of yet, none have returned"

"None? How many have you sent?"

"Twelve."

Gasps and a few curses echoed around him.

"We need to find out what they're planning," Rafe stated, but, before he could continue, the double doors were shoved open, slamming against the walls, and through them sauntered Tehl's wife, as if she owned the place. Tehl caught her eye and swore to himself. The furious glint in her eyes did not bode well for him.

She looked around the room. "Good afternoon, gentlemen. Have I interrupted anything?"

Tehl jerked his chin to the two guards accompanying her. They closed the doors while she smiled as his council scrambled out of their chairs to bow.

His eyes narrowed when Rafe stood, kissed her hand, and whispered something in her ear that made her smile. Zachael and Garreth tossed him questioning glances. He shrugged; he didn't like the exchange any more than they did. He liked it even less when she lifted onto her toes and kissed the corner of Rafe's mouth while watching the table of men. When she turned away, she didn't catch the heat in Rafe's gaze as he eyed her covetously, but Tehl did and he didn't like it. It was true that many men admired his wife, she was after all a beauty, but it was different with Rafe and her actions certainly weren't helping. She was playing with fire, but why?

Sage walked up to Sam and patted him on the cheek a bit harder than was friendly.

"Always the sneaky one, aren't you, brother?"

Sam's brows furrowed at her mocking tone.

Sage skirted around Sam and moved next to his seat. Tehl about choked on his tongue when she leaned down and smacked a loud kiss against his mouth before ruffling his hair. "Hello, husband of mine."

Tehl scrutinized her. Something was definitely wrong.

She plopped down onto the arm of his chair and waved to the group of men. "By all means, continue."

The council members were obviously taken by surprise, some gaping while others watched her through narrowed eyes, no doubt attempting to figure out her angle.

Rafe coughed, eyes twinkling, obviously enjoying her show.

Bloody mischief-maker.

"We were discussing the need for information on Scythia," the rebellion leader supplied.

"Indeed." Sage pulled out a wickedly sharp dagger and, somehow, produced an apple out of thin air.

Where the hell did the apple come from? How did she keep doing that?

She sliced a piece, stabbed it with the blade, and held it out to him. "Hungry?"

Tehl's brows lowered in confusion. "No... I am not," he drew out the words, trying to make sense of her odd behavior. What was she up to?

She shrugged. "Suit yourself." His wife crunched into the apple and gestured with the knife. "So, you need information?"

"Yes," Sam drawled, placing his hands behind his head.

"Perfect. Especially since I have some and you might find it fairly useful."

Suddenly, she had every man at the table leaning forward, both suspicious and eager. She continued to snack on her apple, studiously ignoring them.

Information? Tehl placed a hand on her thigh to get her attention. She stared at it for a beat before placing her dagger against his hand and pushing it off. Point taken. Don't touch her leg.

She grinned at him before biting down on the apple with a loud crunch and smacking her lips.

Tehl twitched. If she smacked her lips in his ear one more time he'd push her off his chair. He hated people chewing in his ear.

"Are you going to tell us your information?" Jaren snapped. "Or just dangle the promise of it in front of us all day?"

Half the table stiffened. The pompous windbag didn't seem to notice, or if he did, he didn't care. No matter how it came about, she was now a princess of Aermia and therefore ought to have been accorded due respect.

"Watch your tone, old man," Tehl warned.

Jaren scowled and his face reddened so much he was almost purple.

"Is he going to explode?" Sage whispered loudly.

Several chuckles, poorly masked as coughs, had Jaren glaring round the table as Tehl held in a groan. Why today? Did she always have to be a thorn in his side?

Abruptly, Sage pushed from his chair and sat on the table's edge, swinging one leg. "As much as I would like to keep you in suspense, Jaren, I have much to do. So," she paused tracing the grain of the table with her blade. "Would it interest you if I told you Scythia will invade soon?"

"That's nothing new, Scythia has been a threat for some time," Garreth stated. "We've suspected invasion for a while now."

"True." Sage locked eyes with Garreth. "But I collected

information that confirms they plan to move against Aermia, and that it will be soon." Sage dropped her eyes and continued to trace the grain. "I have it on good authority that the invasion will be on a scale we have not previously anticipated. It will make the Nagalian Purge look like child's play."

The room stilled, and Tehl's stomach soured.

The Nagalian Purge was the worst crime ever committed within living memory. Two entire races, Nagalian and Dragon, destroyed at the behest of a single nation. Women and children were not spared and every aspect of their cities and culture were reduced to rubble before the surrounding nations even heard of Scythia's betrayal. Then, the warlord had claimed it was necessary to purge the world of the Nagalians and their 'undesirable' and 'debased' ability to communicate with the draconian species.

It wasn't purification. It was genocide.

"Where did you come by such information?" Garreth probed. "I wasn't aware the rebellion had spies in Scythia."

"We don't," Rafe replied while watching Sage.

"You don't know?" Sage lifted her face and took in the council's expression before throwing her head back, roaring with laughter.

Now was not the time for laughter. "Love, could you get to the point?" Tehl growled.

Her head snapped to him and all laughter cut off. "You don't need to use such endearments here my lord. Remember that all these men were witnesses of my sale."

Tehl blinked. He had called her that in public so many times this last month that it now came out naturally. He didn't even think about it. "It wasn't deliberate."

She waved a hand at him, that malicious glint returning to her eye. "It's nothing, but if you insist on using pet names..."

Tehl stiffened and her smiled widened. "I think I will go with *pookie*."

He grimaced.

No. Not now. Not ever.

"Not so fun is it?"

Tehl released an exasperated breath. This was so not the time. Patience, he needed patience.

Sage dismissed him and turned to the table. "Let's expose some secrets, shall we? Pookie, here—" She hitched a thumb over her shoulder at him. "—has been hiding things."

Tehl glanced at Sam and Gav wondering what the hell what going on.

"He's had this information for months."

Tehl's nose crinkled in confusion. He glanced to Sam and Gav who were wearing the same expression.

"What are you talking about?"

She smirked at him over her shoulder. "Imagine my surprise when I discovered the Crown was keeping another woman chained to the dungeon's floor."

His heart sped up. Damn it.

"A Scythian woman."

Gasps filled the room.

"What?" Lelbiel hissed.

Sage's smile turned triumphant just before she turned to Lelbiel, face serious. "You heard me. From the looks on your faces, I can tell you have been kept ignorant of this fact too, just as was I."

"Is this true?" Zachael asked.

"Yes, but she has been useless," Sam interjected. "We have interrogated her for almost three months, but we have gained absolutely nothing. Unless she provided us with any new intelligence, she wasn't noteworthy to the council."

"We still should have known," William commented.

"It wasn't for you to decide," Tehl stated. "Her capture didn't affect you in any way unless she had information to share with us. Which she didn't." Tehl stared at the back of the rebel woman's head. "She didn't feed us lies, as you did, she gave us silence. There was only so much we could do. Her experience has been completely different from yours."

His wife stilled, and his advisors quieted at whatever look was on her face.

Slowly, she turned toward him and spoke, her voice indignant. "So she should be thankful she's been chained to the floor in a tiny dirty cell for ninety days? That's better than what I suffered at your hands?"

He squinted at her trying to see the trap she was weaving. "She made the choice to attack Silva, leaving children without parents and burning homes, so these are simply the consequences of her own actions. She struck first."

"That makes it okay to strike back? To hurt her?"

"She has never been hurt. She's been fed, clothed, and well taken care of. She hardly has reason to complain, all we've asked for is her cooperation. The information she has could save hundreds if not thousands of lives."

"Not that it matters," Sam added. "She's not given us a bloody thing, so it's turned out to be a useless gamble."

"You're more morally corrupt than I thought. Basic human needs are not a privilege, not something to be rewarded, or they shouldn't be," she said softly before pinning Sam with her gaze. "And she's not useless. I spoke with Blaise today."

"Blaise?" Sam scooted forward with excitement. "She gave you her name? She's hardly spoken a word these three months past. What did you do? We've tried everything."

"Not everything obviously. If you had you'd already have known that a little human kindness goes a long way. People don't like to be manipulated, Spymaster." Sage stared his brother down. "They like to be treated as fellow humans and not just assets." A pause. "They are *people*, not things to be used and tossed away, a lesson it seems you haven't learned yet."

Sam flinched and dropped his eyes looking upset. "She's a prisoner of war, Sage. She made her choice when she attacked Aermia."

Her lips pursed, but she didn't argue.

Tehl frowned. Now was neither the time nor the place for moral lessons. It was a war meeting for God's sake and she needed to get off her high horse. This did nothing for the unification of the council, and it was high time for her show to end. She'd made her point. "Are you about done?"

Sage turned placing her boots on his knees and leaned forward. "Not yet, but almost. I don't take kindly to lies of omission, nor do I care to be manipulated. If you think the Scythians are dangerous then you have never been on my bad side."

"Duly noted."

Her eyes narrowed. "I know several of these meetings have happened and yet this is the first one I've been to. I am not your errand boy, your steward, or even your wife. I am your consort, your balance, your judge, and your fellow in arms. Do not think to exclude me." Her hair had fallen around her face framing her flushed cheeks and fiery eyes.

For one moment, he let himself admire her wild beauty. He admitted to himself that her inner fire was appealing. A life with her could actually be enjoyable one day if they could be true comrades in arms, but, until then, it was fight or die. She could have her say but making a scene was not acceptable.

Tehl placed his palms on either side of her thighs and leaned into her space, their noses touching. "I'll make sure you're included but just because we have an alliance and a document that states we are bound, it doesn't mean you are privy to everything that happens in *my* kingdom."

"I understand." A smile flitted across her mouth. "But just because we have an alliance and a document that states we are bound, it doesn't mean you can order me around and exclude me from matters of *our* kingdom."

Stubborn wench. She never made anything easy.

His nose twitched. Cinnamon.

Tehl tipped forward, his nose against her jaw and breathed in. The blasted cinnamon. He loved that smell. A month of sharing a room with her and it permeated everything. Even his clothes smelled like her some days.

She jerked back and crossed her arms. "I am not your mistress, either."

That startled a laugh out of him as he sat back in his chair. "Indeed, you are not."

"As long as we understand each other."

"You're my wife." Her face soured. She didn't like that reminder.

"In name only."

"Not for long." Tehl barely held in the snigger at how her whole body stiffened.

"As long as I say."

"You don't have forever."

"Drop dead."

"Maybe you'll get lucky."

"If only," she muttered.

Tehl studied her. She was a giant pain in his ass, but she wasn't without virtues. As long as she used good sense, Aermia could well benefit from that fire of hers.

Her lips turned down. "What?"

"I think you have the potential to be exactly what Aermia needs."

Her eyebrows rose. "Remember that the next time you try to hide something from me." She swung around and stood on the table.

Tehl rolled his eyes as she strode down it, everyone's eyes on her. So dramatic.

She paused at the end and eyed the group with a grin. "Never underestimate women, gentlemen, especially when provoked."

Rafe stood and held his hand out to her. She ignored him and smiled at Zachael, who stood and offered his hand. Sage accepted and jumped down from the table, then waltzed to the empty chair next to William and flopped into it, lacing her hands across her stomach. "Well, that's taken care of. So where were we gentlemen? What's on the agenda today?"

Silence descended as all the men in the room stared at her, some annoyed, some condescending, and others a bit awed. Tehl cocked his head and watched Rafe stew at the vexing creature his wife was. Seemed she didn't just get under his skin but the rebellion leader's as well.

One by one, his advisers looked back at him.

"Your hands are full with that one," Jaren remarked, eyeing Sage as she fluttered her fingers at him.

Tehl rolled his neck and stared at the ceiling. "You have no idea."

"I heard that."

Tehl tipped his head forward, one side of his mouth lifting. "You were supposed to."

Mason coughed and arched his brows. "Now that we all understand your theatrical skills, we are still anxiously awaiting more information on the Scythian woman."

Her careless smile fell from her face as she straightened in her chair. "There isn't much to tell. She revealed to me that Scythia was coming, time was short, and that we needed to prepare ourselves."

"Did she give you any details, anything specific? Anything more helpful?" Zane asked.

Sage stared at him drolly. "Why yes, she handed over a detailed plan while we were braiding each other's hair."

"Why would she warn us?" Zachael questioned.

"Scythia is founded on the ideal of perfection, on achieving the perfect warrior, love for battle. She warned us so that the battle would be more difficult for them, thus the win more satisfying," Lelbiel explained.

"That makes no sense," Garreth argued.

"Neither did the eradication of the Nagalians in their pursuit of perfection, yet it happened," Rafe pointed out.

"She could be lying. How do we know the information is trustworthy?" Jaren inquired.

"She could be, and we don't, but are we willing to take that chance?" Gav asked.

"We treat this like the threat it is," Tehl stated. He cut his attention to his wife. "Can you get her to speak with you again?"

"Yes."

He turned to his brother. "Sam, will you collaborate with Sage?"

"That won't work," Sage cut in. "She doesn't trust any of you, and certainly not the man who has been interrogating her for the last three months. I need someone else."

"I'll join you."

Tehl glanced at Rafe, his look not quite friendly. "What do you plan to do?"

"Sage and I work well together. We'll figure it out."

Turning to Sage, Tehl met her eyes. "Does that work for you?" It was her choice now.

Her lips thinned, and she shot Rafe a look, but nodded. "Rafe is the best at what he does. If there's anyone who could secure her help, it would be him."

"It's settled then." Tehl's gaze swept the table. "You all have your assignments. We'll meet here in three days to discuss our progress and any other concerns. I have things I need to attend to. Good day." With the dismissal, his advisors filed out of the room.

Closing his eyes, Tehl listened to the murmuring voices of the councilors drift farther away, though neither his brother nor cousin made move to rise, both choosing to remain in their chairs. Tehl heard the door close and the sound of footsteps approaching. One guess as to who that was. He snorted and opened his eyes as Sage kissed Gav on the cheek and sat next to him.

"What about my kiss?" Sam complained.

Sage pierced him with a look. "I am so angry at you right now, Samuel, I don't even want to see your face."

"What did I do?"

"Don't play stupid. You could have come to me with this. You know I would have helped you with her. Yet you stayed silent."

Sam pursed his lips.

His wife rubbed her temples. "But I have a bigger issue to deal with than my anger at you." She peeked at him. "She knows we aren't a love match, Tehl."

Tehl jerked back. "How?"

She shrugged. "I don't know. The best I can figure out is that someone in this room is a traitor or a spy."

Gav blanched. "What led you to that conclusion? There were many in the room when the treaty was negotiated that are not present here."

Sam swore. "She's right. The Scythian woman has been in our dungeon since before the Midsummer Festival. The only ones who both have access to the dungeon *and* know about the treaty are those serving on the council."

"So there's a spy then," Gav growled.

"Yes," Sage replied.

"If it's not one thing, it's another," Tehl grouched.

"Such is the life of ruling," Sage stated.

"Indeed. Welcome to the rest of your life."

CHAPTER TWENTY-FIVE

Sage

The rest of her bloody life.

Sage stared blankly at the princes of Aermia. It truly sunk in for the first time.

It was forever.

Here.

With *him*.

Her body flashed hot and cold.

The crown prince's smile fell, his brow furrowing. "Are you all right?"

His distorted voice reached her ears as pinpricks of light danced across her vision. Stars above, she was going to pass out.

"Sage!"

Sage blinked and jerked her head toward Gav. "What?"

Her friend looked at her with concern. "Are you all right? The color in your face drained, and you swayed."

She pasted on a weak smile and waved away his concern. "It's nothing. I skipped lunch, and all I have eaten is that apple. I am starving, I need meat." Male grumbles of understanding sounded as they accepted her excuse. Carefully, Sage met Tehl's eyes. "Why did you keep me in the dark?"

"I didn't think it was necessary. She had nothing to do with you." The crown prince shrugged. "You've had many new duties and burdens you've taken on since we wed. You didn't need this one on your shoulders too."

She gritted her teeth and sucked in a deep breath. Patience. She needed patience or she'd knock his head off. "And you're the one who gets to decide that for me?"

"It's a trap, brother. Don't answer that question," Sam whispered out of the corner of his mouth.

Tehl glanced to his brother. "I am the crown prince," he said slowly before looking at her. "And acting sovereign of Aermia, not to mention your husband, so yes. I do get to decide."

Sage blew out a breath and clenched the arms of her chair.

"Bad choice," Sam sniggered.

She glared at Sam who promptly turned his snigger into a cough. She turned her neck and stared at Gav attempting to gather every last thread of her control. "I will kill him. That's all there is. How can anyone expect me to spend my life with that blundering offensive oaf?"

Gav smiled at her. "He's what I like to refer to as a very smart-dumb person." A growl from Gavriel's right made his smile widen. "He's not *so* bad. Emma and I used to argue all the time, and we grew up together. You've only known each other a handful of months. You need to keep in mind no one is perfect, Sage, including yourself."

Her lips thinned at the gentle chastisement. Grudgingly, she admitted to herself that Gav was right, but it still didn't excuse the words that came out of Tehl's mouth. "Agreed, no one is perfect, but I am not the one in the wrong this time." Sage looked at her clenched hands and tried to loosen her grip. Gav's large hand came into view and squeezed her hand once.

"What he said has merit."

Sage whipped her face toward Gav. He was taking the crown prince's side?

Gav held his hands up at the hostile expression on her face. "Before you bite my head off, just listen. There was truth in his words, what you're upset with is how he said it, which makes sense because you and he are different. Tehl doesn't see why what he said could be offensive because he was being truthful. You need to explain why it made you angry or he won't understand."

"I am still here," the crown prince cut in.

Sage stared at Gav wishing to bang her head against the wall. "Why me?" she moaned.

His lips twitched as he held back a laugh. "Because you're not the emotionally stunted one."

Sage narrowed her eyes at him and turned her attention to the irritated prince glaring at her. She needed to speak to him like a child. "Do you like to have your opinions acknowledged?"

He squinted for a moment before answering. "Yes."

"Do you like controlling choices that will affect your life?"

"Yes."

"Do you enjoy being belittled?"

"No."

"Do you like being patronized?"

"No."

"That's how your statement made me feel, like I am ignorant and don't understand what's best for myself." Sage paused, noting how his forehead wrinkled in thought. "You don't know me, you don't know what I can or cannot handle. Don't presume to run my life because you are the crown prince. And, as far as we're both concerned, our marriage is a piece of paper, but if we had a real marriage that would mean a partnership, a team, not a man ruling over a woman. I am here to solidify our kingdom, and I can't do that if you don't include me in things that are important."

His eyes dipped to the table before meeting hers again. "I understand."

Sage arched a brow. "Do you?"

"You don't want to me to tell you what to do."

"That's not what I am saying. I want you to speak with me before you make a decision that concerns me."

"Did it occur to you I said nothing because of the situation? Because it was similar to something you experienced, and I—" He paused, running a hand through his hair. "I didn't want it to trouble you."

She straightened in her chair. If he was trying to say he kept the Scythian woman from her to spare her any trauma he had to be lying, but, for the sake of the argument, she would entertain the idea. "If that was the case, you could have just asked and I would have answered."

He scoffed. "Because you're so approachable and reasonable."

She barked out a laugh. "Mmmhmm.. because you've given me so many reasons to be courteous to you."

Sam rolled his eyes.

"Don't you roll your eyes!" Sage stabbed a finger at him. "Think of the information we could have had by now if I had been made aware a month ago."

"*Could* have," Sam emphasized.

Sage smirked. "In a half hour on my first day I received more information from her than you have in the last three months." That snapped the spymaster's mouth shut. Sage threw her hands up. "And why in God's name would you pair me with Rafe?"

"I left the decision in your hands," Tehl barked, "exactly like you just asked me to."

"I was put on the spot in front of your war council, what was I supposed to do?"

"Say no."

"Men," Sage muttered, "you understand nothing."

"It seemed like you enjoyed the spotlight, what with the performance you put on. I thought you would give Jaren a fit."

That brought a smile to her lips. "If you hadn't excluded me from the meeting, which is a violation of the treaty I might remind you, I wouldn't have had to do so."

"Children, children," Sam sang.

"Shut up, Sam," both of them snarled, at the same time.

Sage paused, meeting Tehl's eyes. His eyes crinkled and the corners of his mouth hitched up. Suddenly Sage had to purse her lips just to keep the laughter from spilling out. When Gav gurgled next to her, trying to keep his own humor in check, that was the end of it. All of them burst into laughter, and the tension melted away. Sage felt a lightness she'd not experienced in a while. Shaking her head, she pushed back from the table, still chuckling, and rubbed her forehead. "Well, that is as good a note as any to depart on. It seems I have to go and make plans with Rafe." Sage made a face.

"Do you need assistance?" Sam asked, wiping the corner of his eye and standing.

"No, you nosy thing, I have it handled." Sage waved his forlorn look away and strode toward the door.

"We have a dinner party tonight. It's a dressing-up affair."

Sage smiled at Tehl's grumpy tone. He hated court almost as much as she did. She schooled her features and peeked over her shoulder.

"Eight o'clock?"

He nodded.

"Will there be dancing?"

Sage had to smother another smile at the grim face he wore as he nodded a second time. She turned back to the door and reached for the handle and said, "I'll be sure to wear my dancing shoes." His responding groan brought a full-blown smile to her face. At least he would be as miserable as she was.

When she'd quit the room, the first thing she spotted was Rafe, and, immediately, the smile left her face and tension crept back into her muscles.

He pushed off the wall and scanned her from head to toe. "Little one."

Pausing in front of him, she arched a brow. "That's not the proper way to address a princess." Sage knew it was petty, but she didn't want him acting familiar with her. She wouldn't allow herself to be sucked back into a friendship with him. All he did was ruin people.

She watched with satisfaction as his jaw tightened for a moment. "My lady," he growled through gritted teeth.

Sage nodded to him with a smug grin, walking around him and down the airy hallway. She ignored the prickling sensation between her shoulders; she may not have heard him following her, but that didn't mean he wasn't there. He moved with stealthy feline grace. As she reached the stairs, a large hand gently wrapped around her bicep. Sage stared at the hand and slowly peered up at the large man with raised brows. "Yes?"

He cocked his head then released her, offering his arm. "My lady?"

Her eyes narrowed on him. The surrounding Guard shifted uncomfortably as she stared Rafe down. It was a trap. If she didn't take it, she'd look petty but if she did, he would have control.

"It's not a problem to be solved, Sage, it's an offering."

She bit her lip and hesitantly slipped her arm into his. They were both silent as they descended the stairs. Even when they reached the bottom, he didn't release her but guided her through the palace like it was his own home. Inwardly, she rolled her eyes. No doubt he had been doing his fair share of snooping in the last month. He probably did know it as well as his home.

"I am curious to meet this Scythian woman."

Sage looked at him through the corner of her eye. "I just bet."

"I would like to meet her today."

"No."

"Why not?"

Why not? Because he was dangerous. Rafe wasn't even Aermian. She didn't even know what he was really doing in their country. How could she trust his motives? She couldn't. He was a liar, a fake. Sage felt him staring at her as he tried to figure her out, to read her. She kept her face blank.

"I taught you that mask, little one," he whispered. "You cannot hide from me."

Her teeth ground together for a moment before she answered. "I don't trust you."

He sucked in a breath. "Did you not agree to my help before the war council?"

Sage let a smile play on her lips. "I did, but I did not say in what capacity."

"Oh?"

She halted and looked into Rafe's familiar amber eyes. "I neither need your help nor want it. You cornered me in the meeting, and I didn't appreciate it. You forced my hand."

He shrugged a shoulder with a smirk. "I am a spy, little one, it's what I do."

Sage returned his smirk with one of her own—but hers had an edge. "Indeed, but as you often taught me, the devil's in the details. I never said in what way I would work with you." Her smile turned smug as his faded. "I find myself in need of a bodyguard that can blend into the crowd."

"You want me to be your bodyguard?"

"Yes, unseen, unheard. Zachael and the rest of the men would rip into me if I disappeared into the city without an escort but—" Sage slapped his chest, "—with your protection that takes care of that little detail, thus negating the necessity for a military escort. Meanwhile, I can go and retrieve my real helper."

"Indeed. Might that person have magenta eyes?"

Sage smiled brightly at him. "Indeed. What a lucky guess." She turned her back to him and sauntered toward the doors. Sage flipped her hair and called over her shoulder. "Don't forget a cloak, at the moment you practically scream 'see me'." His grumbling about cheeky women made her smile widen. She couldn't wait to see Lilja.

CHAPTER TWENTY-SIX

Sage

Sage sprinted down the halls, her boots echoing on the marble floor. She was running late. Adjusting the delicate package in her arms, Sage veered to the right, heading toward the infirmary. Hopefully, Mira was still there.

She rushed into the room, slamming the door back. The look on Mira's startled face was priceless as she dropped the sheet she was folding.

"Sage Ramses, what are you are doing?"

Sage halted in front of her friend and pulled her into a quick hug before Mira pushed back and scolded again.

"Where have you been? Sam dropped by looking for you. He questioned me until I finally booted him out of my space. Aren't you supposed to be at dinner?" Mira's gaze flickered to Sage's hair. "Good grief. What happened to your hair?"

Sage blinked at the rapid succession of questions fired at her. "I visited Lilja." She pointed to her crazy hair. "Lilja is what happened to my hair, and, yes, I should be at dinner which is why I am here."

"That makes no sense."

"Yes, it does." Sage huffed. "My ladies-in-waiting will take far too long to get ready for dinner. The crown prince will be as ornery as a badger by this point, so I need someone who can help me tame this beast." She gestured again to her hair. "And quickly."

Mira threw her head back and laughed. "There's no helping that mane."

"Please?" Sage pleaded, batting her eyelashes. "I'll hand over what Lilja sent home for you, if you help me."

The healer perked up, intrigued. "What did she send?"

Sage took a step back and swung the parcel before her. "Fix my hair, and you'll find out."

"You drive a hard bargain. But I suppose I accept," Mira smiled as she moved over to a desk. She peeked up as she dug around in one of its drawers. "You know, I would have helped you without a bribe."

"Just as I would have given you Lilja's gift without your help," Sage retorted, and plopped onto a cot.

Mira yanked a brush out of the drawer and rushed to her side. "This might hurt."

She winced. "I know."

Mira began the painstaking process of untangling Sage's salt-encrusted hair. "You smell like seaweed."

"I know."

"You look like seaweed too."

She reached around and smacked Mira's hip. "I know."

"Will you tell me what Lilja sent? I'm dying here."

"Just some seaweed and herbs."

Mira stilled for a moment. "Sea herbs?"

Sage smiled at the excitement in her friend's voice and nodded. "Sea herbs."

Mira let out a little yip and spun in a circle before attacking her hair with the brush again. "I can't believe she was willing to part with some. Sea herbs are so hard to harvest that they're extremely hard to come by, not to mention expensive. It must be because you're living here now."

"I doubt that's the case," Sage replied with a soft smile. "Lilja trusts you. You are not only skilled but a very caring healer. I'm sure it had nothing to do with me and everything to do with your own kindness."

Mira said nothing for a moment as she began to braid above sage's ear. "Thank you."

"We've been through this: there's nothing to thank me for."

"You've done more than you could've known." Mira tied off the left braid and began on the right. "Before I met you, I thought about pursuing something other than healing. I was so tired of the slurs from men and the vicious comments from other women regarding my profession. The things they would say about Jacob and I...it was disgusting." Mira's voice hardened. "I am his daughter, blood or no blood. It abhors me how people speak of us."

Sage closed her eyes as Mira's fingers worked through her hair. "I'm sorry. People can be cruel, especially when they don't understand something."

Her friend sighed. "I was tired. All I wanted was peace, and to work with my father in the infirmary, to just do what I love. I saw that it hurt Jacob every time someone spouted off something ignorant. I didn't want him punished for my choices so I was very close to giving it all up, both for his sake and mine, but then I met you."

Sage's eyes popped open, and she stilled Mira's hand while twisting around. Mira met her gaze, her face full of so much affection that her heart squeezed. In the most unlikely of places, Sage had found true friendship, a sisterly companion she'd forever cherish.

"Even at your weakest, despite the pain, you worked through it so you'd be stronger. Each nightmare could have kept you cowering in your bed, but you didn't allow them to overwhelm you, you kept pushing forward. Watching you deal with your demons gave me the motivation to face mine and not let the actions and opinions of others steal the joy in my life."

Sage swallowed against the lump forming in her throat. She was so fortunate to have Mira in her life. The woman's heart held more love, compassion, and kindness than anyone she had ever known.

Sage lifted Mira's hand up and kissed the back of it. "You're a gem, Mira."

The healer brushed aside her comment and kissed her on the crown of her head. "The feeling's mutual dear."

Sage twisted back around with a smile.

Mira spat into a bin. "Blech. Even your hair tastes like seaweed."

Sage laughed.

"Time to get you out of here." Mira piled the remaining loose hair high on the back of Sage's head, pinning it and then wrapping the braid around the updo. "Done."

Sage murmured her thanks as she leapt up and opened the package. Deep purple fabric slithered out that Sage couldn't help but caress. Mira halted by her side and Sage absently passed the healer her herbs, her eyes never leaving the exquisite fabric.

"Where did Lilja find that?" Mira asked in awe, hugging her herbs close to her chest.

"I stopped asking since she never gives me a straight answer."

"Sounds like Lilja." Mira plucked the fabric from the cot, her eyes rounding. "How do you wear it?"

Sage smiled. "Just wait and see."

***

After many knots, curses, and giggles, Sage was ready to go. The process had proved more complicated than anticipated, but she was finally done. Sage brushed her hands along the eggplant silk once more. "Well? What do you think?"

"What do I think? Everyone will stare at you for it looks exquisite. It resembles a dress, yet there are no seams, laces, or buttons." Mira shook her head, bewildered. "It's both fascinating and confusing. I'm still not sure how we figured out how to tie that thing together, and I'm sure I couldn't figure it out again if I tried. "

"Let's chalk it up to exquisite craftsmanship." Sage swept the fabric to the side and hugged Mira before hustling to the door. "Thanks for your help, I owe you."

"Yes, you do. How about you get Lilja to cough up another one of those dresses for me but in blue?"

"I can do that." Sage sniggered and paused at the door, craning her neck to look at her friend. "You sure you don't want to quit being a healer to be a lady-in-waiting? I hear there's a position open. Surely, it would be better than working here. I mean, just think of your reputation!" Sage widened her eyes dramatically.

Mira picked up a sheet and tossed it at her. "Get out of here, wench."

Sage laughed as she departed, calling out, "Your wish is my command, harpy."

Her smiled widened at Mira's fading cackle. It felt good to laugh. She picked up her skirts and sprinted to the dining hall taking care not to wrinkle the material. She winced when she heard music drifting down the hall. Swamp apples, they had already started dining. She was *so* late. Tehl would not be in a good mood.

She paused in the shadows just outside the door to arrange her dress, squaring her shoulders. Time to put on a good show for the court.

Sage tipped her chin up and adopted a careless air as she glided into the hall, the silky fabric gliding with her as she moved across the smooth marble floor. Sam spotted her first, arched a brow, and sent her a look as if to say *you're in trouble*. Sage forced herself to stay relaxed, holding her smile instead of sticking her tongue out at him, like she wanted to. She puffed out a laugh. He would, no doubt, figure out a way to crack a joke about how the gesture was somehow provocative.

Tehl noted the direction of his brother's attention and finally spotted her. Sage widened her smile in what she hoped looked like delight. Leisurely, the crown prince stood and moved down the stairs from the dais, wearing his full court smile. Oh boy. He was definitely *not* happy. Her afternoon with Lilja had been so fantastic and now he would surely ruin it. She forced her feet forward and dipped into a curtsey when he reached her. "My lord."

His large hand slipped into hers and lifted her. "My lady," he rumbled deeply, placing a kiss on her cheek. "What in the hell are you wearing, and where have you been?" he hissed in her ear before pulling back, his smile still in place.

Sage snuggled up to him and peered up into his face. "I got caught up."

"Obviously."

"Sorry."

He eyed her dress once more and scowled briefly before once

again schooling his features into something more pleasant. Tehl placed her hand on his arm and turned, guiding them both toward the dais. He blew out a breath and glanced at her from the corner of his eye. "Did you have to wear that?"

Sage dropped her eyes to her dress with a faux smile like he complimented her. "What's wrong with my dress?" she murmured.

"It leaves nothing to the imagination."

Sage bit the inside of her cheek to keep herself from biting out a nasty retort. Most of the women of court were dressed much more scantily. "I am completely covered." And she really was, save a small keyhole on her back. The dang thing didn't even have a slit. "I've worn much more revealing dresses than this."

Tehl helped her up the stairs and pulled her chair out. Sage sat and eyed him as he seated himself.

"What?" he muttered.

"What's so immodest about it?" she asked softly.

"It's not what it covers." His eyes roved down her body and snapped back to her face. "It's how it fits."

"It was a gift from Lilja, and it's lovely." The purple complimented her hair, skin, and eyes. It flowed over her curves and onto the floor, neither too tight nor too loose, just fitted.

The crown prince snorted. "Of course, it was," he muttered underneath his breath. "I agree it is lovely, but it's enticing."

Sage blinked. Did he just compliment her? "And that's a bad thing?"

He blew out a breath. "My problem is that every other man is intrigued by the knots tying your dress." Tehl shifted looking uncomfortable.

"Why would they be interested in my knots?" Sage asked, playing stupid.

His eyes narrowed. "You know what I am talking about."

A smile played on her lips. "I'm sure I have no idea what you mean." Sage wanted to cheer when his nostrils flared.

"Every man is wondering if they tugged just right if it would come undone," he gritted out.

"Oh," Sage fake-gasped, though his obvious embarrassment had her bursting inside with mirth. She stifled a laugh.

"Oh indeed," Tehl growled. "I bet the rotten bastards will all vie to dance with you tonight."

Sage took pity on him and patted his hand. "It would take a lot more than that to get this to come undone. Mira spent a half-hour wrapping me in it."

Tehl plucked a grape from his plate and leaned back into his chair with a grin. "I bet you loved that."

Sage rolled her eyes and snagged a piece of cheese from her own plate. "I swear she was slow on purpose."

The crown prince shrugged one shoulder. "It's a possibility. She has a vengeful streak, that one. Have you done anything to vex her recently?"

"Too many things."

"Enough flirting you two," Sam teased from across the table. "It's bad enough I have to deal with it every day. I don't need to experience it at the table as well."

Good-natured laughs surrounded them. "Leave them alone, they've only been married a month."

Sage dipped her head like she was embarrassed to cover her humor. This was the game they played. Little pieces of truth mixed with deceptions so no one suspected what they were really about. The laughing faded and dinner resumed with soft chatter and the tinkling of silverware.

Over the last month, she and the crown prince had finally settled into a routine of sorts for dinner. They didn't say too much unless others engaged them and that suited them both very well. They stole small touches during the meal that weren't so stolen with many eyes on them. Each of these things was, of course, meaningless to them personally, only a deception to please the people surrounding them.

That evening, Sage chatted a little with the gentleman next to her who looked old enough she feared he might keel over at any moment. When the music changed, Sage met Tehl's eyes. This was always the hardest part for them. She loved to dance, and the crown prince could dance, but they weren't comfortable dancing with each other. It was still hard for them to pretend to enjoy being in each other's arms.

Tehl stood and offered his hand, and Sage slipped into her love struck persona as she accepted his hand. He led her down the stairs to the floor and stiffly pulled her into his arms. They began a slow swirling dance, and she smiled at the couples that whirled past, speaking to him from the corner of her mouth. "You're too rigid, you need to soften."

"Said no woman ever."

Her gaze flew to his and she stumbled a step. His face had not changed but she could just detect some humor in the crinkling of his eyes. "You've been spending too much time with your brother."

A smirk lifted the corners of his mouth, and his eyes flashed down to hers for a moment. "Or yours."

"What?" she asked stupidly. "When did you see my brothers? I haven't seen Zeke and Seb in a good two weeks."

"They had a shipment that needed to be dropped off."

"And they sought you out?" Sage questioned.

"No, I saw them and invited them for a pint."

"A pint?" she echoed. Who was this man and what did he do with her cantankerous husband?

He grinned. "You said that out loud."

That mortified her a bit but she shook her head and focused back on the surrounding crowd. "I still can't believe they didn't come and see me."

"Don't worry, you're still their favorite. I think they had a drink with me only so they could interrogate me for your father."

Now *that* sounded like something her brothers would do. "And?"

He shrugged. "The typical you-hurt-my-sister-and-I'll-kill-you threats, and then they left."

Sage chuckled. "I love those men."

"Of course you would, they're as bloodthirsty as you are."

"Very funny."

Tehl halted at the end of the song and bowed over her fingers. "Thank God it's over," he whispered against her skin.

Sage winked. "You think that now. By the end of the night, you will wish you were still dancing with me." His grimace made her chuckle as Sam sidled next to her.

"May I have the next dance, my charming sister?"

Sage avoided his gaze and scanned the group of women eyeing him. "You have a group ready and willing to be your partner."

"Yep, but I want to dance with you, sis."

"Why do you feel the need to subject me to your company?" she grumbled. In truth, she was still angry with him.

"Because they're empty-headed fools, and I prefer your company."

He wasn't giving her much of a choice. She placed her hand in his and scrutinized her brother-in-law. He had said it without a single drop of irony. Sam pulled her into a slow glide, and they twisted between couples.

"Truly?"

He looked down at her, his face serious. "Yes." He pursed his lips before continuing. "I am sorry for earlier."

The prisoner. Good. He should be.

Turning away from Sam, she watched Tehl parade a star struck young brunette across the floor, who looked as if all her dreams had come true. At least someone was enjoying his grumpy company.

"Sage. I'm sorry."

She peered up at the spymaster and noted true remorse in his eyes. He *really* was upset, it wasn't a ploy or a joke.

"I am angry that you didn't tell me. Out of everyone, Sam, *everyone*, you know I would have been your best asset to retrieve information. We could have spared her some suffering." Sage huffed out a breath while holding on the threads of her serene mask. "And much to my chagrin, I am also a little hurt you didn't *want* to seek my help." She dropped her eyes, staring now at his chin.

Sam pulled her closer and kissed her forehead.

"You're never an asset. I learned much when dealing with you. That's why I didn't seek you out, I wanted you to feel at home here and not like a tool we married into the family to utilize whenever the need arose."

"Careful there," Sage chastised, scanning the people watching them, "or people might think you have a heart."

"Take that back."

She smiled and glanced up into Sam's face. "Never. I know others don't see it, including your family sometimes, but I do. I can spot a mask a mile away, and you, my friend, are rarely genuine, but when you are, I see the good man you hide behind this rake persona."

His gaze sharpened for a brief moment as he scrutinized her face but it quickly faded back to his usual look of casual interest. "You, my dear sister, see far too much."

"And you, my dear brother, hide far too much."

"Touché."

When their dance ended, she was passed from one man to the next for much of the evening, and, as it wore on, each dance and conversation seemed more tedious than the next. Her only reprieve were the dances she took with those on the war council. They knew her and her situation so she didn't have to be fake with them.

Zachael was quick on his feet. Sage should have figured, he was a weapons master, after all. Her dance with William was full of stories and tales, and, by the time she finished dancing with Garreth, her belly hurt from laughing so hard.

She was about to call it a night when a Sae tune began playing. Sage closed her eyes and swayed to the music. The Sae was a dance that was loosely based on myths of the Sirenidae. It was supposed to romanticize the lure and capture of her prey.

"May I have this dance?" rumbled a deep voice she would know anywhere.

Sage turned and stared into liquid golden eyes. That sneaky bastard, leave it to him to corner her before everyone so she couldn't refuse. She bared her teeth at him in what could be called a smile but was actually a warning. "I would be delighted."

Slowly, Sage glided backward, swaying her hips and twisting her arms above her head, keeping her eyes on Rafe as he prowled toward her like the hunter, not the prey. He clasped his large hands around her wrists like shackles and spun her around so her back pressed against his chest. She gritted her teeth, irritated that of all the dances, she had to dance the Sae with Rafe, and that he was taking liberties he had no right to take.

Everything about the Sae was meant to depict temptation without much actual physical contact, only the hands and wrists. Sage spun underneath his arm and slid around his back to his other side. His hand caught hers deftly and reeled her in, his arms crossed in front of her, holding her hostage.

Sage looked across the sea of dancing people and locked eyes with Caeja, a manipulative but beautiful young woman who had no problem making it known she was open to being the crown prince's mistress. The vile woman smiled smugly and draped herself against Tehl. So much for only the wrists and hands. She too seemed to take liberties.

Tehl frowned and maneuvered her into a different position that made Sage smile, not because he moved her but because he must have been even more uncomfortable than she was at the moment.

She slid her foot to the side and slipped to the floor, Rafe holding her hands above her head. He spun her once before yanking her to her feet, once again lifting her hands and drawing an arch with their limbs, leaving them face-to-face. "You look stunning, little one, like a true Sirenidae. You have never been more beautiful."

Her mood soured. He didn't have the right to say those words to her. "Not another word," she hissed while twisting side to side in front of him.

"Am I not allowed to pay my mate a compliment?"

Anger burned through her. Had he lost his mind?

Sage forced her smile to stay firmly on her face. "I am not your mate! If anything, I'm Tehl's mate," she tossed over her shoulder while Rafe continued to spin her. The music crescendoed, signaling the end of the song where the male counterpart thought he had captured his woman. Relief cooled some of her anger. At least the song was almost over.

Rafe pulled her close, their chests not quite touching, and swayed with her, his hands resting on her hips. Ever so carefully, Sage ran a finger across his chest and swooped under his arm to run her hand along his shoulder and then neck. The music stopped. All the men were considered dead. The Sirenidae captured their prey.

The rebellion leader spun, eyes filled with something hot that she deliberately ignored. Sage curtsied to him and excused herself. Not the time to dawdle. Her neck prickled as she bustled out of the dining hall so she glanced over her shoulder, locking eyes with Rafe. She frowned as his lips tugged up into a smug grin.

Arrogant man. Foolish man.

What was going on with him? He was acting out of character. Sage brushed the thoughts aside for another time; she had to make her escape. A bath was in her immediate future.

CHAPTER TWENTY-SEVEN

Sage

Sage took the servants hallways to avoid unwanted company, enjoying her solitude. Every so often, she stumbled upon couples in shadowy corners whereupon she would roll her eyes. It was surprising how many trysts she'd interrupted. You'd think they were more capable of finding seclusion.

She swung around a corner and paused to scrutinize the couple in the shadows. She blinked. Stars above, *really*? Familiar blond curls and wide shoulders. Sam.

She hesitated for a moment not knowing if she should startle them or backup and pretend she never came upon the embrace. After a moment, she backed into another alcove to watch. Who was Sam with? Some kind of redhead.

Sage cocked her head and watched with interest. Something wasn't quite right. Her eyes narrowed. For all the world they looked to be lovers, but something was off. There wasn't heat in the manner of his hold on the woman. And the redhead did not seem to behave in a passionate daze, rather her stance and expression demonstrated alertness and intelligence to the trained eye.

Interesting.

The woman leaned forward, whispering in his ear while scanning their surroundings. Sam slipped a hand up her side and plucked a small folded parchment from her skirts. It was naught but a little cream blur before it was gone, but she'd seen it. An idea took root in her head and she smiled. Could she be right? Time to test her theory.

Purposely she stomped her feet and immediately Sam reacted by kissing the woman and pulling her flush against him. Sage burst around the corner and paused, as if she'd been surprised by their appearance. The woman's eyes widened when she saw Sage, and she jerked back from Sam, seemingly scandalized. Sam peered over his shoulder and smiled at her lazily. "Sister, what a pleasure."

What a damn liar.

She shook her head and moved forward while the woman smoothed her skirt, whispering something in Sam's ear before dropping her head and brushing by Sage.

"You have something," Sage pointed to the pink smear on Sam's face.

He smiled and wiped at his face. "Did I get it?"

"Mmmhmm..." Sage stared after the redhead who was now bustling down the hall. "She was lovely."

"Indeed. Her body," Sam groaned, and then frowned playfully. "You scared her off you know. Now you owe me a date."

She snorted and turned back to the spymaster. "I'm sure you are more than capable of finding your own."

His grin turned rakish. "Many."

"Don't be crass," Sage chided. "Well, I am off to sleep. Are you off to find your bed as well?" she asked as she turned to walk away, leaving her trap open.

"Indeed, but, hopefully, I won't have to do so alone."

Sage smiled smugly. Trap set. "Somehow I think you will."

"Why would you say such a thing? You're trying to curse my good luck."

"I don't think luck has anything to do with it."

His voice trailed behind her. "Thank you. I too like to think my good looks have something to do with it."

"Now, now." Sage *tsked*. "You're getting ahead of yourself. You and I are alike. We don't leave things to chance. We plan and plot."

"What does that have to do with anything?" Sam asked.

"She was pretty, I'll give her that, but next time, find a better actress."

Sage held her breath.

Silence.

Wait for it.

Her smile widened when rapidly thudding boots started chasing her. He reached her side, but Sage kept her eyes ahead, ignoring his burning gaze. Sam cut in front of her and stopped. She halted, her skirts swishing around her feet. "Well?" she questioned.

His deep blue eyes ran over her like he was trying to see her secrets, to figure out what she knew. "Blye is a companion of mine, we have a unique relationship."

"I can see that. What sort of relationship exactly?" she probed.

"One too scandalous for your virgin ears."

"I'm not so innocent."

Sam scoffed. "I can spot them from far away. You have *that* sort of innocence written all over you."

"I'm not the only one."

The spymaster smirked. "I'm not sure what you mean, but if you need any lessons in seduction, I'll be your teacher."

Sage grimaced. "That sounded creepy."

Sam wrinkled his nose. "Oh, God, no. Not like that."

She smiled and stepped up to her brother-in-law, tipping her face up to stare into his eyes. "The funny thing is, Sam." She lifted her hand up and stroked his cheek tenderly. "Your words and action may be right, but it's the eyes that tell the truth." Sage lifted onto her toes and stared down the hall while whispering in his ear. "You're a master, but your lady? She gave herself away. Maybe you should have instructed her better."

She stepped back and moved to depart when he caught her arm.

"You are trouble."

"You already knew that."

"You see too much."

"You already knew that."

His eyes were hard as he studied her. "How?"

"Anyone with eyes could see it."

He scoffed and glanced around. "Not true."

"Will you tell me the truth?"

No response. A little disappointed, she pushed around him. "Goodnight, Sam."

A growl.

"Not here."

Sam pulled on her arm, guiding her down the hallway and up a set of stairs she'd never seen before that seemed to head in the direction of the royal wing. Sage filed its location away. One could never have too many escape routes.

He moved her to a shadowy alcove behind a tapestry and she gaped. How many times had she walked passed it and never guessed what was here? Sage shook her head and leaned against the wall, jerking slightly when part of her bare back touched the cold stone.

312

The alcove was just big enough for Sam to pace. He would grumble, look at her, open his mouth, and then close it as he began to pace again.

Sage yawned and waved her hand. "Are you going to start any time soon?"

"Wait a damn minute, woman. I am trying to figure out how to start."

Sage pushed off the wall and placed a hand on his arm to stop the pacing. "Then let me begin."

He looked down at her and nodded before taking her space against the wall.

"Your spies are women." Sage watched as he tensed, looked around, and reluctantly nodded. A laugh burst out of her at the uncomfortable look he wore. "It's brilliant, Sam. No one would suspect a table wench, a baker's wife, a washerwoman, or a lady of court was dealing in secrets."

"How?" he asked, the muscle in his jaw ticking.

"She wasn't that good of an actress. There was too much awareness in her eyes for it to be a tryst."

Sam cursed and ran a hand through his tangled locks before stabbing a finger at her. "You, you are a troublesome wench."

She grinned. "If you had trained your woman better than she wouldn't have given you away. Most people wouldn't have noticed but anyone with extensive training or experience would have known her as a fake."

"No one in years has ever guessed—" He broke off, swallowing hard.

Sage stepped closer and squeezed his hand. When his eyes met hers, she gave him a genuine smile. "I don't know how your brother and cousin haven't seen through your womanizing disguise but I understand the weight that secrets can have on a person. When you wear the persona so long you're not sure what's really you and what's the mask."

His mouth thinned, but he said nothing.

Sage kept from looking away as Sam stared at her, so many emotions rippling across his face in rapid succession.

"I'll be the person to remind you," Sage offered.

"It's been a long time since I've had that," he whispered.

The longing and vulnerability she heard in his voice made her do something she rarely did with Sam. She hugged him. He was warm and smelled spicy. When her anxiety grew, she pulled back and stepped out of his arms.

"I also want to train the women."

Sam blinked at her then sniggered. "Well, you don't take very long to assert yourself in other people's business now do you?"

"You need me. Between your experience and mine we could make your spies unparalleled in their field."

His eyes glittered with excitement. "I've wanted you to work for me since the beginning."

Sage scoffed. "I will not work for you but with you. We'll be equals, partners."

"There can only be one spymaster."

"There can only be one spymistress." she retorted.

Sam grinned at her. "Spymistress, huh?"

She grinned back. "Spymistress."

She would finally have something of her own again. Something she chose. Something she wanted.

"I guess it's settled then." He pushed off the wall and held his hand out to her. "To the future of intelligence gathering."

"To mischief and information."

"I like the way you think." Sam held his arm out to her. "Oh, spymistress of mine, I would like to accompany you back to your room."

Sage faked a gasp. "You don't have designs on my virtue do you?"

"Never, fair maiden. Too many men have designs on it already. It's getting kind of crowded, and I wouldn't survive the fight for dominance."

An uncharacteristic giggle slipped out that gave way to a carefree belly laugh as she took his arm and began walking toward her chamber. "No doubt you'd figure out how to turn the men against each other and run off with me."

"I'm a lover not a fighter."

Sam peeked out from behind the tapestry and waved her out. He settled the fabric and led her around the corner. Sage smiled at the guards standing outside her door. She frowned as she took in their expression. Garreth looked down right angry.

"Garreth," Sam greeted. "What's with the grumpy face?"

The Elite eyed Sam and then focused on her with an apology in his eyes. What was wrong?

"Are you all right?" Sage reached out to touch his arm but froze when a faint sound reached her ears from her room.

A giggle.

She glanced at Sam who was burning a hole into the door with his eyes.

Stars above. Really?

She took a step forward and placed her hand on the door.

"My lady," Garreth sighed. "Sage, walk away."

She gritted her teeth and pushed the door open, stepping inside.

There on her bed, tangled together, were the crown prince and Caeja. Her heart beat heavy in her chest as the smug woman smiled and squeezed Tehl's muscled bicep. Sage pulled her gaze from the clawed hand gripping the prince to his blue eyes filled with hostility.

She jerked straight and backed out, her gut churning. "Excuse me for the interruption."

Sage paused for a moment realizing that a woman in love wouldn't walk away. She squeezed her eyes shut, morphing her face into anger and spun toward the door.

"Sage, I..."

Sage peered over her shoulder at the two. "Save it. You disgust me. I'm done."

She slammed the door shut behind her. That was...odd. Her eyes burned a little. What was wrong with her?

Sage looked up to find both Sam and Garreth were looking at her in concern. Oh no, did she muck it up? Stepping away from the door, Sage looked between them. "That was convincing, right?"

"What now?" Garreth asked, confusion wrinkling his brows.

"Sage wants to know if her performance was good enough to fool the whore in there with my brother," Sam growled.

The Elite blinked. "You're pretending to be upset?"

"Yes," Sage drew out.

"You're not upset by what you saw?" Garreth nodded at the door.

"No," she said slowly, ignoring the betrayal churning inside her. "Why would I?"

"Because he's your husband, and what he is doing is wrong."

"Technically, I was sold to the Crown. I could have the marriage annulled if I wanted. It's not real." Her heart pinched; they weren't a married couple in the normal sense but she still thought they would be respectful of each other.

A crash and a loud bellow was her cue to leave. Sage backed away from the two men and shrugged. "Let the prince know I'll stay somewhere else tonight, but I will be back by morning before the servants arrive. Make sure his guest is gone by then. Garreth?"

He shook himself and met her eyes. "Yes?"

"Are you going to be guarding through the night?"

"Yes."

"Make sure no one notices her exit, please."

She paused when Sam started in her direction. He placed both of his hands on her cheeks and searched her eyes. "This isn't right, even if you feel like your marriage isn't real. There were oaths." He dropped his hand and touched her cuff. "You wear his cuffs."

"Not by choice," she said lightly pulling his hands from her face. "Don't worry about me," Sage wiggled her eyebrows playfully, "I am the spymistress, I wear many masks, hurt isn't one of them, but I ought to be going. We'll speak more tomorrow."

His lips thinned, but he didn't stop her from walking away. Her joking manner dropped and her lips quivered. Even if they weren't a real couple, no one liked feeling worthless and betrayed.

CHAPTER TWENTY-EIGHT

Tehl

"Get out!" Tehl growled as he shoved the treacherous woman off of him. She stumbled to her feet, looking shocked. He cursed loudly and glared at her.

"Are you deaf? I said get out."

Caeja jerked back a step, tripping on her garish red dress. "But I thought..."

"You thought wrong."

She blinked. "But you invited me to your rooms, and we danced the Sae."

Tehl didn't quite remember it like that. "No," he said slowly, "you are my wife's lady-in-waiting, and you offered to help her undress."

At his statement, a seductive smile replaced the uncertainty. Caeja held her hands out in innocence and took a step forward. The innocence was as fake as she was.

"Well, she wasn't here, so I wanted to lend a hand," she purred.

He snarled, and she froze. In no way, had he given her the impression she was welcome in his bed. He was a married man for heaven's sake, and for all intents and purposes, he was in love.

"I love my wife," Tehl stated.

Caeja barked out a sharp laugh crossing her arms. "If you love her, I'll eat my own hat."

Tehl frowned as she drew shapes on the bed with her finger. He wished she would stop doing that. It was creepy.

"I am not blind, I know when a man is enthralled with one woman."

Her eyes traveled from the bed and met his.

"And you, my dear prince, are not that man. The Methian prince on the other hand..." She *tsked*. "Well let's just say he has an issue with covetousness."

Tehl's eyes narrowed to slits. So he wasn't the only one who took notice. The heated exchange between Rafe and Sage during the Sae was plain for all to see. The small, jealous part of him had reared its ugly head as he had observed their dance. Sage was alive in Rafe's arms. He detected the loathing but there was also something else there. And she hadn't responded to him like that, ever. Was it an act? Was it hate? Or was it something more? He still didn't know.

When she'd excused herself, the rebellion leader had discreetly followed her. Tehl decided to call it a night and see what his troublesome little wife was up to, but Caeja had managed to come along.

"I am here for you if you need anything."

He snapped back to the disgusting woman who was still somehow standing in his room. Tehl had dealt with her flirting and blatant advances for years, but now it would end. He was tired of it.

It saddened him to remember the girl she used to be growing up.

She'd been a wonderful person, but somewhere along the way she'd become a power-mongering harpy. Maybe if someone spoke frankly to her, it would snap her out of her ways.

He drew in a deep breath and stared her down. "Caeja, this needs to stop. As a girl you were precocious, kind, and funny." Her smile widened, and she batted her lashes. "But now all you are is an insipid, shallow wench."

Her smile dropped. "Excuse me?"

"What made you this way?"

Silence.

"Caeja, you need to change. If you act the whore, men will treat you that way."

"You don't know a damn thing about me!" Caeja hissed, rage sparkling in her eyes.

"You're right, and I don't care to." He winced. That was a little harsh but he continued on. "I would be remiss if I didn't straighten you out while I have the chance."

"You're not my father, how dare you speak to me in such a way!"

"You're right, I am not, but I am your crown prince and acting ruler. Remember who you are speaking to." Her eyes dropped to the floor. "Where are your morals, Caeja? You were raised better than this. Your father may be a ruthless man, but he would never wish this type of life on you. Have you forgotten what's right and wrong?" Tehl gestured to her dress. "What are you even wearing? What kind of attention are you trying to attract? You're barely covered. What happened to modesty? You've thrown yourself at me without any thought to your future. Don't you desire a family? A husband who loves you?"

Her lips quivered for a moment before she pressed them together so tightly they turned white. "Yes."

"Then take a good look at yourself, and change, or you'll find yourself in a place you don't want to be." Tehl ran a hand through his dark locks staring at the plush rug beneath his boots. "Now, leave me."

Tehl lifted his head when the swish of her gown signaled her exit.

He needed to find his wife and explain. It had taken a while, but he was beginning to read little things about Sage, and she had been genuinely shocked finding them. She'd recovered well, but he had sensed emotion.

Tehl waited a minute and then pushed off the bed, striding to the door. He wrenched it open and halted at the sight of Sam casually leaning against the far wall.

"Where's Sage?" He looked left then right, nodding to Garreth who jerked his chin up at him in a stiff way.

Hell. Even Garreth was pissed at him.

He spun back to Sam and noted his brother hadn't moved or spoken. Usually he had too much to say. "Where is she?"

Sam shrugged. "I don't know."

"Sam, you keep track of everyone. You're a better liar than that."

Another shrug.

Tehl rolled his eyes. "No comment."

Anger crossed Sam's face surprising him.

"She needs to be alone."

"I need to explain."

"Well, that's for damn sure," Sam snapped.

"Nothing happened." Tehl's fists closed and his jaw clenched. "Caeja instigated it and tricked me."

"Now that sounds like Caeja."

His brother pushed off the wall and strode toward him.

"What I don't understand is the amount of time you spent with her after Sage barged in on you." Sam jabbed him in shoulder. "Are you so stupid to risk everything for *Caeja?*"

"We were talking," Tehl said.

"Is that what they're calling it these day?" Sam snorted. "I know a tumbled woman when I see one."

"She looked tumbled because I shoved her off the bed! Do you really think I am capable of being that callous? We're not a love match but do you think I'd so readily disrespect my wife and my standards?!"

Sam searched his face and visibly relaxed. "You're not a very good liar, and you're one of the most loyal people I know. I should have figured. I am glad I won't have to defend Sage's honor by kicking your ass."

His brother believed him. Tehl let loose a deep breath. "Do you really not know where Sage is?"

"She disappeared right after she walked in on you." His brother's lips thinned. "Rafe sauntered by a few minutes ago."

Tehl straightened at that. The rebellion leader was always lurking. "He was in the royal wing?"

Sam rolled his eyes. "The rebellion leader is everywhere. I doubt there is any place we could keep him out of. He moves like a ghost. I am a little envious sometimes, I'll admit."

That's all he needed, Rafe finding Sage while she was upset at him. After the rough day they'd had... One thing was clear: he needed to find her because the rebellion leader wasn't playing by the rules.

"It's like he doesn't understand that she is taken." Tehl found himself saying. "Doesn't anyone have any respect these days? Sage is a married woman, and I am a married man."

"You might want to speak about that with your bride, then," Garreth piped in.

Tehl craned his neck to look at the Elite. "What do you mean by that? Has she been unfaithful?" The words burned in his mouth as he said them.

Garreth's eyes rounded as he shook his head emphatically no. "No, that's not what I meant. What I meant is that she doesn't consider herself in a real marriage."

"It's real."

"Is it?"

"It's not fake, we share a room every night." Tehl pointed to the cuffs on his biceps. "I am wearing her damn cuffs. What could be more real than that?"

Garreth held up his hands. "I am just repeating what she has previously said. Sage is of the mind that she's been sold, and that she can annul whenever she wants."

"What?" She wanted an annulment? Not in his lifetime. "Like hell that will happen. Plus, there's no one who'd examine her for innocence without my say so."

"Mira," Sam breathed.

Tehl froze. Mira, of course, the blond healer wouldn't care what he threatened her with if she wanted to help Sage. "I need to go." Stars above, why did everything feel so unsecure all of a sudden?

Sam slapped him on the shoulder as he stormed by. "I'll look for her too."

Tehl tossed his thanks over his shoulder before searching all the places he could think of where his little wife liked to disappear to.

Nothing.

He rushed up a stairway and spotted Rafe walking toward him. Tehl swerved and intersected Rafe's path. "Have you seen, Sage?"

Rafe's golden eyes studied him for a moment before answering. "No, I've not seen her since our dance."

Tehl fought back a growl at the memory of how the other man had looked at Sage. "If you see her, tell her I am looking for her, will you?"

Rafe nodded.

"I also don't appreciate uninvited guests in the royal wing.

Especially ones looking for *my* wife late at night."

Every drop of civility Rafe held disappeared. "She's your nothing." He said it simply like it was the truth.

Tehl bared his teeth. "That's where you're wrong." He tapped his cuff. "She's now my everything." Tehl ignored the growl that rumbled out of the dangerous man. "Your covetousness and blatant disregard for the sanctity of marriage tonight could cause the death of many. Sage and I are working as partners the best we can to protect Aermia, and you're just making it difficult." He stepped toe to toe with Rafe, their noses almost touching. "So I'll say it again, stay away from my wife."

Rafe's eyes hardened. "You will *never* deserve her."

Tehl nodded. He may not have been in love with Sage but he did see her worth. "Maybe you're right, but I am thankful you drove her into my home."

He dipped his chin and stalked around the rebellion leader to the grand staircase. Hopefully, he had talked some sense into the man. Tehl snorted. Doubtful. The man was as stubborn as he himself was.

Tehl reached the royal wing, irritated that Sage had disappeared. As he wandered down the hall, firelight flickered underneath a door casting wispy ropes of dancing light on the dark carpets. He followed the light to the door.

A smile.

Sage's old room.

He'd found her.

CHAPTER TWENTY-NINE

Tehl

He pulled in a deep breath through his nose and knocked. Time to prepare for battle.

Silence.

No way. She wasn't going to ignore him. They were going to talk. Tehl pushed open the door and stepped inside.

"Sam, do you ever wait for an invitation—" Sage swung out of the bathing room wearing a playful scowl that dropped at the sight of him.

Tehl clicked the door shut and gaped. She'd changed out of her Sirenidae dress into a long silk nightgown. Tehl scanned her from head to toe. Stars above, she was a lovely woman. His mood soured. A lovely troublesome wench. But even that thought didn't tear his eyes from her. He hadn't seen her in anything like that since they'd been married. Each night she went to bed in her linen shirt and leather pants armed to the teeth with weapons.

"You're wearing a nightgown," he said stupidly.

Her scowl returned. A real one. Great.

"Thank you for stating the obvious. I wasn't expecting any guests. Give me a moment." She spun and disappeared into the bathing room.

"You called me Sam when I walked in." Tehl pointed out as he strode farther into her room. He paused by the fire, enjoying the warmth wrapping around him. "Obviously, you were expecting some company."

"Sam's harmless," she hollered.

What a crock. "Are we still speaking about the same person?"

"He doesn't have any design on my virtue," came her muffled reply.

"Sam has a design on every woman's virtue." His tone was full of disgust. His brother's questionable pastimes bothered him. "Anyone who thinks differently is foolish."

The door swung open revealing Sage in her typical nighttime attire, leather and linen. For a moment, he thought it was a pity she'd discarded the nightgown, but he shook his head and focused on what needed to be said. "We need to talk."

She paused at the dressing table and pulled a brush through her tangled hair which left transparent wet spots on her shirt.

"What about, my lord?"

Damn it, she was using formalities. One thing he had picked up living with her is that when she wanted to distance herself from someone, she was overly formal.

"I want to speak about what you witnessed earlier. I need to apologize."

Her brushstrokes stopped, and she met his eyes. "There's nothing to apologize for. We don't love each other, and it's not my place to judge you." She turned from him and began yanking the brush through her hair. "Is that all?"

Tehl's brow wrinkled in confusion. He explained nothing. Sage believed he had broken his marriage vows and yet she acted like it was something as common as stepping on someone's toes. That it wasn't a grievous sin against her. He'd have been angry if he had caught her in that position.

"So you're not upset that another woman was in our bed?" Tehl waited to see if she would pick up the bait. She said more when she was angry. It lit her up.

"No, technically it's not even my bed, it's yours."

"But I am bound to you," he prodded, trying to get some read on her.

"A written piece of paper, some words, and silver does not constitute a marriage."

Now that was a damn lie. Her words ignited his anger. How could she be so callous about marriage vows? "Do you remember what we agreed upon before we were betrothed?" Tehl asked meeting her eyes in the mirror.

She nodded.

"Have you up held them?"

Carefully, she set down the brush and watched him in the mirror. "I have," she ground out. "And I find it unfair that since you have broken yours, you now question mine." Sage placed her hands on the dresser not losing eye contact. "Have I not been a good wife?"

"Yes."

"Have I not shouldered the responsibilities you heaped upon me without a single complaint until today?"

"Yes."

"Have I not given all to keep your kingdom together?"

"Yes."

"Then how dare you question my morals."

Well, hell. That's not what he meant at all. Tehl took a couple of cautious steps until he stood behind her, placing his hands on her rigid shoulders. "It was not my intention to accuse you of anything. My purpose for seeking you out was to clear the air."

She dropped his gaze to stare at the brush. "Well, you sufficiently cleared the air. Thank you for coming to apologize, but it isn't necessary. Now, if you'll excuse me, I am heading to bed. I'll make sure to sneak back into the suite before the servants come to greet us."

"You'll be sleeping in our room." They would not go to bed angry with each other. His mother always said never go to sleep provoked but to make peace, and he planned to.

Her head snapped up, her eyes glittering with true emotion for the first time. "I may brush aside what you do but that does not mean I will sleep in a bed that smells of another woman. I have more self-respect than that."

Sometimes, he laughed at the oddest times, and this was one of those times.

Her eyes narrowed, and she jerked out of his grasp, rounding the bed and yanking back the covers. "Don't you dare laugh at me."

"I'm sorry, I'm not laughing at you," he wheezed. "It's the situation. You haven't let me speak. You've twisted everything around." Tehl watched her whack the pillows. "Sage."

She ignored him and smoothed the sheets.

"Sage."

"What?" she yelled, her chest heaving.

"I didn't sleep with her."

She whipped out a dagger and stabbed the air with it. "Don't lie to me. I saw what happened with my own eyes. I'm not a fool. I'm a fake but no fool."

"Caeja is a snake."

"On that we can agree," she huffed.

"I swear to you on my mother's memory she did not come to our room for that purpose."

Sage paused in making the bed before sitting on the smooth sheet to stare at him. "Then what happened? She was all over you during the Sae." His wife shrugged. "She's beautiful."

Now it was his turn to scowl. He vividly remembered the rebellion leader taking liberties. "I am not the only one who needs scolding about dancing with another."

His wife rolled her eyes. "I can't even stand the sight of Rafe at the moment. Are you sure you can see properly?"

"I know what I saw, it might not have been you, but the rebellion leader..."

"Rafe is just being Rafe."

Tehl shook his head. They could argue this for hours. "We're getting off topic. Caeja only came to our room so she could help you out of your dress, but when you weren't there she tried to seduce me."

A choked sound came from her throat.

He squinted at her blank face. "Your blank face shows me more than you know. You doubt me, I get it, but this is what happened. She had her damn dress pulled so low she tripped on the skirt and slammed into me. We ended up sprawled across the bed." Tehl cleared his throat when Sage's face cracked, and she sniggered. "When I booted her from our suite, she tripped on her skirt and about brained herself against the wall, again." Tehl sighed. "I don't want her. Ever."

Sage eyed him in the quiet of the room. "I believe you."

He blew out a breath, surprised by how much her answer calmed him. "Thank you."

"But I am still not sleeping in there 'til the bed sheets are changed tomorrow. The whole room reeked like roses." Sage's nose wrinkled up in distaste. "I'm staying here."

"I hate roses."

Sage gasped. "You hate roses?"

"Well, not the flowers, just her perfume. It gives me a headache. If you're staying here, then so am I."

Her eyes narrowed. "This is my room."

Tehl sauntered to the other side of the bed and flipped back the covers. "It's mine."

"It's your father's," she countered. "He gave it to me, now out!"

"A technicality. Plus, my father always said you sleep with your wife no matter what. You never let the sun set when you're upset with each other."

"I thought your mother said that."

"They both believed it true."

Her lips pursed. "Fine. Sleep on the floor."

He pulled off his boots and unbuttoned his vest, tossing it next to his boots before plopping onto the bed. "If I'm in my own home, I don't sleep on the floor."

"Then I'll sleep on the floor."

"Stars above," he growled. "When's the last time you had a good night sleep and woke up without an aching back?"

Silence.

Tehl closed his eyes. "I would like a full night of sleep. I'll just end up moving you in the middle of the night after you experience a nightmare. Save us both some time and sleep; get in the damn bed." He cracked an eye and peeked at her. The anger and fear warring on her face softened him. She was a warrior. Stronger than she knew. "I'll sleep on top of the covers."

Uncertainty still showed in the way she stood.

Time for a different tactic. "What are you afraid of?" She never backed down when challenged.

Her jaw tightened before she stormed around the room, blowing out each of the lanterns and candles. Tehl spied on her through slit lids as she hovered by the side of the bed before making her mind up and slipping in. A smile spread on his face when he closed his eyes. They had survived today and they would survive tomorrow. Tehl jerked upward when a large pillow slapped him in the face.

Sage smiled innocently at him.

"Sorry, I didn't see you there."

His eyes narrowed. Devious wench. Lying down, he watched her build a pillow wall down the entire length of the bed, except for where their heads would rest. Nodding, she lay down and stared at him.

"Don't try anything or I'll stab you."

He couldn't help rolling his eyes. "Like I haven't heard that before."

She nodded and closed her eyes. Tehl's gaze traced over her arching brows, long lashes, full lips, and high cheekbones. It would have been easier if he had been married to a hag.

"Would you stop watching me?" she muttered.

"Sorry," he mumbled, still looking at her.

"If you were sorry you would stop it."

Tehl nodded even though she couldn't see him and turned on to his back. He thus far had found their marriage surprisingly entertaining, and he was finding it more intriguing by the day. "I really am sorry for any pain our misunderstanding caused you."

"You didn't hurt me."

His brows furrowed. "It didn't bother you at all?" He turned his head to look at her. "If it had been you in my position, it would have bothered me."

Sage blinked her eyes open and gazed at him. "It didn't hurt me but I did feel disrespected." She swallowed. "And lacking."

That surprised him. "You're not lacking, that's why I was staring. You may be annoying, but you're also beautiful."

Her eyes crinkled before she laughed. "Tehl, you have a horrible way with words."

"I know."

"And atrocious manners."

"I know."

"But a loyal heart."

He blinked. Sage had said something nice to him. "Thank you."

"Now, stop talking and go to sleep, it's been a long day."

Tehl turned to stare at the ceiling. "You have a brave heart."

The fire crackled, and, it was so quiet, he was sure she didn't hear him. It wasn't until he had just about drifted off, that he heard a soft thank you. Tehl smiled. They would make it through the mess of their lives.

CHAPTER THIRTY

Sage

Fingers and steel trained along her skin, pain kissing her all over. "I will break you..."

Sage jerked away and blinked, her breath sawing in and out of her chest. Frantically, she searched the room for the monster that lurked in her dreams. The room was dark, except for the glowing embers of the fire. She gulped a deep breath of cool air and tore the covers back, swinging her feet to the side of the bed.

It was just a dream, Sage. He's not here. You're okay.

"Sage?" a deep voice rumbled.

She jumped, her hand going for her dagger before she remembered who was next to her. The crown prince. Tehl. It was just Tehl. Sage craned her neck and peeked at him over her shoulder as he stared at her, half asleep, his hair messily tossed across his forehead. Her panic loosened at the sight of him. He wouldn't hurt her and Tehl slept with as many weapons as she did. No one would be able to get past the two of them together.

"Go back to sleep, my lord. It's nothing."

"You sure?"

"Yes."

The crown prince nodded and rustled around in his blanket before falling back asleep with deep, measured breaths. Sage stared at him for a moment, jealous that he'd fallen asleep so quickly. Part of her wanted to whack him in the face with a pillow again and pretend to sleep so that when he jerked awake, he wouldn't know it was she that disturbed his sleep. She stared at him for a beat longer, feeling restless, before deciding to go for a walk.

She slipped on her boots and silently slipped out the door, startling Garreth. When he'd recovered, he raised a brow in question.

"I couldn't sleep. I need to walk." Sage paused, her brow furrowed in confusion. "How did you know where—"

"We always know where the crown prince is."

"That sounds...tedious."

A silly smile turned the corners of his mouth up. "Sometimes."

Garreth turned and whispered to the other Elite posted by the door and walked to her side. "If you'll allow me, I'll escort you."

She wanted to argue, but she also understood it wasn't really a request. Royalty required protection and she was now considered royal. She'd spent time with Garreth in training, so he wasn't a complete stranger, and at least he knew how to be silent. He was almost as sneaky as she and Sam were. Sage nodded curtly and spun on her heel, heading to the hidden room the king had shown her to when she first arrived. He hadn't visited her in a while but today she'd make sure to track him down for some tea or a walk.

Sage pushed into the suite, Garreth on her heels. She paused, waiting for him to close the door, and then hastened to the bookcase. Her eyes searched in the dim light to find the silver leafed book. She pressed firmly on its spine until a faint click sounded and the bookcase rolled to the side, revealing the hidden doorway.

"Stars above, how long have you known about that?" Garreth breathed.

A grin touched her lips at the censure in his voice. "The king showed me when I was being held here." She ignored his cursing and began to descend the dark stone stairwell. "Be a darling and light a lantern. It's pitch dark in here, and I would prefer not to break my neck or have to explain why you broke yours."

He grumbled behind her but soon enough was stepping behind her with a soft light. "I'm not too comfortable with this. The stones are slick as snot, my lady."

Sage waved off his concern and descended the spiraling staircase. It was slow going, but it brought her a measure of peace. When the sound of thundering waves echoed up the stairs, she felt a spark of excitement. "We're close," she said, gleefully.

When they rounded the last corner, Garreth's sharp breath of awe warmed her. He found the sea cave as beautiful as she did.

"It's lovely isn't it?" she asked as she stepped over a porous rock, running her finger over a starfish.

"It's wondrous."

"Indeed."

When they reached the mouth of the cave, Sage sat down in the sand that had turned silver by the light of the waning moon. She pulled her boots and socks off, enjoying the feel of the sand between her toes. Garreth followed her lead, placing his boots and the lantern off to one side. Once he finished doing so, she meandered down to the beach, savoring the feel of the cool breeze as it ruffled her hair.

She listened to the crashing waves and entertained herself, discovering small treasures the ocean had deposited on the beach, curling her linen shirt up to contain them. When her makeshift sack was filled, along with the Elite's hand, she decided it was time to return. Her restlessness had faded, as had the memory of her nightmare, so fatigue weighed heavily upon her.

When they arrived at the cavern's mouth, Sage carefully placed her treasures in the sand so she could pull on her boots. She shuddered when she remembered how she'd previously been forced to walk through the slime since she hadn't any shoes. Never again. She eyed her treasures and then the cave.

Garreth rolled his eyes. "You'll break your neck if you try to haul all of that up the stairs. Leave it for now."

"But..." Sage glanced at the sea loot longingly.

He sighed. "Fine, I'll carry them."

Sage beamed. "Thank you."

"Yeah, yeah. I'm supposed to be an Elite, and yet I find myself a glorified beast of burden," he grumbled some more as he collected her shells and sea glass, this time using his own tunic front.

As they began the long ascent, Sage thought about her quiet companion. Their entire walk had been comfortable. She appreciated the quiet, the peace. It was times like these that she realized just how skewed her perception had been of the Crown and those loyal to it. She'd found true friendship in places she never expected. Sage peeked over her right shoulder at Garreth, smiling. "Thank you for coming with me," she said simply.

The happy smile which lit up his face and eyes was the perfect ending to their walk. "My pleasure."

Sage's smile widened as she weaved back through the cave, approaching the stairs. She eyed the stone steps with distaste and groaned, remembering the long trek ahead of her. "All those stairs to hike up, how miserable."

A snigger sounded behind her. "You're the one who chose to come down here. Didn't you account for the trek back?"

She sniffed. *Now* he decided to have something to say. Sage blew out a breath and took the first step up the endless staircase. After a few flights of stairs, her legs burned and her lungs labored. She really needed to train more. The further they trudged, the more Sage questioned her sanity. Why in the world did she decide to come down to the beach? She paused as something plinked against the stone behind her. "Everything okay?" she asked looking over her shoulder.

Garreth was struggling to hold onto all of her sea treasures and the lantern. He glanced up at her. "Actually, no. Could you hold the lantern for a moment while I adjust your loot? I will lose all of them if I don't figure out a different way to hold them."

She carefully spun on the step and took the lantern from him, trying to hide her grin as the highly trained soldier fumbled with the dainty shells. "And here I thought the Elite could do anything with ease," she teased.

He snorted while he adjusted his hold on her treasures and his tunic. "That sounds like propaganda from Sam."

Sage chuckled as she turned and lifted the lantern to one of the darkened hallways. "Indeed." The darkness was so thick she could only see a few feet down them. There were so many hidden passageways in the castles. It would take her years to explore them all. "I wonder where this one leads," she mused out loud. "Eventually, I would like to explore them all. Do you know where it goes?" she asked, hitching a thumb over her shoulder.

He lifted his head from arranging the shells wearing a teasing smile that quickly shifted to horror.

"Sa—" was all she caught as pain exploded in her head. Spots of light and dark danced across her vision, and the world spun around her. She blinked once and the last thing she saw was Garreth exploding into action while her treasures flew through the air. Then she knew only darkness.

***

Something was thundering, and the pain in her head pulsed with the sound. Where was she? And why did everything hurt? Sage groaned, wishing the pounding in her skull would stop. Groggily, she lifted her head and slit her eyes only to slam them shut as bright light brought on another wave of pain.

Suddenly, the pounding made sense. A horse. She was on a horse.

Her stomach lurched as the horse's speed increased, aggravating her head. How did she hurt her head? Why was she on a horse? She couldn't remember anything.

"You awake, consort?" a familiar voice sneered.

Her breath froze in her lungs and her entire body locked up.

No. It couldn't be.

The arm around her waist tightened and warm breath dampened her neck. "I know you're awake. You can't hide from me, love."

Bile burned her throat and panic clawed at her chest.

No, no, no, no, NO!

"Yes, yes, yes," the deep voice crooned in her ear. "Your training is slipping. I know exactly what you're thinking. Now look at me."

Her body trembled, and she squeezed her eyes tighter closed.

"Defiant to the end?" the monster mused. "Well. He will relish breaking you."

Stop being the victim. Don't let him take you without a fight.

She blew out the breath she'd been holding, hyper-aware of his arm below her breasts.

Open your eyes, Sage. Open them!

She turned her neck and forced them open to stare into ordinary mud-brown ones.

Rhys.

A sinister smile curled his lips. "Hello there, love. Shall we play a game?"

To be continued...

In Book Three of the Aermian Feuds: Enemy's Queen.

Thank you for reading CROWN'S SHIELD. I hope you enjoyed it!

If you'd like to know more about me, my books, or to connect with me online, you can visit my webpage https://www.frostkay.net/, follow me on IG https://www.instagram.com/frost.kay.author/ I'm a total Instagram whore. I can't get enough bookstagram pics. Or like my Facebook page https://www.facebook.com/Author-Frost-Kay

From bookworm to bookworm: reviews are important. Reviews can help readers find books, and I am grateful for all honest reviews. Thank you for taking the time to let others know what you've read, and what you thought. Just remember, they don't have to be long or epic, just honest♡

You've just read a book in my AERMIAN FEUDS series. Other books in this series include REBEL'S BLADE and SIREN'S LURE (more information on the next page).

THE AERMIAN FEUDS:
BOOK ONE

War. Secrets. Betrayal.

Tehl Ramses is drowning; crops are being burned, villages pillaged, and citizens are disappearing, leading to a rising rebellion. As crown prince, and acting ruler, Tehl must find a way to crush the rebellion before civil war sweeps through his beloved kingdom.

Tehl will do whatever is necessary to save his people. Yet, his prisoner is not at all what he expects...

Fed up with the neglect and corruption of the crown, swordsmith Sage Blackwell steps forward to spy on the crown. She knows the risks of rebellion - imprisonment or death - and yet, she's still willing to take them to protect her family.

But when plans unravel, Sage finds herself facing the devils themselves, her sworn enemies, the princes of Aermia.

Two Sides. One Goal: Save Aermia

Katniss meets Lord of the rings in this epic adventure fraught with mistaken identities, untold secrets, and dark promises.
The Aermian Feuds: Novella

SIREN'S LURE

Not everything is as it seems.

Hayjen never believed in myths and nightmares until he came face to face with one. Captured and trapped on a slaver ship, life looks utterly grim. But when mutiny and danger arise, Hayjen is tossed into the ocean's watery depths where death stalks.

Vengeance is Lilja's middle name. As pirate captain of the Sirenidae, she's made it her life goal to destroy Scythia after what they've stolen from her. After one miscalculation, she finds herself cast into the sea with a man's life in her hands. Despite her laws ringing in her mind, she saves him, exposing a secret she's kept for years.

A secret that could destroy an entire race.

Available for only 99 cents!